Also by Camilla Way

Watching Edie
The Dead of Summer
Little Bird

the
lies
we
told

Camilla Way was formerly an editor on the style magazine *Arena* and has written for *Stylist*, *Elle* and the
Guardian. She is now a full-time writer and lives in
outh-east London with her partner and twin boys.

 @CamillaLWay

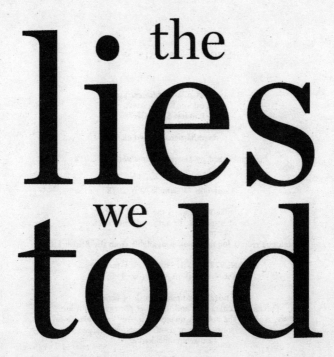

the
lies
we
told

CAMILLA WAY

HarperCollins*Publishers*

HarperCollins*Publishers* Ltd
1 London Bridge Street,
London SE1 9GF

www.harpercollins.co.uk

First published by HarperCollins*Publishers* 2018
1

A catalogue record for this book is available from the British Library

ISBN: 978-0-00-815909-2 (PB b-format)
ISBN: 978-0-00-829436-6 (TPB)

This novel is entirely a work of fiction.
The names, characters and incidents portrayed in it are
the work of the author's imagination. Any resemblance to
actual persons, living or dead, events or localities is
entirely coincidental.

Set in Sabon by Palimpsest Book Production Limited,
Falkirk, Stirlingshire

Printed and bound in the UK by CPI Group (UK) Ltd, Croydon CR0 4YY

For Albert and Sidney

1

Cambridgeshire, 1986

At first I mistook the severed head for something else. It wasn't until I was very close that I realized it was Lucy. To begin with I thought the splash of yellow against the white of my pillow was a discarded sock, a balled-up handkerchief perhaps. It was only when I drew nearer and saw the delicate crest of feathers, the tiny, silent beak, that I fully understood. And suddenly I understood so much more: everything in that moment became absolutely clear.

'Hannah?' I whispered. A floorboard creaked in the hall beyond my bedroom door. My scalp tightened. 'Hannah,' louder now, yet with the same, fearful tremor in my voice, 'is that you?' No answer, but I felt her there, somewhere near; could feel her waiting, listening.

I didn't want to touch my little bird's head, could hardly bear to look at the thin, brown line of congealed blood where it had been sliced clean from the body, the half-open, staring eyes. I wondered if she'd been alive or dead when it happened, and started to feel sick.

When I went to Hannah's bedroom she was standing by her window, looking down at the garden below. I said her name and she turned and regarded me, her beautiful dark eyes sombre, just a trace of a smile on her lips. 'Yes, Mummy?' she said. 'What's wrong?'

2

London, 2017

Clara woke to the sound of rain, to a distant siren wailing somewhere along Old Street, and the low, steady thump of bass from her neighbour's speakers. She knew instantly that Luke wasn't home – not just absent from their bed but from the flat itself – and for a moment she lay staring into the darkness before reaching for her phone: 04:12. No missed calls, no text messages. Through the gaps of her curtains she could see the falling rain caught in a streetlamp's orange glare. Below her window on Hoxton Square came the sudden sharp peal of female laughter, followed by the clattering stumble of high heels.

Another hour passed before she gave up on sleep. Beyond their bedroom door the first blue light had begun to seep into the flat's dark corners, the furniture gradually taking shape around her, its colours and edges looming like ships out of the darkness. The square's bars and clubs were silent now, the last stragglers long gone. Soon the sweep and trundle of the street cleaners' truck would come to wash the night away, people would emerge from their buildings heading for buses and trains; the day would begin.

Above her, the repetitive beat continued to pound and, sitting on the sofa wrapped in her duvet now, she stared down at her phone, her tired mind flicking through various explanations. They hadn't had a chance to speak yesterday at work, and she'd left without asking him his plans. Later, she'd met a friend for drinks before going to bed early, assuming he'd be back before too long. Should she call him now? She hesitated. They'd only moved in together six months before, and she didn't want to be *that* girlfriend – nagging and needy, issuing demands and curfews – it was not the way things worked between them. He was out having fun. No big deal. It had happened before, after all – a few drinks that had turned into a few more, then sleeping it off on someone's sofa.

Yet it was strange, wasn't it? To not even text – to just not come home at all?

It wasn't until she was in the shower that she remembered the importance of the day's date. Wednesday the twenty-sixth. Luke's interview. The realization made her stand stock-still, the shampoo bottle poised in mid-air. Today was the big interview for his promotion at work.

He'd been preparing for it for weeks; there was no way he would stay out all night before something so important. Quickly she turned the water off and, wrapping herself in a towel, went back to the living room to find her phone. Clicking on his number she waited impatiently for the ringtone to kick in. And then she heard the buzzing vibration coming from beneath the sofa. Crouching down she saw it, lying on the dusty expanse of floor, forgotten and abandoned: Luke's mobile. 'Shit,' she said out loud, and as though surprised, the pounding music above her head ended in abrupt silence.

She clicked open her emails and sure enough there it was, a message from Luke, sent last night at 18.23 from his work address.

Hey darling, left my phone at home again. I'm going to stay and work on stuff for the interview, probably be here til eight, then coming home – want to have an early night for tomorrow. You're out with Zoe, aren't you? See you when I do, Lx

An hour later, as she made her way up Old Street, she told herself to get a grip. He'd changed his mind, that was all. Decided to go for a pint with his team, then ended up carrying the night on. He couldn't let her know because he was phoneless – nothing else to it. She would see him soon enough at work, hung-over and sheepish, full of apologies. So why was her stomach twisting and turning like this? Beneath the April sky, grey and damp like old chewing gum, she walked the ugly thoroughfare, already gnarled with traffic, the brutal hulking buildings of the roundabout ahead, the wide pavements filled with commuters pressing on and on, clutching coffee, earbuds in, staring down at phones or else inward-looking, unseeing, as they moved as one towards the white tiled station entrance, to be sucked in then hurtled forward, and spat out again the other end.

The magazine publishers where they both worked was in the centre of Soho. Though they were on separate magazines – she a writer on a finance title, he heading the design desk of an architectural quarterly – it's where they'd met three years ago, shortly before they'd started going out.

It had been her first day at Brindle Press and, eager to make a good impression, she'd offered to make the first round of teas. Anxiously running through everyone's names as she'd sloshed water on to teabags and stirred in milk and sugar, she'd piled too many mugs on the tray before she'd hurried out of the kitchen. The mess when it slipped from her hands and came crashing to the floor had been spectacular; scattered shards of broken crockery, rivers of brown steaming liquid, her carefully chosen 'first-day' dress soaked through.

Fuck. Fuck fuck fuck. It was only then that she'd looked up and seen him, the tall, good-looking man standing in the doorway, watching her with amusement. 'Oops,' he'd said, crouching down to help her.

'Christ, I'm an idiot,' she'd wailed.

He'd laughed. 'Don't worry about it,' he said, then added, 'I'm Luke.'

That evening, when her new team had taken her out for welcome drinks she'd spotted him at the bar, her heart quickening as she met his gaze, his dark eyes holding her there, as though he'd reached out his hand and touched her.

Now, as she approached her desk the phone rang, its tone signalling an internal line and she snatched it up eagerly. 'Luke?'

But it was his deputy, Lauren. 'Clara? Where the fuck is he?'

She felt herself flush. 'I don't know.'

There was a short, surprised silence. 'Right. What, you don't . . . you haven't seen him this morning?'

'He didn't come home last night,' she admitted.

There was another silence while Lauren digested this. 'Huh.' And then she heard her say loudly to whoever was listening nearby, 'He didn't come home last night!' A chorus of male laughter, of leering comments she couldn't quite catch, though the tone was clear: *Naughty Luke.* They were joking, she knew, and their laughter was comforting, in a way, signifying their lack of concern. Still, she clutched the receiver tightly until Lauren came back on the line. 'Well, not to worry. Fucker's probably dead in a ditch somewhere,' she said cheerfully. 'When you do speak to him, tell him Charlie's raging, he's missed the cover meeting now. Later, yeah?' And then she hung up.

Maybe she should go through his contacts list, ring around his friends. But what if he did arrive soon? He'd be mortified she'd made such a fuss. And surely he was bound to turn up sooner or later – people always did, after all.

Suddenly his best friend Joe McKenzie's face flashed into Clara's mind and for the first time her spirits lifted. *Mac.* He'd know what to do. She grabbed her mobile and hurried out into the corridor to call him, feeling immediately comforted when she heard his familiar Glaswegian accent.

'Clara? How's it going?'

She pictured Mac's pale, serious face, the small brown eyes that peered distractedly from beneath a mop of black hair.

'Have you seen Luke?' she asked.

'Hang on.' The White Stripes blared in the background while she waited impatiently, imagining him fighting his way through the chaos of his photographic studio before the noise was abruptly killed and Mac came back on the line. 'Luke? No. Why? What's— haven't you?'

Quickly she explained, her words spilling out in a rush: Luke's forgotten mobile, his email, his missed interview. 'Yeah,' Mac said when she'd finished. 'That's odd, right enough. He'd never miss that interview.' He thought for a moment. 'I'll call around everyone. Ask if they've seen him. He's probably been on a bender and overslept, you know what he's like.'

But his text half an hour later said, No one's heard

from him. I'll keep trying though, I'm sure he'll turn up.

She couldn't shake the feeling something was very wrong. Despite his colleagues' laughter, she didn't really think he'd been with another woman. Even if he had, a one-night stand didn't take *this* long, surely? She made herself face the real reason for her anxiety: Luke's 'stalker'.

Putting the word in inverted commas, treating it all as a bit of a joke, was something Luke had done ever since it had begun nearly a year ago. He'd even christened whomever it was 'Barry' – a comical, harmless name to prove just how unthreatened he was by it all. 'Barry strikes again!' he'd say, after yet another vicious Facebook message, or silent phone call, or unwelcome 'gift' through the post.

But then things had got weirder. First an envelope stuffed with photographs had been pushed through their door. Each one was of Luke and showed him doing the most mundane of things – queuing at a café, or walking to the Tube, or getting into their car. Whoever had taken them had clearly been following him closely – with a wide-angled lens, Mac had said. It had made Clara's skin crawl. The photos had been stuffed through their letterbox with arrogant nonchalance, as if to say, *This is what I can do: look how easy it is*. But though she'd been desperate to call the police, Luke wouldn't hear of it. It was as if he was determined to pretend it wasn't happening, that it was merely an annoyance that would soon go away. And no matter how much she begged, he wouldn't budge.

And then, three months ago, they'd come home late from a party to find the door to their flat forced open. Clara would never forget the creepy chill she'd felt as they silently walked around their home, knowing some stranger had recently been there – going through their things, touching their belongings. But the strange thing was, everything had been left in perfect order: nothing had been stolen; nothing, as far as she could tell, had been moved. Only a handwritten message on a page torn from Clara's notepad was sitting on the kitchen table: *I'll be seeing you, Luke*.

At least Luke had been sufficiently rattled to let Clara report that to the police. Who didn't even turn up until the next day and discovered precisely nothing – the neighbours hadn't seen anything, no fingerprints had been found – and as nothing had been taken or damaged, within days the so-called 'investigation' had quietly fizzled out.

Stranger still, after that, it was as if whoever it was had lost interest. For weeks now there'd been no new incidents, and Luke had been triumphant. 'See?' he'd said. 'Told you they'd get bored eventually!' But although Clara had tried hard to put it out of her mind, she hadn't quite been able to forget the menace of that note – or the idea that the culprit was still out there somewhere, biding their time.

And now Luke had disappeared. What if 'Barry' had

something to do with it? Even as she allowed the thought to form she could hear Luke's laugh, see his eyes roll. 'Jesus, Clara, will you stop being so dramatic?' But as the morning progressed her sense of foreboding grew and when lunchtime came, instead of going to her usual café, she found herself walking back towards the Tube.

She reached Hoxton Square half an hour later, and when she caught sight of her squat, yellow-bricked building on its furthest corner, she was struck suddenly by the overwhelming certainty that Luke would be there waiting for her, and she ran the final few hundred yards, past the restaurants and bars, the black railings and shadowy lawn of the central garden and, out of breath by the time she reached the front door, she impatiently unlocked it before sprinting up the communal stairs to her flat. But when she got there, it was empty.

She sank into a chair, the flat too silent and still around her. On the coffee table in front of her was a photo she'd had framed when they'd first moved in together and she picked it up now. It was of the two of them on Hampstead Heath three summers before, heads squashed together as they grinned into the camera, a scorching day in June. That first summer, the days seemed to roll out before them hot and limitless, London theirs for the taking. She had fallen in love almost instantly, as effortlessly as breathing, certain she had never met anyone like him before, this handsome, exuberant man so full of energy and sweetness and easy charm and who, (inexplicably it

11

seemed to her) appeared to find her just as irresistible. As she gazed down at the photo now, their happiness trapped and unreachable behind glass, she traced his face with her finger. 'Where are you,' she whispered, 'where the bloody hell are you, Luke?'

At that moment she heard the front door slam two floors below and her heart lurched. She listened, her breath held as the footsteps on the stairs grew louder. When they paused outside her door she sprang to her feet and rushed to open it, but with a jolt of surprise found it was her upstairs neighbour, and not Luke, staring back at her.

She didn't know the name of the woman who'd lived above them for the past six months. She could, Clara thought, be anything between mid-twenties and mid-thirties, it was impossible to tell. She was very thin with long, lank brown hair, behind which could occasionally be glimpsed a small, finely featured face covered in a thick, mask-like layer of make-up. In all the time Clara and Luke had lived there she'd never once replied to their greetings, merely shuffling past with downcast eyes whenever they met on the stairs. Every time either of them had gone up to ask her to turn her music down, which she played loudly night and day, she refused to answer the door, merely turning the volume up higher until they went away.

'Can I help y—' Clara began, but the woman had already begun heading towards the stairs. Clara was watching her go when her worry and stress got the better of her. 'Excuse me!' she blurted, and her neighbour froze, one foot poised on the first step, eyes averted. 'It's about the music. Could you give it a rest, do you think? It's all night long, and sometimes most of the day too, can't you turn it down once in a while?'

At first it seemed the woman wasn't going to reply, but slowly she turned her face towards Clara. Her eyes, rimmed thickly in black kohl, landed on her own before flitting away again, as she asked softly and with the faintest ghost of a smile, 'Where's Luke, Clara?'

Clara could only stare back at her, too surprised to respond. 'I'm sorry?'

'Where's Luke?'

She'd had no idea the woman even knew their names. Perhaps she'd seen them written on their post, but it was the way she said it – so familiar, so knowing, and with such a strange smile on her lips. 'What do you mean?' Clara asked but the woman only turned and carried on up the stairs. 'Excuse me! Why are you asking about Luke?' but there was still no reply. Clara stood staring after her. It was as if the world was conspiring in some surreal joke against her. The door to the upstairs flat opened and then closed again and at last Clara went back to her own flat. She stood in her narrow hallway, listening, until a few seconds later the familiar thud of bass began to thump against her ceiling once more.

It was past two. She should go back to work; her colleagues would be worried by now. But Clara didn't move. Should she start phoning around hospitals? Perhaps she should google their numbers – at least that way she would be doing something. She went to the small box room they used as an office and at a touch of the mouse pad Luke's laptop flickered into life, the browser opening immediately at Google Mail – and Luke's personal email account.

For a second she stared at the screen, her finger hovering, knowing she shouldn't pry. But then her gaze fell upon his list of folders. Below the usual 'Inbox' 'Drafts' and 'Trash' was one labelled, simply, 'Bitch'. She stared at it in shock before clicking on it. And then her jaw dropped – there were at least five hundred messages, sent from several different accounts over the past year, sometimes as often as five times a day. She opened and read them one by one.

Did you see me today, Luke? I saw you. Keep your eyes peeled.

And,

I know you, Luke, I know what you are, what you've done. You might have most people fooled, but you don't fool me. Men like you never fool me.

How are your parents, Luke? How are Oliver and Rose? Do they know the truth about you – your family, your friends, your colleagues? How about that little girlfriend of yours, or is she too stupid to

14

see? She looks really fucking stupid, but she'll find out soon enough.

And,

Women are nothing to you, are we, Luke? We're just here for your convenience, to fuck, to step over, to use or to bully. We're disposable. You think you're untouchable, you think you've got away with it. Think again, Luke.

Then,

What will they say about you at your funeral, Luke? Say your goodbyes, it's going to be soon.

The very last one had been sent only a few days before.

I'm coming for you, Luke, I'll be seeing you.

It had been a *woman*, all this time? And he'd known about it for months, had known but hadn't told her – had never even mentioned the emails. Did he know who it was? It was clearly someone who knew *him* very well – knew his parents' names, where Luke worked; knew his movements intimately. Was it the same person who had broken into their flat, sent the photographs, the letters? Perhaps it was a joke, she thought wildly. An elaborate prank dreamt up by one of his friends. But then, where was he? Where was Luke? *I'm coming for you, Luke. I'll be seeing you.*

She was deep in thought when the sound of her intercom sliced through the silence, making her jump violently, her heart shooting to her mouth.

3

Cambridgeshire, 1986

We waited such a long time for a baby. Years and years, actually. They couldn't tell us why, the specialists. Couldn't find a single reason why it didn't happen for Doug and me. 'Unexplained Infertility,' was the best they could come up with. You think it's going to be so simple, starting a family, and then when it's taken from you, the future you'd imagined snatched away, it feels like a death. All I ever wanted was to be a mum. When school friends went off to university or found themselves jobs down in London, I knew it wasn't for me. I didn't want to be a career woman, didn't need a big house and lots of money. I was content with our cottage in the village I'd grown up in, Doug's building business; I just wanted children, and Doug felt exactly the same way.

I used to see them when they came back to our village for holidays, those old classmates of mine. And I'd see how they looked at me, with my clothes from the market and my lack of ambition, see the flash of superiority or bewilderment in their eyes when they realized I didn't want to be just like them. But I didn't care. I knew that what I wanted would bring me all the happiness I'd need.

Year by year, woman by woman, things began to change. They began to change. As we all neared our thirties, baby after baby began to make their appearance on those weekend visits. Of course, I'd been trying for a good few years by then, had already had many, many months of disappointment to swallow, but nothing hit me quite as hard as seeing that endless parade of children of the girls I used to go to school with.

Because I could see it, in their faces, how it changed them. How overnight the nice clothes and interesting careers and successful husbands which had once defined them became suddenly second place to what they now had. It wasn't the change in them physically; the milk-stained clothes or the tired faces, it wasn't the harassed air of responsibility or the being a member of a new club or even the obvious devotion they felt. It was something I saw in their eyes – a new awareness, I suppose – that most hurt me. It seemed to me as though they'd crossed into another dimension where life was fulfilling and meaningful on a level I could never understand. And the jealousy and despair I felt was devastating.

Plenty of women, I knew, were happily childfree, leading perfectly satisfying lives without kids in them, but I wasn't one of them. For as long as I could remember, having a family of my own was all I'd dreamt of.

So, when finally, *finally*, our miracle happened, it was the most amazing, most joyful thing imaginable. That moment when I held Hannah in my arms for the first time was one of pure elation. We loved her so much, Doug and I, right from the beginning. We had sacrificed so much, and waited such a long time for her, such a horribly long time.

I don't remember exactly when the first niggling doubts began to stir. I couldn't admit it to myself at first. I put it down to my tiredness; the shock and stress of new motherhood, or a hundred other different things rather than admit the truth. I didn't let on to anyone how worried I was. How frightened. I told myself she was healthy and she was beautiful and she was ours, and that's all that mattered.

And yet, I knew. Somehow I knew even then that there was something not quite right about my daughter. An instinct, of the purest truest kind, in the way animals sense trouble in their midst. Secretly I would compare her to other babies – at the clinic, or at Mother and Baby clubs, or at the supermarket. I would watch their expressions, their reactions, the ever-changing emotions in their little faces and then I'd look into Hannah's beautiful big brown eyes and I'd see nothing there. Intelligence, yes – I never feared for her intellect – but rarely emotion. I never *felt* anything from her. Though I lavished love upon her it was as though it couldn't reach her, slipping and sliding across the surface of her like water over oilskin.

At first, when I voiced my concerns to Doug, he'd cheerfully brush them aside. 'She's just chilled out, that's all,' he'd say, 'let her be, love,' and I'd allow myself to be reassured, telling myself he was right, that Hannah was fine and my fears were all in my head. But when she was almost three years old, something happened that even Doug couldn't ignore.

I was preparing breakfast in the kitchen while she sat on the floor, playing with a makeshift drum kit of pots and pans and spoons I'd got out to entertain her with. She was hitting one pan repeatedly over and over, the sound ricocheting inside my skull, but just as I was mentally kicking myself for giving them to her the noise suddenly stopped. 'Hannah want biscuit,' she announced.

'No, darling, not yet,' I said, smiling at her. 'I'm making porridge. Lovely porridge! Be ready in a tick!'

She got up, said louder, 'Hannah want biscuit now!'

'No, sweetheart,' I said more firmly. 'Breakfast first, just wait.'

I crouched down to rummage in a low drawer for a bowl, and didn't hear her come up behind me. When I turned, I felt a sudden searing pain in my eye and reeled backwards in shock. It took a few moments to realize what had happened, to understand that she'd smashed the end of her metal spoon into my eye with a strength

I never dreamed she had. And through my reeling horror I saw, just for a second, her reaction; the flash of satisfaction on her face before she turned away.

I had to take her with me to the hospital, Doug not being due back for several hours yet. I have no idea whether the nurse in A&E believed my story, or whether she saw through my flimsy excuses and assumed me perhaps to be a battered wife, one more victim of a drunken domestic row. If she did guess at my shame and fear, she never commented. And all the while Hannah watched her dress my wounds, listened to the lies I told about walking into a door with a silent lack of interest.

Later that evening when she was in bed, Doug and I stared at each other across the kitchen table. 'She's not even three yet,' he said, his face ashen. 'She's only a little girl, she didn't know what she was doing . . .'

'She *knew*,' I told him. 'She knew exactly what she was doing. And afterwards she barely raised an eyebrow, just went back to hitting those damn pots like nothing had happened.'

And after that, Hannah only got worse. All children hurt other kids, it happens all the time. In every playgroup across the country you'll find them hitting or biting or thumping each other. But they do it out of temper, or because the other child hurt them, or to get the toy they want. They don't do it the way Hannah did – for the sheer, premeditated pleasure of it. I used to watch her like a hawk and I'd see her do it, see the expression in her eyes as she looked quickly around before inflicting a pinch or a slap. The reaction of pain was what motivated her. I knew it. I saw it.

We took her to the doctor's, insisting on a referral to a child psychologist – the three of us trooping over to Peterborough to meet a man with an earnest smile and a gentle voice, in a red jumper, named Neil. But though he did his best with Hannah, inviting her to draw him pictures of her feelings, use dolls to act out stories, she refused, point-blank. 'NO!' she said, pushing crayons and toys away. 'Don't want to.'

'Look,' Neil said, once the receptionist had taken Hannah out of the room. 'She's very young. Children act out sometimes. It's entirely possible she didn't realize how badly she would hurt you.' He paused, fixing me in his sympathetic gaze. 'You also mentioned a lack of affection from her, a lack of . . . emotional response. Sometimes children model what they see from their parents. And sometimes it helps if the parent remembers that they are the adult, and the child is not there to fulfil their own emotional needs.'

He said all this very kindly, very sensitively, but my fury was instantaneous. 'I cuddle that child all day long,' I hissed, ignoring Doug's restraining hand on my arm. 'I talk to her, play with her, kiss her and love her and I tell her how special she is every single minute. And I don't expect my three-year-old to "fulfil my emotional needs". What kind of idiot do you think I am?' But the seed was set, the implication was clear. By hook or by

22

crook it was my fault. And deep down of course I worried that Neil was right. That I was deficient somehow, that I had caused this, whatever 'this' was. We left that psychologist's office and we didn't go back.

That day, the day she killed Lucy, I stood looking in at my five-year-old daughter from her bedroom door and any last remaining hope I'd had – that I'd been wrong about her, that she'd grow out of it, that somewhere inside her was a normal, healthy child – vanished. I marched across the room and took her by the hand. 'Come with me,' I said and led her to my bedroom. Her expression, biddable, mildly interested, only made my fury stronger. I dragged her to the bed and she stood beside me, looking down at Lucy's head on my pillow and I saw – I know I saw – the flicker of enjoyment in her eyes. By the time she'd turned them back to me they were entirely innocent once more. 'Mummy?' she said.

'It was you,' I said, my voice tight with anger. 'I know it was you.' I loved that bird. I had inherited her from an elderly neighbour I'd once been close to, and during those years of childlessness Lucy had become the focus of all my attention; a pretty, defenceless little creature to take care of, who needed me. Hannah knew how much I loved her. She knew.

'No,' she answered, and tilted her head to one side as she continued to consider me. 'No, Mummy. It wasn't me.'

I left her standing by the bed and ran downstairs to

the kitchen. And there was Lucy's cage, its door swung open, the tiny headless body lying on the floor beside it cold and stiff. I looked around the room, my eyes darting wildly about. How had she done it? What had she used? She had no access to the kitchen knives, of course. Suddenly a thought struck me and I ran back up the stairs to her bedroom. And there it was. The metal ruler from Doug's toolbox, lying on her table. I'd heard her asking him for it the day before – for something she was making, she'd said. It lay there now, next to her craft things and I stared down at it as nausea rose in me.

I hadn't heard Hannah follow me from the kitchen until she slipped into the room and stood beside me. 'Mummy?' she said.

My heart jumped, 'What?'

Her eyes fell to my belly. 'Is it all right?'

The slight lisp, that pretty, melodic voice of hers, so adorable – everybody commented on it. I bit back my revulsion. 'What?' I asked. 'Is what all right?'

She considered me. 'The baby, Mummy. The little baby in your tummy. Is it all right? Or is it dead too?'

I put a hand to my belly as defensively as if she'd struck me there. Her gaze bored into me. 'Why would the baby be dead?' I whispered. 'Why would you say that?' There's no way she could have known of course that she'd touched upon my greatest fear – that this new baby, our second miracle, would not survive, would not be born alive. It was the stress of my relationship with

Hannah that caused this paranoia, I think. I almost felt as though I would deserve it, because I'd made such a mess of everything with her. My unborn baby would be taken from me, as penance.

As I gazed into her eyes, fear stroked the back of my neck. 'Stay right here,' I said. 'Stay here until I say.'

That night I described to Doug what had happened. 'What are we going to do?' I asked him. 'What the hell are we going to do?'

'We don't know it was Hannah,' he said weakly.

'Who the hell was it, then?'

'Maybe . . . God, I don't know! Maybe it was a fox, or one of the neighbours' kids mucking about?'

'Don't be ridiculous!'

'We have foxes in the garden all the time,' he said. 'Are you sure the back door was closed?'

'Well, no,' I said, 'It was open. But . . .'

'We've had to tell Hannah before about leaving the cage door unfastened,' he added.

This was also true, she loved to feed Lucy, and though she knew she wasn't allowed to open the door without me there, it was possible she had fiddled with the latch. 'OK, but what about what she said about the baby?' I demanded.

Doug rubbed his face tiredly. 'She's five years old, Beth. She doesn't understand about death yet, does she? Maybe she's feeling anxious about having a new sibling.'

I stared at him. 'I can't believe you're saying this! I know it was Hannah. It was written all over her face!'

'And where were you?' he said, his voice rising too. 'Where the hell were you when all this was going on? Why weren't you watching her?'

'Don't you dare make this my fault,' I shouted. 'Don't you dare do that!' On we argued, our worry and distress causing us to turn on each other, sniping and defensive.

'Mummy? Daddy?' Hannah appeared in the doorway, looking sleepy and adorable in her pink pyjamas. She held her teddy in her hand. 'Why are you shouting?'

Doug got to his feet. 'Hello, little one,' he said, his voice suddenly jolly. 'How's my princess? Got a cuddle for your daddy?'

She nodded and edged closer, but then said in a small, sad voice, 'Is it because of Lucy?'

Doug and I exchanged a look. He picked her up. 'You know how it happened?'

She shook her head. 'Mummy thinks I did it, but I never did! Mummy loves her birdy and so do I.' Tears welled, spilling from her eyes. 'I would never, ever hurt Lu-Lu bird.'

Doug held her close. 'I know you wouldn't, of course you wouldn't. It was only somebody playing a nasty trick, that's all. Or a fox. Maybe a naughty fox did it. Come on, sweetheart, don't cry, please don't cry. Let's get you back to bed.' I knew he was fooling himself, too scared to admit the truth, but I'd never felt so lonely, so wretched, as I did at that moment. As they left the

26

kitchen I looked up and caught Hannah watching me over her father's shoulder, her expression impassive now. We held each other's gaze before they turned the corner and disappeared from view.

4

When Clara answered her intercom it was Mac's voice she heard, crackling back at her as though from a different world; an innocent, ordinary place where emails weren't sent that stopped your heart from beating, that turned your blood to ice. 'Jesus,' he said after she'd buzzed him up, 'you look awful. I tried you at work but they said you hadn't come back after lunch so . . .' he paused. 'Clara? Are you all right?'

Without replying she led him to the computer and pointed at the screen. 'Read these,' she said.

Obediently he sat. She watched him as he read, his head bowed, thick black hair sticking out in all directions, his rangy six-foot frame hunched uncomfortably in the small office chair, as though he might uncoil and come

28

springing out of it like a jack in the box. It was good to see him, the band of fear that had been wrapping itself ever tighter round her chest loosening a fraction.

Mac had been Luke's closest friend since school and spent almost as much time at their flat as they did. He was life as she'd known it only twenty-four hours before: nights out at The Reliance, evenings in with beers and a box set, long, hung-over Sunday lunches in the Owl and Pussycat; private jokes and shared history, the comfort and ease of old friendship: he was the mainstay of her and Luke's relationship, witness to their happy, normal life – before everything had become so entirely not normal, before the creeping awareness that everything was very far from normal indeed.

'Holy shit,' he said, when he'd read the last message.

'Did you know about them?' she demanded.

He glanced at her sheepishly. 'Well yeah, Luke told me he'd been getting dodgy emails, but I didn't realize they were this bad, that there were so many of them.'

Clara's voice rose in frustration. 'Why the hell didn't he tell me? I can't believe he kept them from me. They're so nasty – some of them are fucking sick.'

'Yeah,' Mac said. 'He, um, he didn't want you to worry . . .'

'Oh for God's sake!'

'I know, I know. I think he was embarrassed they're from a woman.'

'Are you kidding me? Whoever this nutcase is broke into my flat! She's been threatening my boyfriend. What

29

the hell was Luke playing at, not telling me about it?' She looked at him sharply. 'Does he know who she is?'

Emphatically Mac shook his head. 'No. Honestly, Clara, I don't think he's got a clue.'

She went to the screen and read the last email aloud. '"I'm coming for you." I mean, what the fuck?' She looked around for her phone. 'I'm going to call the police.'

Mac got up. 'I'm pretty sure they won't do anything until he's been missing twenty-four hours. Look, Clara, I think these emails are from some weirdo who wants to rattle Luke – an ex maybe, but I doubt they have anything to do with him not coming home last night.'

'Where the bloody hell is he, then?'

He shrugged. 'Perhaps he's just gone away for a wee while to clear his head.'

'Clear his *head*? Why on earth would he need to clear his head?'

But Mac's eyes slid away from hers and instead of replying he said, 'I've called all his friends, but I guess he could be at his parents' place. Have you tried there?'

The question made Clara pause. 'No, not yet.'

'Maybe you should check with them. It's the first thing the police will do.'

Mac was right. His mum and dad's house in Suffolk was the obvious place Luke would go – in fact she was surprised it hadn't occurred to her before. She'd never known anyone as close to their parents as Luke. Perhaps the emails had rattled him enough to make him want to get out of London for a few days. But in that case, why hadn't he told her?

Looking down at her phone, she hesitated. 'What if he's not there, though? You know what his mum and dad are like – they'll be beside themselves.'

'Aye, you're not wrong there.'

She and Mac stared at each other, both thinking the same thing: *Emily*.

Luke never talked about his older sister and Clara only knew the bare facts: when she was eighteen, Emily had walked out of the family home and was never heard from again. He'd been ten years old at the time, his brother Tom, fifteen. He had told her a few months after they'd started dating, one night at his old place in Peckham, a shared flat off Queens Road in a dilapidated Victorian terrace, where at night they would lie in bed and listen to the music and voices carrying from the bars and restaurants squeezed into the railway arches across the street, trains thundering over the elevated tracks above.

'And you've no idea what happened to her?' she'd asked, astonished by his story.

Luke had shrugged, and when he'd spoken again there was a heaviness to his voice she'd not heard before. 'No, none of us had a clue. She just walked out one day. Left a note saying she was leaving home, and we never heard from her again. It totally destroyed my family; my parents never got over it. Mum had a nervous breakdown and in the end it was better to never mention her. All the pictures of her got put away, everyone stopped talking about her.'

Clara had sat up, appalled. 'But that's *awful*! You were only ten, you must have wanted to talk about her, it must have devastated you and your brother too.'

The hand that had been stroking her leg paused. 'We learnt it was better not to, I suppose.'

'But . . . was there . . . I mean, weren't the police involved?'

He shook his head. 'She went of her own free will. I think that was the hardest part for my mum and dad – she left a note saying she was going, but no explanation as to why or where. My dad told me they hired a private detective to try and find her but it didn't come to anything.' He shrugged. 'She completely vanished.'

And in that moment she'd understood something about Luke that had always puzzled her. Something she'd glimpsed hovering behind the laughter and the jokes, his need to be the life and soul of every party, a sorrow flickering barely there at the edges of him she hadn't quite been able to put her finger on before.

'What was she like?' she'd asked softly.

He smiled. 'She was ace. She was funny and sweet but kind of . . . fierce, you know? I was only ten, and I guess I'm biased, but I don't think you meet many people like her. She was so passionate about stuff, she'd go off on all these rallies and marches, save the whale, women's rights, you name it. Drove Mum and Dad mad because she'd never just stay still and get on with her school work. I was only a kid, but even then I admired her for it, how principled she was, how sure she was about what was right and wrong. And she was a free spirit, you know?' He sighed and rubbed his face. 'Maybe our house was too restrictive for her and she wanted her freedom. Who knows? Maybe that's why she went.'

'I'm so sorry,' Clara had said quietly. 'I can't imagine how hard it must have been for you all.'

He got up, crossed the room to pull a book down from its shelf and handed it to her. It was a thin volume of children's poems. T.S. Eliot's *Old Possum's Book of Practical Cats*. 'She gave me this a few months before she left,' he told her. 'She used to read it to me when I was a kid. It was . . .' he stopped. 'Well, anyway. That's kind of all I have left of her.'

Reverently, Clara had opened it and read aloud the message written on the flyleaf. '"*For Mungojerrie, from Rumpelteazer. Love you Kiddo. Always, E xx*"' 'Mungojerrie?' Clara had queried, and he'd smiled.

'They're the names of the cats in one of the poems – her favourite one.'

He'd been silent for a while before saying, 'Anyway, it's all in the past now,' and he'd taken the book from her hands and pulled her towards him and started kissing her again, to stop her questions, she'd sensed. Whenever she'd tried to bring Emily up after that, he'd simply shrug and change the subject until eventually she'd given up, though she'd found herself thinking about her often, the missing sister of her boyfriend who'd walked away from home one day, never to be heard from again.

Now, with sudden decisiveness she said to Mac, 'I'm going to drive over there.'

His eyebrows shot up. 'To Suffolk? How long will that take?'

She looked around for her keys and bag. 'An hour and a half tops. At least I'll be doing something. I can't just sit here waiting for him, I feel like I'm going mad. And I think you're right – I think that's where he'll be. He's so close to his mum and dad. And if he has gone there because he's freaked out by the emails, I'd prefer to talk to him face to face.'

'OK,' Mac said slowly, 'but what if he's not?'

She glanced at him. 'Then I'll call the police, which is another reason why I should warn Rose and Oliver first. Will you stay here in case he does come back?'

Mac nodded and patted his laptop bag. 'Sure, I've a load of pictures to edit – might as well work here as anywhere else.'

She hesitated. 'Will you call the hospitals too?'

'Clara, I really don't think anything . . .'

'Please, Mac.'

He held his hands up in defeat. 'OK, sure.'

As soon as Clara got into her car, she phoned her office, putting her mobile on hands-free, before setting off across town towards the M11. She was almost at the North Circular before her editor grudgingly accepted her explanation of 'personal problems' and agreed she could have the next day off. After that she phoned Lauren, who confirmed there'd still been no word from Luke all day. Finally she asked to be put through to the security desk where she reached George, the guard who'd been on duty the night before. He told her that Luke had left the building via the back entrance at around 7.30, that they'd had a brief chat about the football and there'd seemed nothing wrong. 'You know Luke,' he chuckled, 'always got a smile on his face.'

As she drove through the London streets she thought about Luke's parents. She remembered how nervous she'd been the first time he'd brought her to The Willows, his childhood home in Suffolk. Rose and Oliver had sounded so impressive; so very much larger than life – and so very different from her own mum and dad.

It had been a morning in late May. The house they drew up to stood alone, stark against the bleak beauty of the Suffolk landscape, the seemingly endless flat fields, the sky vast and blue and cloudless above them. Luke had led her around the side of the building through to a long and sweeping garden, its borders a carefully controlled riot of colour, a white lilac tree at its centre heavy with flowers that filled the air with their sweet powdery scent. 'Wow,' she'd murmured and Luke had smiled. 'My mum's pride and joy, you should see the parties she throws here every summer – the whole village comes along, it's insane.' And there, at the far end of the garden, kneeling at a flower bed, secateurs in hand, had been Rose. She'd stood up when she heard them approach, and Clara's belly had dipped with apprehension. What would this woman, this cultured, educated, retired surgeon, think of her? Would she like her, think her good enough for her son?

But Rose had smiled, and walked towards them, and in that instant Clara had known everything would be OK. This slim, pretty, fresh-faced woman in a pink summer dress was not in the least intimidating. Instead, Clara had been bowled over by Rose's charm, the way her eyes lit up when she smiled, the genuine warmth with which she'd hugged her, her infectious, enthusiastic way of talking. Rose had led her into the kitchen that first day and patting her hand had said, 'Come and have a drink and tell me all about yourself, Clara, it's so lovely to have you here.'

Oliver, Luke's dad, had emerged from somewhere out of the depths of the house, a tall and bearded bear of a man, Luke's features mirrored in his own, his son's kindness and good humour shining from his almost identical brown eyes. He was a university lecturer, the author of several books on art history. Slightly shy, he was quieter and more reserved than his wife but Clara had warmed to him instantly.

In fact, she'd fallen in love with everything about the Lawsons that day: their beautiful, rambling house, the easy affection they'd showed one another, even the way they argued and joked, good-naturedly mocking each other's flaws – Oliver's messiness and tendency towards hypochondria, Rose's bossy perfectionism or Luke's inability to lose at anything without sulking. It was a revelation to Clara, who'd grown up in a house where even the smallest of perceived slights could lead to weeks of offended silence. She had been conscious, that first visit to The Willows, of the strangest feeling of déjà vu, as though she'd returned after a long absence to somewhere she'd once known well; the place where she was always meant to be.

On those early visits Clara would secretly, eagerly, look for signs of Luke's lost sister, but never found any. Emily wasn't in any of the framed photos in the elegant living room, and only Tom and Luke's old preschool paintings were lovingly displayed on the kitchen walls, autographed in their childish scrawls. She had sounded like such a strong and vivid personality from Luke's description, yet even in the small attic room that had once been hers, no trace of Emily remained. She was so carefully deleted from the fabric of her family that it somehow made her all the more present, Clara thought. What had happened to Luke's sister, she brooded; why would someone leave this loving family home so suddenly, then vanish into thin air? The question fascinated her because, despite the Lawsons' warm hospitality, the welcoming comfort of their beautiful home, she could feel the sadness that lingered there still, in the corners and the shadows of each room.

Over the following three years Clara would hear Emily's name mentioned only once. It was at a birthday party for Rose, The Willows full to bursting with friends from the nearby village, ex colleagues of hers from the hospital, Oliver's writer and publishing friends and what felt like the entire faculty of the university he taught at. Oliver had been extremely drunk, regaling Clara with an anecdote about a recent research trip when suddenly he had fallen silent, staring down at his drink, apparently lost in thought.

'Oliver? Are you OK?' she'd asked in surprise.

He'd replied in a strange, thick voice, 'She meant the world to us you know, our little girl, we loved her so very much.' And to her horror his eyes had filled with tears as he said, 'Oh my darling Emily, I'm so sorry, I'm so very sorry.' She had stared at him, frozen, until Luke's brother Tom had appeared and gently led him away, murmuring, 'Come on, Dad, time for bed now, that's right, off we go.'

At last Clara left London behind and joined the M11. It should only take her another hour or so to reach Suffolk. Would Luke be there? She gripped the steering wheel tighter and pressed her foot on the accelerator. Surely he would – he had to be. Unbidden, the emails she'd read earlier came back to her – *It's going to be soon, Luke, your funeral's going to be very soon* – and she felt again the knot of fear tightening in her stomach.

She reached The Willows as the sun began to set. As she got out of the car and gazed up at the house, cawing jackdaws circled above the surrounding fields in the twilight sky. This moment of stillness before nightfall seemed to capture the place at its most magical. It was an eighteenth-century farmhouse, clematis and blood flower clambering over its red bricks, an ancient weeping willow shivering in the breeze. On either side of the low, wide oak door, crooked, crown-glass windows offered a glimpse into the beautiful interior beyond. It was a house out of a fairy story; enchanted and remote beneath this endless empty sky. She approached the door now, taking a deep breath before she knocked. *Please be here, Luke, please, please, just be here.*

She heard the familiar sound of their ancient spaniel, Clementine, bounding to the door, followed by the latch being raised. It was Oliver who opened it. He peered out at her, not seeming to recognize her at first, clearly wary to have someone appear out of the blue, they were so remote and alone out here. Eventually, his expression cleared. 'Good Lord, Clara!' He turned and called behind him, 'Rose, it's Clara! Oh do calm down, Clemmy! Come in, come in, what a lovely surprise. What on earth are you doing here?'

She glanced over his shoulder to the cosy glow of the room behind him and felt the house's familiar pull. She caught the smell of something cooking and pictured Rose in the kitchen listening to Radio Four while she made dinner, a welcoming, irresistible scene of affluent domesticity, so different from the chilly semi-detached she'd grown up in in Penge. But before she could reply, Rose came running up behind him. 'My goodness, darling, hello! Where's Luke?' She looked beyond Clara to the car, her expression pleased and expectant.

Clara's heart sank. *Shit*. 'He's not with me, actually,' she admitted.

Oliver frowned. 'Oh?' he said, adding gallantly, 'Oh well, how lovely to see *you* anyway. Come in, come in!'

But Rose was still smiling at her. 'Why not?' she asked.

'You haven't heard from him, then?'

'No, not since the weekend.'

Before Clara could say anything else, Oliver was ushering her through to the kitchen. 'Come in! Come in and sit down.'

While Rose bustled about putting the kettle on and Oliver chatted about a new book he was researching, Clara leant down to stroke Clemmy, and wondered how to begin.

Finally, Rose placed the tea on the table in front of her and, sitting down, said mildly, 'So, my darling, where's that son of ours?'

Clara took a deep breath. 'Nobody's seen Luke since yesterday evening, around seven thirty,' she told them. 'He emailed me to say he was coming home but he didn't turn up and he doesn't have his mobile on him. He had an important interview today, as well as a big meeting at work . . . but nobody's heard anything from him.' She looked from one to the other of their faces. 'It's just not like him and I'm so worried. I thought he might have come here, but . . .'

Oliver looked perplexed. 'Well . . . perhaps he's gone to stay with friends, or . . .'

Clara nodded. 'The thing is, and it might be nothing, but he'd been getting these weird emails lately, and a few things had started to happen. A break-in at our flat, and dodgy phone calls, and, well, photographs. We hadn't wanted to worry you, so . . .'

'Phone calls? Photographs? What sort of photographs?' asked Rose in bewilderment.

'Whoever it was had been following Luke, taking pictures, I think they were meant to scare him.'

Rose's face suddenly drained of colour behind her carefully applied make-up. 'What did the emails say?'

'They weren't very nice,' Clara admitted. 'Quite threatening, saying they were going to come after him, talking about his funeral . . .'

'Oh God. Oh dear God.' Rose put a trembling hand to her mouth.

'I don't—' Clara began, but was interrupted by the sound of floorboards creaking overhead, then footsteps on the stairs. She looked from Rose to Oliver in confusion. For a strange, chilly moment she wondered if it was Luke she could hear – the disquieting thought occurring to her that his parents had lied to her, that Luke had been here all along. It took her a second or two to recognize the man who appeared at the kitchen door as Luke's older brother, Tom.

They stared at each other blankly for a moment until Tom said, 'Clara! What – where's Luke?'

She watched Tom as he listened to his father explain the reason for her visit. She had never quite been able to get a handle on Luke's older brother. Perhaps it was because the rest of the Lawsons were so welcoming that Tom's reticence was more noticeable, but it had long seemed to her that he kept himself a little apart from his family, that his aloofness almost bordered on disdain. And though he'd always been polite enough to her on the rare occasions that they met, she'd never quite managed to break through his reserve.

It was unusual to find Tom at The Willows at all, in fact. Although he lived relatively nearby, in Norwich, he was not as close to Rose and Oliver as his younger brother, visiting far less frequently than Luke. Unlike Luke, he took after their mother physically, rather than Oliver, having inherited her high cheekbones and blue, almost turquoise eyes – though apparently none of her natural warmth. She remembered Luke telling her once that Tom had split from a long-term girlfriend a year or so before, though Luke hadn't known why. 'That's Tom for you,' he'd said. 'Closed bloody book when it comes to that sort of stuff.'

'He's probably just drunk somewhere,' Tom said now with the elder-sibling dismissiveness she knew drove Luke crazy. She bit back a rush of irritation, and managed to murmur politely, 'I hope so.'

'But what about this stalker person?' Rose asked anxiously.

Tom shrugged and, going over to his parents' extensive

wine rack, helped himself to a bottle. 'Probably some unhinged ex of his,' he said, reaching for a glass. 'God knows he's had enough of those.' He glanced at Clara and perhaps catching her annoyance looked a little abashed and added more kindly, if patronizingly, 'I'm sure he'll turn up soon. I really wouldn't worry.'

At that moment Rose gripped her husband's arm. 'Oh, Oli, where is he? Where is he?'

'Tom's right. He'll turn up,' Oliver murmured, putting a comforting hand over hers, but though his voice was reassuring, Clara saw the worry in his eyes.

She got to her feet. 'I'm so sorry for upsetting you all like this,' she said miserably.

'What will you do now?' Tom asked.

'I'll call the police as soon as I get home, if he's still not back. He'll have been missing for twenty-four hours by then, so hopefully they'll take it seriously.' She looked around for her bag.

'That's actually a myth, you know,' Tom replied.

She blinked. 'What is?'

'That you have to wait twenty-four hours. You can report someone missing whenever you like – the police still have to take it seriously.'

She picked up her bag, ignoring his know-it-all tone. 'Well anyway, I'll be off now,' she said. 'Mac's back at the flat, calling around the hospitals. Just in case,' she added, seeing Rose's alarmed expression.

'Oh God, oh dear, I don't . . .' Flustered, Rose got to her feet.

43

'I'm sure he'll turn up,' Clara said with more conviction than she felt. 'Tom's right, he's probably had a heavy night and is sleeping it off somewhere. I'm only going to ring the police to be sure.'

Rose nodded unhappily. 'Will you phone me when you've spoken to them?' She and Oliver looked so fearful that Clara wished she hadn't come. For the first time since she'd met them, their characteristic energy and vitality seemed to slip, and though they were only in their sixties still, she caught a disconcerting glimpse of the frail, elderly people they would one day become.

'Of course,' she said firmly. 'Straight away.' Quickly she hugged Rose and kissed Oliver on the cheek before raising her hand and giving Tom a brief wave of farewell. 'I'll speak to you soon. I'm so sorry, but I'd better head back now.'

As soon as she got in her car she phoned Mac. 'Any news?' she asked.

'No. The hospitals say no one's been admitted who fits his description – no one who hasn't already been identified anyway.' He paused. 'I take it his mum and dad haven't heard from him?'

'No,' she said quietly.

'Shit.' There was a silence. 'How'd they take it?'

'Not brilliantly. Rose was very upset.'

'Fucking hell, I'm going to kill that dozy bastard when I see him.'

She gave a weak laugh. 'Oh God, Mac. Where the hell is he?'

Mac didn't reply for a moment, and then in a voice completely unlike his, said, 'I don't know, Clara. I really don't know.'

5

Cambridgeshire, 1987

Our son, Toby, was born a few weeks before Hannah's sixth birthday and from the very first moment he was a joy. I adored being his mother; the way his little eyes would follow me around the room, how he'd reach for me as soon as I drew near – the almost telepathic way we communicated. It was as though we were one person; he seemed to melt into me when I held him, his head tucked tightly under my chin, the skin of his body warm against mine. I felt as though finally I was loved and needed in the way I'd always dreamed of being. We adored each other, it was as simple as that, and yes, I guess it did make Hannah feel pushed out a bit.

But I tried hard to make her feel included. I followed the advice in every book I could find about sibling rivalry, did my best to show her she was loved as much as her brother. It almost always backfired. 'Today we're going to have a Hannah and Mummy day,' I told her one morning over breakfast. 'What would you like to do?' I asked her brightly. 'Anything you want!'

She stared balefully back at me as she shovelled Shreddies into her mouth, but didn't reply.

'Swimming? Cinema?'

Still nothing.

'Shopping for a new toy?'

She shrugged.

'Shopping it is then!'

We drove to the nearest town with a large toy store in its centre. 'We can go for tea and cakes first,' I suggested. 'Isn't this fun? Us girls together? You're such a big girl now, perhaps we can choose a pretty dress for you.' She just stared out of the window while I prattled on.

The shop was one of those lovely old-fashioned ones selling tasteful and expensive handmade toys for the sort of parents allergic to plastic. It wasn't the kind of place I usually shopped in, but I'd wanted to buy Hannah something really special and original. We wandered the aisles, but though I pointed out countless dolls, games and stuffed toys, she barely glanced at them, staring back at me with undisguised boredom. I began to lose my patience. 'Come on, love, you can have anything you want, just take a look!'

It was at that moment that I spotted, at the far end

of the shop, someone I used to know from the village I grew up in. I completely froze, my heart pounding at such a strange and unexpected shock. I ducked my head and turned quickly away, hurrying along another aisle. I couldn't face the questions that would have been asked, the inevitable fishing for details as to why Doug and I had left so suddenly all those years before.

Hiding behind a display of teddy bears I looked around for Hannah, my heart sinking when I realized she wasn't there. 'Hannah!' I hissed, 'Where are you?!' At last I spied my former neighbour leaving and heaved a sigh of relief. At that moment Hannah appeared from around the corner.

'I want to go home,' she said.

I was too drained to argue any longer. 'Fine. Have it your way.'

It was as we were leaving that I felt the hand on my arm. I turned to see a middle-aged woman glaring at me with obvious distaste. 'You'll have to pay for these,' she said, tight-lipped.

It was then that I noticed her 'Manager' badge. 'I'm sorry?' I asked.

She held out her hand, filled with what looked like tiny wooden sticks. 'She did this, I saw her,' the woman said, nodding at Hannah. 'You'll need to pay for them. Would you come this way, please?'

I realized then that what she was showing me was the beautiful set of hand-painted wooden dolls from the eye-wateringly expensive doll's house I'd pointed out to Hannah when we'd first arrived. Every single one of them had had their heads and limbs snapped off. I looked at Hannah who gazed innocently back at me.

We drove home in silence. When I unlocked the front door I all but ran to Toby, grabbing him from Doug's arms and burying my face into his comforting, warm little neck, hurrying up to my bedroom and shutting the door behind us.

From the beginning, Doug and I dealt with Hannah's behaviour very differently. I still had the faint scar at the corner of my eye, the sight of Lucy's empty cage stashed forlornly in our garage to remind me what she was capable of. Toby was a very clingy baby who hated to be put down, and occasionally I'd glance up to see Hannah watching us together, gazing over at us in such an unsettling manner that it made me shiver.

So, yes, I guess I was a little over-protective of my baby son, wary and watchful of my daughter whenever she was near. As he was breastfed I always had an excuse to keep him close by me, but soon Doug began to resent me for what he saw as me monopolizing our boy. 'You've made him clingy,' he'd complain when Toby would cry for me the moment he tried to pick him up. It was as though he thought I was deliberately keeping his son from him, but that just wasn't true.

Doug's way of dealing with Hannah was to lavish her with attention, no matter what she did, as though he hoped the force of his love alone might steer her on the right track. If he came home from work, for example, and found her on the naughty step, he would – much to my annoyance – scoop her up and give her a biscuit, taking her with him to the living room to watch her favourite cartoon on TV, while I played with Toby in a separate room. Slowly our family began to divide into two, with Toby and me on one side, Doug and Hannah on the other. It was true that she was much better behaved when she was with her father, but I sensed that she enjoyed the growing rift between Doug and me. I saw the spark of pleasure in her eyes when we argued, how happy she seemed when we ate our meals in offended silence.

A few months before Hannah turned seven Doug and I were summoned, yet again, to the school to talk about her behaviour. We'd had a row earlier that morning and drove there in almost complete silence, Toby sleeping in his car seat behind us, Doug staring grimly at the road ahead. As we drove I brooded over Hannah. Had I caused it, whatever 'it' was? Had the pain of those years of childlessness affected how I'd bonded with my first child? I had felt so broken, so utterly alone back then; nobody had understood, not really – not even Doug. In my misery and isolation had I put up such a self-protective wall between myself and the world that it'd made my heart harder, inca-pable of fully loving and accepting my daughter when she finally came along? Is that what she sensed and railed against? I stared out of my window, trying to fight my tears, until we drew up in front of West Elms Primary.

The school tried its best to be understanding, Hannah's young teacher earnestly offering us strategies and action points to help deal with our delinquent, troubled daughter, giving us leaflets to read, suggesting counselling – before quietly intimating that Hannah would eventually be asked to leave if it continued, that they had the other children to consider, after all. 'Does she have *any* friends?' I asked miserably.

Miss Foxton sighed. 'She tends to select a certain type of child with whom to attach herself; the more vulnerable and easily led types. Hannah can be very persuasive when she puts her mind to it. She'll allow that child to be her ally for a time, and then she'll grow bored and turn on them completely. It's a pattern we've witnessed repeatedly.' Her eyes slid away to the pencil she was fiddling with. 'Daisy Williams is one example, of course. But no, I've never seen her truly *befriend* anyone as such.'

I nodded, remembering Daisy. Shy and eager to please, she was a very pale, thin child with white-blond hair and red-rimmed eyes who reminded me a little of a skinned rabbit. Hannah had homed in on her during the previous school term, enjoyed her new friend's admiration and slavish devotion for a few weeks, before Daisy had been found, tied up with her own skipping rope and soaking wet, in the playground toilet block. Hannah, all wide-eyed innocence, had maintained that they'd merely been playing a game of cops and robbers, and Daisy had eagerly backed up this claim, but from then on the school had done everything they could to keep the two girls apart, at the insistence, I was sure, of Daisy's mother, who glared at me with open hostility whenever we crossed paths in the playground.

After our talk with Hannah's form teacher we walked back to the car in miserable silence. 'Oh, Doug,' I said when I was sitting in the passenger seat.

He looked at me and sighed. 'I know.' He reached over and took my hand, and for a second something of the old closeness between us flickered. He opened his mouth to speak but at that moment Toby woke and began to cry.

I glanced at Doug and began to open my door. 'I'd better sit in the back with him,' I said. Doug nodded, put the key into the ignition and we drove home without another word.

A few days after the school meeting we sat Hannah down and told her what her punishment would be. It was always hard to discipline her because it was difficult to find anything – any treat or toy – that she was genuinely attached to: she literally didn't care if I confiscated any of her belongings. The only thing she really liked to do was watch television. So on that occasion we told her there'd be no TV for a week. I don't think I'll ever forget the look of fury, of pure venom on her face when we gave her the news.

I found the bruise on Toby's arm the next day. Earlier in the morning I'd left him sitting in his little bouncy chair while I got Hannah ready for school. It was as I was fetching her some clean socks from the tumble dryer that I heard his howl of pain. I raced back up the stairs and there he was, red-faced and hysterical, though moments before I'd left him cooing happily. When I went to find Hannah she was sitting in exactly the same spot on her bedroom floor, placidly doing a jigsaw puzzle. She didn't even look up when I came in. It wasn't until later that I found the bruise; a small, angry, purple mark on Toby's upper arm – as though, perhaps, he'd been pinched very hard. I couldn't prove it was Hannah, but I knew that it was. Of course I did.

6

London, 2017

Shell-shocked, Clara and Mac walked back from the police station. When they'd arrived and told their story to the young officer at the front desk, he'd appeared unimpressed at first, listening with studied patience as Clara haltingly went through her story. His attitude had changed, however when, putting Luke's laptop on the desk in front of him, she described the hundreds of threatening emails, the break-in a few months before, the letter and the photographs stuffed through their door.

'I see,' he'd said. 'If you'll just come with me please.' She and Mac had been ushered through to a small, windowless room and told to wait. They'd sat in nervous silence as they listened to footsteps come and go in the corridor beyond the closed door.

When it opened they were greeted by a slender black woman who introduced herself as Detective Constable Loretta Mansfield. Briskly she approached them and shook their hands with a firm dry handshake, her eyes quickly searching theirs as she smiled, before sitting down and placing Luke's laptop on the table between them. 'Right, Clara,' she said, 'I've had a chat with my colleague about Luke, and what we're going to do next is fill in a missing person's report.'

Clara swallowed hard, her mouth dry with nerves as she went over again what she'd told the officer on the front desk, DC Mansfield's calm, almond-shaped eyes flicking up to meet hers at various points in her story.

'And there'd been no arguments between you recently,' she asked, 'no indication that Luke might want out of the relationship?'

'No! And as I said, he's left his mobile and credit card, and he had an important interview at work he'd prepared hard for. We were . . . happy!' she heard her voice rising and felt Mac's hand on her arm.

Mansfield nodded, then opened the laptop and read through the emails. 'I see.' When she looked up again, she cleared her throat decisively. 'OK, Clara, I'm going to hang on to this for now, and talk it over with my sergeant in CID. What I suggest you do now is go home and wait for us to get in touch, and in the meantime, if you hear from Luke, or if anything else suspicious happens, please call us straight away.' She got up and

55

with another brief smile and a nod of her head, indicated for Clara and Mac to follow her.

But Clara remained seated, staring up at her in alarm. 'CID? So you agree those emails could be linked to his disappearance?' She had half hoped to be fobbed off, to be told she was overreacting, that there was clearly an innocent explanation for it all. The seriousness with which Mansfield was taking her concerns caused darts of panic to shoot through her.

'It's possible,' the DC said. 'There could be any number of reasons why he's taken off for a bit. He might have gone out and had a few drinks and not made his way home yet – that happens. Hopefully there's nothing to worry about. But as I said, go home, and someone will be round to see you as soon as possible. We have your address.' She went to the door and held it open, and reluctantly Clara got to her feet.

'Are you all right?' Mac asked as they trudged back down Kingsland Road towards home.

'I don't know. It all feels so strange. You see on the news and stuff about people disappearing, you see those Facebook appeals, and I can't believe he's one of them, it's too surreal. Half the time I'm telling myself there's some rational explanation and I should just chill out, the other half I feel guilty because I'm not tearing through the streets searching for him. I don't know what to do.'

He nodded gloomily. 'He'll turn up. It's going to be OK. They'll find him,' but she could hear the worry in his voice. As they walked she thought about Mac and Luke, and the friendship they'd had for so many years. Of the two of them, Luke had always had the loudest personality, Mac with his quiet dry wit the straight man to Luke's clown. And if Luke's love of the limelight meant he sometimes didn't know when to quit, ensuring he was always one of the last to leave any party, Mac was invariably there to keep his friend out of trouble, bundling him into a cab when he'd had too much to drink, ensuring that he eventually made it home in one piece. Instinctively now she reached out and linked her arm through his, more grateful than she could say for his calm, steady presence. He glanced down at her and smiled, and together they walked on in silence.

She felt desolate when they returned to the empty flat. There was Luke's leather jacket hanging on its peg; on the table by the window was a half-completed Scrabble game they'd abandoned two nights before. The last record they'd been listening to sat silent and still on the turntable. It was as though he'd stepped out only moments before, as though he might reappear at any second with a bottle of wine tucked under his arm, smiling his smile and calling her name. He hadn't taken anything with him – not one single thing a person who was intending to leave home might take.

Mac came and stood beside her. 'Would you like me to stay over?' he asked. 'I could sleep on the sofa.'

She smiled gratefully, suddenly realizing how much

she'd been dreading another night alone. 'Thanks, Mac,' she said.

She was awoken by the sound of her intercom buzzing. Groggily she sat up, looking about her in confusion, surprised to see that she was still wearing her clothes. The fact of Luke's disappearance hit her like a train and she gasped in distress. She remembered she'd gone to lie down while waiting for the police to come, had put her head on Luke's pillow, breathing in the scent of his hair and skin, a feeling of utter hopelessness filling her; nervous exhaustion rolling over her in heavy waves. She must have fallen asleep.

Dazedly she stumbled to her feet and going into the living room saw Mac blinking awake on the sofa. She glanced at the clock: eight a.m. Again the intercom buzzed loudly and she hurried over to answer it. 'Hello?'

'Miss Haynes? DS Anderson from CID. Can I come up?'

He was a large man, Detective Sergeant Martin Anderson. Mid-thirties, a slight paunch, small blue-grey eyes that regarded her from the depths of a ruddy face. A proper grown-up, with a proper grown-up job: even though he was less than a decade older than Clara and Mac, he might as well have belonged to an entirely different generation. She clocked his wedding ring and pictured a couple of kids at home who idolized him. A very different sort of life to the ones led by her and Mac and their friends, with their media jobs, their parties and endless hangovers. He was accompanied by DC Mansfield, who nodded at her and flashed her brief, impassive smile.

'This is Mac, Luke's best friend,' Clara explained nervously as the four of them sat down in the living room. The flat felt very crowded suddenly; a dark cloak of authority and gravity descending upon her home that gave her worst fears credence and made fresh anxiety twist in her belly. Outside on the street someone gave a long, low whistle, a car engine stuttered into life; the world continued as usual, oblivious to the tense, waiting silence of this room.

'I've been passed on the information you gave DC Mansfield yesterday,' Anderson began in a voice that was deep and measured, a faint accent curling around its vowels that Clara's London ears identified vaguely as Midlands.

'I take it you've had no contact from Luke since then?'

Clara shook her head. 'No.'

He nodded. 'In most cases the missing person turns up within forty-eight hours. But due to the harassment Luke's been receiving, we need to make sure there's nothing more to this. I understand there'd been a letter . . . some photographs as well as the break-in a few months ago? Do you have them here with you?'

For the next ten minutes Clara went about the flat, gathering the various items that DS Anderson requested – Luke's bank details, the names and numbers of his friends and family and place of work, a recent photograph, his passport and so on. She moved as if in a dream, stepping around DC Mansfield, who glanced at her apologetically as she conducted her own search, opening various cupboards and drawers. 'What are you looking for?' Clara asked when she found her scrutinizing the bathroom cabinet.

'It's standard procedure,' she said, not answering her question. 'I'm going to need something with Luke's DNA, by the way. Did he take his toothbrush with him?'

Clara shook her head. 'He didn't take anything with him.' She handed over Luke's green toothbrush, leaving her own red one alone in its cup, and tried to fight the tears that sprung to her eyes.

When she returned to the living room she gave DS Anderson everything she'd collected and he nodded his thanks. 'Luke left his mobile behind too,' she said, handing it to him. 'The code's 1609.' The sixteenth of September. Her birthday. She remembered how he'd smiled and said, 'That way I'll never forget.' She watched as that, too, was efficiently deposited into a clear plastic evidence bag.

Anderson turned his attention to Mac. 'And how about you, Mac? How long have you and Luke been friends?'

'Eighteen years. Since we were eleven.' Clara almost smiled at the way this giant Glaswegian was suddenly sitting up straighter, his knees pressed neatly together, meek as a kid in front of his headmaster.

'And there was nothing about his behaviour recently that struck you as unusual?'

'No . . . I don't think so, no.'

Clara glanced at him. Was there something a little strange about the way Mac said that? The brief hesitation before he spoke, something slightly off about his tone? She couldn't quite put her finger on it.

Twenty-five minutes after they arrived, the two officers got up to leave. 'I think I have all I need for now,' Anderson told them. 'I'm going to talk to Luke's parents and his employers next.' He paused, consulting his notes. 'Brindle Press? W1. Is that right?' When Clara nodded he went on, 'We'll also look at any relevant CCTV footage, to see if we can trace his movements after he left work yesterday.' He glanced at Mac. 'And if you could both think about anything that might have happened in the last few weeks that could be relevant – any unusual phone calls, anything out of character he might have said to either of you, or any change in his usual behaviour . . .'

'Yes, yes of course,' Mac and Clara said together.

He nodded. 'We'll be in touch.'

After they left, Clara sank on to the sofa. 'Jesus,' she murmured. She put her head in her hands. 'At least they're taking it seriously, I suppose.' When Mac didn't reply she turned to find him standing with his back to her, gazing out of the window. 'Are you OK?' she asked.

He was silent for a while, and then she heard him mutter something to himself. She stared at him in bewilderment. 'Mac? What's the matter? What is it?'

He turned to face her. 'Jesus, Clara, I'm so sorry.'

'Sorry? What on earth for?'

He raked his fingers through his hair in agitation. 'I really didn't want you to find out like this. But it's all going to come out now – the police are going to talk to everyone – his work, his friends; everyone, and I don't want you to hear about it that way.'

'For God's sake, Mac! Hear about what?'

Mac closed his eyes for a moment. 'Luke's affair.'

The shock was like a body blow, knocking the air from her lungs and leaving her reeling. And when she was finally able to speak her voice was barely more than a whisper. 'Affair? Who with?'

'A girl from work. Her name's Sadie. I think she's . . .'

On the ads team. Blond hair, legs to her armpits. Barely twenty. 'Yeah, I know who she is.' She felt strangely incapable of reaction, as if the information wouldn't quite penetrate her brain. 'How long?'

'A few weeks, maybe a couple of months. But it finished ages ago. Listen, Clara—'

She cut across him, 'A couple of *months*? And is he . . . does he love her?'

His reply was emphatic. 'God, no! No, of course not. He loves you, Clara, I know he does.'

She gave a weak laugh. 'Clearly.'

'It was just . . . oh God, Clara, I'm so sorry.'

She stared at him. 'But he asked me to move in with him! Why? Why do that if you're shagging someone else?'

'He knew Sadie was a huge mistake. He realized it was you he wanted.'

She nodded. 'Great. Lucky me.'

A silence. 'Why the fuck didn't you tell me, Mac?' she asked him quietly. She realized she felt almost as betrayed by him as she did by Luke, almost as hurt by her friend's deceit as by the man who was supposed to be in love with her. She thought of all the times she, Luke and Mac had spent together, when she'd been oblivious to the secret they shared, and her cheeks burned with anger and embarrassment.

'I—'

She glanced at him, her voice suddenly hard. 'Don't tell me. Because you're his best friend. Lads sticking together, right? Some stupid fucking boy code?'

His face was a picture of misery. 'Clara, listen to me . . .'

She waved his words away. 'Does everyone know?' She thought of Luke's large circle of friends – people they socialized with together, met up with at the pub, invited round for dinner, and her humiliation deepened. 'All of you, all his mates?'

'No! God, I don't know. He felt awful about it. He didn't know what to do, he was in absolute bits . . .'

It was then she remembered something. 'That's what you meant about him going away to clear his head,' she said, and the flicker in Mac's eyes confirmed it.

'At first I thought maybe he was with her. But I called her and he wasn't. Then I thought maybe he did go away somewhere to try and sort himself out, get his head straight, but . . . I don't think so. It doesn't add up – not telling work, his parents, me, not taking any of his stuff . . . and the thing with Sadie ended ages ago.'

From outside on the street Clara heard the jingling crash of crates of beers being delivered to the bar on the corner. They sat and listened to it, a sound she associated with summer, with sitting outside pubs on sunlit pavements with Luke, with being happy.

'Clara? Are you OK? I'm sorry. I'm so fucking sorry.'

She looked at his anxious face and suddenly felt so tired she could barely stand. She sank back on to the sofa. 'Just go, Mac,' she said quietly. 'Just go the fuck home now, will you?'

7

Cambridgeshire, 1988

There was a local woman, a childminder named Kathy Philips, who occasionally took care of Hannah for me when I needed a break. She was, in hindsight, a bit slack; her home was haphazard, she had four children of her own, plus at least one other mindee whenever I dropped Hannah off. But she was a kind, no-nonsense sort, and, most importantly, she was willing – by then Hannah's reputation had spread throughout our village; there weren't a lot of people willing to look after her. I was desperate, I'll admit.

I suppose I shouldn't have been surprised that Hannah did what she did. She had told me that morning she didn't want to go: 'They're stupid and boring and their house smells of wee,' was I think how she put it. So this, I expect, was her way of punishing me.

I'll never forget the fury in Kathy's voice when she called. 'Come and pick your daughter up right now,' she spat, before slamming the phone back down. As I drove over there I mentally ran through the possibilities. Attacked one of the other kids? Stolen something? But no, it was far worse than either of those things. Kathy was waiting for me at her door when I pulled up and the expression on her face made my blood run cold. 'She set fire to my son's bedroom,' she told me through gritted teeth.

There was no coming back from that. There was no sweeping that under the carpet – no pretending she'd grow out of it, that it was merely some dreadful phase. Hannah had taken some matches from Kathy's handbag, sneaked upstairs and made a pile of Callum's books, then set fire to them. Kathy, luckily, had smelt the smoke before it had spread too far – but not before she'd burned a large brown hole in the carpet. I hate to think what would have happened if it had been allowed to take hold.

'Callum was being annoying,' Hannah shrugged, when I asked her why she'd done it. By this time she was seven years old.

It was a small village. She had already bullied half the school by then and Kathy wasn't the type to keep anything to herself. Soon everyone would know. Long ago, in my naïve, pre-children days when I used to dream about my future family, I believed I would make friends with all the other local mothers. Our kids would play happily together in each other's gardens; lasting friendships would be formed. Of course back then I believed we'd still be living in our old village, the one I myself had grown up in. But it wasn't to be. Still, I'd hoped very much to be a part of this new community. It was to be a fresh start for us all. Yet here we were: my child was a pariah. She had no friends, was never invited anywhere to play. The other school mums would meet up regularly but never include me. And now this. I didn't know how I'd be able to face going out in public again.

The next day, after dropping Hannah off at school, I drove to Peterborough library. I headed to the Psychology section and began to search. I scarcely knew what I was looking for until I found it, and when I did, I barely noticed my tears as they fell.

When Doug got home from work that night I was sitting on the sofa waiting for him. He'd got back late the night before so we hadn't had a chance to talk properly about what Hannah had done and he looked at me warily as he came in.

'I just want you to listen to me, OK?' I said.

When he nodded and sat down next to me I handed him the wedge of photocopies I'd made that afternoon. He glanced at me, brow furrowed, before flicking through them. I held my breath.

Finally he looked up, his eyes wide. 'Personality

Disorders in Childhood?' he said. 'Early Warning Signs of Sociopathy? Are you serious?'

I leant towards him. 'Doug, it's time we faced facts. We can't continue like this, Hannah set fire to Callum's room, she hurt my eye so badly I had to go to A&E. She killed Lucy . . . then there's the lying, the stealing, the bullying . . .' I could hear my voice rising and I made myself stop and take a breath. 'There's something called Antisocial Personality Disorder and the books say there are certain red flags to look out for.' Eagerly I took the printouts from him and flicked through until I found the one I wanted, reading aloud, '"Antisocial Personality Disorder and sociopathy can be traced back to childhood: desire to torture or kill animals; predilection for arson, manipulation of others. Lack of remorse, apparent absence of emotion . . ."' I looked up at him. 'Doug, there might as well be a picture of Hannah right next to this!'

'Beth,' he said, shaking his head, 'Come on now . . .'

'Why are you denying it?' I asked. 'We could get her help. We could get *us* help.'

'So, what – you want her committed?' he replied, his distress adding a harsh angry edge to his voice. 'Locked up? Are you saying she's – what? – some sort of future serial killer? Is that it?'

'No! No of course I'm not saying that. I'm as scared as you are. I love Hannah! But I know there's something badly wrong with our little girl, and we need to get her help as soon as possible. I know you're frightened, but it doesn't mean that we don't love her. And what – what if she hurts Toby?'

He looked away. 'That shrink we took her to before,' he said there was nothing wrong with her.'

'He said she was too young to make a diagnosis.'

'*Christ.*' He got up and paced around the room, coming to a stop by the window, where he stood looking out in silence. When he finally spoke his voice was tight and strange. 'If this is true, if you're right . . . what if they take her away from us, Beth? What if they say we can't look after her properly, that it's our fault she's the way she is?'

'She's getting worse, Doug,' I said gently. 'She needs help. We all do.'

He nodded, and I held my breath while he continued to stare out of the window. 'OK,' he said at last. 'OK. Let's try to get her another referral.' He glanced at me. 'As long as it's not with that berk in Peterborough.'

He smiled sadly at me then, something he hadn't done, it seemed to me, for a long time, and I could have cried with relief. And I think it was that rare moment of closeness that moved me to say what I said next, to bring up something from years before, that we'd both promised never to mention again. 'I want to talk about what happened, Doug,' I blurted. 'About what we did.'

He knew instantly what I meant, and he became very still. My words hung in the air between us. 'Look, Beth,' he said at last, 'I can't deal with this now . . .'

'Please, Doug,' I begged. 'Just let me talk about it. I

need to. I think about it all the time, don't you? I wake up with it on my mind, the lies we told, that girl's poor family . . .'

His voice was sharp. 'Beth, that's all in the past. We agreed—'

'But, what we did was wrong. It was so wrong, we should never have—'

He glanced at me and the sudden coldness in his eyes stopped me in my tracks. 'You wanted to do it. And we have to live with that now.'

I gaped at him. 'Me? *I* wanted? Doug, we both did.' He shook his head and got to his feet. 'Please, Doug, please don't go.' I started to cry.

He stopped, his back to me, he was very still and quiet, and then with a sudden movement, he went quickly from the room. I heard the front door slam shut. He didn't come back until many hours later, drunk and silent and still too furious even to look at me.

We barely spoke in the following days. I made the appointment with the GP, who referred me to a child psychologist in Cambridge who had a waiting list of several weeks. The loneliness in the days after my talk with Doug was unbearable. I sank deeper and deeper inside myself, brooding over things that should have been left firmly in the past. I knew there was only one person who could help me – the same person who'd provided all the answers once before; who knew our secret, as we knew theirs. It would be such a relief to talk about it, like lancing a wound that had been allowed to fester too long. Of course, I knew Doug would never agree, would be horrified at the very idea of us being in contact again – yet the more I fantasized about making the phone call, the more desperate I became to do it.

8

London, 2017

After Mac had left, his revelation ringing in her ears, Clara sat motionless on the sofa, her shock so absolute that, for now at least, she felt nothing, the world stripped of sound and sensation, like the aftermath of an explosion. But she knew the pain was coming; could sense the tsunami swelling on the horizon, gathering strength, waiting to break.

Her gaze fell to the photograph of her and Luke on Hampstead Heath, her face turned so lovingly towards his, her eyes shining with happiness. *Idiot.* She thought now of all the hundreds of times when he'd appeared to love her. Which of those had been a lie? When had he started to be dissatisfied with her, to begin to draw away, look elsewhere?

She remembered their first date. A hazy summer's evening on the South Bank when suddenly he'd taken her hand and led her away from the crowds, the street performers, the bookstalls, the bars and restaurants, down mossy stone steps to the river's bank, where small groups huddled on the silty sand, smoke rising from a campfire, music from a busker's guitar, the lights of the embankment trailing across the river's surface, the last of the sun falling behind the city's skyline. And when he'd kissed her she'd never felt so deliriously, stupidly happy. Not an expert in these things, she had fallen too deeply, too quickly, entirely forgetting to keep a part of herself back, to put a lifejacket on in case of emergency.

Sadie. Sadie fucking Banks. Did everyone know? Their colleagues, their friends? At that moment she remembered the card DS Anderson had left for her and she pulled it out now, staring down at it until with sudden decisiveness she picked up her phone and dialled the number before she could change her mind, before the tsunami broke and dragged her under.

'DS Anderson.'

She swallowed. 'It's Clara Haynes. I— you—'

'Yes. Hello, Clara, how can I help?'

She forced herself to speak. 'Luke was having an affair,' she said, in the unrecognizable, matter-of-fact voice of a stranger. 'Her name's Sadie Banks, she works at Brindle too. Maybe you should speak to her. She might have a better idea of where he is.' Her voice cracked on the last word and when she hung up the pain crashed over her, dragging her down in its vicious undertow, filling her lungs with grief.

A long time later she sat, head in hands, her face raw from crying. What should she do now? Pack her bags and move out? Had Luke simply left her for someone else? Was that all this was: merely a gutless way of telling her she was dumped, that he hadn't loved her after all?

When she arrived at work the next morning – the thought of staying at home alone in their silent, waiting flat had been unbearable – she hurried towards her magazine's office, keeping her head down, unable to contemplate how she could begin to answer even the most innocent question about where she'd been. Perhaps the police hadn't called there yet, she thought hopefully; perhaps no one had an inkling of the bomb that had detonated in the middle of her life. Making eye contact with no one, she made her way quickly to her desk.

When she looked up from her computer thirty seconds later, however, it was to a ring of her colleagues gathered around her desk, staring down at her.

'Shit, Clara, are you OK?' asked the features editor.

'We had the police here yesterday,' breathed one of the subs.

'Is there any news of Luke, where do you think he is?' asked someone else.

'I don't know,' she stammered. 'They don't – the police, I mean – they don't know either.' She wondered, as she spoke, how many of them knew about Sadie, and felt the heat climb in her cheeks.

For the rest of the morning she tried to distract herself with work, ignoring her colleagues' sympathetic glances, but by eleven she found herself gazing blankly at her computer screen, unable to concentrate on anything except the thought of Sadie sitting a couple of floors below. At last, before she could change her mind, she clicked open her emails and began to type. 'Can you meet me at lunch?'

She waited, heart thumping, for a response, and a few seconds later it came: a one-word reply that said simply, 'OK.'

She'd chosen a café on the far side of Leicester Square, one where they were unlikely to be spotted by any of their colleagues. It was a tacky, overpriced ice cream parlour-cum-souvenir shop, crammed with tourists buying Union Jack tat and clogging the aisle while they confusedly counted out their change. She had made sure she'd arrived early and taken a table at the back out of the way, eyes fixed on the can of Coke in front of her, her fingers nervously shredding a serviette.

For a second, when Sadie appeared in front of Clara, she almost laughed, she was so ridiculously beautiful. Long honey-coloured hair and wide blue eyes, the proverbial traffic-stopping figure. And then she had a sudden image of her and Luke in bed together and felt as though she'd been punched, the pain like a physical blow to the solar plexus. How must she have compared to this goddess? Had he secretly been laughing at her, comparing Clara's short legs and unimpressive chest to this perfection? She found it difficult to comprehend now that she could have been so naive, so self-deceiving as to have believed Luke when he'd dismissed girls like Sadie as too young and too silly to really find attractive – that he found her intelligence and wit preferable to such beauty. What a total fool she'd been.

Wordlessly Sadie sat down opposite her. They stared at each other warily for a moment, each of them waiting for the other to speak. It was Sadie who looked away first. She began fiddling with a bowl of sugar cubes and Clara noticed with a flicker of surprise that her hands were trembling.

'Have the police spoken to you, yet?' Clara asked at last, amazed when her voice came out sure and strong, rather than the tearful stutter she'd been expecting.

Sadie nodded.

She swallowed. 'Well? Have you seen Luke? Do you know where he is?'

At this she shook her head vehemently. 'No! I haven't seen him since Tuesday, at work, I swear to God, Clara!'

'Were you still . . . seeing him?'

She shook her head again.

'How long?' Clara's voice caught and she winced at the indignity of it all. She cleared her throat and tried again. 'How long were you fucking my boyfriend?'

Sadie coloured; a delicate dusky rose staining her flawless skin. 'It only happened once.'

76

Clara gave a snort of disbelief. That wasn't what Mac had said. For the first time her hurt was replaced by an icy disdain for Luke. Beautiful or not, was this lying child what he'd in fact wanted? Really? 'I know that's not true,' she said. 'Didn't you even care he had a girlfriend?'

Sadie's eyes filled with tears. 'I'm so sorry, Clara. We never meant it to happen.'

We. The irony was, Clara had always liked Sadie; they'd often chatted at work dos, laughed together in the pub about Sadie's crazy boss. She'd been too sweet, too eager to please to be considered a threat, not that Clara was in the habit of thinking of other women in those terms. Perhaps she should have been, she reflected bitterly now. 'Why did it end?' she asked.

'He wouldn't . . . he didn't want to leave you. He said he loved you, wanted to marry you,' she began to cry, 'that I . . . was a mistake.'

When Clara didn't say anything Sadie blurted, 'You must hate me. I know you do. But I'm not a horrible person, Clara. I'm really not. I just . . . where do you think he is? Do you think he's OK?'

Clara stood up. 'How would I know, Sadie?' she said tiredly. 'I have absolutely no fucking idea about anything any more.'

Rose called her as she was walking to the Tube later that evening. She hesitated, weariness rolling over her, her finger hovering on the Accept Call button, unsure whether she could face going through DS Anderson's visit with her once again. Eventually she picked up, knowing that Luke's disappearance must surely be even worse for Rose than it was for her. 'Hello,' she said, 'how are you feeling today?'

'Oh, Clara. I can't bear it. I keep going over and over where he could be, whether he's hurt, whether he knows how much we all love him . . .' Her voice gave way to stifled sobs.

'I know,' she murmured. 'I know how awful this is for you.' She hesitated. 'How's Oliver taking it?'

'Very badly. He's dreadfully upset. This all brings back some extremely painful memories, as I'm sure you can imagine.'

'I'm so sorry.'

'I'm worried about him, Clara. He hardly eats or sleeps, just locks himself away in his study, barely speaking to me.'

Clara's heart ached for her. She knew how much Rose loved Oliver; her devotion to him had always touched her, how proud she was of him despite her own considerable achievements. The strength of the Lawsons' marriage was something she'd always aspired to; its generosity and inclusiveness being so unlike the insular, unwelcoming one between her own parents.

'It's such a comfort to us that Luke has you,' Rose went on. 'That we all have you. Knowing you're there looking for him, helping the police. You're like a daughter to us, you know that, don't you, Clara?'

Clara briefly closed her eyes as hurt washed through

her. 'Don't worry,' she said, 'it's going to be all right.'

'I keep thinking about those awful emails. Tell me again what DS Anderson said, he does think they're connected, doesn't he?'

'I don't think he knows yet what—'

'But it must be! The same person who broke into your flat, who took those photographs . . .'

For the briefest moment Clara considered telling Rose about Luke's affair, that she was washing her hands of her son, that he had hurt her too much to care about his whereabouts any more. But even before the thought was fully formed, she knew she never would. Because despite everything, despite all that he'd done, she couldn't do it, not to Luke, and especially not to his parents. After all, it was hardly their fault that any of this had happened. 'I'm going to get on the Tube now,' she said instead. 'I'll phone you as soon as the police get in touch. Try to stay strong, Rose. We'll find him. I promise.'

Sitting on the Northern Line a few minutes later, Clara brooded over Rose's distress. Her mind wandered to a weekend in Suffolk a year or so before. It had been the day of the village fete, an event organized entirely by Luke's parents, to raise funds for a little local girl with leukaemia. There had been stalls and games, live music and dancing, and the whole village had come along, a joyful atmosphere of community and goodwill in the air. Clara had watched as Rose had danced energetically to the band, while a smiling Oliver had organized tug-of-war contests and run the coconut shy. Despite the weeks and weeks of hard work, the time and money that had gone into organizing the event, she saw how they brushed off all congratulations and thanks with self-deprecating modesty. It was only when the parents of the girl for whom the fete was in honour approached and hugged them both that Clara saw how touched and relieved they were by the day's success.

As her train drew into Old Street, Clara got up, reflecting bitterly at how cruel life was. Why was it that bad things seemed to happen to those who least deserved it? Hadn't Rose and Oliver suffered enough? She stepped out on to the platform, resolving that she would do everything she possibly could to help Luke's parents find him.

Mac was waiting for her on the street outside her building when she arrived. He was leaning against the wall, watching her warily as she approached. He raised his hands in a gesture of surrender. 'I just wanted to see how you are,' he said.

She sighed, too tired to turn him away. 'Come up.'

Five minutes later they were sitting across the kitchen table from each other. She took in the familiar, endearing gawkiness of him, the pale skin that looked like it barely saw sunlight – which wasn't far from the truth: Mac was a freelance photographer and spent his nights taking pictures of gigs and music concerts for a living, which meant he often slept during daylight hours. Luke's funny, loyal friend who could usually make her helpless with laughter within seconds, who until yesterday she had thought was one of her closest friends, too. 'Why did he do it?' she asked. 'We've only just moved in together, he told me he loved me! What the fuck was he playing at?'

Mac shrugged helplessly. 'Because he's a bloody idiot.'

'You should have told me, Mac. I thought you were my friend.'

'I *am* your friend. Think about the position I was in. I fucking hated it. But it needed to come from him, not me. I told him to tell you, I told him over and over, you've got to believe that!'

She rubbed her eyes, considering this. 'How did it start between them?' she asked.

'Sadie was in the pub one night after work and Luke got talking to her. Her dad had died recently I think and she was drunk and upset, so he comforted her, told her he was always around for a chat. You know what Luke's like, always wants to be there for people. Anyway, he said after that she used to seek him out whenever she could, they'd meet at lunch now and then, and she'd turn up at the pub after work and make a beeline for him. A few of them ended up at her flat one night and, well, I guess one thing led to another. He told me she wouldn't leave him alone after that, saying she'd fallen for him, he was the only thing keeping her going. He got in too deep, didn't know how to get himself out of it . . .'

'I expect it helped that she looks like a fucking

81

supermodel,' Clara muttered, once again mentally comparing her own looks to Sadie's and finding herself humiliatingly lacking. She was the sort of woman others referred to as 'cute'. Five foot five with a short, Bettie Page bob, a slightly snubbed nose and freckles, she'd long made peace with the fact that she wasn't the stuff of male fantasy – until now, that was, when suddenly every long-buried adolescent insecurity seemed to be rushing back at her with the speed of an express train.

He sighed. 'Look, I'm not trying to excuse him, but he made a mistake, a massive one, he totally ballsed up and he knows it . . . he's truly sorry, I know he is.'

'Jesus,' she said, putting her head in her hands. 'I thought he was so . . . *nice*.'

'He *is* nice,' Mac said. 'He's just a bit of a fuck-up underneath it all.'

'What right has he got to be fucked up?' she said angrily. 'I mean, you've met his parents, seen their beautiful home . . .'

Mac was silent for a while. 'Did he ever talk to you about when Emily went missing?' he asked.

She glanced at him. 'No, not really,' she admitted.

He nodded. 'I moved down to Suffolk from Glasgow right after she disappeared. I was the lanky new kid with a weird accent. The other lads made mincemeat of me, until Luke stepped in. We just hit it off and, well, I was only a kid, but fuck me it was a horror show round at his place for a while.'

Clara frowned. 'Go on.'

'They were all totally destroyed by it. Rose went to bed for months and barely ate or spoke. His dad barricaded himself in his study and Tom went completely off the rails.'

She looked at him in surprise. 'Tom did?' It was a side of Luke's rather uptight, pompous brother she wouldn't have guessed at.

'Yeah, it was like he'd just checked out of the family. He was sixteen by then and hanging out with a bad crowd – off getting pissed and high, that sort of thing, you know? I think Rose and Oliver felt they'd lost their grip on him. But the point is, after that it was as though Luke became the centre of their world, like they became fixated on him. With Emily gone and Tom out all the time, everything began to revolve around him – he was still only ten when she left, remember.'

'What do you mean, "fixated"?'

Mac shrugged. 'They'd never leave him alone. He couldn't move without them breathing down his neck. They wouldn't even go out for the evening without him, even if Tom was around to keep an eye on him. They became obsessed with everything he said and did, his schoolwork, how he was feeling, what he was thinking, every word that came out of his mouth . . . It was intense, like they wanted to make up for how wrong things had gone with Emily.'

Clara frowned. 'OK . . .' she said.

'Well, so anyway, maybe growing up like that made Luke feel responsible for his parents' happiness, for everyone's happiness. Or maybe the attention lavished on him made him a bit selfish, a bit entitled. But you need to hear from him how sorry he is, how much he regrets it. He told me it was over with Sadie, he said it was the worst mistake he'd ever made, that he didn't want to lose you. I believed him. Honestly, Clara, I really think it made him realize how much he loves you.'

She put her head in her hands. 'Where the hell is he? I can't bear this . . . nothingness. There's so much I want to say to him.' She glanced up at Mac. 'Maybe he *has* left me. Maybe he just couldn't find the balls to tell me to my face.'

Mac shook his head. 'No. Not like this, not without his phone, without telling work, his parents . . . me.'

They were suddenly interrupted by an explosion of music from the flat above; a pounding bass so loud it made the ceiling vibrate. 'For Christ's sake,' Clara shouted, jumping to her feet. With a sudden fury she stormed from the flat and up the stairs and began hammering on her neighbour's door. There was no response. The music blared on. 'Answer the bloody door,' she yelled, giving it a kick. 'Open it! Just bloody well open it right now!'

Unexpectedly it swung open. Her neighbour stared back at her, eyebrows raised in mock innocence. 'What?'

'Turn the bloody music down. It's insane. I can't live like this!'

Slowly, and with an infuriating smile on her face, the woman turned and sauntered to her sound system, then flicked the dial down a notch. She turned back to Clara. 'Happy?'

Clara stared at her. She was so very thin, her shapeless oversized T-shirt only accentuating her bony limbs and sharp angles. Her finely featured face, peeping out between curtains of long lank dark hair, was covered by a thick, elaborate layer of make-up that was almost mask-like. She was gazing back at Clara with prickly belligerence. What on earth was her problem? Glancing past her at the flat, Clara saw that it was a tip; clothes and plates and CDs strewn everywhere, a potent smell of dustbins coming from the kitchen. And who the hell listened to trance these days anyway? 'Yes,' she said with icy sarcasm. 'Thanks so much.' She was about to leave when her gaze caught something draped over one of the armchairs. It was a sweatshirt. Luke's sweatshirt. She stared at it in astonishment. A distinctive green and red design with an eagle on the back that he'd bought in New York a few years before. He loved it. She remembered how annoyed he'd been when he'd lost it. When was that, exactly?

The woman followed her gaze. Quickly she began shutting the door. 'I've turned it down, now piss off!' she said, and for a few seconds Clara stood staring at the closed door in astonishment. She remembered how she'd said, 'Where's Luke?' the day he'd gone missing; the strange, knowing smirk on her face. 'Open the door!' she shouted, hammering on it. 'Open the fucking door right now!' But the music pounded on and the door remained closed. Eventually, with a cry of frustration, Clara ran back down to her own flat. When had the sweatshirt gone missing? Had it been around the time they were broken into? That sort of fit, she thought. They'd believed nothing had been taken, but . . . perhaps the reason why the police had no idea how the intruder had got in was because she'd been living amongst them all along. Had she been the one sending the emails?

'Are you OK?' Mac asked when she raced back into the flat. 'You look like you've seen a ghost.'

Without replying, she fetched her phone and found DS Anderson's number. He picked up immediately. 'Hi, it's Clara Haynes,' she said. 'I have something I need to—'

'Clara, I'm glad you called. I was about to ring you. We've discovered something interesting. How soon can you come to the station?'

9

I made the phone call one afternoon while Doug was at work, my fingers shaking as I dialled the number. It began to ring and I felt such a rush of panic I almost hung up. Then I heard the click on the other end, the familiar voice saying, 'Hello?' and the words stuck in my throat. 'Hello? Hello?' a note of impatience now. 'Who is this, please?'

So strange to hear that voice again after so many years, to know that its owner was standing in the house I'd once known so well. In my mind's eye I saw the duck-egg blue wallpaper in the hall, the light falling across the floorboards in two vertical slants. For a moment I was back there again, smelling the familiar smell – a mixture of lavender furniture polish and fresh coffee, the bowl of potpourri on the windowsill – hearing

87

the ticking of the clock above the stairs, looking into those familiar eyes that used to cry so much in those days. I swallowed hard and at last, in a whisper, I said, 'This is Beth Jennings.'

There was absolute silence. 'Please,' I begged. 'Please, please don't hang up. I need to see you. I need to speak to you.' And then I burst into tears. 'Can we meet?'

The voice was ice cold, tinged with fear. 'Absolutely not. We made a deal. You promised.'

'I know,' I said. 'I wouldn't call if I wasn't desperate. I need to talk about what happened. I thought I could live with what we did, but I can't. I just can't. I think we need to put it right, I want to go to the police.'

'No! No, Beth.' There was a long silence, until finally it came. 'All right I'll meet you. But not here. You can't come here. Give me your address.'

Surreal to see that face again, that familiar figure sitting at my kitchen table. Within minutes I was crying again, my words spilling out of me. I talked about everything – about what we did, how the guilt had never left me. I talked about Hannah, my marriage, how I felt I was losing my mind. I realized how desperate I'd been to have someone to confide in, how much I'd missed having a friend. 'What do you think I should do?' I asked desperately, when I'd finally run out of words.

But those eyes remained cold as they looked back at me. 'If you tell the police, we will lose everything. *You* will lose everything. Don't you understand that? What good can come from dragging it all up now?'

'I don't know. I don't know!' I saw that it was useless. Nobody could help me; there was nothing to be done. I bowed my head and cried and cried. I didn't even look up when I heard the chair scraping back, the front door opening and closing once more. It was over. It had all been for nothing.

It was a while before I got to my feet. I made myself take long slow breaths. Toby would be waking from his nap soon and I needed to pull myself together. Slowly I went to the sink and washed my face, then I made myself walk towards the stairs, intending to go up to check on my son, trying to plaster on the necessary smile. I was suddenly desperate to see him, to feel his little body, smell his delicious scent. As I passed the telephone in the hall I replaced the receiver in its cradle – I'd taken it off so we wouldn't be disturbed – and almost as soon as I withdrew my hand it began to ring.

I picked it up. 'Hello?'

'This is West Elms Primary,' the briskly efficient voice said. 'Is Hannah with you, Mrs Jennings?'

'Hannah?' I asked in confusion. 'No. Why would she be with . . . isn't she at school?'

'I'm afraid she's run away again. She must have slipped out of the upper school's gate after lunch. When we couldn't reach you, we called the police. I believe they're on their way to see you now.'

'But . . .' I felt the colour drain from my face. 'How long has she been gone?'

'About forty minutes. As I said, we did try to call you, but . . .'

I hung up and rushed back into the kitchen, my heart pounding. The last time Hannah ran away from school, I'd found her sitting in the back garden on the bench below our kitchen window. It was a warm day today and our kitchen had a stable door, the top part of which I'd left open. Nervously I went to it and looked out, terrified that I would find her there, that she had been there all along. But she wasn't: the garden was empty and I exhaled, relief crashing over me.

And then I turned back to the kitchen and I screamed. Because there was Hannah, standing in the door of the little pantry room that adjoined our kitchen. She must have been hiding in there – must have been there all along. She would have heard everything. She knew everything.

My legs felt weak. 'Hannah,' I said. 'Oh, Hannah.'

She held my gaze for what seemed like an eternity. I don't think I breathed the whole time. And then she walked past me and up the stairs, while I stared after her, fear pounding through me.

The rest of the day was nothing less than torture. I knew I couldn't tell Doug what had happened. He'd told me never to make contact, had been furious at the very idea and would never forgive me for going behind his back. And now this had happened. What if Hannah told Doug? What if she told a teacher what she'd overheard? I could lose everything. Hannah, my marriage, my home . . . maybe even Toby. And the thought of life without my little boy was like a knife to my heart.

During the hours that followed I scarcely took my eyes off my daughter, my heart clenched with panic as I waited to find out what she'd do. But the strange thing was she seemed entirely unaffected by what she'd heard. Maybe she hadn't understood, I told myself desperately. But I went over and over what I'd said in the kitchen, and knew there was no way our conversation could have been misconstrued. How could it? The things she'd overheard were dreadful, horrifying; surely she would have been traumatized to discover what she did.

That night when I tucked her up in bed I lingered for a while on the pretext of tidying her room. I remembered how excited we'd been when we first moved to the house, how we'd looked forward to making our little girl's room perfect for her. Glancing around now – at the walls we'd painted a cheerful yellow, the string of fairy lights draped over her mantelpiece, the large dolls house Doug had built, at all the other little touches we'd spent ages picking out for her but that had always been met with total indifference, I tried to find the words to begin. 'Hannah,' I said. 'Darling?'

She looked at me and waited. At seven years old, she was small for her age still, yet she seemed in that moment to have changed, her face a touch less babyish than it was before; one of those moments you have with children, those startling flashes of realization that they are growing up and away from you right under your nose, that time passes so very quickly. Her hair fanned out across the white pillow, her watchful eyes were fixed on mine.

I made myself take a deep breath, my mouth horribly dry. 'What you heard in the kitchen earlier, sweetheart, it must have sounded so crazy, so silly,' I began, my smile so forced it hurt my face, my voice shrill. 'We were just playing a silly game, that's all! That was Mummy's friend and we were pretending we were in a film or something!' Hannah continued to watch me silently. I licked my lips. 'The thing is, darling, it needs to be a secret. What you heard, what you heard Mummy and her friend saying, the game you overheard, you mustn't mention it to anyone. Do you see? You mustn't mention it to anyone at all, not even Daddy. Do you promise?'

Hannah blinked, her face without expression as she considered me. And then she turned over and closed her eyes, leaving me to stare silently down at her, cold with fear.

10

London, 2017

As Clara walked to the police station a memory came to her of a year or so before, when she had fallen and badly twisted her ankle. Fearing that she'd fractured it, Luke had taken her to the hospital where they'd waited long into the afternoon to be seen. It had been unbearably hot, the waiting area full to bursting with the sick and injured, a palpable cloud of frustration and boredom hanging in the stuffy air.

She'd sat, her leg propped up on a chair while she'd waited, Luke pacing to and fro like a caged tiger. When she'd finally been called to X-ray, she'd returned some time later to find him engaged in a noisy conversation with several waiting patients, including a very drunk man with a tattooed face, a middle-aged woman with a black eye, a couple of pensioners and a teenager who reeked of weed. They'd all laughed uproariously as she approached, Luke clearly in the midst of a long and apparently hilarious story about how he'd broken his leg as a teenager. It seemed that the pall of wretchedness had entirely dissipated, a party spirit in the air now.

She hadn't broken her ankle, but the pain was still eye-watering. 'Wait here a sec,' Luke had said, and off he'd vanished only to appear five minutes later with a wheelchair.

'Are you sure we can take this?' she'd asked, looking at it doubtfully.

'Yep, all sorted,' and he'd raised his hand to wave at a nurse at the other end of the corridor. 'Bring it back tomorrow, Sue!' he'd called and she'd rolled her eyes good-naturedly and nodded. Out on the street he'd pushed her sensibly for a few minutes, before picking up pace and stampeding down the pavements, pretending to career into lampposts and bushes, veering away at the last moment and as they'd headed towards the nearest pub at breakneck speed she'd shrieked and laughed so much she'd forgotten all about her throbbing ankle. Later he'd made her favourite dinner and invited her best friend Zoe around with a bottle of wine to cheer her up. That was the thing about Luke: he could turn any bad situation into something fun. He made everything feel like a party. She looked up to see the police station ahead of her, and taking a deep breath, pushed the memory away.

* * *

DS Anderson ushered her past the front desk and through to a large and busy office where several officers worked, either on phones or tapping away at computers. Nobody glanced up as she arrived, and Anderson led her to a corner desk and nodded for her to sit. There was something different about him today, she thought; a businesslike briskness, a grim purposefulness that made her uneasy. She sat without a word, bracing herself for whatever was coming.

Taking a seat next to her, he pressed the mouse of his computer and the screen flickered into life. 'OK,' he said. 'This is CCTV footage of—'

'Duck Lane,' Clara finished for him, peering closely at the screen. The slightly hazy, bleached-out film showed the narrow dead-end road off Broadwick Street that ran behind the string of office buildings, shops and cafés lining Brindle Press's part of Wardour Street. It was used by delivery vans to offload their supplies to the various businesses' back entrances – as well as being where Brindle employees came to smoke, make private phone calls or take part in periodic fire drills.

'OK, so this is footage from seven thirty-six on Tuesday evening.' Anderson went on, 'If you watch, you'll see Luke leave the building and walk towards Broadwick Street.'

The sudden shock of seeing Luke's image, his posture and gait so familiar, so loved, triggered such a rush of longing that her eyes swam. She stared hard at the screen, watching as he left Brindle and turned to call something over his shoulder, giving a brief wave. 'George,' she murmured. 'He's waving goodbye to George, the security guard.'

Anderson nodded. 'OK. Keep watching.'

At that moment, a blue van appeared, approaching Luke from behind. The second it passed him it stopped, obscuring him from view. She glanced up at Anderson in confusion. 'What . . . ?'

'Wait,' he said. 'The van stops for eight seconds . . . OK, now it's moving off again.' Sure enough, the van continued on its journey to the end of Duck Lane, whereupon it turned right and disappeared from view. Next, Anderson leant forward and with a few clicks of the mouse called up a different camera angle, this time giving a view of Broadwick Street. 'As you can see, Luke doesn't reappear, either before, during, or at any time after those eight seconds that the van stopped for.'

'Well, didn't he just turn right?' she asked. 'Towards Wardour Street I mean?'

Anderson shook his head. 'We've checked all the CCTV footage and Luke doesn't reappear again anywhere in the vicinity, on any of the surrounding streets.'

Clara stared at him. 'So . . . he got into the van?'

'There's nowhere else he could have gone.'

Her mind raced. 'Then it must have been a friend of his driving – or at least someone he knew?'

'Possibly.' Anderson leant back and folded his arms. 'The van stops for eight seconds. We have no way of knowing why Luke got inside.' He paused and looked at Clara. 'What we do know is that the van was stolen from a business address in Ealing, late on Monday evening.'

'Stolen? But . . .'

'We managed to track its onward journey as far as the M20, but we lose ANPR coverage of it shortly after it leaves the motorway and heads in the direction of the Kent Downs, not far from Dover.'

She tried to make sense of what he was telling her, mentally searching for possible explanations, but found none. She shook her head. 'Sorry, I don't . . .'

Anderson switched off the computer and took the seat next to hers, his eyes focused on her face. 'We're doing everything we can to find the van, Clara. And we will find it. But in the meantime we're appealing for witnesses who might have been in the vicinity when Luke disappeared.'

Panic climbed in her chest. 'What about the emails?' she asked at last. 'Do you have any idea who sent them?'

'Not yet, no. We've traced them to several different servers belonging to various internet cafés across London. Not one of them had working CCTV, which might be coincidence but probably isn't. We still have no way of knowing whether the person who sent them is connected to Luke's disappearance. What we do know is that Luke hasn't withdrawn any money from his account since last Monday, nor did he take out any significant sums in the days leading up to his disappearance, which indicates that he hadn't been planning to go anywhere for any length of time. As you know, he didn't take his passport or credit card.'

It was only then that she remembered Luke's sweatshirt. 'I saw something,' she said. 'In my neighbour's flat.'

Anderson listened patiently as she told her story. 'It might not have been his, of course,' she added, 'but it's pretty distinctive.' Her eyes searched the detective's face uncertainly. 'I don't know if . . .'

'We'll look into it,' Anderson told her as he got up and nodded at her to follow. 'We were intending to speak to your neighbours again anyway. I'll let you know what we find out.'

And that was it. She was alone again, standing in the street, looking back at the black bricks of the police station. She turned and began to walk home. Had Luke known the driver of the van? If not, why did he get in it? If it was someone he knew, had he known the van was stolen? It seemed so unlikely – Luke wasn't the law-breaking type, and as far as she was aware, he didn't know any criminals. But if he hadn't known the driver, then why did he get in the van? Had he been forced to? In central London, while it was still fairly light out? That didn't seem likely either. She jumped from possibility to possibility, but came up with nothing.

The quiet emptiness of her flat seemed to close in on her as she restlessly paced its rooms. It was Friday evening, the end of the third day without Luke, and the weekend stretched ahead of her interminably. She thought suddenly of her parents, and realized guiltily that she hadn't yet told them what had happened, that it hadn't even occurred to her to ring them. Quickly she ran to fetch her phone. But returning to the sofa she sat staring down at it for a long, silent moment, before eventually letting it fall, unused, to her lap.

She was an only child, a late and unexpected baby born in Penge to a medical secretary and a bank clerk in their mid-forties. It had always seemed to Clara growing up that Linda and Graham Haynes had never quite acclimatized themselves to the arrival of a child. Clara's presence seemed to constantly take them by surprise, and she spent much of her childhood playing quietly alone, or trailing after them while they visited garden centres, or car boot sales, not entirely sure they had remembered she was there. They hadn't been unkind, not at all, and they seemed to love her, in their way, yet she felt that she had always remained a puzzle to them. They'd looked on, nonplussed, while she devoured books, or spent hours writing stories, and were clearly baffled when she won a place at university – the first in the family to have done so. They'd retired to the Algarve the moment Clara had entered halls and, in their mid-seventies now, were quiet, private people, prone to anxiety, fond of their familiar routines and their own company, though they dutifully phoned their only daughter every other Sunday without fail.

When she'd moved in with Luke she had sensed their

relief – that she was now settled, and no longer their responsibility, and they needn't worry about her any more. The idea of bothering them with news of Luke's disappearance was not one she relished. She realized she also felt obscurely guilty, as though she'd let them down somehow. She suspected too that the second she admitted it to her parents, the nightmare would lose its sense of unreality: the possibility that she still secretly clung to, that this was all some terrible mistake, would disappear.

She gazed around herself at the quiet normality of her flat, its sense of hopeless waiting, her chest tightening and tightening as the silence grew ever louder. She could not stay here: she couldn't stand it.

Her friend Zoe picked up after the third ring. 'Clara? Is there any news? Are you OK?'

She closed her eyes in relief. 'Zo, I know it's not the best time for you, what with the baby and everything, but can I come and stay with you tonight? I—'

'Of course,' Zoe said at once. 'Of course you can.'

Clara burst into tears. 'I just can't . . .'

'Come over,' Zoe's voice was firm. 'Right now. Put some things in a bag, get in the car, and come.'

Zoe lived in a small, end-of-terrace house in East Greenwich with her husband Adam and their new baby, Oscar. Clara knocked and stood on the doorstep, listening to the sound of Oscar wailing from somewhere within, and tried to suppress a fresh, dizzying panic, gripping on to the wall to steady herself. Come on, Zo, she thought desperately. Please answer. And then the door opened and there was Zoe, the sight of her, the relief of it, almost undoing her. She was dressed in dungarees that were covered in something which looked like porridge, her auburn curls tied up in a messy topknot, her face lined with tiredness, her hand reaching out to her as she said, 'Clara, oh sweetheart, come here, it's all right; it's OK.'

Later, in the warm and untidy living room, its floors strewn with baby paraphernalia, Clara finally stopped crying long enough to look up and see six-month-old Oscar watching her from his mother's lap, his big brown eyes wide with fascination. She gave a shaky laugh. 'Sorry, Ozzy, you must think your godmother's a loon.'

'Oh well,' Zoe said mildly. 'Makes a nice change from your own dramas doesn't it, Oz?' She leant over and, squeezing Clara's hand, said, gently, 'Tell me what's been going on.'

So Clara told her, about Luke's cheating, the conversation with Sadie, the blue van and the CCTV footage, the strange woman who lived upstairs. As she talked she felt the knot in her chest gradually loosen fraction by fraction. Despite their lives taking such different directions, despite relationships, careers, motherhood, and all the other myriad experiences that over the years had slowly altered both the people they'd once been and the friendship they'd once had, there still remained between them the closeness and ease they'd known since primary school, and for the first time since Luke had disappeared she felt her churning panic subside a little.

'Holy fuck, Clara,' Zoe said when she'd finished. She shook her head in disbelief. 'I don't know what to say.'

Clara rubbed her eyes tiredly. 'I know he's a cheat and a liar and all the rest, but I can't walk away from it all and let the police deal with it. I can't let Rose and Oliver cope with all this by themselves. And I can't just turn off my feelings for Luke. He's in danger and I don't know what to do to help him. I don't know how to help his mum and dad, who're going through hell, I don't know what the fuck to do about any of it.'

To this Zoe said firmly, 'OK, well right now you don't need to do anything but drink a very large glass of wine – and one for me, too,' she added, 'because I'm still bloody breastfeeding.'

Clara was on her third glass when she murmured, 'I must have been blind, not to see it.' She shook her head in wonder. 'What a stupid *stupid* idiot, thinking everything was wonderful, when it was going on right under my nose. I mean, what kind of moron doesn't even suspect, doesn't even have a clue that her boyfriend's shagging the office sex bomb?'

'Not stupid,' Zoe said, 'just in love. Just absolutely besotted.' She paused, stroking Oscar's head thoughtfully. 'I don't know. Maybe this is a wake-up call, that Luke isn't the perfect man you've always had him pegged as. No one can live up to that. Don't get me wrong,' she said hurriedly, 'it's in no way your fault it happened, the blame's totally on him, but . . . my God you fell for him hard, suddenly there was nothing else in your world but him, and I was happy for you, I really was but . . .' she hesitated.

'But what?' Clara demanded.

She shrugged. 'You were so enthralled by him, by his whole family. All I ever heard was how incredibly clever Oliver was, or about the amazing work Rose used to do for Médicins sans Frontières, or how fantastically well Luke's career was going . . .'

'Sorry if I bored you,' Clara muttered.

'Oh, you didn't, of course you didn't! I got it, I really did, I understood why you grew so close to them all. But what happened to the novel you were going to write? Your own career? Suddenly I stopped hearing about that, it was all about Luke: his job, his talent, his amazing family. As if you didn't deserve him, as if you couldn't believe your luck. But *you* are amazing. *You* are. He was the lucky one. I only wish you realized that.'

They were silent for a while as Clara digested this, until she put her head in her hands and said, 'Christ, Zo, what am I going to do? I've got to find him. I can't bear the thought of him being hurt or in danger, it makes me physically sick!'

Zoe nodded sympathetically. 'You know you can stay here for as long as you like, don't you?' She got up, gently shifting an almost asleep Oscar higher on her chest. 'Adam's away at a work thing tonight. I'm going to put Ozzy to bed then I'll order us a takeaway. I won't be long. Pour yourself another glass.'

Clara sat back and closed her eyes, the wine she'd gulped swilling queasily now in her empty stomach. At that moment, her phone began to ring. It was Anderson's name flashing across her screen and her heart instantly leapt as she picked it up.

'Clara? We've found the van,' he told her.

She sat up. 'Where?'

'It was abandoned in a car park on the edge of the Kent Downs.'

She could scarcely breathe. 'And Luke?'

'The vehicle was empty, Luke and whoever was driving were long gone. However . . .' he paused, 'I have to tell you we found a significant amount of blood on the passenger seat.'

She closed her eyes, the floor seeming to pitch and roll beneath her.

'It will take us a few days to confirm that it's Luke's blood, but—'

'Oh God, oh my God.'

'Clara, we—'

'Is he, do you think he's . . .' she couldn't bring herself to say the word.

There was a pause. 'The amount of blood suggests a significant flesh wound, but it's impossible to tell whether it was a fatal one. We also found blood on the ground within a few feet of the van, which indicates that Luke may have been moved to another vehicle.'

Anderson's words seemed to be coming from somewhere far away, the room felt entirely airless. 'I have to tell you, we are assuming the blood to be Luke's, Clara. The Major Incident Team will be handling the case from now. Which means more officers working on it, a televised appeal, an intensifying of the search . . .'

'You think he's dead, don't you?' Clara blurted. 'You think he's been murdered.'

'No. That is not what I'm saying. But we have to consider it a possibility, which is why we're escalating the search. I will, of course, remain your first point of contact, and if you need to speak to either me or DC Mansfield, please . . .'

Clara barely listened as Anderson's voice rumbled on. When she finally put the phone down, Zoe was standing in the doorway, looking at her in dismay. 'Oh God,' she said, crossing the room in seconds. 'Clara, what is it? What's happened?'

Long after Zoe had reluctantly gone upstairs, unable to fight her exhaustion any longer, Clara sat up on her makeshift bed on the sofa, wide awake as the night rolled slowly past. Though she was desperate to drive straight home, the wine she'd had still sloshed sickeningly in her stomach, and after trying and failing to get some sleep, she grimly drank coffee after coffee, trying to sober herself up. When Oscar woke for a feed at 5 a.m. and Zoe tiptoed down to the kitchen, she found Clara shrugging on her coat.

'You can't go yet! It's not even properly morning,' she cried. 'Stay! Please stay, Clara. Did you sleep at all? Let me make you some breakfast. I really don't think you should be alone . . .'

But Clara barely heard her. 'I have to go. I have to speak to the police, see what I can do to help. I can't just hide out here, while Luke is . . .' tears filled her eyes and angrily she swiped them away. 'I need to help find him.'

She drove home as dawn broke over London, the new morning filling the city with a pale, golden light. She saw barely a soul as she slipped through the silent streets: the occasional homeward-bound reveller, a fox streaking between parked cars; grey puddles of sleeping forms sheltering in shop doorways. The sun was rising as she crossed the Thames, staining the water red and orange, its light catching on the glass and steel of the buildings lining the river. Her body ached from lack of sleep but her nerves were raw and jangling, her mind alert. She would go home and shower, then go to the station to speak to Anderson. She put her foot on the accelerator, her eyes focused grimly on the road ahead.

Parked in her usual spot a short distance from her flat, Clara found she couldn't move. She sat for some minutes willing herself to get out, but the thought of returning home to sit alone with Anderson's words running through her brain filled her with despair. Impulsively she turned the key in her ignition and drove on.

Twenty minutes later she sat at Mac's kitchen table, his face ashen as she described Anderson's phone call. 'My God,' he said, staring at her in disbelief.

'Do you . . . do you think he's dead?' she asked.

'No!' he said sharply and in his agitation got up and began to pace around the room. 'Of course I don't.' He went to the kettle but instead of putting it on, stood for a long time, his back to her, unmoving.

'Mac . . .' she said.

He swung round to look at her, his face white, his eyes wide and frightened.

'Are you OK?' she asked. 'Come and sit down. You look like you're going to be sick.'

'It's just, I wasn't expecting this,' he said. 'I thought . . . I thought he would be home by now, that he would be OK.'

'I know,' she said, 'I'm so frightened. What if he's dead, Mac, what if this bloody maniac has killed him?'

'He's not dead!' Mac said, so loudly it was almost a shout. 'We can't think like that. If he was dead they'd have . . . they'd have found a body. We have to keep positive.' He took a deep breath, then said more calmly, 'The police will find him, I promise, Clara. You said yourself, they're putting more people on it. It's going to be OK.'

She nodded, fresh waves of panic washing over her at Mac's clear distress.

As he made them both a cup of tea she looked around at the familiar disorder of his flat, somewhere the three of them had spent so many hours together, surrounded by the hundreds of photographs that covered every inch of the walls: the bands and musicians he'd shot over the years; the concerts and gigs and festivals he'd documented. A gang of Mac's large circle of friends would often end up here after a night out, it being the biggest space and central to where everyone lived. Sometimes Mac's girlfriend would come along, if he was seeing anyone, but usually, after everyone else had gone home, it would end up just the three of them, talking long into the night, drinking and listening to records.

The flat was situated over two floors, Mac's photographic studio, dark room and bedroom above the kitchen and large living room that housed his vast collection of books and records. The best bit was the building's flat roof where they could squeeze out and sit on summer evenings, looking out over their patch of North London, Highbury Fields behind them, the Holloway Road below.

Now, as she sipped her tea, she spotted a picture on the wall she'd not seen before and getting up, went to look at it. It was one Mac must have put up very recently, unusual in that it showed the three of them together. 'Who took this?' she asked.

'What? Oh . . .' he came and stood next to her. 'My friend Pete, at my birthday last year. Do you remember? I found it the other day.'

She nodded. It was a brilliant shot. A close-up black-and-white in which she and Mac were turned to each other, their heads thrown back in laughter, while Luke grinned straight ahead at the camera. 'What were we laughing at?' she murmured.

'Christ knows. Probably taking the piss out of Luke about something.'

She smiled and he put an arm around her. 'Listen. Why don't you move in here for a bit? I can't stand thinking of you in that flat by yourself. Go and get some things and come and stay for a while. If we're going to lose our minds with worry, we might as well do it together.'

She thought about it. There were other friends she could stay with, but none of them lived as close to her place as Mac did. Staying across the river with Zoe would have felt too cut off from her old life, as though she were abandoning Luke somehow. And she and Mac were the closest people to Luke other than his parents, the two people who cared most about finding him. It made sense. She looked at him gratefully. 'That would be brilliant,' she said.

11

London, 2017

Hoxton Square was almost empty when Clara arrived a couple of hours later, its bars and restaurants locked and silent now, no sign of life on the pavements except for a postman doing his rounds, a homeless woman yawning in her sleeping bag, pouring water from a bottle into her hand for her dog to drink. The sky was filled with a cool, yellow light and behind the black railings shadows lay still and dark upon the lawn. She made her way towards her flat, telling herself she'd stay only long enough to throw some clothes into a bag then drive straight back to Mac's.

Her building was silent as she let herself in and climbed the stairs. She noticed nothing unusual until she put her key to the lock and the door to her flat opened without resistance. She paused in surprise: she had locked it; she knew she had. Fear prickled the back of her neck now as she stepped inside. And as she looked around she gasped in horror. The flat had been completely ransacked. Drawers pulled out, their contents spilled all over the floor, books torn from shelves and left scattered where they fell, the sofa taken apart, wardrobes and cupboards plundered. Nothing had been left untouched. It looked very much as though someone had been searching for something, but what it was, or whether they'd found it, she had no idea.

It was a long time later that the police finally allowed her back in. Clara closed the door behind the officers as they trudged grimly away with their bags and cases of equipment, then she stood alone, surveying the chaos. Who had done this, and why? The downstairs front door hadn't been forced, so how did they get into the building? Whoever it was must have known she hadn't been at home last night. She glanced up at her ceiling, the usual pounding music eerily absent now. The silence seemed to fill the room, travelling to each corner and pressing against the walls and when her mobile rang she jumped in shock then leapt to answer it, desperate to hear another human voice.

It was Anderson. 'Clara. How are you? DC Mansfield told me they've finished searching the flat.'

'Did you speak to my neighbour?' she asked. 'The one I told you about?'

There was a pause. 'She wasn't in when we called,' he told her. 'We've left messages with her to get in touch as a matter of urgency.'

She felt her panic rise. 'But shouldn't you – I mean, what if she knows something? What if she's got something to do with this? Whoever did this last night must have had a key to the main door – what if it was someone who lived here, in the building? Maybe she's got some weird kind of obsession with Luke, maybe—'

'We have no reason to think that at this stage,' Anderson talked over her in the same, infuriatingly calm manner. 'We will speak to her though, Clara, I promise. We are dealing with it. In the meantime, I would suggest you stay somewhere else for a while, at least for the foreseeable future.' She felt a little as she did as a child, when her father told her to go to her room to calm down.

'But—' she said.

'I called to remind you there's a press conference scheduled for later today,' he went on. 'MIT wondered if you'd be prepared to say a few words – talk about Luke, about the sort of person he is . . .'

She closed her eyes. She couldn't think of anything she'd rather do less. 'Is there any news about the van?' she asked.

'Not yet, no. I'm sorry, Clara. I know this must be very frustrating for you, but we are confident that . . .'

She sank on to the sofa, her legs suddenly weak. She listened as he reassured her they were doing everything

112

they possibly could, and when she hung up she stared blankly down at her phone, trying and failing to process the terrifying and utterly surreal possibility that the man she loved might die – might already have been murdered.

Later, she tried to soothe herself with the mechanical, mindless act of righting chairs and refilling drawers, and it was while she was in the tiny, windowless room they used as an office that she discovered the photographs. The metal filing cabinet Luke kept his personal documents in had been upturned, its contents rifled through and scattered across the floor. She began stuffing the various invoices and bank statements back into their slots, but when she attempted to slide the drawer into place she realized that she couldn't. Frowning, she reached in and felt around until she located the obstruction – a large manila envelope that had become caught beneath it. Pulling it out she found three photographs inside – all of them of the same young woman.

She gazed down at the stranger's face in confusion. She was very pretty, but who was she? An ex-girlfriend? In that case, why had they been so carefully hidden away – in a filing cabinet Luke knew she never looked in? They had always been open about past relationships: Luke had often pointed out his exes amongst the faces of smiling friends that gazed from his treasured photo albums. She knew about Amy, his first serious girlfriend from school, and Jade, the one he'd had at uni, and all the others in between and since, but this woman was definitely someone she'd never seen before – she felt sure she would have remembered such a beautiful face. If she was just someone Luke had had a casual fling with before they'd met, then why hide her photographs like this?

The realization seeped into her like cold water. This was no past love, of course, but someone from his present. The hurt spilled through her, biting and acidic. Who was she? Had he loved her? It was the callousness she couldn't bear; the deceit of hiding the pictures in their home, presumably to look at during stolen moments while her back was turned. Clara stood very still, staring down at the wide smile, the dazzling blue eyes. She hadn't really known Luke at all, she saw now, had been like a stupid, trusting child, entirely oblivious to what had been going on right in front of her face, blindly believing in a love that didn't even exist.

At that moment the intercom buzzed loudly, startling her from her thoughts. 'Yes?' she said.

'Clara?'

She frowned, not recognizing the voice. 'Sorry, who . . .?'

There was a crackle of static and then, 'It's Tom. Luke's brother.'

She was so taken aback that she stared at the intercom in blank surprise before pressing the button to let him up. What on earth was he doing here? He rarely came to London, and he had certainly never casually called round like this before; he and Luke didn't have that sort of relationship. Perhaps he had heard about the break-in, maybe Rose had spoken to Anderson already. Yet surely he wouldn't have had time to drive down from Norwich? The sound of footsteps followed by a sharp knock on her door a few inches from her face jerked her from her thoughts and, just in time, she remembered the photographs she was still holding. Hurriedly she stuffed them back in their envelope and into a kitchen drawer, gripped by a sudden shame – that Luke had cared so little about her, that he had felt her worthy of so little respect.

'Tom,' she said dully when she opened the door. 'This is a surprise . . .'

She noticed he looked dishevelled, had dark circles under his eyes, his face unshaven; very different from his usual buttoned up, carefully groomed demeanour. 'I heard about the van,' he said, following her into the living room. 'My mother phoned me last night. I can't believe—' he broke off, looking around himself in alarm. 'Christ, what happened here?'

'We had a break-in,' she told him. 'You didn't know?'

'Break-in? No, I – when did . . . ?'

'I came home this morning and found it like this.'

His eyes widened. 'My God.' He sank into a chair, then listened as she told him about the scene she'd been met with earlier.

She continued with her tidying as she talked, aware of his gaze following her as she moved around the room. She had never been alone with him before, she realized, and she felt oddly exposed in his presence, her movements slow and clumsy beneath his scrutiny. She noticed him pick up the picture of her and Luke on Hampstead Heath and stare down at it, his expression unreadable. She wished that he would go. 'What brings you here, Tom?' she asked.

He looked up, the cool blue of his eyes meeting hers. 'I had to be in town to see a client, and I wanted to see how you are.'

'Really?' She was unable to hide her surprise.

'I'm conscious that you're very much on your own down here, Clara. My parents and I have each other, but . . . well.' He stopped, before adding quietly, 'I'm sorry if you thought I was less than sympathetic when Luke first went missing. I assumed he'd just taken off for a few days – you know how impetuous he can be. I had no idea . . .' he trailed off again, then cleared his throat. 'Do the police have any inkling who might have broken in?'

'No. They've searched for fingerprints, but I guess it'll be a while before I hear anything.' She surveyed the mess hopelessly. 'The problem is there must be so many prints here. And if whoever it was wore gloves . . .' she shrugged. 'I got the impression they were only going through the motions. They haven't got a clue. Not a fucking clue.' She realized that she was going to cry and, desperate not to do so in front of Tom, excused herself and hurried to the bathroom, where she held a towel to her face as she stifled her sobs.

It was some minutes before she felt able to return and she found him standing by the window, staring out

116

at the sky, apparently deep in thought. The silence stretched and though it was in her nature to feel obliged to fill it she sat on the sofa without speaking, unable to summon the necessary energy. She glanced at him, taking in his appearance. He was so different from Luke. They'd both inherited Oliver's tall, broad-shouldered physique, but whereas Luke had his dad's olive skin and softer, more boyish face, it was Rose's pellucid blue gaze, blond hair and strong, symmetrical features that had been passed down to Tom. Even their dress sense was different: Tom's all sharp suits and expensive shoes, the polar opposite to Luke's laidback style of jeans and T-shirts. He was a solicitor, she knew, and it was a job she'd often thought suited him, associated as it was in her mind with a certain dry meticulousness.

He turned suddenly. 'Didn't the neighbours see or hear anything?' he asked.

She shook her head. 'Apparently not. The woman upstairs has been away for a couple of days.' She reflected again how strange that was – seeing as she was usually there all the bloody time, playing her music, night and day. 'The people on the floor below say they didn't hear anything. I guess it must have happened during the night.'

To her surprise he came over and took the seat next to hers on the sofa and she leant away slightly, taken aback by his sudden proximity, the intensity of his gaze. 'I'm sorry,' he said, 'maybe I shouldn't have come. I didn't mean to disturb you – I wanted to make sure you're all right.'

117

'Well, uh, you know. I've been . . . better,' she mumbled.

'Sorry,' he said. 'Stupid thing to say.' After a moment he asked, 'What will you do now?'

She shrugged. 'The police want me to help with a press appeal. Then I guess I'll stay at a friend's tonight. Mac's, maybe.'

He nodded. 'If there's anything I can do to help, or you want to talk, I'm here. I'll leave my number and you could . . . well, anyway . . .' He broke off and she watched him pull a pen from his pocket, then scribble his number on a train ticket.

She tried to hide her surprise. 'Thank you,' she murmured as he passed it to her.

'No problem.'

To her relief, he got up and began to move towards the door.

They stood awkwardly in the narrow hallway. She would normally say goodbye to Rose or Oliver with a kiss or a hug, but that felt unthinkable with Tom. She tried to remember if this dilemma had ever occurred between them before and realized that it hadn't: greetings and farewells were always a nod or a wave from across a room. He cleared his throat. 'Well . . .'

To cover her confusion she darted in front of him and opened the door, saying in a ridiculous, overly bright voice, 'OK then! Nice to see you!'

He nodded. 'Bye, Clara.'

He held out his hand and, thrown by the awkward

formality, she took it, with a small, embarrassed laugh. She felt the coolness of his fingers in hers and something about the way he was looking at her now, his gaze so piercing it seemed to pin her to the spot, rendered her incapable of moving a muscle. He looked as though he were about to say something, but the moment stretched until the sudden sound of a motorbike revving outside broke the silence and his hand released hers, before he turned, and was gone, closing the door quietly behind him.

12

Cambridgeshire, 1989

Funny how it creeps up on you, how the occasional pick-me-up can morph so seamlessly into such a necessary, vital thing. The odd glass of wine used to be nothing more than a treat – a pleasant way to unwind after a long or tiring day, but slowly things began to change. I was never quite able to move on from that moment, you see, the second I turned to find Hannah standing in the kitchen, knowing that she had heard everything, that she knew everything. At night I would go to bed and wait in vain for sleep, only to relive over and over the shock of seeing her by the pantry door, the awful realization dawning in her eyes.

During the weeks that followed I barely let her out of my sight, terrified of what she might do. But to my confusion she almost seemed happier than she had ever been. The concerned phone calls from school all but ceased, the lying and stealing petered out; life ran more smoothly than it had ever done before. I would torture myself for hours trying to work out what this meant. I was terrified of her telling Doug what she knew, aware that there was no way he'd forgive me for going behind his back, secretly contacting the very person he'd wanted out of our lives forever.

Strangest of all, her relationship with her father began to change too. Now, suddenly, I would come across the two of them, heads bent close together, she sitting on his knee, a wide smile on her face as they chatted about her day. It made me feel sick to see Doug's surprise and happiness at the change in his little girl. Occasionally she'd look up and our eyes would meet, and I would feel again that cold lurch of fear. It was as if she was deliberately torturing me.

When the secretary of the child psychologist whose waiting list we had been on finally rang to schedule our appointment, I almost cried as I fobbed her off with excuses. Because of course there was no question of that now. How could I possibly risk a doctor delving into Hannah's mind? How could I risk Hannah telling what she knew? I seemed to live in a perpetual state of cold terror: I had no idea what to do.

So bit by bit, that end-of-day glass or two turned into three, then four. A bottle, sometimes more. I came to expect, then ceased to care about Doug's disapproving glances. 'Haven't you had enough?' he'd say, when I'd reach for the wine yet again at dinner. Sometimes I'd see a closed, tight expression in his eyes when he noticed the empties piling up in the bin. But I never drank during the day, while looking after Toby, for example. I'd always, always wait until he was safely tucked up in bed for the night – at least at first. I couldn't tell Doug, you see; I couldn't tell him what I'd done.

'She seems to have turned a corner, don't you think,' he said with satisfaction one evening, after Hannah had obediently gone off to get changed for bed.

I looked into my wine glass. 'Hmmm,' I said.

'Maybe she doesn't need to see that shrink after all,' he added. 'What do you reckon?'

'Yes,' I said faintly. 'Perhaps you're right. I'll cancel it.' I made myself return his smile. When he went whistling out of the room, I poured myself another, extra-large glass, and drank it in three gulps.

My only joy during this time was Toby. He was the one thing that made life bearable. Hannah knew that. She knew he was all I had.

It was an evening in October a year later and it had been a long and tiring day: I'd slept badly the night before and Toby had been difficult for most of the afternoon – he was two years old by then. I'd promised myself I wouldn't have a drink until both of the children were in bed so I was doing my best to chivvy Hannah along. Toby should have been in bed ages ago but he was refusing to settle, so I'd brought him into the bathroom with me while I kept an eye on his sister.

'Come on now, Hannah,' I said for what felt like the hundredth time, while Toby played on the floor, making a relentless 'brrrrmmm brrrrmmm brrrrmmm' noise as he pushed a toy car around my feet. 'Get out of the bath now – it's getting late.'

She glanced at me dismissively. 'No, I'm not ready to.'

My anger seemed to come from nowhere. I was usually so careful to keep her onside, but I was tired, a bit hung-over from the night before, and there was something in the look she shot me, the disdain in her eyes that just made me snap. 'Get out of the bath right this minute,' I shouted so loudly that Toby jumped and started to cry. 'I'm sick of you disobeying me!'

With infinite slowness, a maddening smirk on her face, she did what she was told. It seemed to take her forever, and I was suddenly desperate for a drink. I passed her a towel. 'Go and put your night things on,' I muttered. 'I'll be two minutes.' I left the room and headed for the stairs, thinking only of the cold bottle of wine I had waiting for me in the fridge.

After I'd poured myself a glass I stood at the sink savouring that first gulp. I could hear Hannah talking to Toby, their voices getting louder, which meant they must have left the bathroom. I closed my eyes, summoning my last scrap of energy, then knocked back the rest of the glass. That was when I heard the scream. I ran from the kitchen, the bottle still in my hand, to find Toby lying at the bottom of the stairs. I heard myself shouting his name as I knelt down beside him. Time seemed to stop: I was senseless with panic. The relief I felt when he got up and threw himself into my arms was indescribable. 'Are you OK?' I asked as he screamed hysterically. 'Oh my darling, are you OK?' Frantically I checked him over for broken bones, but miraculously he seemed unharmed.

I have never known fury like it. When I looked up, I saw Hannah sauntering down the stairs towards me, a serene smile on her face. I admit, in that one brief moment I wanted to kill her. 'What did you do?' I screamed. 'What the hell did you do?'

'Nothing, Mummy,' she said.

'Did you push him, Hannah? Did you push your brother down the stairs?'

She reached the bottom step and considered me. 'Nope. He fell,' she said with a shrug. 'It wasn't my fault.'

And then I did it. I slapped her. I had never once raised a hand to either of my children before but everything seemed to boil up inside me in that moment. My handprint left a livid red mark on her cheek. 'You little bitch!' I shouted. I was completely beside myself, all I could think about was the fact Toby could have died. 'Don't you ever touch my child again. Do you hear me?' I was screaming so loudly I didn't hear Doug's key in the door.

'Beth?' He stood in the hall in his coat, a look of horror on his face. 'Beth. What the hell are you doing?'

The second she saw her father, Hannah began to cry. 'Mummy hit me, Daddy! I didn't do anything! Toby was sad because Mummy was gone so long, she went to get her wine and she never came back – and then Toby fell and Mummy hit me! She hit me and I don't know why!'

I shook my head in disbelief and turned to Doug. 'She's lying. I was only gone a moment. She pushed him!'

His eyes still wide with shock, Doug bent down and took Toby from me, gathering him in his arms. 'OK, little man,' he soothed, 'it's OK, it's OK now.'

'No!' I shouted at him, 'No it's not OK! Nothing is OK! She pushed our son down the stairs!'

His gaze fell to the bottle of wine that in my panic had fallen to the floor. 'You're *drinking*?' he said. 'You're looking after our children and you're drinking?'

'Don't you fucking dare say this is my fault,' I said, my voice shaking. 'I've had one drink. I was gone less than a minute!'

I sank to my knees and pulled Toby away from Doug's arms. 'Darling,' I said, 'tell Daddy what happened. Did Hannah push you, honey?'

But Toby was too hysterical to answer. 'Want Daddy,' was all he said, turning back to his father and burying his face in Doug's chest. 'Want my daddy!' Meanwhile, Hannah's own sobs rose to fever pitch.

I got up and went to Hannah. 'What's wrong with

you? What the fuck is wrong with you?' My anger and guilt and fear mingled, fuelled by the wine I'd drunk.

I felt Doug's hands grip my shoulders as he pulled me away from her. 'Stop it, Beth!' he shouted. 'This isn't helping. Go and calm down, I'll deal with it.'

I looked at Toby, still clutching Doug and sobbing, the satisfied glint in Hannah's eyes, the puddle of wine on the carpet, and ran from the house.

13

London, 2017

Clara was still thinking about Tom when Mac called to say he was on his way over. She stood at the window while she waited, recalling the unsettling intensity of Tom's gaze, the peculiar texture of the air between them as they'd stood together in the hall. Try as she might, she couldn't work him out. He was such a strange mixture of contradictions. At times during his visit she'd seen flashes of sympathy in his eyes, yet there remained that strange reserve, the feeling that he was scrutinizing her intently. Mac had mentioned him going off the rails in his teens, but she couldn't imagine him ever losing control, of him ever being vulnerable or lost. And then there was the distance he kept between himself and his parents, an ambivalence towards them that bordered on disdain, which had always seemed especially cruel after they'd suffered so much already. On the other hand, he'd cared enough about Clara to travel some distance to see her, to check that she was all right. It was all entirely baffling.

Beyond her window the sky hung tepid and sallow over Hoxton Square. She watched as a group of achingly hip twentysomethings appeared at its furthest corner, on a wave of energy and laughter. They passed an elderly man, his chin nearly on his chest, edging with painful slowness along the pavement, a blue plastic bag dangling from his fingers, until at last he crept off down a side street to be swallowed by the council estate that lay beyond view of the square's bustling restaurants and bars.

She turned and considered her flat, its disorder reminding her of the day she and Luke had moved in – the excitement they'd felt as they'd unpacked their belongings and talked about the housewarming party they were planning that weekend. She remembered how happy she'd felt at the prospect of their living together, of waking up every morning next to him.

Her gaze travelled now over their ransacked belongings: the stuff they'd chosen together when they'd first moved in, gathering bits and pieces from markets and junk shops, slowly and lovingly transforming the small, modern, white-walled space into somewhere that felt more like home to her than anywhere she'd lived before.

She was dragged from her thoughts by the intercom's

buzzer. A few minutes later Mac looked around himself in dismay as he stood amidst the chaos of her flat. 'What did the police say?' he asked. 'I mean, they must think this is linked to Luke's disappearance, right?'

'They're not commenting either way. Maybe whoever it was . . . I don't know, but it seems to me they were looking for something.'

'What the fuck for, though?' He picked up a broken ashtray from the floor and gazed down at it. 'Christ, Clara, what if you'd been in? There's no way you're staying here any more.' His worried eyes met hers. 'Get some stuff and come to mine.'

She remembered then the photographs she'd found and went to fetch them. 'Look at these,' she said, watching him closely as he slid the pictures from the envelope and stared down at the unknown woman's face.

'Who's this?' he asked.

She eyed him suspiciously. 'You don't know? Really?'

'No. Never seen her before. Why?'

'At a rough guess I'd say it's someone else Luke was shagging behind my back,' she said bitterly. 'I found them hidden in the office.'

'No way, Clara,' Mac said with complete certainty. 'He would have told me, I know he would. He said Sadie was the only one.'

'Yeah, well, Luke's a liar, isn't he?' she said quietly. 'He's lied to me and he's probably been lying to you, too.' She took the photos from him and angrily stuffed them back into the envelope. 'He probably wanted to sneak a look at them whenever I was out. I mean, for fuck's sake!' She gave a short, exasperated laugh. 'It just keeps getting better, doesn't it? What else am I going to find? A secret wife tucked away somewhere? A couple of kids?'

They fell silent for a while, until, looking around himself Mac said uneasily, 'Why don't we get out of here? This place is giving me the creeps.'

It was while she was in the bedroom shoving clothes into a bag that her mobile rang. 'This is DC Mansfield,' the officer said when Clara picked up. 'Can you come to the station? As you know, the press conference is this afternoon. It would be very helpful if you could say a few words.'

Her heart sank. 'I really don't know if—'

'I would urge you to, Clara,' she said. 'This kind of appeal has more impact if it has the involvement of family and loved ones.'

'But . . . wouldn't his mum and dad be more—'

'Unfortunately they've declined. Understandably, they don't feel up to it right now.'

'Yes. I see . . .' she thought about Rose and Oliver, of the agony they were going through, and then she thought of the abandoned van, the sickeningly blood-stained seat. 'When do you need me?' she asked, glancing at Mac.

They were on their way to the police station when Clara asked casually, 'What do you think of Tom, Mac?'

He looked at her in surprise. 'Tom? Why?'

She shrugged. 'No reason. He came over earlier, that's all. Said he was in town meeting clients and thought he'd see how I was. I mean, you've known him a long time, what's your take on him?'

Mac frowned. 'That's odd, I would have thought all his clients were local to him.' He considered it for a moment. 'I suppose he can be a bit uptight, and he's a bit of a loner, but he's not a bad sort of bloke. I remember Luke telling me they were close when they were kids, but—'

'Really?' She felt a fresh flash of surprise. They'd certainly never seemed particularly close. She hadn't given it much thought before; not having any siblings herself, it wasn't a relationship of which she had experience. She'd assumed the distance between the two of them was due to the five-year age gap, Tom's habit of talking down to his younger brother, or their different personalities.

'Yeah,' Mac went on. 'From what Luke said, all three of the kids were pretty tight before Emily left. I don't know what happened, though. Like I said, Tom checked out of the family after she disappeared, and Luke and his parents became quite wrapped up in each other. Maybe that caused a bit of a rift.' He glanced at her. 'I always got the feeling it upset Luke; I think he wanted to be closer to his brother growing up, but Tom didn't want to know.'

Clara considered this. How hurtful that must have

been, to be rejected by his older brother, especially after losing his only other sibling so young. She realized that Luke had never talked about his relationship with Tom and she hadn't thought to ask. Uncomfortably she wondered now what else she might not know about her boyfriend, what other sorrows Luke might have been hiding, behind his cheerful smile.

When Clara and Mac arrived at the station she was struck by the sense of urgency and purpose in the air. There were a number of new officers to meet, members of the Major Incident Team, including a family liaison officer and press officer, as well as Detective Chief Inspector Judith Carter, a heavy set, rather austere-looking woman who explained to Clara that she was the senior investigating officer on the case, Anderson keeping back respectfully as they talked. Every one of the officers she met was friendly, reassuring and grateful for her assistance, but still she felt entirely overwhelmed. Her natural compulsion to be helpful, to do the right thing, combined with the knowledge that, if she messed it up, Luke's life was at stake, made her heart pound faster and faster, a thick lump of anxiety building in her chest.

Soon she was ushered into a side office where Anderson and the press officer went over with great patience what she would need to say and before she knew it she was hurried into another, larger room, a mic was fitted to her top and she was directed towards a bank of tables in front of a blue screen, the Met's insignia at its centre. She sat between DCI Carter and DS Anderson, TV cameras pointed at her, a sea of eyes trained on her face. Mac stood to the side, and she tried to keep the reassuring warmth of him in her mind while she stared ahead, saying her piece to the cameras. But despite her determination to hold it together, to somehow compel a watching stranger to reach out and help, to make this horrible nightmare end and bring Luke safely back to her, her words stumbled and she clenched her fists so hard she thought her knuckles might burst through the skin.

Afterwards, when the ordeal was finally over and she and Mac were standing outside the station doors staring back at each other, she found she was shaking so violently that Mac had to reach out and clamp her arms firmly to her sides. 'I'm so sorry, Clara,' he said miserably, 'I'm so fucking sorry you're having to deal with this.'

She looked dazedly back at him. 'Mac, I wouldn't be able to cope with any of it if it wasn't for you.'

He hugged her then, wrapping her tightly in his arms and when they drew apart he exhaled a long breath. 'Come on,' he said, 'let's get the fuck out of here and have a drink.'

It made the national news later that night. Clara was sitting on Mac's sofa, half-heartedly picking at some pasta he'd made for her when Luke's face suddenly loomed large on the TV screen. She cried out in shock, causing Mac to rush in from the kitchen and together they watched in silence.

'Fears grow for missing London man, Luke Lawson,' the newsreader said. It was the picture she'd taken of him herself earlier that year, at a bar in King's Cross where they'd all gone to celebrate his twenty-ninth birthday, and for a moment she was back there again, tasting the tequila shots, laughing as the whole bar joined in with an impromptu round of Happy Birthday. Luke smiled back at her from the TV screen with joyful, blameless eyes.

Anderson appeared next, addressing the camera, describing Luke's last-known movements before he was replaced by the CCTV footage of Luke leaving work. She watched as the familiar, denim-jacketed figure with its loose easy gait made its way up Duck Lane. When the film cut to a still of the abandoned blue van she stared at it in dismay. Such a lonely, desolate spot: had Luke really been there? It seemed unimaginable. Next, and most distressing of all, was a close-up of the blood-stained seat.

Finally, there Clara herself was. Huddled between Anderson and DCI Carter, her face deathly pale, her voice shaking as she read from the piece of paper that trembled in her hand. 'My boyfriend Luke is a kind and loving man,' she began. 'We all – his family, his friends – we all miss him so much. If anyone knows anything, anything at all, please, please come forward. We haven't seen him for four days, and we just want him back . . .'

An information number ran along the bottom of the screen as she talked. When she finished, the camera zoomed in on her face, lingering on her tears. After a few more words from the detective chief inspector, the film cut back to the studio, the newsreader soon replaced by a weatherman standing before a map of Britain annotated with swirling clouds of rain.

For two days, Mac and Clara holed up in his flat on the Holloway Road, an anxious, stultifying existence while they waited for news, broken only by aimless walks around Highbury Fields beneath the muggy April sky. On the third day they sat miserably in Mac's local, staring into their pint glasses. 'Shouldn't you be working?' Clara asked him, it suddenly occurring to her that he hadn't been disappearing off at night with his camera as usual.

'I'm taking a break for a while,' he told her. 'Perk of being freelance, I guess.' He looked at her. 'How about you? How long have you got off?'

'A couple of weeks. They said I could tack some holiday time on to that.'

He nodded and each of them silently wondered the same unknowable thing: how long would it be before they were released from this nightmare?

Realizing she could put it off no longer she phoned her parents in Portugal, downplaying the situation for all she was worth – as much out of her ingrained desire not to cause them any trouble as to prevent them from flying over to stay with her: she wasn't sure she could cope with that on top of everything else. 'No, no,' she soothed, 'there's nothing you can do. The police are handling it. I'm sure there'll be good news soon. I'm OK. Honest, Mum, I'm fine. Mac's looking after me, and Zoe. I'll call you as soon as I hear anything.'

Her conversations with Anderson did little to lift her spirits. They had found no identifiable fingerprints in her flat and the upstairs neighbour, who it turned out was named Alison Fournier, a twenty-eight-year-old IT specialist from Leeds, had been traced to her cousin's home in Middlesex, where she'd been staying since a day before the break-in. They had 'no reason to think she was involved', Anderson said.

'But . . . what about the sweatshirt?'

'We're satisfied that it belongs to Ms Fournier.'

'Well, what now, then?' she asked desperately.

'We're doing all we can,' he replied. 'Clara, we are looking into everything, I assure you we're doing our utmost to get to the bottom of this, and I'll be in touch as soon as we have more news.'

'Yes,' she said quietly, 'OK.'

After she'd put the phone down, she met Mac's gaze and he shook his head in silent sympathy.

'This is day eight,' she told him helplessly. 'Day fucking eight since Luke went missing. Four days since they found the van. They've had no useful response to the appeal, he's just completely vanished. How can that be possible? How can anyone disappear into thin air?' Her voice rose in despair. 'What if this is it, Mac? What if they simply give up on him and we never see Luke again? If his mum and dad never see him again?'

'No one's going to give up on him, Clara,' Mac told her firmly. 'They know what they're doing. We have to trust that they'll find him.'

'I feel so fucking useless.'

They sat listening to the rush-hour traffic passing below, the noises from the kebab shop on the street directly beneath them. Through the wall came the applause and canned laughter of the neighbour's TV set. Day was drifting into night, but neither of them moved to turn on the light and a thick gloom settled into the corners of the room.

'Whoever sent the emails knows Luke well,' Clara said. 'Someone he must have been close to once, who for whatever reason holds a grudge.'

Mac frowned. 'Yes, but surely the police have looked into who that might be?'

She nodded impatiently. 'Yeah, maybe, but they said they'd not found anything suspicious.'

'So . . . ?'

'Well, I don't know – maybe we should start looking into it ourselves? Between us we've probably got a good idea of the different girlfriends, colleagues, flatmates and so on Luke has had over the years. Maybe the police have missed something?'

'Hmmm . . .' said Mac doubtfully.

'But they *could* have. You were at school with him, and we both know some of his old uni friends, past flatmates, or colleagues he's mentioned. I'm sure if we start digging . . . maybe the police have missed someone? And no one knows Luke like we do; we'd have a better idea if, say, something was mentioned that sounded off about his past behaviour, or if they said something that didn't fit with what he'd told us. And at least we'd be doing something. I feel like we're going slowly insane here.'

He pulled on his lip. 'That's true.'

'Will you help me?' She looked at him beseechingly until he sighed.

'OK. If it'll make you feel better, sure.'

She smiled. 'Good. We need to make a list of people to approach. Ex-girlfriends from school and uni, old flatmates and female friends, women he used to work with – before Brindle, I mean. Anyone at all that he might have got on the wrong side of, or who might know of someone he fell out with at some point.' She pulled out her phone. 'Get your laptop. Let's start with Facebook.'

For more than an hour they sat side by side in silent concentration. It was slow work: Miles, a friend from Luke's uni days, was still in touch with the sister of Luke's ex-girlfriend Jade. Andrew, who once worked with Luke at the digital publishing company he'd been at before Brindle, was Facebook friends with a woman who'd been on his team there, who herself still kept in contact with a couple more of their female colleagues. Yet despite the difficulty of their task, for the first time in days Clara felt a sense of purpose, and bit by bit a list of women began to emerge.

'I'm worried this could be a massive waste of time,' Mac said.

'Keep going,' she replied, her eyes still on her phone. 'At least it's a start.'

They were about to take a break when Clara noticed the New Message symbol on her Facebook page. She frowned in confusion when she saw she'd been contacted by someone calling themselves 'Rumpelteazer'. But when she read the message, she felt the hairs on the back of her neck stand up. 'Oh my God!' she shouted.

Mac looked up in alarm. 'What? What's happened?'

Wordlessly she handed him her phone. The message had been sent from a locked account, with a blank Profile picture. Mac read it out loud.

'"Clara. I saw you on the news. I'm Luke's sister Emily Lawson. It's very important you don't tell my family I've contacted you. Do not tell the police. Can we meet?"'

Mac's mouth fell open in shock. 'No way,' he said, as he looked from the message to Clara's face then back again. 'No way that's her . . .'

'I don't know. I mean . . .'

They stared at each other. 'Why has she called herself "Rumpelteazer"?' Mac asked.

Clara gave a gasp of realization. 'It's from the book! Luke's book, the one Emily gave him before she left. Don't you remember? The T.S. Eliot one about cats.'

Mac shook his head. 'Is it?'

'Yes!' Her eyes were wide with excitement. 'The message she wrote inside the cover. "For Mungo something, from Rumpelteazer. Love you Kiddo." It's her! It must be! How would anyone else know about that?' She jumped to her feet, feeling a mixture of elation and shock. 'Bloody hell, Mac! Bloody hell!'

'He could have shown it to loads of people over the years,' he said. 'This could be from any old nutcase. Some weirdo who's seen the news story and thought they'd stir up trouble. It's probably some sick joke. Seriously, Clara, I wouldn't—'

'But it *could* be Emily,' Clara persisted. 'No one ever knew what became of her. And her disappearance was pre-Internet, it's not like it was common knowledge.'

'Why all the "no police" drama, though? The "don't tell my family" stuff. Bit cloak-and-dagger, isn't it?'

But Clara was undeterred. 'Look,' she said impatiently, 'we don't know why Emily left when she did, or what she's been doing since. But bloody hell, Mac, what if it *is* her? She's heard about her brother going missing and wants to help? Imagine if, because of this whole horrible nightmare, Emily comes back to her family!'

'But what if it's the nutjob who's been stalking Luke, who's abducted him?' Mac persisted. 'What if this is just some fucked-up trick?'

She turned back to the screen. 'All the more reason to agree to meet them,' she said quietly, and after a moment's thought, she began to type her reply.

14

London, 2017

No matter how frequently she checked her inbox over the following hours, Clara's message to Emily remained unanswered. Perhaps Mac was right; maybe it had been some lonely weirdo with too much time on their hands – yet she couldn't quite shake the hope that it really had been Luke's sister who'd contacted her. While she waited for a reply she imagined reuniting Emily with her family, picturing how ecstatic Rose and Oliver would be to finally see their daughter again, and felt a surge of excitement.

To distract themselves, she and Mac went back to compiling their list of women and by the next morning they had an assortment of names on their list: a mixture of ex-girlfriends, colleagues and former flatmates, people who could count as significant women in Luke's life – none of whom, she had to admit, seemed likely candidates for the role of Luke's abductor. 'I guess it's a start,' Mac said, doubtfully.

'Who shall we contact first?' she asked.

'Luke's first girlfriend, Amy Lowe, I suppose. She still lives in Suffolk, though, so—'

'Right then, let's go,' she said, getting up.

Mac blinked at her. 'What, now?'

'We've got nothing else to do.' She picked up her coat. 'We'll take your car, shall we? Do you have her address?'

He nodded. 'An old school friend of mine still knows her vaguely.'

For the first time since Luke went missing, Clara felt her spirits lift. 'We'll drop in on Rose and Oliver on the way,' she said as they headed for the door.

As they eased slowly through the London traffic, Clara again checked Facebook. Since she'd appeared on TV there'd been a constant stream of messages from friends and well-wishers asking her how she was, whether there'd been any news, telling her they were thinking of her. And though she was touched by their concern she'd grown to dread their messages appearing in her inbox, feeling obliquely guilty when the only possible reply she could give was, 'No, still nothing I'm afraid.' Today, however, she checked through them eagerly, yet over twenty-four hours since she'd first contacted her, there was no reply from 'Rumpelteazer'. Perhaps it *had* all been a sick joke. She sighed and allowed her phone to drop to her lap. She glanced at Mac. 'What was she like, this Amy?'

He shrugged. 'Nice. She and Luke were pretty serious back then. I know he was really keen on her.'

She remembered the pictures she'd seen in Luke's photo albums. An attractive, curvy teenager, with big blue eyes and blond waves – the sexy girl-next-door type that the boys at school always went for. In the photos she and Luke invariably had their arms around each other, surrounded by happy crowds of friends, faces flushed, eyes shining, taken at some party or other. She felt another pang of doubt; it seemed so unlikely that someone so sweet-looking could have sent such threatening emails.

She stared out of the window, watching as the city's outskirts segued into the green and yellow fields of Essex. For a while they drove in silence, each lost in their own thoughts, until Mac fiddled with the stereo and Bowie's 'Life on Mars' filled the car. A memory of the three of them listening to it on other, happier trips returned to her, visits to Glastonbury and Camp Bestival, someone's wedding in Hampshire to which they'd travelled in a huge convoy of cars filled with all their friends.

She glanced at Mac. The stress was beginning to take its toll on him. Although on the surface he was keeping it together, trying to put on a brave face for her, she could tell that underneath he was starting to fray. He seemed to have a perpetual haunted look in his eyes, a queasy pallor to his skin as though he'd barely slept for days. 'Thanks,' she said to him quietly, 'for doing this with me. I don't know what I'd have done without you through all this.'

'Don't be daft. You and Luke are my best mates,' he said. 'What else was I going to do?'

She smiled and, staring out of the window again, she thought about Mac for a while. She'd often wished he would find a girlfriend, worried he might feel awkward tagging along with her and Luke all the time. But on the subject of his love life, Mac had always been intensely private. Occasionally he'd disappear for a few months, alluding vaguely to someone new he was seeing, and sometimes he'd even introduce them to her, but none of the girls ever seemed to last. 'She's not the one,' he'd said once, when pushed. 'So what's the point?'

'Our Mac's a hopeless romantic,' Luke had laughed.

'Oh well,' Clara had said encouragingly, 'the right one's out there somewhere, you'll see.'

'Aye,' he'd grinned. 'I expect she is.' And then he'd changed the subject.

They were less than a mile from The Willows when a reply from Emily finally arrived. Her heart leapt. *When can we meet?* it said. *I can come to London.*

'What shall I say?' she asked Mac excitedly. 'Shall I tell her I can see her tomorrow?'

He glanced at her in alarm. 'You've got to make sure it's really her you're talking to first. You can't just go

145

and meet any old weirdo off the internet, it could be anyone.'

'Yeah,' she said reluctantly. 'I suppose you're right.' It seemed such an incredible thought, to find Emily at last, she could hardly begin to believe it might happen. She looked at Mac. 'What was Emily like, do you think? I mean, I know you didn't move to the area until after she'd left, but I guess Luke used to talk about her to you?'

He thought for a moment. 'Not much, to be honest. She was always kind of present, in the sense that you knew they thought of her all the time, but no one ever mentioned her. I do remember Luke saying she was a big character, quite stubborn and fiery, you know, into her politics and good causes and so on, but that's about it. Rose especially took her disappearance so hard, I guess they all got used to not talking about Emily in front of her.'

When they drew up to The Willows not long after, Clara felt a small lurch of shock when she saw Tom's black Audi parked in the drive. It hadn't crossed her mind that he would be there today, and she sat staring at it, lost in thought. Mac glanced at her in surprise as he began to open his door. 'Aren't you coming?' he asked.

'Yeah. Sorry.' She undid her seat belt and followed him to the house.

When Oliver opened the door, Clara was shocked at the change in him. It was as though he'd aged a decade since last she'd seen him and she saw reflected in his face the same careering horror she'd endured herself those past few days; a vertiginous, eternal freefall where you almost longed for the ground to hit you, because that final violent impact must surely be better than this dreadful, endless plummeting.

'Oh, Oliver,' she said as she hugged him, 'it's good to see you.'

Releasing her, Oliver smiled faintly and shook Mac's hand. 'Mac, come in,' he said quietly. 'Glad to have you here.'

Silently they followed him through to the kitchen. But as soon as she walked into the room, Clara was struck by its strange, taut atmosphere and she froze inside the door, confusedly taking in the sight of Rose seated at the table, her head bowed, her face in her hands, while Tom stood over her with an expression of such anger on his face that Clara's first instinct was to rush to stand between them, to shield Rose from her son.

Before she could move, however, Tom turned and, his eyes briefly meeting hers, abruptly moved away, crossing the room to the window where he stood looking out at the garden.

'Rose?' Clara asked in bewilderment. 'Are you all right? What on earth's happened?'

For a moment, when Rose raised her head and looked at her, Clara hardly recognized Luke's mother, her expression was so tortured, so desperate, it seemed to contort her face into someone else's entirely. But seconds later it had passed, the old Rose returning once more. She wiped her eyes, a shaky smile on her lips as she said, 'Nothing! Nothing's happened, darling. Or, you know . . . everything.' She looked at Mac. 'Goodness, Mac,' she said weakly. 'How lovely it is to see you too.' She didn't move, though; it was as if she was pinned to her seat and the four of them stood looking at each other, while Tom remained at the window with his back to them, radiating hostility.

Finally, Clara threw Mac a beseeching look and he grimaced, crossing the room to Tom and putting a tentative hand on his shoulder. 'Hello there, pal,' he said. 'Long time.'

It was three long silent seconds before Tom turned to him and, clearing his throat, said, 'Yes. Good to see you, Mac.' They shook hands. 'How are you?' he added, at last managing a thin smile. The strange, taut atmosphere lifted a fraction. Rose jumped up, saying briskly, 'Well then! Who would like some tea?'

'Let me do that,' Clara begged. 'Please, don't get up.'

But Rose waved her away. 'No, no, don't be silly. I'm fine!' She began bustling about, patting her husband on the arm while she went to fill the kettle. 'So,' she said, a little more brightly, 'tell me what brings you here!' Suddenly she paused, her hand flying to her mouth as she asked, 'Oh! You don't have any news, do you?'

Clara saw the half hope, half dread in her eyes and said quickly, 'No, no news.'

And in that instant Rose seemed so desolate, Clara

could hardly bear to look at her. Instead she gazed around the room, which she noticed was in an uncharacteristic state of disarray. The usually pristine surfaces were covered in piles of junk and dirty plates, the air, which was once full of the scent of fresh flowers or cooking smells, now had a stale, sour whiff. A kind of panic rose in her. *No*, she wanted to say, *please don't do this, don't fall apart. You're Rose and Oliver! You can't give up on him, not yet*. To cover her dismay she said weakly, nodding at the window, 'Garden's looking lovely, Rose.'

To this she gave a wan smile. 'Oh, I've not been out there in a while, I'm afraid. Usually by this time I'd be gearing up for our annual spring garden party, sorting out the invites for the village and so on . . .' Her smile faltered. 'It doesn't seem so important any more.'

At this, Tom made a strange, bitter sound and strode abruptly from the room. The four of them stared after him, until seconds later they heard the front door slamming shut. Clara and Mac glanced at each other in amazement.

'So,' Rose said, as though nothing had happened. 'What brings you here?'

Haltingly, Clara and Mac explained their plan. 'We might not find anything, of course,' she told them, 'but at least we'd be doing something . . .'

There was a silence, until Oliver nodded and, not meeting their eyes, said, 'Well, yes . . . if there's anything we can do to help . . .'

Clara looked anxiously at Rose, who said quietly, 'Whatever you think's best, darling, of course.' She got up. 'I'm very sorry. I hope you don't mind, but I think I need to go and lie down now.'

They watched her go, Oliver sinking into a chair, staring after her with such a look of helplessness that it made Clara's heart hurt. She thought about Emily's email, wishing she could tell them about it, praying that one day soon she'd be able to give them the news they'd waited for so long.

Tom was outside when they left the house, leaning against his car and gazing out across the fields. A thin veil of drizzle hung in the tepid air and crows cawed and circled overhead. He turned when he heard them crunching across the wet gravel towards him and levelling his gaze at Clara said quietly, 'I'm sorry about that.'

She felt a rush of indignation on Rose's behalf and was relieved when Mac answered for them. 'Don't worry about it,' he said. 'It's a difficult time. Are you OK?'

'Yeah. You know . . .'

She was conscious of his eyes on her still and busied herself with fiddling with her phone.

'What are you both doing here?' he asked, and listened while Mac quickly ran through their plan.

'We're starting with Luke's first girlfriend,' he told him, 'Amy Lowe. Did you know her?'

Tom shook his head. 'Not well. I'd left for university

by the time they started going out. Are you off there now?'

'Yeah, she lives outside Framlingham, apparently.' Mac checked his phone and read out the name of Amy's street.

'I know it,' said Tom. 'I'm heading in that direction myself. I'll show you the way if you want to follow me.' He paused, and finally Clara looked up and met his gaze. 'Actually, there's a pub nearby called the Kestrel,' he said. 'I could do with a drink, if you . . . ?'

'Sure,' Mac shrugged, before she could make up an excuse. 'We'll follow you there.'

As they pulled out of The Willows' driveway and began to follow the black Audi, Clara expelled a long breath. 'God, that was weird,' she said. 'What the hell was going on between Tom and Rose?'

'Christ knows.'

'As if she hasn't got enough on her plate without him laying into her too,' she said angrily. 'He's so bloody strange.'

'I know,' he murmured. 'I guess they're all very upset.' After a while, he said, 'They looked awful, didn't they, Rose and Oliver?' He flicked his indicator and followed Tom as he turned left, away from the village. 'Poor bastards. I can't believe this has happened to them again.'

Clara watched the countryside slip past her window, the hedgerows and verges beginning to burgeon into spring, and thought about Rose. When they'd first met a few years before, Rose had been in her mid-sixties and newly retired, enjoying a 'life of leisure', as she'd laughingly put it. Gardening, cooking, taking holidays in Europe with Oliver, relishing her new-found freedom after such a long and distinguished career in medicine. Clara had seen pictures of her taken in her forties and fifties: a good-looking, impeccably dressed woman whose eyes had shone with intelligence and purpose and responsibility, but now, though she was still all of those things, there was a softness, an ease and comfort about her too that Clara thought made her even more attractive.

She recalled a time a year or so earlier when she'd first caught a glimpse of that other Rose, the coolly capable doctor she'd once been. It was a weekend in November and they'd all taken a walk together through the frost-covered fields. Rose and Clara, slightly ahead of the others, had come across a hare caught in a barbed-wire fence. It was bleeding, its face contorted in fear and pain. While Clara had cringed and fretted uselessly at its suffering, Rose had knelt and carefully freed it, but rather than hopping away, the animal had lain there, eyes bulging, still bleeding profusely. 'Poor thing,' Rose had murmured. 'It's dying. I think it'll be kinder if I just . . . don't look, darling, if you'd rather,' and then she'd picked the animal up and deftly wrung its neck. And though Clara had felt a little sick, she had been filled with admiration for Rose's unflappable efficiency, her ability to get on with what was necessary, no matter how unpleasant or bloody.

'I wonder what Rose and Oliver were like,' she said now, 'before Emily left, I mean. I met them so many years afterwards, I can't imagine how it must have changed them.'

'They were quite a big deal by the sound of things.' Mac replied. 'Rose was head of paediatric surgery at the hospital, and Oliver had written his first book, which had got a lot of attention – TV appearances and so on. They were pretty well known in the area, very active in the village, fundraising and all that, then there were all the huge parties they used to throw. Luke told me their house was always full of people.' He glanced at Clara. 'So yeah. I'd say they had it pretty good.' He shook his head sadly. 'It's just so fucking tragic the way things turned out. They don't deserve it, they really don't.'

Tom was waiting for them in the pub when they arrived. It was a beautiful Tudor building with low black beams and wide oak floorboards, roaring fires and battered leather sofas. 'They've got quite a decent menu here if you feel like eating something,' he said, his manner markedly more relaxed now he was away from The Willows.

Mac glanced at her. 'I am pretty hungry actually. What do you think?'

She shrugged, suddenly realizing that she couldn't remember the last time she'd eaten a proper meal. 'All right,' she nodded and forced herself to return Tom's smile.

For the first ten minutes or so after they'd ordered, she listened to them discuss their old school and the local people they knew. She watched as Tom slowly became more at ease and talkative, the way people generally did in Mac's company. He had a self-deprecating humility that even the chilliest of people tended to warm to, a willingness to listen and let the other person lead. It occurred to her that she and Mac were pretty similar in that sense. Was that what had drawn Luke to them both, she wondered? And was it that same lack of ego, her readiness to take a back seat and let him shine that had allowed him to cheat on her with Sadie, to treat her with so little respect? She remembered a girl she'd once lived in halls with, who'd said with a mixture of pity and scorn, 'You're such a people-pleaser, aren't you, Clara? Doesn't it get dull?' She felt a rush of contempt for herself now and with effort pushed the thought away, forcing herself to turn her attention back to Mac and Tom.

They were talking about the area of Norwich where Tom lived, but though he was chatting quite easily there still persisted the sense that he was keeping something of himself back, only allowing them to see a fraction of his true self; the same guardedness that had always made her feel instinctively wary of him. She remembered the scene between Rose and him earlier and shook her head in silent frustration: he was impossible to work out.

'Cash only,' the waitress said when their bill arrived

and they'd each got their cards out. 'Machine's broke. There *was* a sign at the bar,' she added wearily.

The three of them exchanged glances. 'Shit, I don't have any, do you?'

'Nope, was going to card it.'

'There's a cash machine at the post office down the road,' Tom said, getting up. 'I'll go; it won't take a minute.'

But Mac stopped him. 'No, you stay, pal, I need to return a work call anyway,' he said, waving his mobile at him.

As she watched Mac leave, Clara glanced at Tom. 'It was good to see your mum and dad before,' she said coolly, adding pointedly, 'I like them very much.'

After a pause he returned her gaze and smiled, saying with no hint of rancour, 'Yes. Everybody does.'

At that moment a different waitress arrived and began wiping down their table and they lapsed back into silence. She noticed after a while that the girl was taking an inordinately long time at her task, and realized she was distracted by Tom, staring at him with open admiration as she wiped the same spot over and over on their table. It was true, she thought without much interest, he was very good looking, but there was something supercilious about his face that prevented him from being truly attractive. She looked at him then and froze in surprise to find his eyes fastened on hers. A little flustered, she said quickly, 'I was trying to remember something Luke told me once, about Emily.' Immediately she wanted to kick herself for bringing up his sister so clumsily. She saw Tom's eyes darken and silently wished she'd found a more gentle way to broach the subject.

'Oh yes?' he said, once the waitress had moved away.

She fiddled with a beer mat. 'He was telling me about a game he used to play with your sister when you were all kids, but I can't remember what it was. Do you have any idea?'

'No,' he said quietly. 'I'm afraid not.'

'Right,' she said, trying to hide her disappointment.

'Oh, except, it wasn't a game, as such . . . but there was a song they used to sing before Luke went to bed – she used to like reading to him then tucking him in at night. '"Five Little Monkeys" it was called – you know that rhyme? "Five little monkeys jumping on the bed, one fell off and bumped his head . . ." Luke used to bounce around on the bed while they sang it. It was a kind of ritual between them . . . is that what you meant?'

She nodded. 'Yes,' she said, 'yes, that was it, thank you.' For a moment she pictured Luke as a boy, and felt a wave of sadness. When she next looked up it was to see such wretchedness on Tom's face that she felt a stab of guilt. 'Oh, Tom, I'm so sorry, I didn't mean to upset you, I—'

He shook his head. 'It's not your fault. It was just, when she went, it was . . . a bloody awful time, you know?'

'I can't even begin to imagine.'

156

'Listen, Clara,' Tom said, leaning forward, the intensity of his gaze returning. 'There's something I need to tell you.'

She looked at him in surprise. 'What is it?'

At that moment, the door opened and Mac appeared, brandishing their cards and cash. 'Sorry – the machine was broken,' he said. 'I had to go to the one at the petrol station.' He looked from one to the other of them. 'Everything all right, is it?'

Tom dropped his gaze from Clara's. 'Everything's fine,' he said, abruptly getting to his feet. Let's pay at the bar, shall we?'

Amy Lowe lived in a small house down a cul de sac of 1930s semis. Clara and Mac paused in the front garden for a moment, taking in the broken swing set and stack of roof tiles piled high amongst the weeds. On the chipped front door was a peeling sticker with the words 'BEWARE OF THE DOG', illustrated by a toothy Doberman. From inside they could hear the sound of a TV at top volume, a girl's voice wailing, 'Mummy he hit me! Jakey hit me, he did! Mummeeeeee!!!' They glanced at each other and shrugged, before Mac pressed the bell.

A boy of about six answered. He was dressed in a Superman onesie and the small round face below his buzz cut was covered in freckles. He glared at them suspiciously. 'You selling stuff?' he asked. 'Mum says she don't want any.'

157

Mac laughed. 'No. We just want a word with—'

Suddenly Amy came up behind him. 'Yes?' she said sharply. 'Can I help you?'

She'd changed little since her teenage years, Clara thought. A fraction heavier, a few lines here and there, but still the same doll-like eyes, the tousled blond curls, the careless, unassuming attractiveness. Her face cleared. 'Oh my God!' she said in a thick Suffolk accent. 'Mac!' She smiled then, and for a moment she looked sixteen again, exactly as she had in Luke's pictures. 'Haven't seen you for years! What the bloody hell are you doing here? I thought you lived in London these days?'

'Hi, Amy, good to see you,' Mac said. 'This is Clara, Luke Lawson's girlfriend.'

At this Amy gave a start of recognition. 'Yeah,' she nodded, 'I saw you on the news, it's all anyone's talking about around here.'

'I'm sorry to turn up out of the blue like this,' Clara said. 'I . . . we wondered if we could have a word with you?'

She frowned in surprise. 'If you want. Come in.'

They traipsed after her down the narrow hallway, its walls covered in pictures of Amy in a wedding dress next to a chubby, grinning groom, the living room they passed on the way to the kitchen seemingly full of kids crowded around the telly where some kind of Wii tournament was going on. ''Scuse the mess,' Amy muttered. The kitchen was a pleasant, cosy room with lilac walls and a round pine table around which were crammed several chairs. 'You want a cuppa?' she asked, removing a pile of washing from the table.

Once they were all sitting down with mugs of tea, she raised her eyebrows questioningly. 'So what's all this about then? I told the police when they came before that I hadn't really spoken to Luke for years. Occasionally I'll bump into him in the village at Christmas or whatever, but it's never more than "Hello, how's it going" or what have you.'

Clara glanced at Mac. 'We're trying to build a picture of what Luke was like when he was younger,' she said cautiously.

Amy blinked at her, nonplussed. 'Yeah, that's what the police said, and like I told them—'

'We're trying to find out anything we can, to see if we can work out what happened to him,' Mac said.

'Right,' Amy said, still looking mystified. 'Well, he's not here, is he?'

There was a silence. This, thought Clara, had been a really bad idea. They must look completely barking mad. Suddenly Mac got up and went over to a photo stuck on the fridge. 'Shit,' he laughed. 'Is this you and Mandy Coombs?'

'Yeah, that's us!' Amy's smile lit her face once more. 'Think it was my eighteenth,' she took the picture down and handed it to him. 'Still a nutter – see her all the time!'

Clara listened while they reminisced about a club they used to go to in Ipswich. When there was finally a break in the conversation, she asked, 'Do you have any of Luke and you? Pictures, I mean?'

Something passed across Amy's face and she turned away. 'No, I got rid of them years ago.'

'Oh,' Clara said. 'Right . . .'

Amy shrugged. 'Past is past. Ancient history, isn't it?' She looked at Mac. 'Sorry, can you keep an ear out for the kids? Just going to have a quick ciggie in the garden.'

When she'd gone, Clara and Mac glanced at each other, eyebrows raised. 'Maybe we should go,' Mac said. 'We're not going to find out anything here. Guess it was a bit of a long shot . . .'

But had there been something strange about Amy's expression, Clara wondered, her desire to leave the room so quickly? 'Hold on,' she said.

Following Amy into the garden she found her standing next to a trampoline strewn with toys, shivering while she puffed on a roll-up. Clara smiled apologetically. 'I'm sorry about this,' she said. 'I know you and Luke were a long time ago, it's just . . . no one knows what happened to him, he's completely disappeared. The police don't seem to be getting anywhere, or not that they're telling me anyway. I'm trying to work out if there's anyone from his past who might know something.' She paused and, her voice catching, added, 'We're all so worried about him, his mum and dad, Mac, we're getting desperate.'

Amy's face softened. 'Look,' she said. 'I'm sorry he's disappeared, I am, and I hope he's OK. But it's not like we kept in touch. I don't exactly have great memories of my relationship with Luke.'

Clara looked at her in surprise. 'Really?'

The other woman stared at her for a moment, and then she turned decisively away, her face closed again. 'I don't want to talk about all that, to be honest. And like I said to the police, there's nothing I could tell you that would bring you any closer to finding Luke. I don't know anything.'

Clara's despair hit as if from nowhere, like a bus slamming into her at full speed. After the shock of him vanishing, the news about Sadie, the ridiculous hope she had felt to be finally doing something proactive, she realized now how stupid she had been, how pointless it all was. She sank down on to a rickety garden chair and put her head in her hands.

'You all right?' Amy's voice was suddenly near.

She looked up. 'Sorry, I'm sorry. We'll leave you in peace. I don't know what I'm even doing here, to be honest. You must think we're mad.'

Amy sighed and sat down next to her. She thought for a moment, then rolled herself another cigarette. 'You want to find out what he was really like back then? Behind his perfect image, I mean?' Clara glanced at her in surprise to hear the note of bitterness in her voice. 'Well, look, I expect he's changed by now, grown up a bit, but OK. I'm not sure it'll help but I'll tell you, if you really want me to. But come on now, stop crying.'

Clara nodded and wiped her eyes. 'Thank you,' she said.

Amy sighed. 'I got pregnant when I was sixteen and he dumped me, leaving me to have the abortion on my own. I was quite far along in the pregnancy when I realized and the whole thing was horrendous. I was devastated.'

Clara stared at her in shock. 'I'm so sorry,' she faltered. 'I had no idea.'

Amy shrugged.

'Did anyone else know about it?' Clara asked.

She laughed. 'Everyone thought the sun shone out of Luke Lawson's arse. No one would ever think badly of him. In fact, everyone always acted like I was bloody lucky to have a spoilt posh lad like him.' She grimaced and added, 'He was a selfish little shit, all said and done. I'm sorry, but he was.' She glanced at Clara. 'Perhaps he's changed. But all he cared about back then was what people would think, especially his parents, how it would fuck up his plans to go to uni, how a baby wouldn't fit in with his perfect bloody image. He dropped me without a backward glance. But no, I didn't tell anyone what had happened. I guess I felt . . . ashamed, somehow.' She sighed. 'Now I'd like to go back in time and give my head a wobble, tell myself to have more self-esteem and then give Luke Lawson a good kick in the nuts.'

As Clara listened, shock reverberated through her. Amy's tone was so disparaging, painting a picture of a man she barely recognized. 'Anyway,' Amy said, throwing her cigarette butt away. 'That's all I've got to tell you.' She got to her feet. 'I'm sorry, but I better get on now. Kids' tea and that.'

Clara thought of the pictures of the chubby, smiling groom in the hall. 'Will your husband be home soon?' she asked.

Amy snorted. 'Probably. I wouldn't know.' Clara stared at her in confusion and she laughed. 'He lives two streets away with someone else.'

'Oh, I'm sorry, I thought—'

Amy made a face. 'I keep the pictures up for the kids' sake. They're still a bit messed up from it all.' She wrapped her cardigan around herself and headed for the door. When she reached it she paused. 'Funny,' she said, 'how it's always us women who are left to deal with the shit men leave behind, isn't it?'

Later, as they began the drive home, Clara told Mac what Amy had said.

'Jesus,' he said, 'I had no idea.'

'He never said anything to you?'

'Not a word. I . . .'

'What?'

He shook his head. 'I thought I knew everything about him,' he said quietly. 'I really thought we told each other everything. Obviously not.'

She stared out of the window at the passing countryside and thought about Luke at sixteen, how he'd been little more than a kid himself, how panicked and scared he

163

must have been at the prospect of becoming a father. But if Amy was telling the truth – and she was certain that she was – there was no excuse for the way he'd behaved towards her. She realized that, for the first time since they'd met, she felt ashamed of him. She remembered Zoe saying how quickly and how deeply she had fallen for Luke, and it was true, but had her infatuation made her blind? If he was capable of behaving so badly towards Amy, who else might he have crossed? If Amy wasn't responsible for Luke's disappearance – and a gut feeling told her she wasn't – then some other woman had sent the emails, stolen a van to take Luke off to God knows where. But who was she, and what had Luke done to provoke her?

When they finally joined the motorway she sighed and picked up her phone. After a moment's thought she wrote her reply to Emily:

> I need to know you are who you say you are. You sang a song with Luke when he was little, before he went to bed every night. Do you remember what it was?

She forced herself to put her phone away, telling herself that she needed to be patient; that Emily probably wouldn't reply for ages. Her willpower lasted less than fifteen minutes, however, and to her surprise when she next looked there was already a message waiting for her.

> Five Little Monkeys, it said. Where do you want to meet?

There's a bar called The Octopus on Great Eastern Street, Clara wrote, her heart thudding with excitement. Would that suit you? I could meet tomorrow, any time.

The reply was instant:

I'll be there at six. Please, Clara, it's very important you don't tell anyone. I'm trusting you.

Clara looked at Mac. 'Bloody hell,' she said. 'We're on!'

15

After Doug told me to leave I ran blindly through the streets of our village, barely aware of my surroundings as I made my way towards Saint Dunstan's Hill. When I got to the top I sat on a bench and looked out across the darkening fields. I don't think I'd ever felt so desolate, so frightened. All I knew was that Hannah had pushed Toby. I *knew* she had.

I thought about her as a newborn, how tiny and beautiful she'd been. Doug and I had treated her as though she was made of the finest glass, we had barely been able to contain our happiness in those early weeks. We had waited so long for her, had been through so much, and now there she was, so utterly perfect, we could scarcely believe our luck. And then little by little, as the months and years had passed, the doubts had crept in.

I must have sat there for more than an hour, watching as the lights of the scattered villages grew gradually stronger as the darkness gathered. From a distant church I heard a bell toll nine. My thoughts chased each other. My rage towards Hannah had been instantaneous, the thought of her hurting Toby triggering something primal and instinctive within me. I didn't know how we could continue now, how I could ever trust her around my little boy again.

At last, cold and exhausted, I turned back towards home. When I reached my street I hesitated at our gate and took a gulp of air to steady myself. There was nobody about; no sound from the other houses, an eerie stillness in the air. When I let myself in, the hall was in darkness. I stood and listened. Had Doug gone to bed? Suddenly I heard a faint sound coming from the kitchen. A creak of a chair, perhaps a sigh. I crept nearer and pushed open the door. There, sitting at the table, was Doug. The only light in the room was the one that glimmered dimly from the oven's hood.

I whispered his name but he didn't look up, so I edged a fraction closer. 'Doug?' Filled with a sudden, nameless fear I asked, 'Has something happened? Is it Toby? Talk to me!'

He shook his head. 'Toby's asleep.'

Quietly I sat down next to him. I saw that he had

167

been crying and instinctively I put my arms around him. I think it was the first time we'd touched in months.

At last he began to speak. 'When you left the house, I looked around at Hannah and the expression on her face . . . she looked so . . . *happy*. She was smiling, Beth. Actually smiling. And when she caught me looking at her it was as though she flicked a switch.' He put his head in his hands. 'Toby told me, he told me that she'd pushed him.'

I noticed that his hands were trembling and I reached over and took one in my own. 'He said she told him to go and find you, and when he got to the top of the stairs . . .' He looked at me, his eyes full of horror. 'She could have killed him.'

'I know,' I said.

'But why?' he said desperately. 'Why is she like this? Is it something we've done?'

I chose my words carefully. 'From what I've read, people like Hannah have no empathy, no conscience. I don't know why she is the way she is, but she's dangerous, Doug.'

'Then we need to get her the best psychiatrist we can find! We can turn this around, I know we can. She's eight years old . . . we can get her help, can't we? We should never have cancelled that psychiatrist. Can we get another appointment? Maybe we could go private, get seen sooner.'

I closed my eyes, knowing I had to tell him the truth.

'Doug,' I said. 'We can't do that. We can't let her talk to a doctor.'

His eyes shot to my face in surprise. '*Can't?* Why?'

I had no choice but to tell him. I could barely look at him as I described how I'd made the phone call behind his back all those months ago, how I'd discovered Hannah in the kitchen, how she'd overheard everything, knew everything. 'I'm sorry,' I cried when I saw his horrified expression. 'Oh, Doug, don't look at me like that! I'm so sorry. I didn't know what else to do. I was so frightened, I thought it would help, I needed to talk to someone.'

'But, Beth, if Hannah tells anyone. If she tells . . . oh, Jesus, Beth, we're in it up to our necks!'

I nodded. 'I know.'

'But what do we do?' he asked.

'We keep Toby with us at all times,' I said. 'We never, ever leave him alone with her. We'll . . . just have to try to manage her, watch her . . .'

He sank back into his chair and we stared up at the ceiling, to where Hannah lay sleeping in the room above. Around us the night settled into the corners of the house, the darkness outside growing denser, the moon hidden now behind thick cloud. From somewhere in the fields beyond our street came the solitary scream of a fox, before it, too, lapsed back into silence.

The next day was a Saturday. When Hannah came down for breakfast Doug and I were already up and waiting for her. She froze in surprise to see us sitting at the table together. She turned to Doug. 'I don't want her here!' she said. 'She's going to hurt me again! Don't let her hurt me, Daddy.'

'Hannah,' Doug said, calmly. 'Stop this. Stop right now. We know that you pushed Toby.'

Her eyes darted to me and then back to her father. She folded her arms. 'No I didn't!'

'Yes, Hannah,' he said. 'You did, and I know you've hurt him before.'

She looked like the child she was at that moment. Thwarted. She stood, barely four feet tall in her Winnie the Pooh slippers, her hands balled into fists. She screamed, suddenly, running to him and pounding at his belly. 'Stop it, Hannah,' he said, holding her at arm's length, his face red. 'Stop it right now. I want you to tell me why you've done this. Why did you want to hurt Toby? Hurt us? We're your mummy and daddy and we love you.'

'Well I don't love you. I hate you! I'm going to tell everyone what you did! I know what you did and I'm going to tell on you! I'm going to tell the police!'

Doug flinched at her words and I saw the triumph that flashed across Hannah's face. I stepped towards her. 'Good,' I said, as calmly as I could. She stopped and stared at me in astonishment. 'You do that. You tell the police what you know, and your father and I will be put in prison – and you will go into care. Do you know what that means?'

She hesitated, watching me intently, the look in her eyes so familiar; so eerily old beyond her years: assessing, calculating.

'It's where children go when they don't have a mummy or daddy to look after them any more,' I continued. 'You will be sent to a children's home, with lots of other children, where you'll have to do what you're told. You won't have any of your things, none of the nice food you like to eat. It'll be like school, all day every day, with grown-ups making sure you follow all their rules. Do you want that, Hannah? Really?'

'I don't care,' she said, but I could hear the uncertainty in her voice. 'I hate you. I hate you and Daddy and Toby. I don't want to live here anyway!'

'If that's what you want, then go ahead,' I said quietly. 'Go ahead, Hannah, tell whoever you want.'

There was complete silence for a moment, my eyes met Doug's across the room. And then, all at once, I saw the fight go out of her. She sat down at the table and sullenly filled her bowl with Shreddies. We had called her bluff, and, for now, at least, it seemed to have worked.

And so began an uneasy truce; a watchful, distrustful co-existence, during which we stuck to our promise, never leaving Hannah alone with her brother for a moment, using a constant, exhausting cycle of punishment and reward to get her to go to school and keep her behaviour under control. And there was peace for a time. For five years, in fact, until she was thirteen.

At the age of eleven she went to the nearest secondary school, the same one all the kids from the village went to, and though she had no friends, neither were there any more incidents of bullying or violence. She had no hobbies, no connection with the world beyond her love of television, something that I would worry about incessantly – I still loved her, you see, back then. So when she showed an interest in computers we were pleased, saving up to buy her a PC for her bedroom. I thought it could do no harm; when she spent more and more time alone in her room, I told myself that it was a good thing she'd found something she liked doing.

We never gave up trying, I want to make that clear: we never stopped trying to reach her, to make her feel loved and wanted. But the truth was she didn't want our love. And when you're met with hostility or indifference over and over it becomes almost impossible to keep on trying. My priority was my son, to make sure Hannah never had a chance to harm him again. Her spending her free time in her bedroom made that easier, I'll admit.

I'll always wonder I suppose if she was secretly planning what she went on to do. I like to think not; I like to think that she was happy, in her own way, or at least content during that time. But, truthfully, I think I've always known that my daughter is only ever really happy when she's hurting others. If I'm honest I think, back then, she was just biding her time.

*　　*　　*

172

Our one joy during those years was Toby. Our funny, sunny little boy. As a pre-schooler, despite what she'd done, he would follow Hannah around like a baby duckling, his face lighting up whenever he saw her. But her active, clear dislike of him eventually took its toll and by the time he was five and she was eleven, he barely acknowledged her.

We rarely went out as a family; instead, either Doug or I would take Toby by ourselves, but despite everything, he grew up to be a happy, kind and loving little boy. We were extremely close, he and I. He told me he loved me every day, made me presents while he was at school. I loved him so much.

I remember him saying once, 'Hannah hates me. She hates you and she hates Daddy.' By then my heart had started to become less sensitive. 'Well, Hannah is Hannah,' I said. I didn't try to hide it or deny it any more. 'Her eyes are funny,' he said. 'They scare me.' There was nothing I could say to that. He was right: there was a quality there, an absence I suppose you'd call it, that you didn't want to dwell on for too long.

There was one incident that has always stuck with me. When she was twelve, a new neighbour popped round to introduce herself. She came in and I made us both a cup of tea. I remember feeling so pleased, because the rest of the villagers ignored us, more or less. When she left, I said goodbye to her at the door and turned to find Hannah standing on the stairs, watching us. She saw me notice her and made her way to the kitchen to get herself a glass of milk. I thought nothing of it at the time, but later that day while I was in my room I heard the sound of her voice.

When I went to investigate I looked through the crack of her door to see her standing in front of her mirror, talking to herself. 'Goodbye now, Carol, so nice of you to call round,' she said. It was exactly what I'd said to the neighbour a few hours before. She practised it over and over until she had the intonation, the inflexion, just right. 'Goodbye now, Carol, so nice of you to call round!' She copied the exact way I'd smiled, the little wave I'd given. It made the hairs on the back of my neck stand on end.

Did I know what she was back then? Could I have stopped her? Years later, of course, at Hannah's trial, they had no hesitation in using the term I couldn't bring myself to say out loud. Sociopath. That's what their expert witness called her, that beautiful summer's day, the afternoon light pooling through the small, rather dingy windows while she stood in the dock awaiting sentencing. But when she was still a young child, I prayed that I was wrong about her; that she'd grow out of her problems, that it would somehow all go away. And for those five years she behaved herself. She kept out of trouble. I suppose I allowed myself to hope that it would all somehow be OK.

16

London, 2017

Turning the corner into Great Eastern Street, Clara saw the Octopus Bar ahead of her and slowed her pace, suddenly gripped with nerves. Perhaps Mac had been right: perhaps she was crazy to do this alone. 'What if it's the nutcase who's been stalking Luke?' he'd pleaded. 'It's too risky. Let me go, please, Clara – let me go instead, just to make sure.'

But she'd brushed away his concerns, her gut telling her that Emily was who she said she was, that meeting her today would be the first step to reuniting Rose and Oliver with their daughter, a thought too exciting to risk by going back on the promise she'd made. 'I said I'd go alone,' she'd told Mac stubbornly, 'so that's what I'm going to do.' Besides, the person who'd sent the messages had known about the song Luke and Emily had sung at bedtime, they knew about the T.S. Eliot book. It had to be her. So she'd left Mac waiting at his flat, beside himself with worry, promising she'd call him as soon as she could.

Clara paused a few metres from the bar now and pretended to check her phone before glancing up and down the street. It was ten to six, the pavements fairly busy with office and shop workers beginning their journeys home. She felt a stab of fear now that she was so close and for a moment contemplated turning back. Just then, a burst of evening sunlight penetrated the clouds and the passers-by lifted pleased, surprised faces to the sky. Surely nothing bad could happen here, in such a public place?

Encouraged, she walked on and when she entered the bar was relieved to see that at least half the tables were already taken. There was a low buzz of music and conversation in the air and the barman smiled cheerfully at her as she approached. Her body tensed with anticipation and nerves, she scanned the room. There were no lone drinkers, male or female, and she relaxed a little, glad that out of the two of them it was she who had arrived first.

When she'd bought her drink she chose a seat that gave her a good view of the street – close enough to the large plate-glass window to be able to see people as they approached. The minutes passed slowly. Six o'clock became six fifteen, then twenty past. Restlessly she glanced around. It was a nice place, simply decked out without any of the self-consciously hip touches so many bars in the area were afflicted by: no ironic taxidermy on the wall, no neon flamingos, or jam jars used as cocktail glasses. Just an ordinary bar with an unpretentious, after-work crowd. She settled back into her seat and continued to wait, her eyes fixed on the door.

It was quarter to seven before she admitted to herself she'd been stood up. The disappointment crushed her. She realized at that moment the biting anxiety she'd felt since Luke disappeared had been temporarily lifted by the prospect of finally meeting Emily, and it was only now as she slowly and despondently began to gather her coat and bag, that she realized how desperately she'd wanted it to be true. The despair she'd been feeling since the day Luke had gone missing returned now with renewed strength: everything seemed entirely hopeless once more.

The sound of smashing glass turned her attention to the bar, where she saw the guy who'd served her earlier looking down at a dropped tray. He grinned ruefully at her when their eyes met, and she smiled her sympathy back. When she turned again to her table, it was to find a woman standing in front of her and she jumped in surprise.

'Clara?' the woman said, and with a quick, tentative smile, added, 'It is you, isn't it?'

The stranger was so unmistakably Luke's sister that at first Clara could only stare at her in stunned silence.

She was slim and slightly younger looking than her thirty-seven years, strikingly attractive and dressed in a simple T-shirt and jeans. Her hair, thick and dark like her brother's, framed a finely featured face that had large brown eyes the replica of Luke's. Even their mouths, with their wide, full lips, were identical. 'Oh,' said Clara, jumping to her feet. 'Oh my goodness, it's you, isn't it, it's really you!' She wanted to hug Emily but she seemed so nervous, as though she might bolt at any moment, that she just stood with her arms by her side, drinking her in.

When they'd sat down Clara gave a shaky laugh. 'I thought you weren't coming.'

Emily's voice was low and soft, with the same gentle middle-class Suffolk accent as her brother's. 'I'm sorry I'm late,' she said, before adding anxiously, 'You didn't tell my parents you were meeting me?'

Clara shook her head. 'No.'

'You told no one? Are you sure?'

For a split second Mac's face flashed into her mind but before she could even process the thought, she heard herself say, 'No. I promise. I didn't tell a soul.'

At this Emily relaxed a fraction, though she continued to scan the room with quick nervous glances.

What was she so scared of, Clara wondered. Because there was no doubt about it: Emily certainly seemed afraid of something. She was like a tightly wound spring, as though at any moment she might jump out of her chair and run off into the night. 'Would you like a drink?' Clara asked, the normalcy of the question sounding utterly surreal in the circumstances.

'No. No thank you, I'm afraid I can't stay long.' She tucked her hair behind her ears and the smile that flickered across her lips was one of such sweetness that Clara smiled back.

'I'm so glad you came,' she said.

'When I saw you on the news, I couldn't believe it . . . that it was my brother you were talking about.' Emily shook her head in wonder. 'When they showed his picture . . . seeing him again after all these years, all grown up . . .' Her eyes swam, and instinctively Clara reached over and put a hand on hers. 'I've missed out on most of his life. He was ten years old when I last saw him and I've thought about him every single day since. When I saw you, I couldn't . . . I couldn't not contact you.'

Clara was about to reply when Emily leant down and pulled something from her bag. 'I have something to show you,' she said, handing her a small, creased photograph.

Clara gazed at the faded picture in amazement. It was of Luke aged about four, wearing stripy pyjamas and a huge toothy grin. Behind him stood Emily, a gangly, pretty girl of around twelve, her arms wrapped tightly around her brother's shoulders, her smile a replica of his. In the background was the living room of The Willows, its walls painted an unfamiliar green.

'Oh my goodness,' Clara murmured.

'I carry it with me everywhere,' Emily said. 'And this one too.' She passed her a second picture, which showed herself aged about fourteen or so and standing between a smiling, much younger-looking Rose and Oliver in the back garden of The Willows, each of them with a glass of champagne in their hands. They looked so relaxed and happy, Clara thought; such a stark contrast to how battered by grief and worry they were now. 'How are they?' Emily asked. 'How are Mum and Dad?'

There was such anguish in her face that Clara felt her throat thicken with sympathy. She paused, searching for the right words. 'They're not good, Emily,' she admitted. 'Luke's disappearance . . .'

Emily looked so sad that Clara couldn't help herself any longer. 'Emily, what happened to you? Where have you been all this time? What happened when you were eighteen?'

But it was as if the shutters slammed down in her eyes and she looked away.

Into the tense silence, Clara said miserably, 'I'm sorry. I don't want to push you, it's just . . . your mum and dad, it would make them so happy to know that you're OK. Can I tell them I've seen you, that you're alive and well? It would—'

'No!' A group of people sitting at the next table glanced over at them in surprise and Emily stared down at her hands for a long moment. When she spoke again, her voice was very quiet. 'I hope, soon, I'll be able to go home. When all this is over, when we've found Luke,

I will go back to my parents. But you must let me do that myself. I don't want someone else to break the news to them, to fill them with hope when I don't know how long it will be before I can go back to them.'

'But—'

Emily leaned forward, gazing at her urgently. 'It wouldn't be safe, for my parents, or for me, if I return home now. You have to trust me, Clara. But I will go to them. When they've found Luke, I will go home, I need more time, that's all.'

Clara searched Emily's face. 'What do you mean,' she said, '"it wouldn't be safe"? What are you frightened of? If you're in danger, you must—'

'Clara,' Emily cut her off. 'I can't talk about it. If you can't promise me that you won't tell them, I'll have to leave.' She half rose from her seat and Clara put her hand out to stop her.

'No, please stay, please. I promise. I just . . .' she trailed off uncertainly. It didn't make any sense, and she didn't know if she could bear to keep something so huge from two people she loved so dearly. But it was clear that Emily wasn't going to explain herself now. Finally, she said, 'Do you promise you will go to them, when Luke's found?'

Emily nodded. 'I promise, Clara. All the attention should be on him now, on finding him. There's nothing I want more than to see them again. I'm just asking you to keep this secret for a while longer.'

And what if we don't find Luke? The unwelcome

thought snaked its way through Clara's mind and with effort she pushed it away. Reluctantly she nodded. 'OK.'

A man by the bar went over to the jukebox and within moments the soulful strains of a Joan Armatrading song filled the room.

'What are they like now,' Emily asked, 'my mum and dad? I've tried so hard to imagine them over the years; to picture them as time passed, but it's difficult after so long.'

Clara stared down at her drink as she thought how to answer. 'Before Luke went missing they were . . . happy, in a way, I guess. But you must know that they never got over you leaving. How could they? They don't talk about you because it's too painful, but I know that they think of you every day.'

'I had to go,' Emily said, her voice so low now, Clara had to strain to hear her. 'I had no choice.'

Clara nodded, desperate for an explanation but knowing better than to push for it again and, her gaze falling to the photos in her hand, asked, 'Don't you have one of Tom?'

'No,' she replied. 'No, I don't have a picture of Tom.' And there was something in her tone that made Clara stare at her in surprise, but before she could speak Emily asked quietly. 'Do you see him ever?'

'No – that is, only now and then. He lives in Norwich, so . . . but, um, he's well, I think. I mean he seems quite well. Desperately worried for Luke too, of course, but . . .'

The barman came over at that moment and wiped down their table, and they waited until he'd finished. 'Tell me about Luke,' Emily asked when he'd gone. 'Have the police any idea what happened to him? Is there any news at all?'

Slowly, while the bar filled up around them, Clara told her everything that had happened since Luke's disappearance: the threatening emails she'd found, the break-ins, the police enquiry that had so far come to nothing. 'Mac – that's Luke's friend – and I have decided to try and find out who it might be who hates Luke enough to do all these things,' Clara said, describing their visit to Amy and the list of women they had yet to see.

Emily listened to her with rapt attention and when she'd finished, gave Clara a sad smile. 'I could tell, when I saw you on the news, how much you love my brother. And I bet he loves you too. I bet he loves you so much.'

An unwelcome picture of Sadie's face flashed before Clara's eyes but she pushed it away. 'I just wish I knew what had happened to him,' she said. 'To vanish into thin air . . . it's . . .' she shook her head.

'It must be so hard for you.'

They were silent for a moment, then Emily asked, 'You were talking about my parents. Be honest with me: are they coping, do you think?'

Clara considered this. 'They're strong people, and they're trying to stay positive, but yes, they're deeply upset. I don't think they're sleeping or eating properly, and I have to admit I'm worried for them.'

Emily nodded, and after a moment Clara said cautiously, 'I'm sorry, but I have to ask because it might help us find Luke. I can't help thinking . . . it's such a coincidence that first you disappeared, and now Luke, too . . . I thought maybe the two might be linked. They're not, though, are they? I mean, they can't possibly be . . . ?'

Emily's gaze held Clara's for a beat or two, her expression unreadable. 'Is that what my parents think too?'

Clara shook her head in surprise. 'I don't know.'

Emily looked away. 'No,' she said. 'They aren't linked.'

Just then, a group of men in business suits came through the door on a wave of noise and cold air. It was dark in the street now. The lights inside the bar burned brighter, the atmosphere deepening into something more raucous and drunken. Emily glanced nervously around her. 'I have to go,' she said. 'I've stayed too long. I have to get back . . .'

'So soon?' Clara asked in dismay.

'I'm sorry.' Emily got up. 'I have a very long journey.'

'But where are you going back to?' Clara asked desperately, getting to her feet too. 'Where do you live?'

She turned away without answering, and Clara picked up her things and hurried after her into the street. They stopped and regarded each other. 'I'd like to meet you again – if you want to?' Emily said.

'Yes,' said Clara eagerly. 'Yes, please. You can message me anytime.'

At this Emily reached over and surprised her by taking both her hands in hers. 'Clara, I can trust you, can't I?' she said. 'When I saw you on the news, I felt I could trust you. I wasn't wrong, was I?'

She shook her head, unable to look away from Emily's gaze, its quiet intensity reminding her suddenly so much of Tom. 'No,' she said, 'you weren't wrong.' Then, as she watched, Emily pulled her hood up so that it half obscured her face. She looked around her, shooting quick, nervous glances at passers-by. 'I better go,' she said. 'I'll be in touch,' and without another word she set off, slipping away through the crowd. Clara watched her go, adrenalin shooting through her now their meeting was over. But then something strange caught her eye. Just before she lost sight of Emily completely, Clara saw, or thought she saw, someone who looked very much like Mac. He was walking not far behind Emily – in fact, as Clara strained to see, it almost looked as though the two were in step, as if, in fact, they were walking side by side. A moment later they turned off down a side street and disappeared, swallowed by the London night.

She stood staring after them in confusion. Surely it couldn't have been Mac? That made no sense at all. At last she turned away and, finding her phone, clicked through her contacts until she found his number. But when she rang it went straight to voicemail. She listened to the answerphone message in surprise. He'd said he'd be waiting for her to call, desperate to hear how it went.

So why wasn't he picking up? Eventually she put her phone back in her bag and began walking towards the Tube. It can't have been Mac, she decided. It was pretty dark and the street had been crowded; she must have been mistaken. She'd go straight to his place now and then she'd know it hadn't been him.

Now that she was away from Emily, her anxiety at keeping something so momentous from Rose and Oliver returned. Could she really do it? What had Emily meant when she said that it would be dangerous for her to go back to them? It made no sense. Guilt nagged at her. But perhaps Emily was right that everyone's focus needed to be on Luke now, and it was true it wasn't Clara's place to break the news to Rose and Oliver if she wanted to do it herself. Plus Emily had promised she'd go to her parents as soon as Luke was found. It was so hard to know what to do for the best, but finally she came to a decision. She would give Emily a week. Whatever happened in that week – and she hoped to God they would find Luke – she would tell Rose and Oliver herself if it looked like Emily wouldn't. Besides, the last thing she wanted was to give Rose and Oliver false hope, tell them she had found their long-lost daughter only for her to disappear off the face of the earth again – that surely would be too heartbreaking for them. No, she would keep quiet for now. Hopefully she'd see Emily again soon and be able to unravel more of the mystery then.

When she reached Old Street she paused, gazing off

towards the station in the distance. A group of laughing teenage girls clattered past her in high heels, followed by a drunken man weaving along in the gutter behind them, clutching a can of cider. A cool breeze picked up. Across the road was the narrow side street that led to Hoxton Square. She hadn't been back to her flat for days and she suddenly longed to go home: to the quiet and privacy of her own space, to be surrounded by her own things, to take a shower and make a cup of tea and take stock of everything that had happened without feeling she was encroaching on anyone else, hospitable as Mac was. And what if Luke had come back while she'd been away? What if he had phoned or written or left a message? Before she knew it, she found herself crossing the road at a run.

It was gone eight now, the square's bars and restaurants busy, straggles of people standing around outside them smoking and chatting in the cool spring air. When she reached her building she glanced up at its three rows of windows and paused. Only the first floor showed signs of life; electric light shining through the gaps in the curtains, the shadow of a figure crossing the room. The Japanese couple who lived on the floor below her, she thought. Her own floor, and that of the flat above – Alison? Had that been her name? – was in darkness. Perhaps she would just go up to collect some more clothes, she told herself. Have a quick check round to make sure all was well. It would only take a few minutes, after all.

As she climbed the stairs and passed the first-floor flat, she heard the noise of a TV, of the scraping of cutlery and a toilet flushing from within; comforting, ordinary sounds that eased her nervousness. When she reached the second set of stairs she hit the light switch on the wall, but the hall and stairwell remained in darkness and she swore under her breath. Holding her key in her hand she ran up the next flight and felt around for that floor's switch, but it, too, gave no response when she pushed it. She shivered, mentally cursing her landlord, and glanced quickly up the stairs to Alison's flat, but all was quiet. Perhaps she was still away, she thought. When Clara reached her own door she pulled out her mobile and used its light to guide her to the keyhole.

Once inside her flat she hurried around hitting every switch until the rooms were bathed in light, then stood looking about herself. It was still in disarray since the break-in, and the place had a sad, abandoned air. Something that had been niggling her ever since she'd received the first message from Emily returned to her now. She got up and went to the living room, taking down a small wooden box tucked away out of sight on one of the bookshelves. Opening it she breathed a sigh of relief. Inside, untouched still, was the T.S. Eliot book Luke had shown her all those years before. Ever since they'd moved into this flat he'd kept it with a few other precious bits and pieces in the same place. It had not been touched, she was sure of it – the box was still covered in a thin layer of dust from where it'd sat untampered with for half a year. She put the box back on the shelf.

Wandering into the bedroom her hip knocked against the chest of drawers and something fluttered to the floor. Picking it up she saw that it was the valentine's card Luke had given her a few months before, a line drawing of one of Picasso's doves on the front. Inside was written, simply, *Love you, Clara, always will.*

She went to the wardrobe and pulled out his favourite T-shirt, a faded Stone Roses one he used to wear in bed. Holding it to her face she breathed in his scent. A rush of memories hit her; his face, his kiss, the way he said her name, the smell of his body first thing in the morning. An image of the van's bloodstained seat flashed before her and she sank on to the bed, tears choking her. At this moment, more than ever before, she felt sure that he was dead, that she would never see him again.

Suddenly she was desperate to get out of there. It had been a mistake to come; his absence far more brutal here between these silent walls than it was at Mac's. She realized it didn't even feel like home, not any more: whoever had broken in had destroyed that sense of safety and sanctuary. Hurriedly she wiped her eyes and, snatching up an empty carrier bag, began to fill it with clothes. Leaving the flat, she closed the door behind her, using the light from her phone to make sure she'd double locked it.

As she stood standing in the hall's blackness grappling

with her keys, she thought she heard a sound from the floor above. She stood stock-still. What was that? 'Hello?' she called. Nothing. And then, the name unfamiliar on her lips, 'Alison, is that you?' Again, silence. 'This isn't funny,' she shouted. 'If that's you, say something.' Still nothing, yet she couldn't shake the feeling there was someone there. Suddenly, it was as if the air was ripped in two by a deafening roar of music. Her heart lurched at the shock and involuntarily she screamed, before hurtling down the stairs, the music stopping as abruptly as it had begun the moment she reached the main door. She bolted out of the building, gasping for air in the cool, orange-lit darkness of the street. Across the square voices drifted over to her from the string of bars and restaurants. She turned, and, her heart still pounding, set off at a run towards the station.

17

Cambridgeshire, 1994

Those few brief years of peace ended not long after Hannah turned thirteen. She seemed, physically, to change overnight – or perhaps I hadn't been looking, maybe I had grown used to letting my gaze flicker over my daughter, it being too painful to linger on her for too long. Whatever the case, I remember vividly the morning I looked up from my breakfast and noticed something I'd failed to see before.

'What?' she said, as she sullenly emptied some cereal into a bowl.

'Nothing.' But though I lowered my gaze I couldn't help but watch her from the corner of my eye as she began to eat. Toby, seven by then, was halfway through his Cheerios, engrossed in a comic. Doug had already left for work, and Hannah was eating her breakfast as she stood by the window, having long ago refused to join us at the table.

Perhaps it was the too-small T-shirt she was wearing, or the angle in which she was standing, but for the first time I noticed the small breasts that had begun to bud on her chest, the waist that had become more defined, the thickening of her hips. My eyes travelled to her face. It was, as usual, half hidden behind a wild tangle of hair, but I saw now that it had begun to lose some of its childish plumpness, her features becoming more certain – the beauty she'd always had becoming more distinct.

I can't quite put into words the emotion that filled me. But I guess, mainly, it was a kind of panic. As long as she was physically still a child I was able to fool myself that there was still time – for things to turn themselves around, for her to grow out of her difficulties, for me to become the sort of mother who knew how to deal with someone so clearly out of step with the world. The realization that she was growing into an adult triggered a sort of terror in me, because it meant that soon it would be too late for me to work out how to help her, to change the course on which her life was going. Perhaps I had a premonition of how badly things would end for us all. It terrified me: in that moment of clarity I was utterly terrified.

Nevertheless I took a deep breath and chose my words carefully. 'Hannah, I was wondering if you would like to come shopping with me at the weekend?'

Her head shot up. 'Can I get some new computer games?'

'I thought we'd look for some bras for you, some toiletries . . . or new clothes, perhaps. We could even get your hair cut. What do you say?' I heard the wheedling edge my voice always seemed to have when talking to her and cringed, but forced myself to continue smiling brightly.

Her glance fell downwards to her chest and I steeled myself for her embarrassment, but her expression when she next looked up was one of ambivalence. For a while she held my gaze, before she plonked her bowl back down on the work surface and muttered, 'Don't want any,' before turning and walking away, the conversation clearly over as far as she was concerned.

Nevertheless in the following weeks I bought her a variety of bras in different sizes, hoping that some of them might fit. I bought her some shampoo, deodorant, some sanitary towels and tampons, some nice new clothes that I chose with painstaking care. I even bought her a book about puberty. It broke my heart, of course; every purchase driving home the fact that this should be so very different: an opportunity to guide her lovingly through this important life stage, a chance to bond amongst the rails of Topshop. I tried not to mind, had long ago told myself to let go of the fantasy relationship I'd always longed for, but it hurt all the same.

Days later I found the clothes and toiletries dumped, still in their packaging, in the bin. She never wore the bras I bought her; as her breasts grew bigger she let them flop around beneath her grubby T-shirts. She began to smell. Though she never talked about school I knew she had no friends, and could only imagine how she must have appeared to the other children: the smelly kid. The school weirdo. I felt so sorry for her, but my pity was useless. She didn't want it. Really, it was self-pity, I suppose, and it's amazing how even that turns to nothing after a while: even the hardest things become acceptable, just another part of life.

Her bedroom door remained firmly closed. I would stand outside it and listen sometimes while she played her computer games, the sounds of simulated death and destruction seeping between the cracks, before I'd creep away and leave her to it, turning up the television or closing the kitchen door. I told myself that at least she was safe, and happy, in her own way.

It was less than a year later when everything changed. I don't know how long she'd been sneaking out at night before I realized what she was up to. It was three in the morning and I was in the kitchen getting a glass of water when she came creeping in through the front door. I screamed, seeing her so suddenly, so shockingly, in the dark hallway. 'Hannah,' I said, once my heart had calmed, 'what the hell are you doing? Where have you been?'

She shrugged. 'Nowhere.'

I stepped towards her, wincing at the pungent smell

of cigarette smoke. 'Where have you been?' I demanded. 'Who have you been with?'

As I spoke, Doug appeared at the top of the stairs, rubbing the sleep from his eyes. 'What's going on?'

Hannah shrugged, a sly smile on her face. 'Nothing. Just went out. What's wrong with that?'

'You're only fourteen!' I said. She took her coat off and threw it over the banister, stumbling as she did so. It was then that I realized she was drunk. We stared after her with open-mouthed astonishment as she climbed the stairs, pushing past her father as she did so. A moment later we heard her bedroom door slam shut, and Doug and I stood staring back at each other in dismay.

No matter how much Doug and I threatened, begged and cajoled over the following weeks, Hannah continued to make her midnight escapes. We tried everything: took away her allowance, put extra locks on the door, we even hid her shoes – but nothing worked. She must have been getting money from somewhere, because she continued to come back smelling of alcohol and I often found boxes of cigarettes in her coat.

'You're too young to be doing this, to be out by yourself at night,' I pleaded when she returned close to dawn one morning. I had long since stopped being able to sleep, my anxiety and worry for her keeping me awake while I waited for her to return.

She smirked. 'I'm not by myself.'

'Then who are you with?'

She shrugged. 'Friends.'

'What friends?'

'No one you know.'

'There are bad people around,' I told her. 'Bad men who take advantage of young girls like you. Don't you understand that, Hannah? Don't you realize it's not safe?'

'So what? I'm having fun.' And then she'd sneer and add, 'You can't stop me. You know you can't.'

She was right, of course. She knew that the secret she held over us ensured we would never try to force the issue. We were too afraid of what she'd do, and she understood that only too well.

Gradually, the scruffy, shapeless T-shirts and tracksuit bottoms disappeared to be replaced with miniskirts and tight, low-cut tops; she would often go out with her face plastered inexpertly in make-up. It terrified me. Sometimes the police would bring her back, drunk or high. There they'd stand in our living room, describing how they'd found her at a squat party they'd searched for drugs, or hitching home alone at night, or getting stoned at bus stops with God knows who.

She loved that, the police involvement. Absolutely loved it. She'd watch us with her kohl-lined eyes, a smirk on her face while the police officers sat in our living room reminding us that she was a minor, that it was our responsibility to ensure she didn't come to harm. She knew how terrified we were of them, that she could blow open our secret there and then with just a few choice words. And I would think of my sleeping boy upstairs beneath his *Star Wars* duvet and grit my teeth and say, 'Yes, officer, we're sorry. It won't happen again.'

I grew used to the hostile looks from my neighbours, who no doubt thought it was all our fault, that if she were their child, they would have done things differently. No doubt they would have, but they didn't have to deal with someone like Hannah, someone utterly devoid of conscience or love for us, someone who wouldn't think twice about exposing us if we tried to force her hand.

Eventually, filled with a burning shame and dismay, I took to leaving packets of condoms in her underwear drawer when I knew she was out. She caught me only once. I turned to find her watching me from her bedroom door, the expression on her face one of amused enjoyment at my discomfort.

We thought of moving away, but what would have been the point? The situation would have stayed the same wherever we went. And we liked our village. We both worked in the area – I had found a job at the medical centre in the next town, resuming the nursing job I'd had before Hannah came along, and I loved it there, situated far away enough for no one to know me, or Hannah. Besides, we'd had to leave our home, fleeing my childhood village once before. I couldn't face doing it again.

There were many, many nights that Doug and I spent driving around the nearest towns looking for her. Toby wrapped in his duvet, sleeping in the back. They were dark and desperate times; I was convinced we'd eventually find her left for dead in the street. I was permanently terrified for her, I lost almost two stone, the knot of fear that seemed constantly to lie in the pit of my stomach preventing me from eating. But though those months were unbearable, she always stopped short of going too far, staying just enough out of trouble to ensure that the police and social services never followed through with their many threats to remove her from our care. She was smart enough to know that, if that happened, the freedom her hold over us afforded her would be curtailed. And besides, she had bigger fish to fry, as we were soon to find out.

It was an ordinary morning, not long after she'd turned sixteen. Toby, who was ten by then, was getting ready to walk to school. I was dressed in my nurse's uniform in preparation for another shift and Doug was clearing the breakfast things away. I didn't even look up when she came into the room, though I was surprised she was out of bed. She had finished school without a GCSE to her name and, having flatly refused to re-sit them, spent her days at home, rarely surfacing before noon as she slept off the night before. I remember I glanced at Doug, and my first hint that something was wrong was the expression of astonishment on his face. It was then that I turned and looked at my daughter.

Of all the awful things she had shocked us with over

the past couple of years, nothing could have prepared me for how she looked that morning. Because it was an entirely different girl who stood before me now. Her usual rat's nest hair was clean and neatly brushed. And though I had assumed she'd long ago thrown out all the nice clothes I'd bought her, today she was dressed in a pretty coral jumper and a plain, knee-length denim skirt. Her make-up was subtle, the black nail varnish removed, as was the nose ring and multiple ear studs she'd taken to wearing lately.

She didn't look at us as she made herself some toast. Doug, Toby and I stared at each other in mute disbelief.

'Hannah,' I said nervously. 'You look very nice today.'

She looked up then, but though she raised her eyebrows mockingly, she didn't reply.

'Going somewhere?' Doug asked.

'Nowhere special,' she said. We watched as she finished her breakfast, and then she got up and left the house. I didn't find out for a long time what she was up to. And when I did, it was far too late to stop her.

18

London, 2017

Clara closed the door to Mac's spare room and sat down on the bed, listening as he moved around the flat turning off the lights, before going into his own room. On the table was a pile of books he'd left there for her, and she smiled at his thoughtfulness. She wasn't sure she'd be able to sleep. From the moment they'd said goodbye outside the bar, Emily had haunted Clara's thoughts. Their meeting had done nothing to shed light on the mystery of her disappearance, leaving Clara more plagued by questions than ever.

She longed to see her again, yet nearly two days had passed and she'd received no more messages from Emily, leaving her with the nagging worry that she might have vanished as suddenly as she'd appeared, their meeting already taking on the unreality of a dream.

When she'd told Mac she thought she'd seen him that night he'd stared back at her blankly. 'Of course I wasn't there,' he said in confusion. 'You said I couldn't come. I was right here, waiting to hear all about it.'

'I tried to call you, though – it went straight to voice-mail.'

He looked at her, mystified. 'Sometimes my phone loses signal in this flat, but . . . Christ, there's no way I wouldn't have picked up if my phone rang, you know that!'

She considered this. The signal thing was true; his flat seemed to be in a bit of a black spot reception-wise – she'd experienced herself, several times, the frustration of pacing its rooms, waving her iPhone around, trying to pick up a signal. She gazed back at him. He was telling the truth, she could see that. She must have been mistaken – and no wonder, when she'd been so stunned by her meeting with Emily. Plus, the street had been crowded and dark, and they'd been so far away.

For the past two nights she had lain awake, going over and over every moment of her and Emily's conversation. Had Clara scared her off by asking too many questions? Or was something, or someone, preventing her from making contact again? When she finally slept her dreams were plagued by visions of Emily in distress, trapped somewhere dark and terrifying, her face morphing into Luke's. She'd often wake, her throat constricted with fear, too anxious and upset to go back to sleep.

Wherever she went, whatever she did, Emily was never far from her thoughts and she began to dread Rose's calls, the guilt she felt when she heard her voice almost unbearable, knowing that with a few choice words she could put an end to so many years of uncertainty. Yet she couldn't shake the suspicion that Emily was somehow protecting her parents by refusing to see them; that telling Rose and Oliver might put them in danger. And though Emily had said that her and Luke's disappearances weren't linked, Clara wasn't entirely sure she had believed her. Also, she had given her word she'd let Emily go to them herself when the time was right. There was nothing she could do except wait and hope that Emily would get in touch again – and that the next time she did, Clara would be able to unravel a little more of the mystery of what happened to her twenty years before.

Next on her and Mac's list of women to contact was Jade Williams, the girl Luke had dated while he was at university. She tried to remember what he'd told her about this, his next serious relationship after Amy, and recalled now that he'd been unusually evasive when she'd asked him about her, had wanted in fact to change the subject as quickly as possible. She had assumed at the time that things had ended badly between them and, not wanting to pry, hadn't pressed him further.

It was the twelfth night without Luke, and she and

Mac were sitting at his kitchen table, half-heartedly playing a game of gin rummy and listening to music. She had phoned her parents earlier, and after that Zoe had called, as she did almost daily, but though it was always comforting to talk to her best friend, still it felt as though she and Mac were alone in this nightmare, bound together in a hideously tense waiting game, jumping each time the phone rang, talking incessantly in painful, circular conversations about what might happen next. Through the open window the evening sounds of the Holloway Road drifted up to them; a siren's wail, the rumble of buses, a man shouting into his phone outside the kebab shop below.

Clara eyed Mac above her hand of cards. 'So what was she like then, this Jade? Luke never said.'

He frowned, trying to remember. 'Bit of a party animal, good looking, quite posh. I only met her a couple of times though; me and Luke were at different unis.'

She picked up a card from the pile. 'Why did they split?'

'As I recall, she finished with him. He was quite cut up about it.' He thought for a while, brow furrowed. 'Actually, there was something odd about their break-up, now you mention it. I remember him calling me upset that Jade had ended it out of the blue. Said she'd accused him of something that wasn't true.'

'Accused him? Of what?'

'That's just it, he wouldn't say. He was really down for a while. I saw him in the holidays and he wasn't his old self at all.' He picked up a card then shrugged. 'The next time we spoke, he was over it.' He gave a half-smile. 'You know Luke, not one to dwell on things too long.'

Jade Williams – now Spencer – lived in a smart Georgian townhouse in Lambeth. Pinning her down to a time she could meet had proven tricky, and when at last a day was agreed, Mac had to work, so Clara went alone. She stood on the front step after she'd rung the doorbell, taking in the freshly painted olive green door, the pots of well-tended geraniums and the antique glass lantern that hung above her head. It was a quiet, leafy street with expensive cars parked outside each carefully reno-vated house.

The woman who answered was tall, attractive and blond, immaculately dressed in a chic trouser suit that made Clara instantly conscious of her own jeans and trainers. From behind her a red setter came bounding on to the step, wagging its tail and enthusiastically sticking its nose into Clara's crotch. 'Clara? How nice to meet you,' Jade's smile was sincere but distracted as she ushered her inside.

She led Clara down to an enormous basement with an open-plan kitchen, tasteful and expensive looking with duck-egg blue units and white marble worktops. Clara perched at the rectory table and watched as Jade flew around making tea, talking in rapid, breathless flurries as she told Clara about the interiors company she'd started with her husband – 'Honestly we've been working like dogs, our poor baby barely recognizes us, though luckily we've got the most wonderful nanny' – and the alterations they'd had done to the house – 'That's the thing about buying around here, anywhere bigger than a shoebox and you have to expect to completely gut the place . . .'

Clara tried to imagine what she would have been like when she was younger and dating Luke. It was a strange idea. Had she always been so intimidatingly self-assured? She couldn't quite picture them together.

'So what can I do for you?' Jade asked, suddenly businesslike now that two delicate cups of ginger tea sat on the table between them. 'Your email said you wanted to talk about Luke Lawson.' She leant forward, her eyes wide. 'So awful, isn't it? Though, as I told the police, I'm not sure what I can possibly do to help . . .'

'I know this must seem strange,' Clara said, 'the police, as you probably know, haven't come any closer to finding him . . .'

'Yes. So I gather. I heard they'd found a van? So odd. Dreadful. You must be out of your mind.'

Clara nodded. 'I am, we all are. My friend Mac and I are trying to find anyone who might have held a grudge against Luke. You were close to him once, and if there's anything you can think of, anyone he might have got on the wrong side of, or who might have something against him . . . '

'Hmm,' Jade said, as though mulling it over. 'People

who might have disliked Luke.' She pursed her lips. 'He was a very popular lad at uni. Lots of friends, so . . .'

'You were together a couple of years?'

'More or less.'

'Do you mind me asking why you split?'

Jade's smile remained exactly the same, it was only her eyes that became a touch cooler. 'It's rather personal, actually. And a long story.' She took a sip of her tea.

Clara nodded. 'Of course. I'm sorry . . .'

She must have looked desolate because Jade sighed. 'The thing is, Claire—'

'Clara.'

'Clara, sorry. The thing is, Luke Lawson . . . all that, was a long time ago. I really don't think I can help you.'

'I understand, and I'm sorry for bothering you.' There was a silence, and Clara felt her spirits sink. This was hopeless. The whole thing was hopeless. She shouldn't have come – it had been a stupid idea to think she'd find anything out by sticking her nose into Luke's past like this. She was about to get to her feet when a thought struck her, and because she had nothing else to lose, asked, 'Did you love him?'

For a moment Jade's poise slipped a little, and someone younger and far more vulnerable took her place. 'Yes,' she said quietly. 'Yes, I did, at first, very much.'

'At first?'

She dropped her eyes. 'As I said, it was a long time ago. Nearly a decade, in fact.'

'I know. I'm just trying to get a picture of him, to work out why anyone would want to hurt him. If there was a side to his character I didn't know, it might help track down whoever has done this to him. I don't know where he is. My boyfriend has disappeared, possibly murdered, and no one has a clue where he is or what's happened to him.' She pressed her fingers to her eyes, forcing back her tears.

Jade got up to fetch her a tissue. 'Look, please don't upset yourself,' she said, and then, as if she'd suddenly come to a decision, she went on: 'The fact is, Luke cheated on me. We were very young, and you know what it's like at uni, all the parties, everyone drunk most of the time. Luke and I got together in our first term and it was great for a while. But halfway through our second year I found out he'd slept with someone else.'

Clara looked at her in surprise. 'Who with?'

'A friend of a friend. I didn't believe it, not at first. I went to find the girl myself. And as soon as I confronted her, I knew it was true.'

'I'm so sorry.' She remembered how she'd felt when she'd found out about Sadie, and she winced in sympathy.

Jade stared down at her cup. 'It wasn't just that he'd cheated on me,' she said very quietly. 'The girl was telling everyone that he'd pressured her into it, that they'd kissed but then she'd changed her mind and he'd pestered and pestered her until she gave in. And afterwards, Luke started harassing her . . .'

'*Harassing* her?'

'She said he turned up the next night, and when she said no and showed him the door, he began bombarding her with texts, turning up at her place, trying it on with her. She said he was a nightmare, and in the end she reported him to the university. God, I felt so ashamed – you can imagine the gossip.'

Clara's eyes widened in astonishment. 'Did you talk to him about it?'

'Of course. He was very upset, burst into tears in fact, admitted that he'd got hammered at a party and kissed the girl, but denied everything else. Said she was lying, insane, that she'd come on to him, had wanted to take things further, then made it all up about him harassing her because he'd turned her down.'

'Jesus. And did you believe him?'

She paused. 'I didn't know what to believe.'

'But . . . didn't this girl show you the text messages she said he'd been sending her? The missed calls and so on. I mean, did she have the evidence?'

'No. No, she didn't. She deleted it all. She said that as soon as he sent her a message it freaked her out so much she got rid of it, that she didn't want to give him headspace.'

'Well . . . she could have been lying,' Clara said desperately. 'She could have made it up.'

'Yeah, she could have.'

'OK, so . . .'

Jade shrugged. 'Why would she lie about it? She was so certain, so sincere. You can usually tell, can't you, when another woman's lying to you. In the end the uni let him off with a warning. Typically, he got no comeback, apart from me dumping him of course, and a reputation for being a pest, but the general feeling was "naughty old Luke, boys will be boys" sort of thing. He continued to swear blind that the girl was lying, and he certainly had no trouble getting another girlfriend. Let's be honest, it's the sort of thing that happens all the time, just the sort of shit women are expected to put up with, be flattered by, even.'

Clara thought about it. About a time at a party when she was a teenager, a lad she'd fancied buying her shot after shot after shot, then, later, things going too far, too quickly, him not taking no for an answer until she finally managed to push him off. She'd told no one, worried it had been her fault for leading him on. Jade was right that it happened all the time, in different forms. A friend who often slept with her boyfriend when she didn't feel like it because she couldn't stand his endless moods if she didn't, the time Zoe had been hit on by her flirty boss, who'd then made her life miserable when she'd turned him down. They were ordinary men, not monsters leaping out of bushes: friends, boyfriends, colleagues, getting drunk, getting carried away. A bit selfish. A bit entitled.

She remembered the emails Luke had been sent: *Women are nothing to you, are we, Luke? We're just here for your convenience, to fuck, to step over, to use or to bully. We're disposable. You think you're untouchable. Think again.*

'Did you tell the police about this?' she asked.

Jade shifted in her seat, looking slightly uncomfortable. 'No, it's not something I like to dwell on. And there's no way it would have anything to do with Luke going missing now, so I didn't think it was relevant.'

'Can you remember the girl's name?' she asked.

'Of course. Her name was Ellen. Ellen Michaels. We have a few Facebook friends in common from our uni days and I saw that she'd got married recently, in fact. She's living in Hong Kong now.' Jade was silent for a bit. 'I wonder if she thinks about it ever, about what happened with Luke.'

'So what did Jade say?' Mac asked her later that evening 'Anything interesting?'

They were slumped on his sofa, picking at a stir-fry she'd made for them. And to her own surprise, Clara found herself saying, 'No. Not really. Bit of a waste of time, to be honest.'

He nodded. 'That's a shame. So who's next on the list?'

'A couple of his old colleagues,' she said vaguely. 'I'll get on to them tomorrow.'

She realized that she couldn't quite face telling Mac what Jade had told her. He would, she knew, be as horrified and shocked as she was, yet she also knew that his loyalty to Luke might lead him to defend his friend, suggest that the girl was exaggerating perhaps, or even making it up, and though part of her was desperate to believe that, to be persuaded that the person she had loved for three years was incapable of behaving so badly, she also couldn't quite face hearing it brushed aside, denied or disbelieved either. She watched as Mac got up and began to clear the plates away, and when he smiled at her, she smiled too, before turning back to the TV.

She thought about Luke, about his exuberance, his easy charm, how she and Mac had always laughed at the way luck seemed to follow him, wherever he went, how he always seemed to get what he wanted, always came out on top. It suddenly didn't seem so funny any more. She thought about Amy and Jade and Ellen and the way Luke had treated them. Excuses could be made, of course. He was young and frightened when he'd got Amy pregnant. Perhaps Ellen *had* been exaggerating. Why then, did she feel so utterly sick to her stomach? Again she thought of the emails Luke had been sent. *You think you've got away with it. Think again, Luke.*

Who'd sent that email? She was pretty certain it was neither of the women she'd met over the past few days. The woman, Ellen, who'd made the accusation at university was living in Hong Kong now with a new baby, according to her check-ins and photos on Facebook, so was unlikely to be driving Luke around Britain in a stolen van. And Amy hardly seemed like a revenge-crazed psychopath either. She felt drained by the impossibility of it – there could be countless women that Luke had wronged in some way, women she had no hope of knowing about, let alone tracking down. It was hopeless.

19

A few days after they'd met at the bar, Emily contacted Clara again, asking if she could meet her somewhere private. And though she was elated to hear from her, Clara's heart sank when she realized that the only possible place she could take her to was her own flat – Mac, after all, was not supposed to know about their meeting. The memory of her last visit there, that strange, eerie sense of being watched, the sudden, terrifying burst of music exploding down the stairwell still haunted her, and she sat for a long moment in Mac's living room, staring down at Emily's message before she typed her reply.

She was grateful the following afternoon as she let herself into her building that Emily had at least agreed

212

to meet in daylight. When she reached her door she paused and listened, glancing fearfully up to Alison's floor, but all was silent now. She busied herself with tidying up, thankful that she wouldn't be alone for too long.

Sure enough, Emily arrived on the dot of two. When she opened the door Clara was struck afresh by her similarity to Luke, the almost identical way they smiled; the exact shade of their eyes. She watched Emily as she moved around the living room, her fingers trailing over shelves and ornaments as she drank everything in. When she came to the photograph of Luke and Clara, she picked it up and studied it. 'Tell me about my brother,' she said. 'Tell me what he's like now. He was such a lovely little boy, so kind and funny and loving. Is he still like that?'

And Clara heard herself replying, 'Yes, yes he is,' because, despite the disturbing things she'd learnt about him over the past few days, the Luke she'd known *had* been kind and funny and loving – at least to her.

'We were so close when we were kids,' Emily said wistfully. 'What sort of man is he now?'

So Clara told her everything she could think of: how Luke had travelled around Asia in his gap year, the university he'd gone to, the friends he'd made, his career, the music and books he liked. She told her about the Luke who made the best roasted sea bass she'd ever tasted and did the worst impression of Michael Jackson she'd ever seen, the Luke who cared about his friends and his family, and her.

Emily listened avidly, her legs curled up beneath her where she sat on the sofa next to Clara, her head resting on her arms, her quiet, thoughtful gaze upon her face. 'You love him very much, don't you?' she said, and mutely Clara nodded. Outside on the street the thudding bass of a car stereo swelled then faded, a child cried out one long, plaintive wail, yet up here all was quiet and still.

She felt strangely shy in Emily's presence here in her flat, far more so than she had at the bar. She wasn't entirely sure what Luke's sister wanted from their meetings, sensing that there was something more to it than the simple desire to keep abreast of the search, and she could only conclude that talking to her somehow made Emily feel closer to her family, a connection to her parents and brothers after so many years apart. But that, too, didn't seem quite right. Hoping to get her to open up, Clara asked tentatively now, 'What was it like growing up at The Willows? It's such a special place – it must have been idyllic.'

Emily's eyes lit up. 'Oh, it was! Mum and Dad built such a wonderful life for us, you know? That big lovely house, so full of people, so many parties, they'd both met so many interesting people through their careers, and they welcomed everyone – you'd be just as likely to be sitting down to dinner with the local dog walker as with the local MP.' She paused, lost in thought. 'But I think Mum, despite her career and devotion to Dad, loved more than anything just being our mother. Her family has always been everything to her, she put so much love and time into making our home beautiful for us all. It was perfect.' She smiled sadly, 'You're right, we were very lucky.'

'They've always been lovely to me,' Clara told her. 'I was so nervous before I met them, I was afraid they wouldn't think I was good enough for Luke, but I couldn't have been more wrong.' She paused, remembering the talks she'd had with Rose over the years, how sometimes Rose had felt more like a mother to her than her own ever had. It struck her now for the first time that perhaps Rose had had similar thoughts, substituting Clara for her own lost daughter, that it was Emily she'd been thinking of when she'd wrapped Clara in one of her warm hugs or given her advice while they'd cooked or gardened together.

She glanced at Emily and the sadness on her face made her catch her breath. 'It must be hard for you to talk about them,' she said.

But Emily shook her head. 'No, I want to.' She looked at Clara. 'They were always very close, Luke and my parents. Are they still?'

'Incredibly so. That's what makes it all the more heartbreaking, seeing Rose and Oliver so desperate.'

Emily nodded and, unable to stop herself, Clara leaned forward and said, 'You obviously love your family so much. What made you leave? You said it would be dangerous to go back to them now, but—'

'Clara . . .' Emily began, a warning in her eyes.

'I know, I know. I'm sorry, I know you don't want to talk about it, but if you're in danger still, if you think your parents might be in danger . . . surely we should go to the police? I can help you!'

But Emily looked away and a silence stretched between them, before Clara pressed gently, 'Why did you want to meet with me? I mean, I know you wanted to talk about Luke, find out how the search is going, but . . . I get the impression there was another reason . . .'

Something in Emily's face altered and Clara understood that she was right. Carefully she reached out and touched Emily's arm. 'If there's anything you want to talk to me about, you can. I want to help you.'

Abruptly Emily got up and went to the window, staring down at the street below. 'Clara, please don't . . .' she began. In her agitation she swiped a hand through her hair, an unconscious, nervous gesture that caused the T-shirt she was wearing to rise a few inches.

Clara felt her heart almost stop. 'Jesus,' she said in alarm. 'What happened to your back?'

Emily turned to face her, hurriedly tugging her T-shirt back into place. 'Nothing. It's nothing,' she said.

Clara got to her feet, shock propelling her across the room to where Emily stood. Without another word she lifted the fabric and recoiled in horror. The skin on the lower half of Emily's back was grotesquely scarred; puckered and discoloured as though it had been terribly burned. 'Emily,' she whispered, 'what happened to you?'

But Emily jerked away, her eyes widening with something close to panic. 'Please, Clara, don't—'

'When did this happen?'

It seemed to Clara then that the expression in Emily's eyes changed, something dark and harsh and bitter transforming her into someone else entirely, so that Clara gave an involuntary shiver. 'It was a long time ago, when I was seventeen,' Emily said.

'Seventeen?' Clara shook her head in confusion. 'When you were still living at home? I don't understand—'

Emily stared at her and Clara held her breath, sure that Emily was going to tell her something and she leaned forward, again touching her arm. 'Emily,' she said, 'you can tell me. Who did this to you? How did it happen? If you're still scared of whoever it was, if they're preventing you from going home, I'll help you. You can stay here with me, I'll go to the police with you, it will be all right, I promise.'

Tears spilled down Emily's face, her eyes searching Clara's. 'I—' she began, but at that moment Clara's phone started to ring, startling her into silence. 'Who's that?' she asked nervously.

Inwardly Clara cursed herself for not muting her mobile before Emily arrived. She felt sure that she'd been about to tell her something. 'I don't know. It doesn't matter. Emily, please—'

'You should answer it,' insisted Emily, turning away.

Clara shook her head and took hold of her hand. 'No, Emily. Please talk to me.'

Emily only stared at her, her expression unreadable. The phone rang off. 'You should see who that was,' she said. 'It might be important – the police, or . . .'

Knowing she was defeated, Clara nodded and went to her bag. 'It was Tom,' she said in surprise when she looked at her phone. Just then a bleep signalled a voice-mail message and she put it to her ear. 'Clara?' Tom's voice was harried. 'I'm in London. I need to speak to you. I tried looking for you at Mac's but I guess you must be at your place. I'm coming over. I'll be there in half an hour.'

She frowned, staring down at her phone. 'That was Tom, he's on his way over. I wonder what he—'

But Emily had already snatched up her coat and was making for the door. 'I have to go.'

As Clara stared at her in surprise she scrabbled with the door handle. 'Emily, calm down!' she said, going to her. 'It's all right. Let me do it, I—'

The look of panicked desperation Emily shot her stopped Clara in her tracks. 'You won't tell him, will you, Clara?' she begged. 'You won't tell Tom I was here? Please, Clara, you must promise.'

'Of course I won't. I promise, hey, Emily, calm down. I won't tell—'

But Emily was already out of the flat and heading for the stairs, the hood of her jacket pulled up high around her face.

'Emily, wait!' Clara called, but there was no reply. She watched until she disappeared, waiting until she heard the main door slam below before she went back into her flat. She stood, stunned, her heart thumping, then sank on to the sofa. The expression on Emily's face when she realized Tom was on his way had been one of pure terror. Her thoughts raced, remembering now the scene she'd witnessed at The Willows, Rose so cowed, so defeated as Tom had towered over her. Then she recalled how Mac had told her Tom had gone off the rails after Emily left, getting involved in drugs and drink and a bad crowd. And Mac had said something else, too – that Rose and Oliver had become so protective of Luke they wouldn't leave him alone in the house – not even if Tom was there. Her unease deepened. Had it, in fact, been Tom they'd been protecting Luke from?

Who had hurt Emily so badly when she was seventeen? Why was she too scared to go back to her family now? From the little Luke had told her about his sister, he had painted a picture of someone strong and single-minded, yet the woman Clara had met was someone intensely vulnerable, and clearly traumatized. Something else occurred to her. Tom had been in London the day her flat was broken into, turning up out of the blue only a few hours later, looking as though he'd barely slept. Then there was the fact Emily had treasured photos of Luke and her parents, but not one of him – had visibly flinched at the mention of his name.

She sat up straighter, her heart accelerating as she looked at her watch. Ten minutes had passed since Tom's phone call. She suddenly realized she didn't want to be alone with him. She needed to get out of the flat.

When she arrived on the Holloway Road half an hour later she stood on the street looking up at Mac's windows. Though she'd tried to call him on her way over he hadn't picked up the phone. She rang the bell now and waited, desperate to talk to him about what had taken place at her flat, but the intercom remained silent. Where was he? He knew that she was meeting Emily today; had told her he'd be waiting for her to come back and tell him all about it. So what was going on? Stepping back from the door she looked up at his windows, before catching the eye of Mehmet, the owner of the kebab shop.

'You all right there, my darling?' he called.

She went in. 'Have you seen him today?' she asked, breathing through her mouth to avoid the stench of sweating meat.

'No, my love, not since this morning.'

She nodded, fingering the keys Mac had given her when she'd first started staying with him. She'd never just let herself in before because she'd never needed to and it felt a bit intrusive to start doing so now.

'Some bloke called round for him an hour or so ago though,' Mehmet went on, turning down the radio from which Taylor Swift's voice blared, 'but I don't know if he had any luck. I nipped out the back for a fag when he started knocking.'

Tom, she thought. Murmuring her thanks, she was about to leave when Mehmet added something that stopped her in her tracks. 'He's definitely in, though.'

She looked at him in surprise. 'Mac? How do you know?'

'When I came back after my cigarette I heard him crashing around like a herd of baby elephants – and he hasn't left the flat since, I've been right here.' He raised his eyebrows at her. 'Thought he was going to come through the ceiling at one point. What's he doing up there, rearranging the furniture or something?'

The narrow staircase that led from the front door to Mac's flat was silent as she climbed it, a sense of foreboding rising inside her with every step. When she reached the top she found his front door ajar. 'Mac?' she called nervously, but there was no response. Gingerly she gave it a push.

It took a few moments for her to make sense of the scene she was greeted with. A repetitive scratching sound filled the air, and she listened to it in confusion until it dawned on her it was the sound of the needle rasping against the dead wax of a record on the turntable, the noise amplified by Mac's prized Bowers and Wilkins speakers. To her right, the living room was a mess of upturned furniture and scattered belongings, even the TV had been knocked to the floor. Just like her flat the week before, Mac's had been completely ransacked. She tried to call his name again but fear made the words stick in her throat. It was only when she turned towards the kitchen that she saw his legs sticking out from behind the half-closed door. She cried out, her shock making the noise fight its way out past the knot of fear in her throat.

'Mac!' She ran to him, having to shove the door to prise it open against the weight of his body, then she fell to her knees next to where he lay. A thin line of blood trickled across the pale linoleum floor; his skin was a deathly white, his eyes closed. 'Mac,' she cried, 'Mac, wake up, oh please, oh God please wake up!' On the floor next to him was an unopened bottle of wine, its glass smeared with blood. Presumably it was what had been used to hit him with. Sobbing now, she searched desperately for a pulse and cried out in relief when she felt the faintest flutter at his throat. 'OK,' she said, 'OK, you're OK,' and, her hands shaking, she scrabbled about in her pocket until at last she found her phone and called for an ambulance.

It was almost 11 p.m. and Clara stood on the street outside University College Hospital blinking into the darkness, sick and disorientated after the bright glare of the intensive care unit. For several hours she had sat by Mac's side, only letting go of his hand to be inter-viewed by the police and speak to Mac's mother on the phone. He had woken, once, opened his eyes and, finding Clara there next to him, had smiled briefly. She had bent her head and cried with relief.

He was stable, at last; the doctors telling her that he

would make a full recovery, that he had been 'very lucky', but that she should leave him now, should go home and get some rest.

Suddenly the enormity of it all, the shock of finding him, the horrible fear that he might die, the hours of stress and lack of food hit her with full force and she staggered towards a lamppost, leaning against it as her legs almost buckled beneath her, choking back the bile that flooded her mouth. She realized she was shaking violently.

'Excuse me, are you OK?' A passing nurse on her way into the hospital's main entrance stopped and looked at her in concern. 'Are you feeling unwell?'

'I'm fine.' Clara managed a weak smile. 'Thank you. I'm just . . . tired.'

'You all right getting home?'

Clara nodded and moved on, fighting her exhaustion. Where could she go to tonight? Not to Mac's, of course. She couldn't encroach on any of her other friends either, not at this time. The only possible place she could go to was her own flat. She stood there, hating the thought of it, swaying with tiredness. After a few moments, her heart sinking with resignation, she flagged down a passing taxi. 'Hoxton Square, please,' she said.

When the cab dropped her off she paused outside, staring up at the windows. Her heart jolted when she saw that there was a very faint light on in the top floor flat. Alison. She swallowed hard and let herself in. Once she was on her own floor she stopped and listened, but all was silent. Inside her flat she hastily switched on all the lights as well as the television, knowing that she might go slowly mad if she sat in silence, jumping at every sound and creak from above. As she passed her door again she noticed a piece of paper she'd not seen before, lying on the floor. It was a note from Tom. She stared down at it. Even the sight of his handwriting chilled her. How had he got into her building to post it through her door? Perhaps one of the downstairs neighbours had found it in the entrance hall and brought it up for her. Still, unease shifted inside her. '*Clara*,' she read, '*I must talk to you, it's very important. I called round but have to return to Norwich now. I could drive back to London tomorrow. Can I see you then? Please call me to let me know. Tom.*'

Relieved that he had left town she sank on to the sofa, the enormity of what had happened hitting her afresh. She saw again Mac lying unconscious on the floor. Could Tom possibly have been responsible? But why on earth would he want to harm Mac? Tiredness rolled over her in heavy waves yet she felt too wired, too on edge to sleep. Turning down the TV's volume, she listened hard, but heard nothing.

She went to the kitchen and found a bottle of wine, pouring herself a large glass, and then another and another. When she felt sufficiently drunk she went to bed, her tired mind full of thoughts of Tom. Had he been involved in Luke's disappearance? Was that why

Luke had got into the blue van, because his own brother had been driving it? And what part had he played in Emily's disappearance? Had he caused the horrific scars she'd seen on her back? But why would Tom want to hurt his brother or sister – or Mac? On and on her thoughts raced until finally, exhaustion and drunkenness getting the better of her at last, she fell into a deep sleep.

She dreamt that she was being chased, her lungs screaming for air as she ran down darkened streets, her faceless pursuer close on her heels. She was aware as she ran of the overpowering smell of burning, and mingled with the frightening confusion of her nightmare was the horrifying sensation of the skin on her back blistering and melting. She woke gasping for breath, fear gripping her when she realized that the pain in her lungs and throat persisted. Half raising herself up, she saw smoke billowing through her room, the passageway beyond her bedroom door glowing and flickering with red light, the crackle of fire filling her ears.

She couldn't move. Smoke filled her eyes and lungs, a scream of terror caught in her throat. Suddenly, she saw a figure standing in her doorway and her heart lurched with fright. It was only when they reached her bed that she recognized the slender form and long lank brown hair. It was the woman who lived upstairs. The last thing she saw before she blacked out was Alison looming over her.

20

Doug, Toby and I stared at each other in astonishment after the front door closed behind Hannah. 'Where's she going?' whispered Toby. 'Why's she dressed up like that?'

'Could she . . . do you think she's found herself a job?' Doug hazarded.

It seemed unlikely. 'A boyfriend?' I said, conjuring up an improbable picture of a nice, clean-cut lad for whom Hannah, blinded by love, had transformed herself. Whatever had triggered this extraordinary change it must have been momentous. And I should have been over the moon: instead of her usual slovenly attire she looked like an ordinary, if very pretty, teenager on her way out to meet her similarly wholesome friends. She was up and out of the house by 8 a.m. when normally I could barely get her to surface before noon, bad-tempered and stinking of last night's cigarettes and beer. But the way she'd looked at me, a certain glint in her eye, had made me uneasy. I knew my daughter. I knew when she was up to something.

My eyes met Doug's and we gazed at each other uncertainly. 'Mum?' Toby's voice was worried. 'What's going on?'

I turned to him and made myself smile. 'Who knows? But come on now, love, it's time for school. I'll get us all a takeaway for our tea later, shall I?'

He smiled back, clearly relieved. 'OK, Mum.'

But the feeling of disquiet stayed with me. After Toby and Doug had left I went upstairs to Hannah's bedroom and nervously opened her door. I was usually too afraid to look in there, fearful of what I might find – a glimpse inside her head was not something I normally relished. It was always a disgusting mess anyway and today was no exception: clothes were strewn everywhere, dirty plates and mugs littered every surface. In fact, everything looked exactly as it always did. I backed out and went to work myself.

But I couldn't stop thinking about her. She'd looked so completely different. Could it possibly be that Hannah had somehow grown up, turned over a new leaf and decided to become an ordinary, functioning member of society at last? I allowed myself to indulge in that fantasy all day.

When I got home from work, however, it was to find

that she was dressed again in her usual grubby attire. The nose ring and eyebrow piercing were back in place, as was the thick black eyeliner and bad attitude. The fresh-faced and presentable young woman of earlier had completely disappeared, and my daughter was as hostile and as unreachable as ever.

But from then on, once a week, the same thing would happen. Hannah would appear early for breakfast dressed in pretty, fashionable clothes, her hair neatly brushed and with subtle make-up in place. Sometimes she'd return within an hour, her face like thunder as she stormed upstairs to lock herself in her room, but usually she'd stay out all day, with a pleased, self-satisfied expression as she strolled back through the front door. After a while I gave up asking where she'd been: I could sense she enjoyed my confusion far too much ever to tell me.

A few weeks later the phone calls began. She always seemed to be expecting them, always ready and waiting by the upstairs extension, snatching up the receiver as soon as it began to ring. She'd mumble a 'hello,' then pull the lead into her room, shutting the door and talking in hushed whispers.

In the end I couldn't stand it any longer: I decided to follow her. It was a warm day in September. She came down as usual all dressed up and as soon as she left the house I called into work, quickly leaving a message to say I'd had a family emergency and wouldn't be in until later. When I emerged on the street I saw her disappearing around the corner and got into my car to follow her, keeping a safe distance behind and parking out of sight when I saw her waiting at the bus stop.

I followed her bus to the nearest town and when she got off I parked and saw her hurrying towards the train station. Inside, I saw her queuing at the ticket office and I managed to stay hidden behind a magazine stand while I listened to her ask for a ticket to a town in Suffolk, twelve miles away. I knew I'd never be able to get on the train without her seeing me, and I wouldn't be able to get there before her in my car, so for that day, frustrated and more confused than ever, I gave up and went home.

The following week, however, I was ready for her. As soon as she came down for breakfast I made an excuse about wanting to get to work early and drove straight to Suffolk. I arrived in a large market town not very far away from the village Doug and I grew up in. When I got there I parked and, sure enough, ten minutes later saw her emerging from the station. Keeping a safe distance behind, I followed her as she headed into the town's centre. Eventually, to my astonishment she came to a large building with a sign outside that said, 'Crofton Hill Sixth Form College'. As I loitered at the gate I saw her approach a bench near the main entrance, then sit down to wait.

At eleven o'clock students began to pour out of the college doors and a tall, pretty, dark-haired girl a year or so older than Hannah walked towards my daughter with a wide smile on her face. When she reached her, Hannah got up and the two girls hugged. I was dumbstruck. Who on earth was she? Was Hannah secretly studying here? I was utterly confused. I watched as the two linked arms – such an easy, affectionate gesture, and so unlike anything I'd seen my daughter do before that my astonishment deepened. When they turned in my direction I hurriedly ducked out of sight, concealing myself behind a parked van. A few minutes later I saw them heading back into town so I followed them to a café where they sat down together at one of the outside tables.

I watched them for about an hour. Hannah looked so carefree and happy, so entirely different from her usual self as she smiled and laughed that I felt a wave of sadness, even jealousy for this stranger, whoever she was. When, finally, the girl looked at her watch and grimaced, they both got up and hugged again, before going their separate ways, leaving me to drive home alone, still entirely confused.

For three weeks I remained none the wiser, and then, one morning everything suddenly became horribly clear.

It was a Sunday, and Doug had taken Toby to rugby practice as usual. Hannah had barely shown her face all morning and I was about to start the ironing. I happened to be standing right next to the downstairs phone when I heard Hannah come out of her room and pause on the landing. I knew she was in her usual spot, hand poised over the receiver, ready to lift it as soon as it rang. This time I was ready for her and as soon as it started ringing I snatched it up myself. My heart thudded, had Hannah heard the click? Apparently not. The person on the other end was speaking. 'Becky, is that you?'

Becky?

'Yes! How's it going?'

'Fine, you know, college work and stuff . . . '

'Ugh, how'd it go with that essay?' my daughter asked.

There followed a conversation about schoolwork, annoying teachers and favourite TV shows. The usual chatter of your average teenager. I should have been used to it, should have heard this or something like it all the time. But I didn't. Because this wasn't my daughter talking, not really. I knew Hannah – I knew she wasn't this girl, the sort of ordinary teenager I'd long given up wishing she'd become. This was Hannah pretending to be someone else entirely. It reminded me of the day I'd overheard her impersonating me talking to the neighbour: today, too, each girlish giggle, breathless exclamation, was nothing more than an act. It was both fascinating and utterly chilling.

As I listened, it became clear that Hannah – or 'Becky' – was claiming that she, too, was at a sixth form college taking her A-levels and after some more chat about coursework and deadlines, the conversation turned to me and Doug. 'What's going on with your parents, anyway?' the girl asked.

'Doing my head in as usual,' Hannah sighed. 'I wish my mum and dad were like yours. They sound so great, you're so lucky.'

The girl snorted. 'You're joking, right? They don't give a shit about what I want. Mum just wants me to go into medicine like her so she can show off to all her friends, and Dad only cares about his own work and what my brothers are doing.' She sighed. 'They don't take me seriously at all. Like that Greenpeace rally I went on last week, I tried to talk to them about it and they just nodded and asked me if I'd done my bloody revision. I mean, who cares about that? Half the planet's being destroyed and they're worried about a fucking mock Biology exam. So as usual we ended up having a row. They don't see how important this stuff is to me, and I'm sure I'm going to fail my exams anyway, sometimes I feel like giving up.'

'No you're not,' Hannah replied. 'I wish you believed in yourself more.' Mock sternly, she added, 'OK, repeat after me: My name's Emily Lawson and I'm going to ace all my A-levels. Go on, do it!'

I barely heard as the girl gigglingly obeyed. I felt as though I'd been sucker-punched, the air knocked clean from my lungs. I don't remember what they said after that, only that afterwards I went into the kitchen and felt the room spin around me. As I clung to the table, I was dizzy with shock.

Emily.

Emily Lawson.

Oh please God, no.

Suddenly, everything made sense.

21

London, 2017

Her head felt full of cotton wool, her mouth and throat dry as sand. She became aware of the strong whiff of disinfectant mixed with the boiled-veg-and-gravy smell of school dinners. Her closed eyelids prickled. For a while she drifted, sleep ebbing and flowing.

'Clara?' A voice from far away, then the gradual drift forward into consciousness. 'Clara, can you hear me?'

A sudden sharp awareness of pain in her throat and chest, each breath a dragging rasp. She opened her eyes, daylight harsh against her retinas. A face leaning in that was female, middle-aged, framed by a dark bob. The features took shape, a stranger's patient gaze upon her. Clara tried to speak, 'Uh—'

'Well, good! You're awake.' The voice was briskly kind.

All at once the memories rushed back: her smoke-filled flat, the looming threat of Alison, and her fear returned in one violent rush. She tried to raise her head.

'How are you feeling?' The stranger's face was nearer now; pale pink lipstick, crow's feet around wide blue eyes, a white coat.

'What happened?' Clara asked.

'You were in a fire. You were brought in last night suffering from smoke inhalation. I'm Doctor Patricia Holloway. We had to sedate you in order to examine the extent of the damage to your lungs and throat.'

'Alison. She . . . it was her . . . in my flat . . .'

The doctor got up and wrote something on her clipboard. She shot her a sympathetic glance. 'I'm sorry, I don't have any information on what happened. The police were here earlier, they'll be back later, I'm sure.' She smiled. 'The good news is you're going to be fine. You were remarkably lucky.'

'But . . .'

'Try to relax now. You're quite safe.'

It was half an hour later when Anderson knocked on her door. He looked incongruous here, besuited and authoritative amidst the pale green hush of the hospital room. He also looked exhausted, and she had the vague memory of him saying he had one-year-old twins at home. 'How are you feeling?' he asked, sitting heavily down on the chair by her bed. She caught the faint whiff of coffee and cigarette smoke.

'I . . . don't know. What happened? Did Alison . . . did you catch her? It was her . . . she tried to kill me.'

He considered her, brow furrowed. 'It was Alison Fournier who alerted the emergency services, Clara. She and your downstairs neighbours dragged you out of your flat. She helped save your life.'

She stared at him, stunned. 'But . . . are you sure? I mean, how did she get in?'

'Your door was open when the couple in the flat below went to investigate the smell of smoke.'

Clara shook her head, unable to make sense of this new information. 'Open? But—'

'Were you alone when you went to bed?' he asked.

'I – yes. Yes, of course I was . . .'

'And you shut the door to your flat securely?'

'Yes! At least, I think so.' She remembered how upset she'd been about Mac, the wine she'd drunk, her wooziness as she'd fallen into bed. The door had been closed though, she was sure of it.

'How's Mac?' she asked. 'Is he OK?'

Anderson nodded. 'He's going to be fine. He's been discharged already.' He leaned forward, fixing her with his tired grey eyes. 'The fire was caused deliberately. Officers found a bottle of lighter fluid in your lounge near where it looks to have started. If you're quite sure you closed the door behind you when you got home last night, whoever got in must have used a key.' He paused. 'Is there anyone apart from yourself who has a copy?'

She pulled herself more upright in the bed, aware

suddenly that her head ached horribly. 'I . . . no. I changed my locks after it was broken into last week.'

'How many copies of the key did you make?'

'There were three, one I dropped off at the letting agent, the other I kept, and the only other one I left at Mac's. I went to stay with him after the break-in.'

Anderson nodded. 'I see.'

She stared at him, the fog in her brain slowly clearing. Her throat still felt horribly sore. 'Whoever broke into Mac's flat yesterday turned it upside down, they were looking for something. They could have taken my key. It was in my bag in Mac's spare room.'

'We'll look into it,' Anderson said.

She remembered Emily's visit to her flat and, her words coming out in a rush, blurted, 'I think it was Tom.'

He looked up sharply. 'I'm sorry?'

'I think it was Tom Lawson, Luke's brother, who attacked Mac and set fire to my flat.'

Anderson blinked. 'And what makes you say that?'

Quickly she told him how Tom, who never came to London, had been in the city the first time she'd been broken into, how he'd turned up at hers shortly afterwards. How the day that Mac had been attacked he'd texted to say he'd just been over there, then that same night her flat was set on fire. She didn't mention the scene she'd walked in on between him and his mother, the strange feeling she'd always got from him, Emily's palpable fear at the mention of his name.

236

Anderson nodded slowly. 'And why do you think Mr Lawson would want to hurt you?'

'I don't know! I don't understand any of it!' A nurse came in and they watched her in silence as she cheerfully took Clara's blood pressure, and wrote something on her clipboard before leaving again. 'What about Alison? Is she all right?' Clara asked.

'She'll be fine – minor smoke inhalation. But she was very lucky. You both were.'

And with that he got up to leave, trailing distracted promises he'd be in touch. Clara lay back, her eyes on the window by her bed.

Outside, the sun shone brightly through a fine mist of drizzle. She could almost smell the damp grass and flower beds of the hospital grounds below. Spring suffused the world beyond the airless, seasonless confines of this room and she listened to the sounds of the hospital; the bleeps of the machine next to her bed, the brisk clip-clop of a passing stranger's shoes, the continuous swish and thump of unseen swing-doors.

She felt utterly, horribly alone – who would visit her, who would even know that she was here? Did her parents know? Would they come? She was surprised how desperately she wanted to see them both. She closed her eyes, trying to fight the waves of anxiety, and when she opened them she found Mac standing at her door, his familiar face triggering such a rush of relief in Clara that she had to choke back a sob. He crossed the room in three quick strides and when he reached her took her hand in his. 'Are you all right?' he asked. 'I couldn't believe it when I heard. I had no idea you were here, Anderson told me and I came straight over. I phoned Zoe, she's on her way too.' He stared down at her, and she saw that he was close to tears. 'I'm so sorry, Clara, I'm so fucking sorry this happened to you.'

'God, it's so good to see you,' she told him. 'I'm fine, I'm fine, and don't be silly, this is hardly your fault. But what about you? I've been so worried, how's your head?'

He grimaced and turned to show a large shaved area of scalp, the exposed white skin severed by an ugly scar. 'Attractive, huh?'

Her eyes widened. 'Jesus. What did the doctors—?'

'It's only a scrape,' he said, waving her concern away. 'I'm far more worried about you. Anderson said you're going to be OK, but how do you feel?'

'I'm so scared, Mac. Who'd want to kill me, or hurt you? Who the fuck is doing this to us?'

He took the seat Anderson had vacated and put his face in his hands, taking a long breath. 'I wish I knew,' he said at last. Reaching over, he squeezed her hand. 'Tell me about the fire. What happened exactly?'

So she described how she'd woken to billowing smoke, the sight of Alison looming over her. 'Anderson said she saved me, but who on earth started it?' When he shrugged helplessly she asked, 'And how about you? Do you have any idea who hit you? Did you see who it was?'

'No. I was standing in the kitchen with my back to

the door. It all happened so quickly. I had music playing, the kettle was boiling, whoever it was crept up behind me . . .' Tiredly he ran his fingers through his hair. 'I've been back to my flat, it's a right state.'

She leaned forward. 'Was anything missing? I think whoever it was must have taken the key to my flat, that's how they got in. It was in my bag in your spare room. Did it look like someone had been through it?'

He shrugged. 'I don't know. Everything was a complete mess, but I'll check when I get back.'

'And nothing of yours was taken?'

'My Leica's missing – you know the one I take everywhere with me? Why, out of all the expensive kit I've got in my flat, they'd only take that, I've no idea.'

She hesitated. 'Look, this is going to sound crazy, but I think it's Tom. I think Tom did all this.'

His eyes widened in surprise. '*Tom*? Why?'

Quickly she told him about Emily's visit, the panic and fear she'd seen on her face when Tom had called to say he was on his way over. 'She had the most awful scars on her back,' she said, shuddering as she remembered Emily's disfigured skin. 'She said it had happened before she left home all those years ago. Mac, I think Tom's got something to do with why she's too scared to go back to her family. The look on her face when she thought he was coming over – seriously, she was absolutely terrified. And before, when my flat got broken into, Tom turned up straight afterwards, out of the blue. Then he called me and said he'd been around to yours

239

the morning you were attacked. He's been in London every single time something weird or awful has happened. Surely that's got to be more than a coincidence?'

Mac stared at her. 'I've known him for years, I just . . . I mean, why would he . . . ?'

The door opened at that moment and Clara started in surprise. 'Alison!'

Her neighbour stood in the doorway, one hand still on the handle. 'I've been discharged so I thought I'd come and . . .' she trailed off, her eyes shifting nervously from Clara's face to Mac's, to the floor.

'Are you OK? Were you hurt?' Mac asked, breaking the surprised silence.

Alison shook her head. 'No, not really.'

In the harsh brightness of this room she seemed even more wraith-like than ever, Clara thought, but her face, scrubbed clean now, looked far younger and prettier without its customary mask of make-up. Clara stared at her wordlessly, not knowing what to say to this woman who had saved her life, yet had always been so prickly and antagonistic towards her. 'The police told me what you did,' she said at last, 'I don't know what to say . . .'

Alison shrugged. 'It was the people downstairs who found you, it was them really, not me.'

Clara nodded. 'Still . . . I mean, thank you – it doesn't seem enough somehow, but thank you.'

No one said anything for a moment or two, until Alison mumbled, 'Well anyway . . .' she moved as if to leave, and Clara and Mac exchanged a glance.

'Wait,' Clara said. With effort she pulled herself out of bed, wrapping her thin gown around her as she went. 'Are you sure you're all right?' she asked.

But instead of answering, Alison blurted, the words escaping from her mouth almost involuntarily, 'Have they found Luke? Is there any news?'

And it was the desperation, the misery in her eyes that made something click inside Clara at last. She stared at her. 'Something happened between the two of you, didn't it?'

Mac glanced at her in surprise, but Clara kept her eyes on Alison, who scowled, her gaze shifting away. 'No,' she said, 'don't be stupid.'

A beat or two, then, 'Alison, I just want to know. I think something did happen, and I think that's why you've always been so weird towards me.'

At this, Alison's face changed, her chin dropping to her chest, and Clara understood now that her spiky belligerence had merely been a cover for something else, that she was far more vulnerable than she first appeared. 'Look,' she said gently, 'I'm only asking you to tell me the truth. After everything that's happened, I think I deserve that, don't you?' Clara waited, her gaze never leaving Alison's face.

Finally she spoke. 'Nothing happened,' she muttered. 'Not really.'

Clara nodded. 'But you wanted it to?'

Alison shrugged.

'How did it start?' Clara asked.

241

At this, Alison burst into tears, covering her face with her hands. 'Come and sit down,' Clara said, leading her to a chair.

'My boyfriend left me,' Alison began, her voice thick, the pain clearly still sharp. 'Luke and I got chatting on the stairs one day. Then I got locked out of my flat and he invited me in for a beer.' She glanced up at Clara. 'You were out.'

Clara sighed. 'Go on,' she said.

'He was so nice to me, and I thought . . .' she coloured now, 'he told me I was pretty, that I'd find someone else.' She wiped her nose with the cuff of her jumper and gave a loud sniff. 'After that he'd stop and chat if he saw me. I gave him my phone number and he'd text me. Nice stuff, you know? Telling me I was . . . Well, anyway, it started to mean a lot to me, the attention, you know . . . he'd pop up to see me sometimes when you weren't in.'

Clara nodded. 'And did something happen between you?'

Alison met her gaze and shook her head. 'No.'

There was another silence, and Clara wondered if the younger girl would clam up again, but it seemed instead that she wanted to unburden herself now that she'd started. 'I wanted it to,' she admitted. 'I told him that I was falling for him.' She shook her head, a flash of anger in her eyes now. 'I thought he felt the same way. But then he changed, started being funny with me, acting like it had all been in my head, he didn't think of me like that. And I was so fucking angry with him . . .'

242

'So that was what all the loud music was about, the dirty looks on the stairs,' Clara said.

Alison glanced away. 'He made me feel good about myself for the first time in ages, then there you'd be, the two of you, so happy together, rubbing my face in it. I wanted to make him see how bad I felt. And I guess I thought that him and I could be together if it wasn't for you.'

As Clara listened she felt the creeping heat of anger inside her. Stupid, *stupid* Luke. What had probably meant nothing more to him than a bit of harmless flirting had clearly meant much more to this silly girl.

A silence fell as Alison crossed her arms defensively in front of her, her pale face closed and truculent once more.

'Look,' Clara said. 'You helped save my life, I'm not about to give you a hard time for flirting with my boyfriend. Trust me, Alison, whatever went on between you and Luke is the least of my problems.'

Alison nodded.

'Will you be all right?' Clara asked.

She got up. 'Yeah,' she shrugged, 'course I will.' She made towards the door, but once there said stiffly, reluctantly, 'I'm sorry, all right?'

Clara nodded, and she and Mac watched as Alison closed the door behind her.

22

Cambridgeshire, 1997

I'd kept the newspaper cuttings. I don't know why. Doug had no idea, of course – he'd have been livid if he'd ever found them. We were supposed to forget all about it, pretend we'd played no part in the whole horrible tragedy. But it didn't seem right to throw them away. I felt I owed it to her – Nadia – to remember, that I shouldn't get away guilt-free or ever be allowed to forget what happened that day. Her poor family. Her poor mother. They never found out the truth. And I had to live with that – we all did. So I hid the cuttings in between the pages of a book tucked away at the top of the bookcase in our bedroom. I never looked at them, I didn't need to. I knew what they said by heart.

But after I overheard Hannah on the phone to Emily, after it all fell into place, I took down the book – a thick Jackie Collins I was certain neither Doug nor Hannah would ever want to read – and there they were, the two separate folds of newspaper, yellow with age. It had been sixteen years since I'd last read them. I smoothed out the first one and even the headline brought it all back, those awful feelings, the guilt.

East Anglian Gazette, 25 April 1981
FEARS GROW FOR LOCAL MISSING WOMAN AND CHILD

Police have discovered no new leads on the whereabouts of Nadia Freeman, 19, from Bury St Edmunds and her three-week-old baby, Lana. Ms Freeman is said to suffer from complex mental health issues that had intensified following the birth of her daughter in March.

Nadia's mother, Mrs Jane Freeman, 56, said, 'We are all desperately worried for my daughter and granddaughter. They are both so vulnerable. I want Nadia to know that she's loved, that we will help her, no matter what she's done. I only want to see my daughter and my baby granddaughter again. We are all so dreadfully worried.'

Police are urging any members of the public with information to come forward.

It's that bit from Nadia's mother that's so awful to read. Knowing the pain she must have felt, the uncertainty. Knowing I could at least have given her the information to end her suffering, that it had been my own selfish desires that had prevented me from doing so. The picture of Nadia, too, is almost impossible to look at, but I force myself to. That young, pretty face, so familiar. Those eyes that haunt me still.

The second article, written a month later, is almost too much to bear, but again I make myself read it. Why should I get to hide it away? I owe it to her to remember.

East Anglian Gazette, 30 May 1981
BODY OF MISSING LOCAL MOTHER FOUND

A coroner's verdict of suicide has been reached in the case of 19-year-old Bury St Edmunds woman Nadia Freeman whose body was found a fortnight ago on the beach at Dunwich, by dog walkers. Earlier sightings had put Ms Freeman at a known suicide spot, 'Widow's Cliff'. She was last seen less than a mile away with her baby daughter, in a distressed state. Extensive searches are being held by police for the body of her three-week-old daughter Lana, but fears are growing that the baby might have been washed out to sea. Nadia had been suffering from poor mental health at the time of her disappearance.

So there it was. I knew what had really happened to Nadia of course, knew what really led to her death. And now, sixteen years later, the truth was about to come out. Why else would Hannah befriend Emily Lawson, if not to punish us all for what we'd done?

23

London, 2017

Mac smiled encouragingly at Clara from the driver's seat of the battered Ford transit van. 'Ready?' he asked. As they turned the corner out of Hoxton Square on to Old Street the boxes of Luke's belongings – his records, books and clothes that had survived the fire, along with the few pieces of his furniture she'd been able to salvage, slid and bumped heavily against each other in the back. She hadn't known what else to do with his things. Her landlord, a middle-aged and heavily Botoxed Russian, had been clear he wanted the flat vacated sooner rather than later. 'Decorators coming tomorrow,' he'd said, eyeing her disapprovingly when she'd met him at the flat, as though he suspected the damage to his property was more down to carelessness on her part than anything else. She and Mac had packed up her and Luke's stuff in one grim and depressing afternoon, and while Mac's had seemed the most sensible place to store her own belongings, Zoe not having the room, they'd been at a loss at first about what to do with Luke's.

'How about taking them to Suffolk?' Mac had suggested. 'Rose and Oliver could look after them until . . .' As his sentence tailed off their eyes had met briefly, then skittered away. The unanswerable question of how and when this nightmare would end hanging in the air between them.

'I better start looking for somewhere to live,' Clara had said into the silence, turning back to the box she was packing with books.

'You know you can stay with me for as long as you need to, don't you?' Mac had said.

She'd nodded. 'I know. Thank you.'

'Have the police been in touch?'

'Anderson rang earlier. He said they're doing more door-to-door enquiries, looking at CCTV and so on. But it all feels pretty hopeless, to be honest.' She'd got up, then, to carry the box to the door, where she paused, staring down at it. 'I don't know what to do,' she'd said. 'Perhaps I should go and see my parents for a while, although I need to go back to work, soon . . .' she broke off. It felt entirely impossible to comprehend a future beyond the question of where Luke was, her life on perpetual, agonizing hold until he was found.

Now, as they edged slowly through the Saturday-afternoon traffic, her gaze flickered unseeingly over Kingsland Road. It would take them a couple of hours to get to Suffolk and she sat back, mulling over the past two days. Once she'd confirmed that her keys had indeed been taken from her bag in Mac's spare room, Anderson had said little to indicate they'd come any closer to finding who'd been responsible for the break-ins. On the subject of Tom, the detective sergeant had remained tight-lipped. 'We are pursuing that line of enquiry, yes,' was all he'd say on the matter.

Although Mac had an impressive selection of new locks fitted to his door, her sleep had been plagued by dreams that someone was trying to break in, nightmares from which she'd jerk awake several times each night, heart thumping, to begin each new day feeling more exhausted than ever. As the van progressed through East London, her thoughts turned yet again to Emily. There'd been no word from her in the few days since they'd met, and Clara found herself thinking of her increasingly often. What if Emily had just vanished again? Should she tell Rose and Oliver about her, or should she trust Luke's sister that she would contact them herself very soon? Her tired mind struggled to find answers and finally she closed her eyes and tried to sleep.

An accident on the motorway meant they didn't arrive at The Willows until five. The sun was beginning to set over the surrounding fields, the sky already tinged with night when they knocked on the door, and Clara shivered in her coat as they waited. After a while they knocked again, but when there was still no sign of Rose and Oliver she glanced at Mac in confusion. 'Do you think they've gone out?'

He frowned. 'They knew we were coming, though. Bit weird, isn't it?'

Walking to the side of the house, she cupped her hands to peer through the window, and it was only then that she noticed its shutters were closed. She tried to think if she could remember ever seeing them closed before, and realized she couldn't. Looking up at the higher windows, it seemed the house was in total darkness. 'Mac,' she said, 'this is really strange . . .'

It was at that moment that they heard a sound from within, followed by Rose's nervous voice, 'Hello? Who is it, please?'

'It's us, Rose. Mac and Clara,' Mac called. 'Are you OK?' They heard bolts being drawn back and finally the door opened.

The Rose who peered out at them was so gaunt and ill-looking that Clara gasped. 'What's happened?' she asked anxiously, feeling suddenly afraid. 'Why are the windows shuttered, and the door bolted? Are you all right?'

Rose stared at her strangely before nodding. 'Yes. Yes, of course.' She opened the door wider and, glancing quickly behind them from left to right, added, 'Come in, both of you. Please, do come in.'

Even in the dark gloom of the interior Clara could

see that the house's sad air of disarray had worsened since last she'd visited. When they reached the kitchen she and Mac paused inside the door, shooting nervous glances at each other as Rose silently filled the kettle then stood motionless, staring blankly down at it in her hand. 'Rose,' Clara said, going over and gently taking it from her, before leading her to a chair at the cluttered table. 'Are you sure you're OK? I'm worried about you.'

'Worried, darling?' Rose asked faintly. 'About me? Why should you be worried about me?' She began to cry, the tears seeping out down her pale, make-up-less face. 'It's I who should be worried about you.' She put her hand to her mouth as a sob escaped. 'After what happened to you,' she glanced at Mac, 'to both of you. I'm so sorry, I'm so dreadfully sorry.'

Clara knelt down next to her and took her hands. 'Sorry? Oh, Rose, why are you sorry? None of this is your fault. How could it be?'

At that moment Oliver appeared, their dog, Clemmy, at his heels. Mac stepped forward to greet him but received barely a glance, as though Oliver could see nothing or no one but his wife. 'Rose,' he said, his voice full of tenderness. 'Oh, darling, why are you crying? Don't cry, please don't cry.' He went to her and put a gentle hand on her shoulder. She looked up at him, fixing him with her gaze, something that Clara couldn't read passing between them and then, to Clara's astonishment, Rose very slowly and very deliberately removed his hand from her shoulder and got up. She stared back at her husband, a look on her face of such coldness, of such breathtaking dislike, that Clara felt her heart jolt in shock. And then Rose turned and left the room, leaving the three of them to stare silently after her.

Later, as they were unloading Luke's belongings from the van, Clara said quietly to Mac, 'What the hell is going on?'

He shook his head. 'I have absolutely no idea.'

At Oliver's request they brought the boxes and furniture up to Luke's old bedroom. When they reached his door, Mac opened it and stopped. 'Christ. I haven't been up here for years,' he said. He wandered over to a skateboard propped against the wall, then looked up at a Beastie Boys poster above the bed, the words 'Fight For Your Right To Party!' emblazoned across it, and smiled sadly. 'The times we spent up here, smoking out of the window, smuggling up beer, talking about girls. This used to be my second home.'

He sat down heavily on Luke's bed and to Clara's surprise put his head in his hands, his shoulders heaving as he began to cry.

Clara stood, stricken at the sight. She realized she had never seen Mac cry before; that throughout the days since Luke had gone missing he had remained unfailingly strong – far stronger than she herself had. It had been he who had comforted her, who had listened to and looked after her. The thought of him giving in to the despair that had threatened her so often, made dread rise inside her. She went to him. 'Mac,' she said, 'it's going to be OK.'

He wiped his face and exhaled a long breath. 'I'm all right. Ignore me. It's just being here, seeing his stuff again, you know?'

She nodded, sitting down next to him. 'We've got to believe that he's going to come back to us,' she said, trying to put some conviction into the words he'd used to comfort her so many times. 'We've got to keep going, try to keep positive.'

'Clara,' he said, turning his face to hers, and the expression she saw there was so strange, so desperate, so unlike any she'd ever seen there before that she felt a chill.

'What?' she said. 'What is it, Mac?'

He held her gaze for a moment, before finally dropping it. 'Nothing.' He took a gulp of air and stood up. 'Nothing. You're right. Got to keep positive.' He took her hand and pulled her up. 'Come on,' he said. 'Let's get this over with.'

She nodded, and together they went back down to finish unloading the van.

When Rose next appeared she looked very different; her hair neatly brushed and her make-up carefully applied. She smiled at them as she came into the room, but made no mention of the scene earlier. 'I hope you'll stay for dinner?' she said.

Mac and Clara exchanged glances. 'It's getting rather late, Rose, the traffic . . .'

Her face fell. 'But maybe you could stay the night? Oh, please say you will. It would be so lovely to have you here.'

'Well . . .' Rose's face was so beseeching that Clara shot Mac a questioning look.

'Of course,' he said, shrugging, 'if you want us to.'

For the first time that day, Rose's face brightened with something resembling her old, charming smile. 'Oh wonderful! Mac, you can have Luke's room, and Clara can have Emi— the spare room.'

After a pause Clara turned to Oliver and asked as casually as she could, 'Have you heard from Tom recently?'

He shook his head. 'No. Not for a few days actually, though that's not unusual. Why do you ask?'

She looked away. 'Oh, no reason.'

He nodded absently and the moment passed, but she wondered what Anderson's enquiries were leading to, whether her suspicions would be proven correct. It was almost too terrible to think about, that it could be Tom who was behind everything, that the person responsible had been among them all along.

The evening passed slowly. They sat down together for a meal – a half-hearted affair of sausages and mash – and though Clara and Mac did their best to make conversation, the strange, stiff atmosphere between Rose and Oliver remained. There was a sense of waiting, of impending doom, and they were both relieved when Rose took herself off to bed early, Oliver padding up not far behind her.

Clara and Mac took their drinks into the living room. 'My God,' Clara said, flopping on to the sofa. 'I had no idea they were in such a bad way.' She shook her head miserably. 'I feel so sorry for them both.'

'I know,' Mac nodded grimly, taking the armchair opposite her. 'They look terrible. Do you think they're even eating properly? Maybe we should try to get them some help, contact their GP or something . . .'

Wearily she rubbed her eyes. 'I can't stop thinking about Tom. I wonder where he is, whether the police have talked to him yet. I tried to call Anderson earlier but he didn't pick up.'

'Do you really think he's involved?' Mac asked her doubtfully. 'It seems so . . .'

'Yes,' she said emphatically. 'I do.'

There was silence for a while, both of them lost in their own thoughts. A fire Oliver had lit earlier crackled in the grate, an unwelcome reminder of what had happened at her flat only three nights before. Even Clemmy seemed on edge tonight, restlessly pacing the room, ears pricked as if alert to something they couldn't hear.

Finally, Mac asked cautiously, 'How are you feeling now about what Alison told you?'

She sighed. 'To be honest, it just made me wonder

what the hell else Luke was up to that I didn't know about. Which reminds me,' she added, getting to her feet again. 'Remember that picture of the girl I found in Luke's filing cabinet?'

'Yeah. Any idea who she is yet?'

She shook her head. 'No, but I haven't had much chance to think about it. Hang on, I'll see if I can find it.'

When she reached Luke's old bedroom she went straight to his filing cabinet which they'd wedged in the corner earlier, two bags of Luke's clothes balanced on top of it. She rifled through his papers before she came to the manila envelope. When she returned to the living room she slid the pictures out and passed one to Mac.

'I wonder who she is,' he said as they both stared down at the stranger's beautiful face.

'Must have been someone else he was shagging,' she replied. 'I mean, it has to be, don't you reckon?'

'I guess, seems a bit young, though—'

They were interrupted by a noise from outside. Clemmy sat up, her hackles raised, a low growl emanating from her throat. Clara's chest tightened in fear. There it was again, followed by the sound of a car door slamming. 'What was that?' she asked, alarmed.

They sat very still and listened, their eyes widening when they heard footsteps crunching on the gravel outside the front door, followed by a loud barrage of knocks. They looked at each other. 'It's half past ten,' Mac said. 'Who the fuck would be out here at this time?'

There was the sound of a key being put to the lock followed by someone swearing, a voice saying, 'Mum? Dad? Why's the door bolted?'

'It's Tom!' Clara said, another jolt of fear shooting through her, while Clemmy continued to growl.

The hammering intensified. 'Mum? What's going on? Let me in!'

Fear nestled in Clara's chest. What was he doing here? Did he know she'd told the police about him? Had he come to hurt Rose and Oliver? When Mac got to his feet, she put a hand out to stop him. 'Wait,' she said. 'What if he—'

'I can't leave him out there battering the door in.'

She followed him into the hall and watched as he drew back the bolts. When he opened it, Tom stood looking at them in amazement. 'Mac? Clara? What the hell are you doing here?'

'We brought some things of Luke's up after the fire,' Clara replied, her heart still pounding in fear.

He nodded distractedly. 'The fire, yes, my God, are you OK? I couldn't believe it when I heard—'

'Yes, yes, I'm fine. Thank you,' Clara replied. She tried to smile but it died on her lips. Nobody moved.

Tom glanced past them. 'Where are my parents?'

'They've gone to bed,' Mac told him. 'They asked us to stay tonight. They're actually in a pretty bad way, mate. We don't want any trouble.'

Tom stared at him. '*Trouble*? What are you talking about? Look, I've had a long day. I've just been questioned

258

by fucking plod for three hours and I need a drink.' Pushing past them both he strode into the kitchen. Following him, they watched as he took a bottle down from the wine rack. He poured himself a drink and downed it, then immediately poured another, watching Clara steadily above the rim of his glass.

Clara and Mac exchanged a glance. 'Tom, what are you doing here?' Mac asked again.

He considered him for a moment. 'Well, not that it's any of your business, Mac, but I've come to talk to my parents.'

There was a belligerence about him, a wildness she'd not seen before. She thought about how Mac had said he'd gone off the rails as a teenager, and she saw in him for the first time now a slightly unhinged, unpredictable side to him. 'They're asleep,' she told him.

He finished his second glass and continued to stare at her. 'Are they? Are they really, Clara? Well, maybe it's time they woke the fuck up.' He slammed his glass down on the table and went into the hall. Raising his voice he shouted up the staircase, 'Mum? Dad? Wakey-wakey!'

Rushing over to him, Clara put a hand on his arm and cried, 'Tom! What are you doing?'

'Something I should have done a very long time ago,' he replied. Raising his voice again, he called, 'Get down here now! It's time to wake up.' He looked at Clara and muttered, 'It's time we all fucking woke up.'

Without another word he strode into the living room

and flung himself on to the sofa where he sat motionless, morosely staring ahead.

Clara watched him in horror. Should she call the police? Glancing at Mac, she began to edge towards the hall, to where she'd left her bag hanging over the banister. If she could only get to her mobile without him seeing, she could go somewhere out of earshot and call 999. Without thinking, she let the photograph in her hand drop.

But before she could escape Tom leant forward and picked it up. 'What's this?' he asked.

She stopped in her tracks. 'Nothing. Just a photo of Luke's I found,' she said nervously. 'I don't know who it is. I found it in—'

Tom frowned in confusion then looked at her strangely. 'You don't know who this is? What are you talking about? This is Emily, of course. This is my sister Emily.'

There was absolute silence. And then Mac and Clara said at exactly the same time, '*What?*'

'My sister.' He stared down at it. 'I didn't know Luke had this picture of her, I thought my darling parents destroyed every last trace of her. Guilt can make you do all kinds of crazy shit, after all.'

But Clara wasn't listening. 'Emily? *This* is Emily?'

Tom looked back at their astonished faces in surprise. 'Well, yes. Of course it is. Why? Who did you think it was?'

'But I've met Emily,' Clara said, her voice rising in panic. 'This isn't . . . '

'You've *met* . . . ?' He stared at her. 'No, you haven't. She disappeared almost twenty years ago. How could you possibly have met her?'

She glanced around at Mac, but saw he was looking now for something in his bag. 'I was contacted by someone who said they were Emily,' she said, turning back to Tom. 'I met up with her in a bar, she came to my flat. If this is Emily, then who have I been meeting?'

They stared back at each other.

'Clara?' Mac had pulled out his laptop and was turning it on. He brought it over to them. 'This is the person you've been meeting, isn't it?' She looked down at the laptop screen, and there was a picture of Emily, or at least the person who'd said that she was. It was a slightly blurred photo taken of her profile, surrounded by a crowd of people.

'Where did you get this?' she asked Mac.

He flushed and looked away. 'I took it. When you said you were going to meet her in the bar that first time . . .' He met her astonished gaze. 'I was worried!' he said defensively. 'I know you didn't want me to come with you, but I needed to make sure it wasn't a trap, that you weren't meeting someone dangerous. I'm sorry. I waited in a doorway down the road from the bar, then when she left you I followed her to see where she was going. It all seemed so suspicious.'

Her eyes widened. 'So I did see you that night! I thought I'd imagined it.' She turned back to the picture. 'Where did you follow her to?'

'Shoreditch Tube. I had my Leica around my neck as usual. When she was buying a ticket, I took a picture of her but she turned around and saw me. I just brazened it out and kept walking, got on the Tube and went home.'

Clara stared at him in horror. 'What camera did you say it was?'

'The Leica, the one that—'

'Went missing from your flat?'

'Yes.'

'Could she have followed you home that night?'

He thought about it. 'I suppose. I didn't see her, but it was busy, rush hour, there were a lot of people.'

'So she could have followed you. She could have broken in later and stolen it from your flat, knowing you had her picture stored on your camera?'

He looked at her. 'Yes, I suppose so,' he said.

'So if this person isn't Emily,' Clara said, 'then who the fuck is she? Who have I been meeting with?'

Tom was still looking at the picture on the laptop screen. 'I know her,' he said. 'I know this woman.' They turned to stare at him. 'I met her when I was qualifying in Manchester, about – what? – ten years or so ago. Her name's Hannah.' He shook his head in confusion. 'But I don't understand. Why is she pretending to be my sister?'

'How did you know her?' Mac asked.

'She answered an advert for a room in a house I shared. We gave the room to someone else, thank God,

262

but after that she seemed to be everywhere. Wherever I went – supermarket, pub or gym or whatever – there'd she'd be. I'd turn around to find her staring at me. If I approached her, she'd just walk off. It was really fucking weird. Then suddenly, she disappeared. Vanished out of the blue and I never saw her again.'

Clara listened to him in amazement. 'But who on earth is she? None of this makes any sense.'

At that moment they heard footsteps on the stairs, and Oliver and Rose, crumpled and dazed in their dressing gowns, came into the room. 'What's happening?' Oliver asked. He started in surprise when he saw his son. 'Tom? What are you doing here?'

Clara glanced at Tom, then said to Rose and Oliver. 'Something very strange is going on.'

Rose put her hand to her mouth. 'What?' she said nervously. 'What is it?'

'I found this picture in the flat,' she said, passing it to her. 'I thought it might be someone who . . . well, anyway, I didn't know who it was.'

Rose visibly flinched when she saw it. 'Emily,' she whispered, her face stricken.

Oliver came and stood behind her and the two of them looked down at their daughter's face in silent anguish.

'The thing is,' Clara said, 'after the TV appeal I was contacted by someone saying they were Emily.'

Their eyes shot to her face. 'What?' said Oliver faintly.

'I met with her . . . and a while later I found this

263

picture in Luke's filing cabinet, not knowing that this was the real Emily.'

Rose and Oliver had gone very white. 'What did she look like, this woman?' Rose said, her voice little more than a whisper.

'Here,' Mac said. 'I have a picture of her.' He passed them his laptop and they stared down at it for a long time.

Rose began to shake uncontrollably. 'Oh,' she said. 'Oh dear God, Oliver.'

'Do you know who she is?' Tom demanded.

After a silence Oliver said, 'Yes. We know who she is.'

Rose's voice was loud. 'Oliver,' she cried. 'Don't! Do you hear me? Don't you dare!'

While the others watched, open-mouthed, Oliver sank heavily into a chair. He still held the laptop in his hands. At last he sighed and said, 'Enough now, Rose. Enough.' The two of them stared at each other for a long moment before finally Oliver turned back to Tom. 'This woman is Hannah Jennings,' he said quietly. 'She's my daughter.'

24

The Lake District, 2017

When I think of my old life, the one I left behind, it's our village in Cambridgeshire I picture, the house we lived in for sixteen years – Doug, Hannah, Toby and I. I sometimes wonder if our old neighbours ever think of us; if they remember the family that used to live between them in that quiet row of cottages below St Dunstan's Hill. But of course they do: how could they not? After all, for a while Hannah Jennings was a household name, the Jennings family front-page news. How, after so much horror, could anyone possibly forget who she was, and what she did?

In my late twenties, when Doug and I still lived in Suffolk, I worked as a nurse on the paediatric ward at the General, where Rose Lawson was completing her specialist training in paediatric surgery. She must have been around thirty then, but she was already very highly regarded in the hospital, and it was clear that all the senior consultants thought she had a bright future ahead of her. It must take a special sort of person to be a surgeon, I've always thought, all those years and years of training, all that ambition and talent and single-mindedness you must need.

On the ward she always remembered our names, would often stop to ask after our families, and chat to us about hers. She'd been married a few years I think to her husband Oliver, and they had a beautiful baby girl named Emily. I remember once, one Saturday morning, bumping into them at the large Sainsbury's in town. Doug and I were there together doing the weekly shop when I spotted them. Oliver was a tall, very good-looking man, and they looked so happy, so close, laughing about something together, and I was struck by what an attractive, perfect-looking family they made. When Rose spotted us and came over we smiled and introduced our husbands. I knew Oliver was a university professor and a published author and I was a little in awe of him, both Doug and I were, but in fact he was nice, really – you could see he was quite sweet, a bit shy even, despite all his success.

We chatted for a while. Rose told us they'd recently bought a huge house called The Willows, not far from our own village. A 'complete wreck', she called it, and laughed about how they were going to have to spend years doing it up and how they were both hopeless at that sort of thing. So Doug told them he was a builder and gave them a bit of advice, offered to come out and take a look at it, which they seemed very pleased about.

On the way home I thought about them; about their gorgeous daughter and how content they all looked. I'd stopped taking the pill not long after Doug and I were married, and the worry, the anxiety, had already firmly set in by then, because month after month, year after year, my period would turn up regular as clockwork, and I suppose deep down, I knew something was very wrong. So as we drove home I thought about the Lawson family and closed my eyes and wished and wished with all my heart that we'd be as happy as them one day too.

Despite how nice she was, it was still unusual for someone like me to strike up a friendship with someone like Rose. Even though we weren't very far apart in age, we were poles apart in terms of class and education. But in fact, six months after that meeting in Sainsbury's we did become friends, because of a series of events that led us to forming an unusual sort of bond. I suppose it was a case of luck, of being in the right place at the right time – or so it felt back then. Looking back of course, I'm not sure how 'lucky' our friendship really was, when you think about what went on to happen.

*   *   *

It began because I was temporarily placed on the maternity ward, due to a staff shortage. Of course, as a paediatric nurse I was well used to working amongst children, had learnt to shut my private longing away in a little box inside myself when dealing with my young patients. But the maternity ward was a different matter. The placement coincided with a brief but unsuccessful pregnancy that had ended in miscarriage. It was the first time I'd actually managed to get pregnant and so much excitement and relief and hope was wrapped up in that positive test result. Doug and I could barely contain ourselves, walking around with our hearts in our mouths, almost too nervous to breathe, praying that finally, finally, everything was going to be OK.

But a few weeks later I felt the first cramping pains. I tried to persuade myself it was nothing sinister, but then the headaches came, the faintness, and finally, as I knew it would, the spots of blood that grew heavier and heavier until there was no doubt that my baby was seeping away from me before it had barely had a chance to begin. I was devastated, absolutely inconsolable. Doug tried to keep positive: it was good news that I could at least get pregnant, he said, perhaps next time it would 'stick'. He held me for hours as I sobbed, but it didn't help, nothing did.

And then, by the cruellest twist of fate imaginable, there I was, two days later, placed on the maternity ward. I had to witness baby after baby being born into the world, had to continue as though the sight of each one didn't feel like a knife to my heart, but there was one in particular that completely crushed me. Candice, she was called, a teenage drug addict, whose baby, like the two she'd had before it (or so I'd heard), was whisked away into care by social workers as soon as it was born, the mother stony-faced, unblinking, indifferent it seemed to me then – though I suppose now, looking back, that she wouldn't have been, not really. It broke my heart, the unfairness of it all. I would have given everything I had to be that baby's mum.

It was 1980. The use of IVF, or 'test-tube babies' as we called them then, had hardly begun; it was considered an almost freakish thing in those days, 'weird science'. It certainly wasn't available to someone like me and wouldn't be for years. Perhaps, eventually, I would have come to terms with it all; perhaps I would have gone on to happily adopt like many millions of couples do. But I was very far from that state of mind back then: it was like a physical, desperate need that was bigger than myself, that I couldn't control or contain.

That particular morning, the morning of the baby who was taken into care, I fled from the delivery room and shut myself in the first store cupboard I came to. I clasped my hands to my mouth but I couldn't help it; I sobbed and sobbed and sobbed. And then the door opened and to my horror Rose Lawson walked in, absorbed in a list she held in her hand, presumably of supplies she was after. She stood stock-still when she saw me. 'Beth?' she said, astonished. 'What on earth's the matter? What's happened?'

269

I couldn't speak, and it was so like her to do what she did next. She didn't say another word and as though it were the most natural thing in the world she walked over to me and hugged me. Such an instinctively kind thing to do, I've never forgotten it. I cried and cried until the shoulder of her white coat was sodden and bit by bit she got it all out of me.

'Beth, I'm so very sorry,' she said, and I could tell that she was. Someone tried to come in but she put her foot against the door and said in a grand sort of voice, 'This one's taken, thank you very much. Try the next one!' and then she winked at me and I laughed. She talked so much sense that morning, she was so gentle and comforting. 'Listen, my love,' she said, 'I know things feel very, very bleak right now, but you will be a lovely mum one day, I know you will. You're still so very young. In a year, or two years, things will look different, you'll see.' The words would have sounded like platitudes on anyone else's lips, and I suppose they were, but nevertheless they did help because I could tell she meant them, and having someone like her saying them did make me feel less hopeless about it all.

After that day, whenever I passed her in the wards, or saw her in the canteen or the tea room or whatever, she would make a point of stopping me, to ask how I was and put a hand on my arm. It was nice, supportive – I didn't feel any better about my situation, but I did feel less alone.

And then something entirely unexpected happened

that solidified our friendship – or our connection, I suppose you'd call it – even further. Because I had grown used to looking out for her, taking special notice when she was on shift at the same time as me, a few months later when I was back on the paediatric ward I noticed a change in her. She'd always taken such good care of her appearance – beautifully cut and coloured hair, lovely make-up, nice clothes – but suddenly she seemed to let herself go entirely. She'd turn up to work looking haggard and ill, her clothes crumpled, her face lined with tiredness, as though she hadn't slept in days. There was clearly something very wrong, but I felt too shy to ask – it would have seemed too forward, I think.

A few weeks later, however, I came across her in the Ladies. I was washing my hands at the sink when she came out of one of the cubicles, her eyes red and raw as though she'd been crying. 'Oh,' I said before I could stop myself, 'Rose, are you all right?'

She went to a sink as though she hadn't heard me, and then stared down at the running water without moving. I didn't know what to do. After a while I put a hand on her arm. 'Rose? Is there anything the matter? Can I help?'

She looked up, as though she hadn't known I was there. 'Oh,' she said, 'oh, Beth. I'm – no – I'm fine,' but then she started to cry.

'Rose, what's happened?' I said.

She waved me away. 'No, no, please, don't be kind. Please, I couldn't bear it.' She pulled a hand towel from

271

the dispenser and put it to her face, then gave a half laugh through her tears. 'Ridiculous. I can't seem to stop crying. Oh please ignore me, Beth, you're very kind. It's just I have no one to talk to, no one at all.'

'But I'm sure you have lots of friends,' I said, surprised.

'Oh yes,' she agreed dispiritedly. 'I'm very lucky.' And then she whispered, 'I just feel so ashamed.'

'Well you could tell me,' I coaxed, 'I wouldn't tell anyone.'

It was then that she broke down and began to cry as though her heart was broken. 'Oh, Beth, it's such an awful mess.'

On impulse I put my arms around her, just as she had done to me all those weeks before. 'What am I going to do?' she said. 'What on earth am I going to do?'

And then she told me what was wrong, how Oliver had confessed to having an affair with one of his students at the university. 'She's nineteen,' Rose said. 'Nineteen! He said it just happened, that it got out of control, that he'd tried to end it but she became obsessed with him. He says she's unstable, that he hadn't realized how fragile she is and that . . . that he's sorry, and . . .' she broke down again, too distraught to go on.

'Oh,' I whispered. 'Oh Rose, I'm so sorry.'

'It's all so sordid,' she cried, 'so humiliating. How could he do it to us, Beth? To me and Emily? How could he?'

I don't think she meant to tell me so much. I think

272

it was like a dam breaking, that it was a relief to confide in someone. She said she couldn't face anyone finding out, her family, her friends, I think she only talked to me because I was so removed from her personal life. And people have always said I'm a good listener, perhaps she felt safe unloading it all on me. Eventually she stopped crying. 'I have to go,' she said. 'I'm due to see a patient any minute.' She took a gulp of breath and dried her eyes, but she looked so hopeless still, so crushed.

'Do you want to meet for coffee tomorrow?' I asked her. 'We could go somewhere in town, if you like, away from the hospital, I mean.'

I wanted her to see that she could trust me, that I'd keep her secret, that nobody from work would find out. I thought she was going to turn me down but to my surprise she looked at me gratefully, 'Are you sure?'

After that, we fell into the habit of meeting up once a week or so. We'd go for coffee in an out-of-the-way place in town, or sometimes I'd go to her lovely house, The Willows, when Oliver wasn't in. We were unlikely friends, but friends we became. I honestly think I was the only person in the world she could talk to. And I thought how strange and sad life is, that someone like Rose with all the grand and important friends she must have, had only me, a near stranger, to confide in. How different people are, aren't they, from how they first appear? I tried my best to comfort her because I felt so sorry for her. She told me that she wanted to forgive

Oliver, that he knew he'd made a horrible mistake, that he regretted everything.

'Can you forgive him, though?' I asked, surprised. I tried to think how I would feel if it were Doug cheating on me. I didn't think I would be able to get past it, to be honest, not if we had a baby.

A strange expression came over her face and suddenly she didn't look quite so vulnerable any more. In fact, she looked quite fierce. 'I will not let that *bitch* destroy my family,' she said, and she sort of spat the words at me and I remember being shocked. 'I will not let that happen,' she said.

A week or so later she came looking for me on the ward. She looked dreadful, I could tell something was very wrong. She pulled me into an empty office, her face deathly white. 'She's pregnant, Beth,' she said. 'Nadia. The girl my husband has been *fucking*.'

I'll never forget her saying that word. I'd never heard her swear before, she just wasn't the type. But she said it with such bitterness, such venom. My hand flew to my mouth. 'Oh no!'

'She's due in two months!' she cried. 'Two months! Oliver said he's only known a month, that he couldn't face telling me before, but he's lying, of course. And now she's started calling the house. She won't leave us alone. She said that unless he leaves me for her, she'll tell everyone about their affair.' She shook her head in dismay. 'His career will be over, Beth, we'll have to leave, everyone will find out at the hospital – everyone will know. All our friends and colleagues and family . . . oh, Beth, what shall I do? Everything, our lovely life, our lovely family, it will all be ruined! It will be so humiliating, so utterly humiliating.'

She was beside herself. I tried to comfort her the best I could, but I didn't know what to say. After that night I didn't see her for a while. She took some time off work and then, what with one thing and another a few weeks slipped by, though I worried about her constantly. Occasionally I'd see her but she was always busy or rushing off somewhere. When, finally, we did arrange to meet I thought she seemed calmer, more resigned to it all, as though she'd begun to come to terms with it a bit. I knew the girl – Nadia – was due to have her baby in late March, and when the date came and went I was surprised when Rose didn't ask to meet me. I assumed she'd decided to accept it, to get on with her life.

And then, one night, at around nine o'clock when Doug and I were just settling down to watch TV, there was a knock on the door. We looked at each other in surprise and when I went to answer it, Rose and Oliver were standing on our front step, Emily beside them asleep in her buggy. 'What's the matter?' I asked. 'What's happened?' They looked so odd, staring back at me like that, their eyes so big and frightened.

It was Rose who spoke first, and her voice was strange, not like her usual one at all. 'Beth,' she said. 'You have to help us. You're the only one who can.'

25

For a long moment in the living room of The Willows, no one moved, as though frozen by Oliver's words. It was Tom who spoke first. 'What?' he said faintly. 'She's your *what*?'

At this, Rose made a low moaning sound and dropping her head began to cry bitterly into her hands. Nobody moved to comfort her. Clara looked at each of their faces, shock reverberating through her. This, surely, was some sort of joke? She glanced at Mac, but he, too, was staring at Oliver in astonishment.

'Before you were born, when Emily was still a baby,' Oliver said, 'I had an affair with one of my students.' He paused and his eyes met Clara's until, embarrassed, she looked away. 'I was a stupid, weak fool, and I have

276

no excuse, I have no defence. I know now that it was the very worst mistake of my life and I have regretted it every single day since.'

He turned to Tom. 'I don't deserve forgiveness, but I want, at least, to try and explain.' There was a pause, the silence broken only by the sound of Rose crying. 'Her name was Nadia, she was a student of mine. We became close, and I suppose I was too infatuated, too flattered, to realize how troubled, how . . . unstable she was. It wasn't until later that I learned quite how unstable.'

Clara stared at him in horrified fascination. This brilliant man, this loving father and devoted husband, whom she had admired, *loved*, from the first moment they had met, was a cheat? Had betrayed his wife and child for the sake of a vulnerable woman far younger than himself? Something hard and bitter lodged in her throat as she listened to him speak. For the first time since she'd met him she suddenly saw Oliver very differently. Her gaze turned to Tom and she saw that he was very still, his eyes fastened on his father's face.

'Your mother was completely blameless,' Oliver went on. 'Emily was only a baby, it was an unforgivable betrayal for which I was entirely responsible. When I came to my senses and ended things between Nadia and me . . .' he paused, and swallowed, glancing at each of their faces, 'I didn't know that she had already fallen pregnant with my child.'

Rose's head whipped round at this. 'Don't, Oliver,' she cried. 'You promised me!'

Oliver's voice was tender: 'Rose, don't you see? There's nothing we can do now. She's won. Hannah's won.'

At this, Tom's head shot up. 'What the fuck are you talking about, Dad?' he said. 'What do you mean "she's won"?'

Oliver flinched at his anger. 'When Hannah was a baby, she was adopted by a woman named Beth Jennings and her husband. She grew up believing they were her natural parents, but then, when she was seven, she found out the truth.'

'That you were her real father,' Tom said coldly.

'That, and what happened to Nadia, to her mother.'

Tom shook his head in frustration. 'Well, what did happen to her?'

Oliver glanced at Rose, something passing between them, fraught with pain. Rose cleared her throat and said, 'She died. Nadia died. It was all my fault.'

Clara shot Mac a look of stunned disbelief. 'What do you mean?' she asked.

'When Oliver finished things with Nadia, after he'd confessed to me about the pregnancy, she became obsessed with him,' Rose said. 'She persecuted him – both of us – she wouldn't leave us alone. She said she was going to expose him to his university, finish his career.' She turned to Tom. 'Your father told her he would provide for the child, but that wasn't enough for her. She wanted *him*. She became manic, obsessed, she wouldn't be happy until she had Oliver to herself, until he left me and Emily for her.'

278

There was absolute silence, the three of them staring at her mutely. 'I arranged to meet her,' Rose continued. 'I wanted to make her see sense. And if that didn't work, I decided I'd offer her money, enough to leave the area, to start again somewhere else. I asked her to meet me somewhere we wouldn't be seen. I used to walk the dogs along Widow's Cliff, above Dunwich beach, you know. It seemed like as good a place as any, equidistant to where we both lived. It was usually deserted and I knew she'd make a scene.'

Rose hesitated, her eyes gazing unseeingly at the window as she remembered. 'She was quite calm at first. But when I told her what I was offering, that I'd pay her to go away, that Oliver didn't want her and never would, she went crazy. She had her daughter in her pram, and Emily was sleeping in her pushchair. She started ranting and raving, shouting that it wasn't fair that Emily had her father but her daughter wouldn't. And then . . . and then . . .' Rose broke down, crying into her hands.

The three of them exchanged horrified glances. 'What?' Tom asked. 'What happened to her?'

'She jumped,' Rose whispered. 'Without any warning, she stepped off the edge and she jumped, leaving her poor baby alone up there with me! I ran to the edge and looked down, and her body was . . . oh God it was so awful, so horrible, her body was there, on the rocks below, before she got swept away.'

'Jesus Christ,' Tom whispered.

'We found out later that she had made suicide attempts before, had been diagnosed with bipolar long before she met your father. I didn't know what to do,' Rose cried, 'I was in shock. I took the baby, took her from her pram, and put her in the pushchair with Emily, and then I ran. I thought people would say I pushed her, or that I made her jump, or I had driven her to it, that when it all came out about your father and her, it would look like I'd engineered the whole thing. I wasn't thinking straight, I panicked, I just ran, I didn't know what else to do!'

For a long moment after she had finished speaking, Rose and Tom stood silently in the centre of the room, while Oliver sat, his head in his hands. Beyond the window, clouds moved in front of the moon, the endless empty fields stretching on beneath it cast suddenly into darkness.

26

Suffolk, 1981

I didn't notice the baby, not straight away. Rose and Oliver both looked so awful, were in such a state, that it took me a few moments before I saw the tiny creature wrapped in a blanket in Rose's arms. And it's funny but I realized immediately; before they said anything, I had already guessed whose she was. 'Oh, Rose . . .' I said.

'Beth, we need your help,' she replied.

That was when Doug came into the hall. 'What's going on?' he asked, taking in the sight of the four of them.

But Rose didn't shift her eyes from mine. 'There's been an accident, Beth,' she said, her voice low and strained. 'There's been a terrible accident and you have to help us.'

Once we were all seated in our living room you could

have heard a pin drop as Rose began to tell us what had happened. When she got to the part where Nadia jumped, I gasped, and Doug got to his feet. 'And you didn't call the coast guards, the police?' he asked, incredulously. 'What the hell were you thinking? You just *ran*? You took the baby and ran?' He turned first to Oliver and then to me. 'For God's sake, we need to tell someone!'

Rose stared at him, her face still drained of colour, her eyes wide and bright. In her arms the baby began to stir.

'Doug,' I said firmly, 'sit down,' and he was so surprised that he did what I asked. I went to Rose and gently lifted the child from her arms. God, she was tiny. She was so, so tiny. I suppose my nurse's instincts kicked in because I suddenly felt very calm. 'Do you have formula and nappies for her?' I asked. When Rose didn't reply, just gazed at me blankly, I had to go to her and take hold of her shoulder while I said it again, loudly and slowly. I noticed that she was trembling quite violently.

At last she nodded. 'Yes, yes, I – they're in the bag beneath Emily's pushchair. We stopped on the way. There was some milk still left in the bottle that she had with her. I think . . . I think maybe it's breast milk.' She clamped a hand to her mouth then. 'Oh God,' she cried. 'Oh God!'

'OK,' I said. 'Good.' When I'd got the bag I turned to Doug, handing him a bottle and a tin of Cow & Gate. 'Just follow the instructions on the side.'

It was then that Oliver spoke for the first time. 'I'll do it,' he said. 'I mean, please, if I may?' He looked so meek and uncertain, so very different from the dashing, charming man I'd met that day in the supermarket. In fact, he looked more like a cowed, frightened . . . well, wimp is the only word I can think of, to be honest. I felt a sharp cold flash of disdain. I looked away and nodded, and he followed Doug into the kitchen.

Rose began to cry again. 'That poor woman,' she said. 'Oh, Beth, that poor, poor woman.'

And it's funny, because there I was, a baby in my arms, Rose's desperate, frightened eyes staring back at me, the knowledge that a woman had died that night, and yet I felt completely calm. Here they were, these big important people, so clever, so successful compared to me, sitting in my living room, miserable and terrified and wanting me to make it all better for them. I held her to me, little Lana as she was called then, and knew what Rose was going to ask me to do.

When Oliver came back in with the bottle of milk, he hesitated, then passed it to me. 'Would you like to do it?' I asked him. I raised the baby slightly, offering her to him, and I saw his eyes dart to Rose, saw her briefly shake her head, and, deflated, he dropped his gaze and turned away. I will remember forever the disgust I felt for that man right then. I had thought that he and Rose were so admirable, people to look up to. I realized in that moment how very wrong I'd been.

I turned to Rose. 'What are you asking us to do?'

To her credit, she didn't bother beating around the bush. 'You want a child,' she said bluntly, 'you want a baby. I can arrange everything, all the hospital paperwork so you can get a birth certificate saying she is yours.'

Only Doug was surprised. He looked from one to the other of us in confusion before the penny dropped. 'Are you completely out of your minds?' he said. 'This is absolute madness! You need to go to the police and tell them what happened. We want no part of this. We could be arrested. Aiding and abetting it's called, or . . . or obstructing the police or something. Absolutely not. This is your mess, not ours.'

'What if they think I killed her?' Rose cried. 'That I pushed her! It will all come out who she is, they'll say I did it out of revenge. Even if they don't blame me there will be such a scandal! My career...' She turned to me, pleading: 'You are our only hope, Beth. Haven't you always wanted a child? Now you can be a mother at last. Please, Beth. Please!'

Silently I turned to Doug.

'No,' he said. 'Absolutely not! If you want to adopt a baby then we can do it through the proper channels. We can't get involved in this. If the police find out we've taken a kid that doesn't belong to us, forged a birth certificate . . . if they found out we knew what happened to that poor woman and didn't tell them . . . What about her relatives? Her family? It's wrong, Beth, you know it is.'

I looked down at the baby. I knew Doug was right,

but God, she was so beautiful. I loved her immediately, I think. She was so defenceless and alone, her mother was dead, her father didn't want her – what would happen to her now? I lifted her to my face and breathed in the delicious smell of her scalp. I think I already knew by then that I'd never be able to let her go.

Suddenly, Oliver seemed to find his voice. 'All we ask is that you have her tonight. We can't be seen with her, people will start asking questions. Please, just have her tonight and think about it.'

Rose caught hold of my hand. 'I'm begging you, Beth, please help us.'

Doug shook his head and I pulled my hand away from Rose's. 'Doug,' I said, 'can I talk to you in the kitchen?'

Once we'd shut the door behind us, Doug hissed, 'There is no way we're doing this, Beth.'

'Doug,' I began, but he cut me off.

'The very idea is insane. We can't take in someone else's child! A woman died tonight, we should tell the police!'

We must have been in there for half an hour, arguing back and forth. I think I wore him down in the end. 'It's one night,' I promised him. 'Just one night. Let the baby have a good night's sleep in peace and we'll decide what to do in the morning. Please, Doug,' I said. 'Please.' I think he knew that there would be no talking me out of it and eventually, reluctantly, he agreed. 'One night,' he said. 'That's all.'

We went back to the living room. 'All right,' I said. 'We'll look after her tonight.' I could hardly look at Oliver as he thanked us, his eyes full of shame and gratitude.

After they had left, Doug and I took care of Lana. We fed her, changed her, and made her a makeshift bed next to ours. She was such a good little soul; so peaceful and quiet. I did with her what I'd never allowed myself to do with any of the babies I'd looked after in the hospital: I closed my eyes and held her to me and let myself pretend she was mine. She seemed to fit in the crook of my neck so perfectly, it felt so right to have her snuggled against me.

When she was sleeping peacefully, I took a deep breath and steeled myself to talk to Doug. 'I know the circumstances are awful,' I began cautiously, whispering in the darkness, 'but this, surely, is the answer to our prayers. You heard Rose, she'll get us the necessary paperwork so we can get a birth certificate saying she's ours. They'll think Lana died with her mother, that her body was lost at sea. No one need ever know.'

He kept repeating the same thing, saying it was morally wrong, that we could get into terrible trouble. I thought I'd never change his mind. But when Lana woke a few hours later in the middle of the night, I passed her to him while I went to make up her milk. When I came back, he was sitting on the end of the bed holding her, an expression on his face as he gazed down at her that I'd never seen before. It was a scene I'd imagined so many times throughout those endless years and years of hope and disappointment, and I felt a lump lodge itself in my throat. I sat down next to him and silently passed him the bottle.

'I was thinking,' he murmured as we watched her drink. 'What if you're right? What if this *is* our only chance? If we never did manage to have our own, or for some reason couldn't adopt. What then?' He looked at me. 'You'd never forgive me, would you?' He sighed and added, 'I don't think I'd ever forgive myself.'

I closed my eyes. Could this be true? Could we really be about to do this? Careful not to disturb Lana, I put my arms around him. We both watched as she fell asleep again, her little head with its beautiful thick dark hair on his chest. Our daughter. I felt overcome with happiness.

The days following our decision were utterly surreal. The practicalities of adjusting to new parenthood, the fear of what would happen if we were discovered, the guilt we felt about her real family, was interspersed with the pure joy of having Lana so suddenly and unexpectedly in our lives. She was absolutely perfect. We decided to call her Hannah after my grandmother, and that was when it began to feel as though she was really and forever ours. But there was a huge amount of fear and anxiety too. We had to keep her existence secret from the world while we worked out how to pass her off as our own. Luckily, the house we lived in then was down a lane, set slightly apart from our neighbours, so there was nobody to hear her when she cried. We would take it in turns to drive to a town far away from our village to buy her formula and nappies.

We knew we had to come up with a plan. I thought if we were going to commit to such a huge lie, then it had to be to everyone – to all our friends and family – and we would have to move away from the Suffolk village we'd lived in all our lives. I resigned from my job at the hospital. Doug had wanted for some time to expand his building business, so he applied for a loan, and the idea was to move from the area and start again. We began researching villages and areas in Cambridgeshire, the next county, miles away from our village, where no one would know us.

Two weeks after Hannah came to us, I went to the local pub to have a drink with friends, and broke the news that Doug and I had decided to split up. In the shocked silence I told them that I was going away for a while to stay with a friend from the hospital while I worked out what to do. I knew the gossip would spread like wildfire. Later that night, I took Hannah, drove to a town near the Cambridgeshire village we'd chosen to move to, and stayed in a hotel while I looked for a house to rent. Doug gave notice to our landlord and a month later, came and joined us.

My parents had moved to the Lake District after I had married Doug, so the fabrications we had to weave, though difficult, were not impossible. When I announced my 'pregnancy' to them I said that, because of my previous miscarriages, we'd waited four months before telling them. Later we said that as the baby had arrived a month early she'd had to spend several weeks in the hospital's neo-natal intensive care unit – a place where only the child's parents are allowed to visit. Finally, citing problems with the move and so on, we were able to put off their first visit for a further couple of months. Hannah was a naturally very small baby, so when my parents did eventually get to meet their grandchild they didn't guess that she was in fact far older than we said. It was very difficult – I hated lying to them, but what else could I do? Doug's own mother had died some years earlier and his father, who lived in Devon, was not the type to be much interested in newborns, so that at least was easier.

As far as local friends were concerned I told them that Doug and I had got back together after our split when we'd found out I was pregnant, and we were now living happily together in Cambridgeshire. Yes, I hurt some feelings, burnt some bridges, but, well, it was a small price to pay.

In the event, everything seemed to go our way. I took that as a sign it was meant to be. I told myself, although it hadn't happened in the best of circumstances, that wasn't our fault. We'd had nothing to do with Nadia's death and Lana would have had to have been adopted by someone eventually, so why not us, who had waited for so long and so desperately for her? I guess I made myself not think about Hannah's real-life family, the grandparents who were mourning both her and Nadia's loss. I read the newspaper reports about Nadia's suicide and put them away, out of sight, locking my guilt firmly away as I did so.

So, suddenly there we were: new house, new village, new daughter, new life. God, I was so happy. I thought I had it all, that my dreams had come true at last. Soon it felt as though we truly were just an ordinary, natural family. Doug was as besotted with her as I was and took to fatherhood right away, doing his fair share of nappies and night feeds, cuddling and playing with her as often as he could. He was so proud of her; we both were.

And later, when the small, niggling doubts crept in, I ignored them at first, telling myself that it was nothing, that I was imagining things. Occasionally, when I couldn't sleep at night and the worry that something wasn't quite right with Hannah loomed larger, I would torture myself, wondering if her antipathy towards me was because she wasn't really mine; that she sensed I wasn't her real mother, or even that I was imagining things because of the guilt I still felt at the dreadful way she'd come into our lives, at all the lies we'd colluded in. But always, at least in the beginning, I'd push the doubts from my mind, because I wanted so badly for it all, at last, to be completely perfect for Doug and me.

27

Suffolk, 2017

From the hallway, the clock above the stairs struck one.
The fire had long since died out; the coldness that seeped
into the corners of the room made Clara shiver inside
her thin jumper. They were all of them seated now: Clara
and Mac on the large and uncomfortable chesterfield,
Rose and Oliver in the two creaking armchairs. Clemmy
lay on the floor at their feet, emitting the occasional
uneasy grumble, her eyebrows shooting up unhappily
towards first one, then the other of her owners. Only
Tom still stood, his back to the window, listening to his
mother speak. He continued to drink steadily, pouring
again and again from the bottle of wine, watching Rose
grimly from above his glass.

'We cut all ties with Beth and Doug,' Rose went on.

'We all agreed it would be better that way,' her voice rose imploringly as she looked from one to the other of their faces. 'We got on with our lives, what else could we do? The police had rightly concluded Nadia's death was suicide, assuming she'd died alone, and that . . . that . . . Lana had been lost to sea.' She looked at Tom. 'And later, when first you, then your brother came along, we just wanted to put the whole dreadful business behind us.' She paused, seeming to shrink inside herself as she said in a low, fearful voice, 'It wasn't until seven years later that Beth suddenly contacted me out of the blue.'

'What did she want?' Clara asked.

'She was hysterical, saying she wanted to go to the police, that we needed to confess everything. It was a horrible shock, as you can imagine, I had no idea why she was so upset. I tried to get her to calm down, but she became so worked up that in the end I agreed to meet her. When I got there she was still in a state, saying Hannah, as they'd named Lana, had become violent, that she was frightened of her. She said the child had started a fire at her babysitter's, had hurt her son, that her marriage was falling apart because of it all. She was convinced Hannah was mentally ill – that she'd inherited her mother's psychiatric issues and that now she – Beth – was somehow being punished for deceiving everyone the way we did. I tried to reason with her but she was beside herself, saying she wanted to go to the police, that she couldn't stand the guilt any more and wanted to confess that they'd taken the child illegally. She kept talking about how Nadia had died, how wrong it had been to pass Hannah off as their own. Most of all, she believed Hannah needed professional help, that doctors would need her real medical history. The more I tried to talk her out of it, the more upset she became. I decided the best thing for me to do was to leave. And I told her not to contact me again.'

There was complete silence. Clara looked across the room to Oliver, who was still slumped in a chair, his head in his hands as his wife talked.

'I thought,' Rose continued, 'or rather I hoped very much that would be an end to it. But it wasn't, of course.' She looked up and met Clara's eye. 'Because Hannah had been there all along, in the kitchen where we were talking, was hiding in the next room, listening to our conversation. She had heard everything Beth and I said. She was seven years old and she knew everything – who her real parents were, how her mother had died. Everything.'

Clara put her hand to her mouth. 'Oh my God, that poor kid.'

Rose glanced at her with the smallest flicker of confusion, almost, Clara thought, as if Hannah's suffering hadn't occurred to her in all of this. 'I didn't find out for many years that Hannah had overheard us, not until I saw Beth again,' she went on, 'and by then it was far too late. In the meantime she grew up, becoming more and more disturbed, fixated on what she'd learned. She became obsessed with Oliver and me, with all of us – her "real" family as she thought of us. She knew the hospital

Beth used to work in and tracked me down there. After a while she began to skip school, getting the train over here and following Oliver to work, or standing outside the children's school, becoming more and more resentful.' She turned to Tom. 'She saw you kids as having the perfect life, the life that she should be living.'

'Didn't you confront her?' Tom asked angrily. 'Talk to her?'

'We didn't know!' Rose cried. 'Even Beth had no idea until years later. Hannah always kept her distance, never approaching us, or letting herself be discovered. We had no clue that she even knew about us! And then, when she was sixteen and Emily had just turned eighteen, she engineered a way for the two of them to meet. They became friends.'

'And you still had no idea who she was?' Clara asked.

'No! She told Emily her name was Becky, and she never came here to the house, not that I'd recognize her if she did. We knew Emily had a new friend but I didn't make the connection. Why would I? The Jennings lived miles from us in Cambridgeshire, I had no idea Hannah knew about us all, I had no reason to suspect.'

'So how did you find out?' Mac asked.

At this Rose began to cry again. 'One night Hannah told Emily. She told her everything. Who she really was, that Oliver was her father, that she and Emily were half-sisters, that we'd given her away to near strangers to be rid of her.'

'My God,' Tom said.

'But it was worse than that. Hannah knew I'd been the only person present when her mother died, and over the years she had convinced herself that it was I who killed her, that I'd pushed her!'

'And Emily believed her?' Tom asked.

Rose wiped her eyes. 'I don't think so, thank God. I told her it wasn't true of course, that I'd seen Nadia jump, but it didn't stop her being furious with both of us. Furious that Oliver had had an affair, that we had kept from her that she had a half-sister, that I'd "covered up" for her dad. She said we disgusted her, that she'd never forgive us. You know what she was like, how principled she was, so sure of what was right and wrong. There was nothing we could say to make her stay, she was such a stubborn, headstrong girl. She said that she was leaving, that she never wanted to see us again. What could I do? She was eighteen! I couldn't force her to stay!'

'So you just let her go?' Tom said.

'Oh, darling, she was so, so angry with us. I thought she would go away for a few days, a week or so, and then she'd come back once she'd calmed down. And she was legally an adult, I couldn't stop her. But she didn't come back. We tried to look for her, but it was no use. And the next day Hannah called us, taunting us, telling us that she knew where Emily was, saying we deserved it, that she'd make us pay for the rest of our lives, that she'd drive each of you away from us, one by one.'

'You should have told me!' Tom cried. 'You had no right to keep this from me!'

'We wanted to spare you . . .'

'But you didn't! You didn't! Are you that crazy? Did you not think I suspected something? That I didn't hear you and Dad talking in corners, whispering away when you thought Luke and I were in bed? Then one night I heard you say it outright. I heard you telling Dad it was his fault she had left, that Emily would never forgive him for what he'd done, that she'd left because of him.'

Rose's face fell. 'You heard that?'

'Why do you think I couldn't bear to be around you any more? I knew you knew why Emily had gone. Guilt was written all over your faces. I didn't confront you because . . . well because I was fifteen, it was easier to just get drunk, take drugs, stay out all night, bury my head in the sand. But I hated you, I bloody hated you for lying to me, for pretending you had no idea why our family had fallen apart.' He turned to his father. 'I knew it was your fault, that you made her go. I just didn't know why.'

Clara stared at him, suddenly everything that had confused her about him making sense, and she felt a rush of pity.

'And then when Luke went missing,' Tom continued, 'again your reaction didn't add up. Just like when Emily left, I could tell you were hiding something. It wasn't shock or bewilderment I saw on your faces, it was guilt. I saw the looks that passed between you, and then I overheard you, Dad, begging Mum's forgiveness, promising that Luke would be OK. And when I asked you outright in that fucking kitchen, the day Clara and Mac came round, when I asked you if you knew where Luke was, you denied it! You lied! I *knew* you were lying. And now I know why. It's her, isn't it? The person who has Luke, it's this fucking woman! Hannah, my half-sister.'

Rose nodded miserably. 'Yes,' she whispered.

'And does she know where Emily is?'

'We don't know. Sometimes she likes to taunt us, telling us she does, other times she denies all knowledge. We've never known what to believe.'

'What does she want from us? Why did she approach me in Manchester all those years ago?'

'Revenge,' said Oliver quietly. 'And money. Once she'd made contact with you in Manchester she phoned us constantly, telling us that she'd seen you, that she was going to tell you everything, that there was nothing we could do about it. That once she'd finished with you you'd never want to see us again, would disappear from our lives like your sister. She told us it was all going to come out . . . my affair, giving her away as a baby, the ridiculous lies about her mother's supposed murder, all of it. She knew she couldn't prove any of it to the police, so hurting us through you kids was the best way she could think of to punish us. We were trying to protect you from it all!'

'Jesus fucking Christ! And you didn't think to tell me about it? You didn't think I had a right to know about the nutcase who was hanging around me?'

Oliver hung his head. 'We paid her a lot of money. Thousands and thousands of pounds to leave you alone. She was broke, homeless, a drifter, she'd . . . been in a lot of trouble throughout her life, drugs, prison . . .'

'*Prison*?' Clara asked.

'We paid her the money and it worked. We didn't hear from her for ten years. I hired a private detective to track her down, keep an eye on her. Her life . . . it spiralled, she was a junkie, a prostitute, constantly in trouble with the police. She was in no fit state to continue to wage her war against us, so she left us in peace for a time.'

Clara couldn't keep quiet any longer. 'This is your daughter. Your daughter! As much your flesh and blood as Emily! Didn't you care? Didn't you feel any guilt, any responsibility for this woman? Jesus, Oliver! I can't believe what I'm hearing!' Oliver kept his head bent, unable to meet her gaze. She felt a burning dislike for him.

'But why after ten years did she get it together to go after Luke?' Mac asked. 'It doesn't make sense. Why now?'

Rose shook her head. 'We don't know.'

Tom drained his glass of wine. 'When did you guess that Hannah was behind Luke's disappearance?' he asked.

Oliver glanced at him. 'Hannah sent us a picture of him, saying he was with her. She said that she wanted more money, that if we didn't give it to her, she'd hurt him. So we gave her what she asked for, then she said it wasn't enough. She said if we paid her more she'd let Luke go. We've been going out of our minds, Tom. We know it's not money she wants, she wants to torture us, this is her revenge, that's why she's keeping it going, the longer she can cause us pain, the better she likes it.'

'Why didn't you tell the police?' Tom asked next. 'Surely that was the first thing you should have done?'

'We didn't dare!' Rose said. 'She seems to know everything about us. Every move we make – when we speak to the police, what we talk about with them, our conversations or meetings with Clara, you name it, she somehow knows about it. We couldn't work out how she was doing it, even if we used public telephones, she'd know what we talked about, it's terrifying. She said if we told the police about her, she'd know and she'd kill Luke immediately. We couldn't take that risk. And then . . .' her voice faltered and she took a gulping breath. 'And then she sent us pictures of Luke, to warn us what would happen if we did.'

'Pictures?' Clara asked, feeling sick. 'What pictures?'

Oliver pulled his phone from his pocket. 'This is the last one that Hannah sent us.'

'Let me see that.' Tom's face drained of colour as he took the phone from his father and stared down at its screen. Wordlessly he passed it to Clara. It was a picture of Luke. He had a large and vivid bruise across his face, a split lip, and his skin behind his scars was horribly pale, his eyes staring glassily at the lens.

Clara gasped in horror as she swiped to the next photo. It showed Luke's bound arms, covered in hundreds of small, weeping knife wounds. 'Oh no,' she whispered, 'oh God.'

'We've been waiting to hear from her, to tell us what to do next,' Rose said. 'We're so frightened.' Fresh tears fell from her eyes. 'She's dangerous, Tom. She's so very dangerous.'

A coldness spread through Clara. 'How dangerous?' She looked at Oliver. 'When you said she went to prison, what was it for?'

28

Cambridgeshire, 1997

They say that personality disorders, including sociopathy, can come about due to a mixture of biology and circumstance. A neurological malfunction, often inherited, that can be exacerbated by trauma in childhood. I've had a lot of time to think about it over the years, in fact I've thought of little else, but I still don't know why Hannah became the person that she did. Perhaps she did inherit her mother's psychiatric issues, perhaps the discovery of where she came from that day, aged seven, detonated a bomb that been sitting idle, waiting for its touchpaper to be lit. I guess I'll never know for sure. I try my hardest not to dwell on the reasons why any more. I last saw Hannah – I no longer refer to her as my daughter – over twenty years ago. I never want to see her face again.

After I overheard Hannah on the phone to Emily that day, pretending to be 'Becky', I was thrown into a panic. I didn't know what to do for the best. I knew I should call Rose to warn her, but I felt paralysed. Should I talk to Hannah first, try to dissuade her from her plan, whatever that might be? I needed to find out what she was intending to do. When she ended the call to Emily, I waited in the kitchen for her to come down, my head in turmoil, until I heard her door open and, a few seconds later, her tread on the stairs.

She glanced at me as she entered the kitchen, but as usual said nothing, coldly ignoring me as she went to the cupboard and started rooting around for food. I can still see her now. She was wearing black leggings and a T-shirt that might once have been white, her face a mess of last night's make-up that she hadn't bothered to wipe off. Yet still her beauty made me catch my breath. I thought again of the strange, fake voice she'd used on the phone, how she'd called herself 'Becky', and I shuddered. At last I steeled myself and cleared my throat. 'Hannah?'

She straightened up, a packet of biscuits in her hand. 'What?'

I swallowed hard and braced myself. How had I become so afraid of my own daughter? 'I know you've been meeting Emily Lawson,' I said. 'I overheard you on the phone with her this morning.'

302

I saw surprise register on her face. For a few seconds there was absolute silence, and then she did something I hadn't expected her to do in a thousand years: she started to cry. As I looked on, amazed, at the tears rolling down her face, she put the biscuits down and came over to where I was sitting at the table. She took the seat opposite mine, put her head on her arms, and began to sob.

Funny to think that I still loved her then, that the sight of her in pain could make my heart twist in sympathy as though it were my own that was breaking. 'Oh, Hannah,' I said. 'Oh my darling, what is it?' I reached across the table and took hold of her hand. It was the first time she'd let me touch her in years. 'Tell me, please, tell me what this is all about.'

It took her a while to compose herself. When she did, she wiped her eyes and said in a voice so small and desolate that it brought a lump to my throat, 'I just want them to love me – my real family, I mean. I want to know them, to understand where I come from.' Her eyes brimmed with tears again. 'Ever since I found out about my real mother and father, I've felt so confused.'

I was astonished. This was the first time she'd ever brought up what she'd overheard all those years before. 'I had no idea you felt like this,' I stammered.

And then, suddenly, and to my horror, a wide smirk broke across her face. 'Jesus, you're stupid,' she said.

As I recoiled she snatched her hand away and slowly shook her head as though dumbfounded. 'You actually bought that, didn't you?' She laughed loudly, a harsh, ugly sound. 'I always knew you were a fucking idiot, Beth,' she went on, 'but I didn't know you were quite this retarded.'

She got up and, walking around the table towards me, leant down and put her face so close to mine that I could smell the cigarettes on her breath. 'What I actually want to do is to fuck them up,' she said quietly. 'And not just the Lawsons – all of you.'

'What do you mean?' I asked, my voice shaking.

'I've been watching them,' she said. 'Watching them for years. My brothers and sister, my father and his dear wife. Sometimes I'd go every day, catching the train over there, following them to school or work.' She paused, raising her eyebrows at me. 'They have a nice life, don't they? A lovely, happy life. While I've been stuck here in this shit hole with you.' I flinched, and she laughed. 'How did my mother die, Beth? I heard you talk that day to Rose, I heard her say that she was with my mother when she died, about her body being found in the sea. Rose pushed her, didn't she?'

My eyes widened in shock. 'No! No, Hannah,' I cried. 'Of course not! Your mother jumped, she committed suicide.'

'I don't believe you. Rose killed her. Because my mother slept with her husband. Rose murdered her.'

I shook my head in shock and pity, that she had convinced herself of such a dreadful thing. 'Hannah, your mother was very unhappy,' I said firmly, 'she was ill, she died by throwing herself into the sea.'

'No! She wouldn't have left me. I was her baby. I was all she had. Rose murdered her. My mother would never have left me alone like that.'

'Hannah, that's not true,' I cried. 'Your mother jumped, she took her own life. I'm sorry, but it's true. It was suicide.'

A look of infinite hatred flashed in Hannah's eyes then. 'Rose did it, and then she and my father gave me away like I was a fucking stray puppy.'

'Hannah—'

'You all lied to me. All of you. You are all responsible, and you're not going to get away with it. None of you.'

I stood up. 'Hannah, please, Doug and I, we love you so much, we've looked after you since you were a baby, we have always thought of you as our daughter. I only ever wanted you to be happy!'

She turned on me then. 'Happy? I have never been happy here. You never loved me, not like you love Toby. I felt it, always, and when I overheard you and Rose talking that day I finally understood why: because I'm not yours. You lied to me my whole life and I'll make sure you get your fucking punishment too.' She turned to go. 'But first it's Oliver and Rose's turn.'

'What are you going to do?' I cried.

She glanced back at me. 'All these years I've been watching them, following them, seeing how they doted on those kids of theirs. Those three spoilt little pricks have had everything they ever wanted. So one by one

I'm going to show them what their father's really like. Maybe then Oliver will wish he'd treated me a bit better, maybe he'll regret how he threw me away.'

And then she walked slowly from the room, leaving me staring after her, reeling in shock.

I heard her go out an hour later. The first thing I did was to try to call Rose to warn her, but the phone rang and rang until in the end I gave up. I paced the house, adrenalin and fear shooting through me while I went over and over what Hannah had said, driving myself mad trying to work out what her next move might be. What did she want with Emily? What was she planning to do? No matter how many times I tried Rose, there was no answer: nobody picked up, nobody, it seemed, was home.

When Doug got back later that evening I pulled him into the kitchen and shutting the door in case Toby should overhear us, told him what had happened. 'I can't get hold of Rose,' I said anxiously. 'Maybe they've changed their number since the last time I saw her, it was nine years ago, after all.'

'Christ,' he said, looking at me in dismay. 'And you have no idea where Hannah has gone?'

'No. She left but she didn't say where.'

At that moment, Toby came in. 'What's up?' he asked, stopping dead and looking from one to another of our faces.

'Nothing!' I said brightly. 'Nothing at all. Go and wash your hands for tea, will you?'

We tried to eat a normal meal, but I couldn't stop the panic pulsing through me. The look in Hannah's eyes had been so triumphant, so spiteful. Maybe she'd been bluffing, I told myself, maybe I should just wait and see, but I couldn't ignore the fear that was slipping and sliding in the pit of my stomach, and though I kept trying Rose, no one picked up. As the clock crept closer to ten o'clock, I made up my mind. 'I'm going to drive over there, to Suffolk,' I told Doug.

He looked worried. 'Maybe I should come with you.'

'No,' I said decisively. 'Wait here with Toby in case Hannah comes back. She was probably only trying to scare us.'

It took me forty minutes to drive to The Willows, the clock on my dashboard telling me it was ten forty-five when I pulled up outside. I half expected the house to be in darkness but in fact I could see a light burning brightly from the living room. They must have changed their phone number, I thought, and remembered how Rose had told me never to contact her again, the last time we'd met. When I knocked, the look on Rose's face told me all I needed to know. She nodded silently at me to come in, and when I followed her into the kitchen Oliver was there, white as a sheet. Fear trailed its fingers along my spine. 'Do you know?' I blurted. 'That Hannah has been meeting with Emily? I came here to warn you, I don't know what she's planning to do but—'

'You're too late, Beth,' Rose replied quietly. 'Emily got a phone call and she went out, saying she was going

307

to meet her friend Becky. When she came back she knew everything. It was Hannah she'd been meeting all along, she'd told her everything.'

I sank on to a chair. 'Oh, Rose.'

Her face twisted in pain. 'She's gone,' she said. 'Emily has gone. We don't know where she is. She says she never wants to see or speak to us again. She hates us, she thinks we're monsters!' And then Rose told me what had happened. Emily had come home from seeing Hannah, beside herself with fury. 'She kept shouting, "Is it true? Is it true?" She knew everything. About Oliver's affair, Nadia's death, how Hannah had been given away. Hannah even told her that I had killed Nadia, that I'd pushed her into the sea in revenge for sleeping with Oliver!'

'My God,' I said. 'Did Emily believe her?'

She put her head in her hands. 'I don't know. I hope not, I don't think so . . . I don't know! She said that even if it wasn't true, it was still Oliver's fault she jumped, that he drove her to it.' Rose burst into tears. 'And she said I was as bad as Oliver, because I'd known all along about Hannah, about Oliver's affair and Nadia's death, and didn't tell her. She said I'd covered up for him, that I was as disgusting as he was. God, it's all such a mess. She hates us, absolutely hates us.'

I looked at Oliver, and he put a hand on his wife's arm, but she snatched it away, continuing to cry bitterly. 'She said she never wanted to see us again, that we repulsed her, and then she ran off and locked herself in her bedroom. When I went up to see her an hour later she was gone, there was only a note, saying she never wanted to see us again.' Her eyes welled with fresh tears. 'I don't think she'll ever forgive us.'

'Oh, Rose,' I whispered. 'I'm so dreadfully sorry.'

'Why didn't you tell me she'd been there that day?' she asked angrily. 'That she'd overheard us talking? We would have had some warning, we could have been prepared!'

'Because you told me not to contact you!' I cried. 'And I had no idea that she would go looking for you all, that she'd been watching you all this time and would eventually do this! How could I have known? I told you nine years ago that I wanted to come clean, that I wanted to put this right, but you said no, you told me to stay out of your life and leave you alone!'

I stayed with them for a long time, and it was gone midnight by the time I left. On the drive back, the feeling of dread built and built. Would Hannah be home when I returned? What would I say to her if she was? I thought about Emily, how distressed she must be, and then of Oliver and Rose, their shock and devastation. It made me think of Toby, of how I'd feel if he told me he hated me and the idea of it made me physically sick. I longed suddenly to be home with him and Doug, and I put my foot on the accelerator and headed back as fast as I could towards Cambridgeshire.

As I turned the corner into our road it was almost 1

a.m., and I was met by a scene of such pandemonium that at first my eyes couldn't make sense of it. The street was full of our neighbours, black smoke billowed from the upstairs windows of our home. My stomach dropped. I heard the sound of sirens, followed by two fire engines screaming down the street after me. I screeched to a halt then scrambled out of the car, stumbling and tripping in my haste as I ran towards my burning house.

Doug and Toby died that night. I could describe the horror of those hours, the brutal, freeze-frame panic as I watched the firefighters battle their way through the bonfire of my house, the endless awful waiting for my husband and son to be saved. And when all hope was lost, their bodies being dragged out into the cold night air, I remember the arms and hands of strangers, neighbours, police, restraining me, stopping me from running to them, the ungodly sound of my scream.

I could describe the aftermath, the blind stumbling through what remained of my derelict life. But I won't. I can't relive it all again. I will tell you only the facts, of what she did, Hannah, of how she paid me back.

After she left Emily, she bought petrol, two cans of it, from the local garage, then walked the streets with brazen carelessness with one in each hand. And finding the house in darkness as she'd expected (assuming, I suppose, that I too was safely tucked up in bed), she set to work. Afterwards, a neighbour saw her running from the flames across the fields. Somewhere her plan must have gone wrong because she was found by the police less than a mile away, badly burned herself. I imagine she wanted me to die too, but in the end the outcome was probably better for her. She had said she wanted to punish all of us: what greater punishment could there be than allowing me to go on living?

The trial lasted seven days. There was never any question of her being acquitted, the evidence against her was too overwhelming – not least the CCTV footage of her buying the petrol that day. And in fact I don't think she actually cared about being caught; her aim was to destroy as many lives as possible, by whatever means, so her punishment was the least of her concerns.

The trial attracted a fair amount of media attention – the tabloids, especially, baying for her blood. TEEN SLAYS FAMILY, that sort of thing. They, like me, wanted retribution. Yet the Hannah who appeared in court defied all expectations, knocked the wind out of the jury's sails with her doe-eyed fragility, her tears and her beauty. She looked much younger than her years as she stood in the dock wearing a simple, childlike dress, trembling and remorseful, a beautiful yet troubled waif in desperate need of help.

The prosecution tried their best: calling in a psychiatrist as their expert witness who said he was certain Hannah posed a significant and ongoing threat to society. They even got Kathy Philips, Clara's old childminder, to describe how Hannah had set fire to her son's room all those years before. But despite all this, despite the fact that she deliberately burnt down her family home, in the end her fate hinged on the performance she gave, the jury's belief of whether she intended to kill or not. She sobbed as she said she hadn't meant for the fire to spread, that she'd tried to go back to save her father and brother, that she had the burns on her back to prove it. The jury was divided, uncertain, and in the end the murder charge was reduced to involuntary manslaughter, and because of her age, she got just five years.

At first I was shocked that she didn't come clean about the discoveries she'd made, had shied away from a heartrending description of how she'd found out, aged seven, the awful truth. Such a pitiful tale could only have worked in her favour, after all. But I think she knew that there was no need. That story was too valuable to be given up so easily, when she still had so much more suffering in store for her father, and for Rose.

I could have told the police myself, confessed to them about Hannah's real mother, how she died, how Rose and Oliver and I were involved in it all, but what good would that have done? My child was dead. I thought of the two Lawson boys, so young still, and I didn't think I could be responsible for destroying their lives too. I was drowning in grief, only capable of wishing with all my heart that I'd died with Doug and Toby that night, as I'm sure Hannah knew. I wish I had died too.

29

Suffolk, 2017

As Rose described the fire and Hannah's trial, Clara felt cold waves of panic wash over her. *This* was the person who had hold of Luke? This *murderer*, this madwoman? And Rose, Oliver – they had known it all along? She stared at them, anger and shock mingling with her despair.

It was Tom who spoke first. 'How old was he, the boy?' he asked, his voice scarcely louder than a whisper.

Rose hung her head. 'Ten. Toby was ten years old.'

'Jesus! Oh Jesus Christ!' He got up and paced the room, coming to a halt in front of his father. 'She's killed before, what's to stop her doing it again? What's to stop her from murdering Luke too?'

Oliver looked up at his son imploringly. 'If she was

going to kill Luke she would have done so by now, not continued to send pictures and taunt us like this. She knows if she kills him there's nothing to stop us going to the police. It wouldn't be in her best interests; she wants us to suffer for as long as possible. It's a game to her, that's all. It's our punishment.'

As Clara listened to Oliver talk, she remembered how frequently Hannah had enquired after her father and Rose's wellbeing during their meetings, how avidly she listened when Clara described their suffering. Her desire to see Clara wasn't just to keep abreast of the police search; it was an opportunity to revel in the havoc she had caused.

Rose got to her feet then and, approaching her son, put her hand on his arm. 'Tom, you have to understand that Hannah has never given us a straight answer about Emily's whereabouts. Sometimes she says she knows, other times she denies it. She might have some information, no matter how small, that could let us know what happened to her. If the police catch Hannah before us, she'll never tell us. She would go to prison and keep quiet just to spite us. At least this way, if we do what she wants, there's still a chance she could tell us something, anything, that might help us find Emily.'

'Christ!' Tom shook off his mother's hand. 'What the fuck are we going to do, then? How are we going to find Luke?'

There was silence, and then Clara said, 'She doesn't

314

know that I know who she really is, yet. She thinks I still believe she's Emily.'

Tom looked at her. 'That's true.'

'So if I arranged to meet her again, one of us could follow her, to see where she goes.'

Mac shook his head. 'It's too risky, she knows what we all look like, even me, she'd spot us a mile away.'

'Then who?' said Tom.

The following morning, Tom, Mac and Clara sat in a café in Greenwich, nervously looking at the door. 'Do you think she's going to come?' asked Mac.

Clara nodded. 'She wouldn't let me down.'

A moment later, a tall, auburn-haired woman with a baby strapped to her chest walked through the door.

It took nearly half an hour to bring Zoe up to speed. When they'd finished, she looked at them, speechless with shock. 'Holy fuck,' she said at last, shaking her head. She looked at Clara. 'Why didn't you tell me this was going on?'

Clara took hold of her hand. 'I'm sorry. But will you do it? I wouldn't ask if we weren't absolutely desperate. We just need you to follow her as far as you can.'

'If there's any sign of anything dodgy, if you feel like she's spotted you, or you feel nervous in any way, turn straight around and come home,' said Mac.

'Only follow her as far as you feel comfortable,' Tom added. 'If she leads you somewhere isolated, don't go any further.'

Zoe looked from one to the other of their tense faces, then down at a fast-asleep Oscar. Finally she looked up and, meeting Clara's gaze, said, 'Of course I'll do it.'

Clara closed her eyes. 'Are you sure? Are you absolutely sure?'

Zoe gave a wry smile. 'Are you kidding? A chance to leave Oscar with Adam and go and do something more exciting than puree carrots? Hell yeah.'

While Mac and Tom breathed a sigh of relief, Clara chewed her thumbnail unhappily. She felt a fresh surge of anger towards Rose and Oliver. This was their mess, their doing, yet they'd jumped at the chance to send a young woman they didn't know, a young mother, into danger to help clear it up. 'What if it goes wrong?' she asked.

'Like you said, Hannah doesn't know me; she doesn't know what I look like. I'll keep way back. Listen, Clara, I'm going to do this, you'd do the same for me. I'm not stupid, if I start getting a bad vibe, I'll back the fuck off. But let's give it a try, yeah? Let me help you find Luke.'

'And if she lives out of London? Miles away? What if it's a wild goose chase?' said Mac, worriedly.

'As soon as it looks like she's heading out of town, I'll abort mission, OK?' Zoe replied. 'Seriously, guys, it'll be fine.'

Later that day, as Clara sat with Tom and Mac, she sent the message to Hannah: *Can we meet?*

316

The reply came quickly: *Of course. Do you have any news?*

'What shall I say?' she asked the others.

Tom thought about it. 'We need to give her a reason to meet us. We can't afford for her to drop contact now.'

Clara gave it some thought, then typed, *There's been an interesting development that I want to talk over with you.'* And she pressed Send.

For the next hour or so they waited for a reply. 'Maybe she's on to us,' Clara said nervously to Tom. 'Your mum said that she somehow seems able to track their every move. What if she's twigged that I know she's not Emily?' She sighed in frustration. 'Where the fuck is she?' she muttered.

Finally, another message came through: *Tomorrow? Same bar as last time?*

Sure, Clara wrote, feeling a rush of relief. *I'll see you there at six.*

She put her phone down and looked at first Tom and then Mac. 'Looks like we're on.'

30

London, 2017

Clara felt as though a balloon was slowly expanding inside her chest. Whenever she checked her watch, time seemed to have stood still, though it seemed hours since last she'd looked. Rose and Oliver had driven down from Suffolk and the five of them were now sitting around Mac's kitchen table, restlessly waiting for the moment when Clara would leave to meet Hannah. 'We're coming with you,' Rose announced. 'After Zoe follows her and finds out where Hannah lives, I mean. We're going to come with you to confront her.'

Tom shook his head. 'No, you and Dad should stay here.'

'We're coming,' Oliver told him grimly. 'It's us she's doing this for. We need to try and reason with her.'

'And I need to know for certain if she knows where Emily is,' Rose added. 'I need to look Hannah in the eye and ask her what happened to my daughter.'

Clara felt the tightening in her chest intensify. She couldn't stop thinking about Doug and Toby. If Hannah was capable of killing them, what else might she do? Was Luke even still alive? She checked her watch again: it was only quarter to four.

The minutes passed so tensely that despite her fear, Clara was almost relieved when it was finally time for her to leave. 'Remember,' Tom said as they all anxiously gathered around her in the hall, 'if you think she's on to you, just make your excuses and leave. We've got Zoe's number, we'll tell her to back off too.'

She nodded and took a deep breath, looking from one to the other of their anxious faces. 'Don't worry,' she said, sounding far more confident than she felt. 'I'll be fine.'

The journey from Highbury to Old Street seemed to take forever, her nerves winding tighter and tighter as the Tube rattled through the black tunnels. By the time she reached East London she felt sick with fear. She emerged on to the street to find that a cool wind had picked up, sending scraps of litter dancing across the pavement as she walked. At last she spied Great Eastern Street ahead of her and as she turned into it her mobile buzzed, causing her to almost leap out of her skin. It was a text from Zoe: *I'm at the pub a*

*little way down from The Octopus. I'll call you as
soon as I can afterwards.*

And then Clara was at the bar. To her relief there
was no sign of Hannah yet, and she took a seat at the
same table as before. There was the same quiet, early
evening buzz in the air and the same barman smiling at
her from behind the bar. She both longed for and dreaded
Hannah's arrival. Would she be able to tell, just by
looking at her, what was going on? Fear and adrenalin
surged through her. Right at that moment a shadow fell
across the table.

'Clara?' Hannah was dressed as usual in dark jeans
and a hoodie. She tucked her hair behind her ear in a
familiar nervous gesture that had once seemed endearing,
but now seemed entirely staged, her smile oozing warmth
and gentleness. It was utterly chilling how convincing
she was.

Clara forced herself to return her smile, digging her
fingernails into the palm of her hand, endeavouring to
keep her voice steady as she said, 'Hi, Emily, it's good
to see you, how are you?'

'I'm OK.' Hannah sat down and they stared at each
other for a beat or two before she said, concern
furrowing her brow, 'God, you look awful, are you all
right?'

'No, I'm not,' Clara said quietly. 'Emily, after we last
met my flat was set on fire. Luke's friend Mac was
attacked, and his camera stolen. I wanted to talk it over
with you, I know how concerned you are about how

the search is going. I thought I should let you know. To be honest, I'm still really shaken.'

Hannah leant forward, her eyes wide with shock. 'Oh my goodness, Clara, that's terrible. You poor, poor thing, I'm so sorry. Were you hurt? Are you OK?'

Clara nodded. 'I'm fine, and so is Mac, but yes, it was awful.' She took a sip of her drink, an excuse to look away from Hannah's intense gaze. This was the single most difficult thing she had ever had to do.

Hannah shook her head. 'I don't know what to say. How are my mum and dad? This must have really rattled them.'

'About as well as you'd expect,' Clara replied. She hesitated, 'Oliver, especially, is in a bad way. I'm worried about him, I mean, he's not a young man . . .'

It was almost imperceptible, the flicker of pleasure in Hannah's eyes, but it was definitely there. 'And the police?' she asked. 'They have no new leads?'

'No, nothing. It's incredibly frustrating,' Clara sighed. 'Sometimes I think they'll never catch this person, whoever they are.'

Hannah nodded sadly. 'We mustn't give up hope,' she said. 'They'll find Luke, I'm sure they will.'

After a pause, Clara said, 'It's so good to talk to you, I feel like I'm losing my mind with worry. Having you to talk things over with . . . I don't know, it makes it easier somehow.'

Hannah smiled her sympathy. 'I'll do whatever I can to help.'

They lapsed into silence, watching the bar slowly fill up. Clara made herself smile shyly. 'It was so lovely hearing you talk about your childhood with Luke the other day,' she said. 'I don't know why, but I found it comforting, somehow, hearing about what he was like as a little boy.'

At this Hannah smiled warmly and with such apparent sincerity that Clara could only stare at her in horrified fascination. 'Oh, he was such a great kid!' she said. 'So funny, you know? Such a big personality. We used to have such good times together, all of us.' Her eyes grew wistful. 'My parents were the best. We kids always felt so loved and wanted, it was wonderful.'

As she listened, Clara felt icy fingers walk up and down her spine. It was almost as though Hannah had persuaded herself she really *was* Emily, adored child of Oliver and Rose. She remembered how Rose had said that Hannah would skip school to spy on them all, watching their every move, like a kid with its nose pressed up against a sweetshop window. A chilling thought struck her: if Hannah's vendetta was partly fuelled by jealousy, or a sense of injustice that Emily was treated like a beloved daughter while she herself had been cast out, if it was Emily's place in the family that she coveted, would it have been necessary for her to get rid of Luke's sister entirely? Nobody had seen Emily for twenty years. As she listened to Hannah talk, unease moved inside her like cold water.

They discussed the police search next, Hannah asking

question after question for all the world as though she didn't already know the answers. Just when Clara thought she would crumble under the strain of it all, Hannah glanced at her watch. 'I must go,' she said. 'But I'm so glad I've been able to talk to you.' Her eyes met Clara's. 'I hope you know that you're not alone in this. If ever I can help, in any small way, I want you to know I'm here for you.'

'Thank you,' Clara said gravely, relief overwhelming her as they both got to their feet. On the street, Hannah took Clara's hands in hers, exactly as she had the time before. It was all she could do not to snatch them away.

'Keep strong,' Hannah said, looking deep into her eyes. Now that they were standing so close to each other, Clara felt her fear return two-fold as she forced herself to meet Hannah's gaze. Something must have shown in her face because Hannah tilted her head, her eyes quizzical. 'Are you OK?' she said.

'I—' Clara stammered.

'What, Clara? What is it?'

As Hannah's hands tightened on hers, she had the overwhelming sense of suffocation, an instinctive compulsion to run. Her mouth dried. 'Nothing,' she whispered, 'nothing at all.'

Hannah nodded. 'This must all be so hard on you.' She smiled compassionately again and the moment stretched until, all at once, she released Clara's hands, pulled her hood up around her face and with a final, brief look of sympathy she turned and left, leaving Clara standing alone, her heart pounding, as she watched her walk off down the street.

Relief surged through her at the knowledge that her part was over, at least for now. But when she looked across the street and saw Zoe emerge from the pub opposite then set off slowly after Hannah, Clara's fear returned. What the hell was she doing, letting Zoe get caught up in this? She wanted to run after her and drag her friend back, but, terrified that Hannah would turn and see her, she made herself set off up the street the way she'd come. She'd barely reached the corner, however, when anxiety got the better of her and she stopped and turned, hoping to catch one last glimpse of Zoe before she disappeared from view. And then she gasped. Because there Hannah was. Not walking away from her as she'd expected, but standing stock-still not far from where they'd parted, her eyes fastened upon her.

Clara felt a jolt of shock. Unable to help herself, she glanced across the road, seeking out Zoe and, sure enough, she spotted her friend standing by a bus stop a few yards further on, pretending to look at her phone. Panicked, she looked back at Hannah. Had she seen her eyes dart across the road? Had she given Zoe away? What on earth was Hannah doing, anyway? Uncertainly she raised her hand to wave, shooting her a questioning smile. Hannah's face remained expressionless for a beat or two, then abruptly she nodded and turned, continuing on her way.

Across the road, Zoe met Clara's frightened gaze and shrugged. Clara scrabbled for her phone. 'Zoe,' she said when her friend picked up. 'She's on to us, I'm sure of it. Let's give up, it's too dangerous. Don't follow her, I'm sure she knows what's going on.'

But even as she replied Zoe turned and continued following Hannah down the street. 'No way, I'm not giving up now. Fuck knows what all that was about, but I'm certain she didn't look at me once. I'm going to keep following her. I'll speak to you soon.' And with that, she hung up.

Swearing loudly, Clara watched as they both disappeared from sight. Frantically she dialled Mac's number.

He picked up on the first ring. 'Clara? Thank God. Are you OK? Hold on, I'll put you on speaker.'

Quickly she told them what had happened. 'I don't know what to do! Zoe thinks Hannah didn't see her, but what the fuck was she doing? Why was she staring at me like that? The expression on her face was just – oh God, I'm really worried, I've got a bad feeling about this. I think you should call Zoe, Mac, and tell her to back off, I—'

But Rose's voice cut through her garbled words. 'No! Don't call it off! Please, Clara. Please let Zoe find out where she lives.'

She closed her eyes. The desperation in Rose's voice was tangible. She heard Tom speak next. 'Mum's right,' he said. 'It's our only chance.'

She released a long, pent-up breath. 'OK,' she said

reluctantly. 'OK. I'm on my way back now. I'll see you soon.'

When she returned to Mac's flat, the air was thick with tension as she took a seat amongst them in the kitchen, four pairs of eyes fastened on her face as she described to them what had happened, recounting every single word and gesture, careful not to leave anything out, beginning from the moment Hannah appeared in front of her and ending with the strange shock of turning to find her standing motionless in the street, watching her.

When she'd finished, an anxious silence hung in the air and they sat staring at Clara's phone, which she'd placed on the centre of the table, waiting for Zoe's call. 'Christ, when will she ring?' Clara asked shakily.

'Surely she should have phoned by now?' Rose asked.

'Not necessarily,' said Mac. He looked at Clara and tried to give her a reassuring smile, adding, 'I'm sure it'll be soon.'

It was half past eight – an hour and a half since Clara had left Zoe to follow Hannah – when the phone eventually rang. Clara leapt on it, putting it on speaker. 'Zo?' she said. 'Oh thank God, are you OK?'

'Yes, it's me,' she said, her voice breathless and exhilarated above the noise of traffic in the background. 'I'm fine. I'm on my way back now.'

Clara closed her eyes, relief washing over her. 'What happened? Where did you follow her to?'

'To her flat, I think. At least I assume it's where she

lives. Acton, to be exact, north-west London. I followed her to Liverpool Street Tube, then got on the Central Line. I was about to give up, because by the time we got there the carriage was practically empty. But I don't think she had a clue I was following her. She didn't look at me once. She got off at Acton and the streets there were fairly busy. Luckily she lives not too far from the station and there was a noisy gang of drunk lads who walked between us almost the whole way, so I think I was safe.'

Tom cleared his throat and, raising his voice, asked, 'What does her place look like?'

'Total dump. Massive old Victorian building, about five floors, a flat on each one, I'd guess. She let herself in then a light went on in a ground-floor window, so I'm pretty sure that's hers. I went around the back of the building and there's this sort of parking area, and a back door, too, which again I think must be hers. I've got the address for you, I'll text it.'

When Clara hung up they all stared at each other wide-eyed. 'Fuck,' said Tom.

'So what do we do now?' asked Mac, nervously.

'We wait,' said Oliver. 'We wait until the middle of the night, when she's least expecting us, and then we go round there.'

'But then what?' said Tom. 'She's not just going to answer the door and welcome us in, is she?'

'No,' said Clara quietly. 'No, she's not.'

31

London, 2017

It was 2 a.m. when they set off for Acton, the five of
them in Tom's car. Clara looked out at the dark, mostly
empty suburban streets. She couldn't seem to stop shivering, despite the fact that Tom had turned the heating
up full. In the trapped tension of the car they listened
to the satnav's incongruously dulcet tones guiding them
ever nearer to whatever it was that was waiting for them
at their journey's end.

She put her cold hands in her jacket pockets and,
feeling something sharp, withdrew her fingers with a
start. Before they left, Mac had pulled Tom and her
aside. 'I think you should take these,' he'd said, and
when she looked down she'd seen two small kitchen
knives in his hand.

She'd backed away. 'No! Are you crazy? I don't—'

But Mac had pleaded with her. 'We don't know what she's going to do when we get there. She's crazy, dangerous. Hide it in your pocket. Please, Clara, just in case, OK?'

She'd glanced at Tom and when he'd shrugged and taken one, she'd reluctantly done the same.

'You have reached your destination,' the satnav informed them primly when they eventually turned into a wide street lined with enormous detached houses. Clara looked out at the silent buildings as their car crept slowly along, scanning each door for its number.

'Number 82 must be up there, on the corner,' Tom said, steering the car into a space and cutting the engine. Nobody moved.

It must have been quite a wealthy area once, Clara thought. Each of the grim, hulking Victorian buildings housing but a single family and their servants. Now, however, it had a decidedly uncared-for air, every house divided into many flats or bedsits, the paintwork peeling, the front gardens overgrown, a sense of transience and decay. Somewhere further down the street a loud party was in full swing; drunken shouts mingling with music pounding from some unseen window. Here though, all was quiet and still.

'Well then,' Clara said, glancing at the others uncertainly.

Number 82 was even shabbier than the rest, situated on the corner of the street, its front garden strewn with litter, six bells on the door. From somewhere further down the road a door slammed, making Clara jump, footsteps pounding on tarmac accompanied by low laughter that quickly disappeared into the silence once more. A lone car swept past. 'Let's check around the back first,' Tom murmured.

Just as Zoe had said, they rounded the corner to find a small car park, empty but for a beaten-up Renault and a moped missing its front wheel. Clara nodded towards the house's back door, a pile of over-spilling bin liners outside it. 'That must be the door Zoe was talking about,' she whispered. 'Do you think it really does lead to Hannah's flat?' She shivered at the thought that they were so close.

They all glanced at each other. 'Listen,' Mac said. 'I think I should stay out here, just in case. I can stop her if she tries to run out this way, and call the police if I need to . . .'

Tom nodded and looked at Rose. 'You stay here, too,' he said.

'Absolutely not,' she replied. 'I've come this far. I want to see her, speak to her. I need to do this, Tom.'

For a moment he looked as though he would argue but eventually he shrugged and nodded. 'Let's go then,' he said. The four of them went back to the front of the building, leaving Mac behind. As they left, Clara turned and gave him a final wave.

It was 2.40 a.m. At the front door they paused on the bottom step. Every window was in darkness, the ones on the ground floor shielded by heavy curtains. They glanced at each other nervously, then stared at the line of bells, most of them with indecipherable labels beneath peeling Sellotape, 'Flat A' written in smudged black ink on the first.

In a sudden decisive movement, Tom climbed the steps and pressed his finger on the top floor flat's bell. They held their breath. When there was no response, his hand moved to hover over the next one but before he could press it, the intercom clicked and crackled. 'Who the fuck is this?' a deep male voice growled.

'Sorry, mate,' Tom said, 'I think I—'

'Fuck off or I'll call the police.' There was a click then the intercom was silent once more.

'Let me try.' Clara pressed the next bell and they all waited. No answer. Then the one below. A crackle, then a sleepy, female voice with a Jamaican accent, 'Yeah, hello?'

'I'm sorry,' Clara said, 'But I'm afraid I've locked myself out, I live on the ground floor and I forgot my key. I'm really sorry, could you—'

The woman kissed her teeth. 'Fuck's sake.' The door buzzed. They were in.

In the communal hallway they looked at each other with wide eyes. It was horrible; the carpet threadbare and stained, piles of takeaway delivery leaflets and unclaimed post littering the floor, the walls dirty and scrawled with graffiti, mould creeping over the dirty paintwork, a musty, sour smell in the air. And at the far end a filthy, battered-looking door. 'That must be it,' Tom whispered.

Clara turned to the others. She swallowed hard. 'So we do this like we planned?' she said. 'You all need to stand back out of sight.' Wordlessly they nodded, flattening themselves against the wall.

Fear dragged its fingernails down Clara's spine as she approached the door and knocked. Seconds dripped by in absolute silence. She brought her fist up and knocked again, harder this time. She strained her ears to listen and thought she heard the faintest sound from within. 'Hannah,' she said, her voice emerging from her lips as a croak. She cleared her throat and forced herself to speak louder. 'Hannah, it's Clara.'

There was silence, but Clara felt her there, listening. Her voice shook as she said, 'I'm alone. But I have my phone ready to call the police. I just want to talk to you.'

And then Hannah's voice loud through the door: 'Leave now, or I'll kill him. Get the fuck away from here.'

Clara shrank back, her heart pounding. When they had discussed this in Mac's kitchen, gone over and over how they could get Hannah to open her door, the plan they'd come up with had seemed feasible. But here, now, with Hannah only inches away, it felt absurd, impossible, like using a penknife to fell a tree. And if it didn't work, what then? What would happen to Luke? They must have been crazy to take such a risk. She took a deep breath. 'Hannah,' she said. 'I know everything. I know what happened to your mother. I know how she really died.'

Again there was silence. Clara could feel the hard thump of her heart in her throat. And then Hannah spoke. 'You're lying,' but there it was, Clara was sure: the faintest ghost of uncertainty.

'No,' she said. 'No, I'm not. Let me in. Let me in to see Luke and I'll tell you what happened to Nadia. Rose told me the truth, Hannah. She told me how your mother really died that night.' The only sound now was her own frightened, panting breath. 'Hannah,' she said again, 'open the door.'

Nothing, only a thick, impossible silence. 'Your mother talked about you, before she died,' Clara told her. 'She said something to Rose that I think you'll want to hear. Let me in, Hannah. I'm here alone. I just want to see Luke.' And then, suddenly, there it was: the sound of a lock being turned. Clara briefly closed her eyes, and when she opened them again there Hannah stood. They stared at each other for barely a moment before Tom pushed past Clara with such violence it sent her stumbling and he shoved Hannah hard back into the flat as she let out a cry of surprise and rage.

'You fucking cunts,' Hannah spat before Tom gripped her by the throat and slammed her head against the wall.

'Where's my brother?' he shouted. 'Where's Luke?' He propelled her now into the flat, the others on his

333

heels. Clara felt around for a light switch, and the five of them flinched at the sudden harsh cold brightness, blinking dazedly as they looked around themselves. The flat was small and dismal, in a similar state to the entrance hall with an added stench of decades' worth of stale cigarette smoke. Off the narrow hallway was a living room, a tiny kitchen and three more rooms, each with their doors closed. 'Luke?' Tom shouted. 'Luke, are you here?'

A loud thump came from the furthest room and Clara darted towards it. 'In here!' she cried, but when she tried the handle she found that it was locked. The thumping continued. She turned to Hannah. 'Open it! Where are the keys?'

When Hannah didn't move, Oliver went to the door and tried the handle, putting his weight against it, but it wouldn't budge. He turned back to Hannah. 'Give us the key,' he said.

Her face stretched into a sneer. 'Fuck you.'

'Enough, Hannah!' Oliver shouted. 'Enough! It's over. Open the door.'

'No, it's not over,' she said. 'It will never be over.'

With a cry of frustration Clara went to one of the other doors and, finding it unlocked, switched on the light to find a bedroom with a mattress on the floor, a small wooden cabinet by its side, on top of which was a key. She snatched it up and went back to the locked door. Inserting the key with shaking hands she turned it and pushed the door open. The room was in darkness

334

but when she found the switch she cried out in horror. There was Luke, lying on the bed, gagged and bound with thick electrical tape, his eyes bulging at her as he let out a desperate, muffled cry.

Clara stood frozen as Rose ran past her. Throwing her arms around her son she cried, 'Oh my darling, my darling boy,' and then Oliver was there too, kneeling down and cutting Luke free with one of Mac's knives before he too took his son in his arms.

Luke coughed and spluttered when his gag was removed, crying out with desperate relief. He looked dreadful: thin and bruised, with blood all over his T-shirt, his eyes hollow in his pale drawn face, his arms covered in knife wounds, some of them large and weeping. When Luke looked past his parents to where she stood he said her name with such relief and longing that she jolted out of her paralysis and went to him, holding his thin body to her tightly, all the tension and confusion and fear of the past weeks surging out of her in one loud sob.

Finally she felt him stiffen in her arms and she turned to follow his gaze to where Hannah now stood by the door, her arms still held tightly behind her back by Tom, her eyes bright, almost febrile with excitement. Luke rose unsteadily to his feet and went to her, crossing the room in a burst of energy and fury. 'You fucking crazy bitch,' he shouted, his face red with rage, 'you fucking evil cunt!'

Hannah laughed. 'Temper temper, Luke.'

'I'll kill you, I'll fucking kill you!'

'Oh for God's sake, stop whining,' Hannah said. 'I fed you, didn't I? Sometimes?' She raised her eyebrows. 'Even took you to the potty when you needed it.'

Clara saw Luke's face burn with humiliation. And then she did something she'd never done before. She went over to where Hannah was standing and she hit her full in the face, so hard that the sound rang out into the room, her palm smarting with the force.

Hannah gasped, her eyes flashing briefly with anger before she recovered and, setting her face in a sneer, said, 'Well, look who's found a pair of balls at last.'

Clara looked at her in disgust. 'What now?' she asked. 'You'll go to prison for this! What was the point?'

'What was the point?' Hannah asked. '*This*.' She gestured towards Rose and Oliver, broken and desperate before her. 'This was the point.'

'You said you'd leave us alone,' Oliver said. 'We paid you thousands to stay away from Tom, to stay away from all of us. You said that would be the end of it!'

'Yeah, well. That was until I saw Luke again.'

'Saw him where?' asked Tom.

She shrugged belligerently. 'I'd just come out of rehab, some bullshit thing the courts sent me on last time I got arrested, and I was begging outside Leicester Square station. There he was, like a gift. I recognized him instantly.' Her face lit up as though she was revisiting a favourite memory. 'So I followed him to work, and later I followed him home, and it all came back to me.'

She glanced at Oliver. 'What you did, how you gave me away. There I was, scrabbling about for money, fucking strangers to get by, no place to live, and I thought, I wonder how my dear old dad's doing.'

She paused, fixing Oliver in her gaze. 'I got into the habit of keeping tabs on him, and I discovered something.' She glanced at Clara and laughed. 'Turned out lovely Luke isn't such a nice boy after all, is he? Turned out he was fucking the office slapper. And I thought, wow, the old apple doesn't fall far from the tree, does it?' She turned her hard gaze on Oliver again. 'I saw that he was just like you, pretending he was such a decent, stand-up guy while all the time he was a disgusting, sleazy bastard. A dirty fucking user.' She smiled. 'Like father, like son.'

There was absolute silence. All the amusement drained from Hannah's face as she continued to stare at her father. 'And that really fucked me off,' she said softly. 'Brought it all back. So I started sending him the emails, messing with him, showing I was watching him, that I knew what sort of man he was, and after a while I realized I could kill three birds with one stone: give Luke what he deserved, get some more money out of you, *Daddy,* but most of all,' she turned her gaze on Rose now, and the expression on her face, the icy hatred in her eyes, made Clara shudder. 'Most of all, I'd give you, you murdering bitch, a taste of your own medicine.'

Rose paled. 'What are you talking about?'

337

'I might have left you alone for a few years, but that doesn't mean I ever forgot what you did. You killed my mother, you took her from me – why shouldn't I take something from you? Why shouldn't Luke die, it's only what you deserved.'

'You were going to kill him,' Clara whispered, the cold realization seeping into her, how close they'd been to losing him.

Before Hannah could reply, Rose cried, 'I had nothing to do with your mother's death! She jumped!'

'Bullshit.' Hannah's face was full of loathing. 'She wouldn't have left me. She wouldn't. I was all she had. You were the last person to see her alive. You killed her.'

Rose stepped towards her. 'Listen to me! Your mother was angry, she was out of control! She was extremely ill and she jumped.'

'I don't believe you.'

'Where's my daughter?' Rose asked desperately. 'Do you know where she is, what happened to her? Tell me where Emily is, for God's sake, tell me!'

'She's dead,' was the triumphant reply. 'That's right! She died the same way my mother did, booted into the fucking sea.'

All the colour and light drained from Rose's face. 'No . . .' she shook her head. 'No . . . I don't believe you. You're lying, I know you are.'

Hannah laughed. 'I said I'd meet her up on the cliffs at Dunwich. Told her I wanted to go and remember my mother.' She smiled mockingly. 'She thought she was so noble, going there with me, standing by the poor abandoned sister she never knew she had, cutting off her parents and striking out on her own to prove a point. My God, she was full of it – such a tedious sanctimonious bitch! I was doing the world a favour, to be honest. But anyway, now you know. Beautiful, isn't it?' She looked at Rose and Oliver. 'Your daughter and my mother had the same resting place. Kind of poetic, don't you think?'

Rose stared at her in horror. 'No,' she whispered. 'It's not true.'

Oliver, who until then had been watching in stunned silence, suddenly cried, 'There was no body! If you were telling the truth, her body would have washed up sooner or later.'

Rose looked round at him hopefully. 'Yes,' she said. 'Yes, that's right. There was no body. There would have been, wouldn't there? There would have been a body!'

Hannah laughed. 'Yeah well, maybe there's a little pile of Emily bones on a faraway beach somewhere. Fuck knows, who cares?'

'I don't believe you!' Rose shouted again. 'You're lying. There would have been a body. There would have!'

Hannah stared at her thoughtfully. 'She cried out for you, you know. Just as she fell, just as she realized she was going to die. She cried out for her mummy, like a baby. Did I cry, Rose, when you killed my mother? Did I cry too?'

Oliver's face was full of hatred and despair. 'She jumped. Your mother jumped!' He broke down in tears then, doubled over in pain, as Tom pulled out his phone and called the police.

32

The Lake District, 2017

I live in a quiet village, more a hamlet really, not far from Windermere. A remote and peaceful place, somewhere my past could not follow me, or so I thought. I moved here from Cambridgeshire after Doug and Toby died to be near my elderly parents, and when they died too, I stayed. I've built a simple, solitary life for myself, just me and my little dog Rufus, and if the other inhabitants of this tiny community know my story, if they remember the grim details of my murdered family from the newspapers before I came to live amidst them, they've kept it to themselves, and for that I've been grateful.

But now Hannah's face is once more front-page news, her trial a media circus, a tabloid editor's dream. It has everything, after all: two beautiful teenage girls, an affluent successful family torn apart by adultery, kidnap, suicide and murder – and not one of us who played a part in the whole awful business has escaped without blame. Each of our actions another scrutinized detail in the story that has had the nation gripped these past six weeks.

Who knows what the outcome will be? Hannah will almost certainly be sent back to prison – there'll be no wriggling her way out of this one. How she kidnapped Luke, how she confessed to Emily's murder – though she's denying that now, of course. But what of the rest of us? Oliver's affair with Nadia, her death, the abduction of baby Lana. Such a tangled, complicated web.

It's become clear that Hannah's allegations about her mother's murder can't be substantiated. After all, who would believe the desperate rantings of a proven liar, killer and kidnapper, over someone like Rose, who's presented herself so well throughout this trial? A retired surgeon in her late sixties now, responsible for saving the lives of countless children, years of charity work to her name, beloved by her colleagues and community. A dignified, gentle soul. Yes, there's a lot of public sympathy for Rose, a feeling that she's suffered enough. That will please her, I'm sure – it always was so important for her to be liked.

Oliver hasn't come out of it quite so well. Because there were others, apparently, and plenty of them, all ex-students of his, before, during and even long after his affair with Nadia, most of whom have come out of the woodwork telling their stories about how they too were victims of 'Cheating sex-pest prof', providing the perfect combination of titillation and schadenfreude the British public so enjoy.

As for my part in it all, my involvement in baby Lana's story, the general feeling is I'll get off lightly. I too have suffered enough will be the view: my murdered husband, my murdered child. Yet I should be punished, I want to be. I have carried the guilt for decades for what I did to Nadia's grieving family. Her parents died without ever knowing the truth and for that I think I should pay.

Still, by hook or by crook, the mess will be made sense of, people will be punished while others will go free, the feeding frenzy will eventually die away until someone else's tragedy replaces it. Of course, what almost nobody knows, what they will never know, is what Rose confessed to me the night of Nadia's death, the night they brought little Lana to our door. They don't know that when Doug took Oliver to the kitchen to make up the bottle of formula, Rose turned to me, her eyes wide with panic.

'Beth,' she said, 'Beth, I have to tell you something.'

I looked at her stricken face in surprise. 'What's the matter? What is it, Rose?'

And that's when she told me. 'I pushed her, Beth,' she whispered. 'I pushed her.'

I stared at her in shock.

'I arranged to meet her, I wanted to explain to her that she needed to stop, that she'd never have Oliver, that he was my husband and she had to stop her harassment. But she was so arrogant, so awful, taunting me, goading me, telling me how Oliver had pursued her, that he . . . that he slept with lots of his students. It was lies, all lies! I lost my head, I don't know what happened, I just wanted her to stop. To stop talking, stop ruining everything. I thought of my darling little daughter and our lovely life and this girl, this silly, awful girl, was laughing at me, laughing at all of us, telling me I had no idea, that I was deluded, that everyone at the university knew what my husband was really like.'

'Rose,' was all I could say. 'Oh God no, Rose.' I didn't want to hear any more, I wanted her to stop, to block my ears from hearing it.

'I pushed her. Oh, Beth. I pushed her. I wanted her to die, just for a moment, I wanted it. Even as she fell . . . for a second I was glad.' She looked at me, her eyes full of horror. 'Oh, Beth, what has happened . . . what has happened to me? What am I going to do?'

I could hear Doug and Oliver talking in the kitchen. I had only seconds to decide. 'Shush,' I said. 'Shush, Rose. Stop and let me think.' She watched me anxiously, her eyes never leaving my face. 'Rose,' I said at last, 'you must never tell another soul about this. No one, not ever. Does Oliver know?'

She shook her head. 'You're the only person I've told.'

'OK. Good.' I could hear the others, about to come back in. 'She jumped, Rose,' I said. 'OK? It wasn't your fault.'

344

She nodded, her frightened eyes wide. 'Yes.'

'It'll be our secret, no one ever has to find out.'

'You'll never tell anyone? Do you promise?'

'I promise.'

It's a detail I've always carefully omitted over the years, when I've told myself the story of how Hannah came into our lives. Because it casts a rather different light on things, doesn't it? I wanted Lana for myself, you see. I knew it from the moment Rose appeared on my doorstep that night. If Doug had known the truth behind Nadia's death, he would have gone to the police, I have no doubt about that. So when I promised Rose I would keep her secret, it was myself I was thinking of, deep down. I can't pretend otherwise any more, no matter how hard I've tried to wipe it from my memory. It was so I could keep Lana for myself. Does that make me as bad as Rose? Yes, actually, I rather think it does.

And so, of course, I did keep the promise I made to Rose that night. I didn't tell another soul. In fact, neither of us spoke of it again, not even the day Hannah overheard us talking in the kitchen. All she heard was Rose saying she'd been the last person to see Nadia alive, that everyone would think she'd killed her, and Hannah, not wanting to believe her mother would abandon her by choice, put two and two together herself. So for years I kept Rose's secret – until, that is, the day that Emily found me.

It was seven years after the fire, seven years since Hannah told Emily that she was her sister, and what her father had done. Seven years since the day she disappeared. I don't know how she found me here in such a remote spot – my old neighbours, I suppose, or perhaps the clinic where I worked passed on my new address. She knocked on the door one afternoon out of the blue. I remember my stomach dropped like a stone to see her standing there – I recognized her immediately from the day I'd followed Hannah to Suffolk, when she was pretending to be 'Becky'. 'Emily,' I said. 'You're Emily Lawson, aren't you? What are you doing here?' It was as though a ghost had appeared on my doorstep. Deep down I had always believed that, like Doug and Toby, she was dead too, another of Hannah's victims.

'May I come in?' she asked. She had Rose's clear blue eyes, Oliver's thick dark hair, such a very pretty girl – or woman, I should say; she was twenty-five years old by then.

She said she knew who I was, that I was the woman who'd brought Hannah up, the woman whose husband and son Hannah had murdered. She told me she was living in France now, scraping by as a waitress in a hotel.

Of course I invited her in, and we sat together in my kitchen. 'Do your parents know where you are?' I asked. I had seen Rose briefly after the fire, before I moved up here, so I knew how desperate she was to find her daughter still, though I hadn't spoken to her since, not once in seven years.

Emily hesitated, and looked down at her hands. 'No,' she said eventually. 'I haven't spoken to them since I left.'

346

'Aren't you going to see them? Aren't you going to tell them where you are? That you're OK?'

She shook her head, her eyes filling with tears. 'I miss them all so much,' she said. 'But I felt I couldn't go back, not after what my father did. I can't go back and pretend it never happened, that I don't know about Hannah, that I don't know how he gave away his own baby. I couldn't live with it, keeping their awful secret for them, letting my brothers grow up not knowing they had a half-sister somewhere.'

I nodded. 'But why are you here, Emily? Why have you come to see me after all this time?'

'Because . . .' she glanced down and, following her eyes to the curve of her belly, the penny dropped. 'You're pregnant,' I said.

She gazed at me with those beautiful blue eyes. 'I was going to stay away. But it doesn't feel right, now. I want my family to know I have a child.' She began to cry.

'Then go to them,' I said.

'I want the truth, Beth,' she replied. 'I have to know.'

'Know what?' I asked, playing for time, because I suddenly knew what she was going to ask me.

She hesitated, then she looked me full in the face and said, 'Hannah told me that my mother pushed Nadia. That she murdered her. Is it true?'

'Murdered her?' I echoed. 'Why do you think that?'

'Hannah told me. She was so certain. So absolutely convinced of it. I need to know if it's true, if my mother really did it. Because if she is capable of such a vile thing, then I know I can never go back, I never want to see her again.'

I stared back at her. And I still don't know what made me say it, only that I was still overwhelmed with resentment and pain. I'd lost my family, and I admit I did blame Rose. It was all her fault that Toby and Doug were dead. Why should I lie for her? Why should I tell Emily her mother was innocent, let them be reunited, rebuild their perfect, charmed life when mine was in tatters, when I had nothing left? I'd asked Rose for help once and she'd walked away – why should I help her now? So I said it. I told her the truth, I looked Emily in the eye and said, 'Yes, it's true.'

She gasped, her face drained of colour. 'It is?'

I wanted to take it back then and there, because I saw that Emily hadn't really believed it, that she couldn't believe her mother could have done such a wicked thing. I saw that she'd wanted me to tell her that of course her mother was innocent, so she could go back to her family, build bridges with her father, carry on with her life, and in a few seconds I'd taken all that away. 'Emily,' I said, 'go and see your parents, they love you – whatever they've done, they love you very much. Go and see them, I've lost my family, don't lose yours.'

But she turned away from me. 'I can't.'

'But where will you go? What will you do? Are you still with your baby's father?'

She shook her head. 'We split up,' she said quietly. 'He's not interested. I don't know what I'll do now. I

348

got friendly with a girl from Glasgow last summer, I still have her address. Maybe I'll look her up, try to get a job up there.'

'Will you be all right?'

She looked at me sadly. 'I guess I'll find out.' She wiped her eyes. 'Never tell them, Beth. Do you promise me that? Never tell my mother you saw me today.'

'I promise,' I said.

She nodded, and we looked at each other for a moment more, before she got up and left, closing the front door quietly behind her.

I often think of her, and wonder where she is now, what happened to her. I like to think that she has her own family somewhere, a happy life, in Scotland maybe.

Perhaps I should tell Rose; she still thinks her daughter is dead, another of Hannah's victims. Telling her the truth would be the right thing to do. But then I think of that day in the kitchen, all those years ago, how she wouldn't help me when I begged her to, after all I'd done for her. I warned her what Hannah was like, but she left me to it. And now Rose has come out of it all, the trial, everything, completely free of blame. Revenge is a strong word, but perhaps it's a kind of justice for what she did, to Nadia, and all that happened, later, to my own child. And I suppose I liked the idea of Emily being free of it all, being free of Rose and Oliver, that she, at least, out of all of us, could have the chance to start her life again, somewhere else.

33

London, 2017

It was her final day of giving evidence and as Clara walked from the court she turned to take one last look at the large, white stone building she hoped never to set foot in again and felt a euphoric surge of relief. It was early September, warm still, and breezy, the trees that lined the wide bus-congested thoroughfare showering their first leaves upon the sun-dappled pavement. She pulled out her phone and, seeing that there were two missed calls from Luke, halted mid-stride.

Since being discharged from hospital, Luke had been living at The Willows while he recovered from his ordeal. She had made the journey to Suffolk to see him only once. They'd walked across the fields behind his parents' home, finally able to talk alone for the first time since they'd found him in Hannah's flat. As they'd walked she'd stolen little glances, and she saw how he was altered by what he'd been through. It wasn't just the scars that were still visible on his arms; she noticed that his eyes, once so full of complacent good humour, belonged to someone more uncertain now. The easy smile that had once perpetually hovered around his mouth was long gone. She'd been conscious of his hand swinging by his side, painfully aware that once it would have instinctively snatched up hers.

He told her that he'd met Hannah one night in a pub. 'I was at the bar and she was standing next to me. She looked kind of lost, so I smiled at her, made some small talk, and she said she'd been stood up by her friend. So I bought her a drink.'

'Right,' Clara said, keeping her gaze focused on the horizon as they trudged through a meadow full of cowslip. She had been determined that there would be no recriminations while she listened to his story, but now hurt and bitterness rose up inside her and she had to swallow hard to control it.

Glancing at her, Luke's eyes widened. 'No, nothing like that, Clara, I swear! But . . . I don't know, there was something about her . . . I can't explain it, it was like I knew her somehow, like I'd always known her. She was interesting, we talked about music and art and stuff; she'd been to the same festivals and gigs I'd been to, liked the same films, even been to the same exhibition I'd gone to the week before. Everything that came out

of her mouth, all her opinions, were just spot on, I was
. . . drawn to her, I guess. The conversation flowed
between us, she seemed so switched on, so interesting.
You know what I'm like, I love meeting people, talking
to new people, we hit it off, that's all.'

She nodded stiffly. 'So what happened next?'

'We said goodbye, and I put her out of my mind. I
thought it had been nothing more than a pleasant evening.
I certainly never thought I'd see her again. But as I was
leaving work a month or so afterwards, she pulled up
beside me in this van. She called out my name and seemed
surprised to see me, asked where I was going and when
I said I was on my way home, she told me she was
heading east herself and to get in, she'd give me a lift.'

'And so you got in,' Clara said.

He glanced at her. 'Believe me, I have regretted it
every minute of every day since. I was fucking stupid.
It was pure impulse, spur of the moment.' He shrugged.
'I just thought, fuck it, why not?'

'Christ, Luke!'

'I know. I know. She had a bottle of that whisky I
like on the passenger seat, and I was really surprised,
because not many people know about it, and it's my
favourite. But anyway, when I mentioned how much I
liked it she asked if I wanted a bit, and it had been a
long day so I took a few swigs while we chatted . . .
The next thing I knew, I woke up in a pitch-black car
park in the middle of fucking nowhere.'

'The Downs.'

'Right.' He stopped talking and she heard his breath catch in distress. 'My wrists and ankles were bound. She had a knife. Told me to get out of the car and when I wouldn't she cut me, said she'd do far worse if I didn't do as I was told. I was still so groggy and confused . . . she got me out of the car and there was another one parked a few feet away, she loosened the rope around my ankles just enough so I could shuffle and told me to get in it and we started driving again.'

'And you drove back to London?' Clara frowned. 'Why did she do that?'

'To confuse the police, I guess.'

Clara tried to imagine how it must have felt to have been in that car, how terrified he must have been. As if reading her thoughts, Luke said, 'I was scared witless. It was surreal, waking up like that, I thought it was a joke, a prank, you know? And then she cut me, and I suddenly realized I was in big fucking trouble, that she was completely off her head. The drive back to London, I kept drifting in and out of consciousness as she started talking about my dad, about Emily, but none of it made sense. I realized she was the one who'd been sending me the emails and photos, and the more she talked, the more crazy I realized she was, and the more it dawned on me what deep shit I was in.

'I still thought I'd be OK, though.' He laughed bitterly. 'I mean, I'm tall and fit, you know? I thought she'd take her eye off the ball and I'd escape somehow, I always *am* all right, aren't I? I thought I'd get out of this OK in the end. But when we got back to London we pulled up in the car park outside her building, she had the knife, kept prodding me with it 'til I was bleeding all over, she'd gagged me so I couldn't shout out, and then she made me get out of the car. When she opened the back door to the building and told me to go inside, I thought no fucking way, so I didn't move.'

'And then what?' Clara asked.

'She told me Emily was inside. That my sister was waiting for me in there. It was all so crazy, but in my weird, drugged-up state I kind of thought it might be true.' He shook his head as he remembered. 'And I was still so certain that I'd be able to knock her out or something, so I thought, OK, I'll go along with it, see if she really does know anything about Emily. I'd wondered for twenty years what had happened to her and here was this nutter saying she knew something. I thought I'd still be able to get out later, she was only one skinny woman, after all. I don't know, I was too cocky, too curious.'

'So you went in?'

He nodded. 'My legs were still loosely bound so I couldn't kick but I could shuffle, so, yeah, I walked in.' He ran his hand over his face as he remembered. 'Fucking idiot that I am.'

Luke told her how Hannah had pushed him into a pitch-black room, how he'd fallen to the floor and she'd locked the door. As he reached this part of his story he had to choke back his tears. 'She didn't come back for two days. I just had to lie there, waiting. Pissing myself, not eating or drinking.' Angrily he swiped his tears away, his face burning at the memory. 'She barely gave me any food or drink, I was always tied up, so I couldn't even go to the toilet without her help.'

'Oh, Luke.'

'I still dream about it,' he said. 'I dream about it all the time. Waking up in that car, the knife, that fucking room. I have flashbacks every day.' His voice broke and he began to cry. 'I don't think it'll stop. I don't think it'll ever stop, Clara.'

She'd put her arms around him then and they'd stood for a long time, her holding him as he cried, the feel and smell and touch of him so familiar she had to fight hard not to give in to the sudden longing she felt.

'You could have died,' Luke said. 'She took my keys. I didn't know she was going to go to the flat and look for those pictures of Emily. I don't even know how she knew they were there.'

'What did she want with them?' Clara asked.

Luke shrugged. 'I guess she wanted to make sure you didn't twig she wasn't Emily. Or else . . . I don't know, she seemed kind of obsessed with her, maybe she just wanted to destroy them, fuck knows what was going on in her head. She came back saying she couldn't find them, that if I didn't tell her exactly where they were, she'd burn the place down. So I told her they were in the filing cabinet, but she said she'd looked and they weren't.' He shook his head. 'And then she went back and set fire to

355

the flat.' His face crumpled, 'She came back that night stinking of smoke, crowing over what she'd done, I was so fucking scared that you'd been killed.'

'They had slipped behind the drawer,' Clara told him, 'I found them by accident.' She stared at him. 'But I don't understand why you never showed them to me.'

'I rescued them from the house when Emily first disappeared, when Mum was hiding every last one of them away. I wanted to save them for myself. I never looked at them though, I couldn't bear to. Her going missing was the worst thing that had ever happened to me. It was too painful to look at them, so I put them away out of sight.'

A soft breeze swept across the fields, and they walked on until they reached a stile where they sat for a while, looking out across the meadow. The hazy sky was streaked pink and gold as the day faded into twilight. It was perfectly still, perfectly silent, the smell of the earth and grass filling her nostrils, the dying sun warm on her skin. She would miss this place.

'How are your parents doing?' she asked.

For a while he carried on gazing up at the sky, but at last he said, 'Dad's moved out. Mum, unsurprisingly, doesn't want anything to do with him since all those other students came out of the woodwork.'

Clara nodded. 'I'm so sorry,' she said.

He was silent for a while. 'What my mum's had to put up with from him, lying and covering for him for so many years. I hate him for what he put her through.'

'I know,' Clara murmured. Uneasily though her thoughts returned to that night in Hannah's horrible flat, to when Hannah had accused Rose of her mother's murder. She had seen it, just for a second, Rose's reaction, the flicker of guilt in her eyes, gone almost before it was there. She glanced back at Luke and firmly pushed the thought away.

Suddenly he took hold of her hand. 'I love you, Clara,' he said desperately. 'I love you so much. Please don't leave me, I can't get through this without you.'

'Why on earth would you want to stay with me, Luke,' she said, 'when I was clearly never enough? When you slept with Sadie behind my back?'

'But you are enough!' he cried. 'I don't know, I can't explain it . . . Clara, I've always known that I'm a selfish idiot, that I do the wrong thing, that I hurt people. And then there you were, always so good, so decent and honest, and I wanted to be like you. I thought maybe I could learn to be a better person if I was with you. Sadie was a mistake, a stupid one-off mistake. Please, Clara, give me another chance.'

'But it wasn't one-off!' she said.

'I slept with her once, I swear, Clara. I know that doesn't make it OK, but it was a terrible, stupid mistake that I regretted immediately.'

She thought about this. 'I don't believe you,' she said simply. 'Mac told me it went on for a while.'

Luke shook his head, his face desperate. 'But that's

not true, I don't know why he would say that. I told him it was only once and that's the truth!'

But she had pulled her hand away. 'And then there's Amy, Jade, Ellen – the way you treated them.'

His eyes widened. 'I admit I behaved terribly to Amy. I was so scared of letting my parents down, they were still so devastated over Emily. But Ellen was a complete nutcase. She lied, Clara, she fucking lied! I kissed her once, when I was drunk, when Jade and I were going through a rough patch. She wanted more, she wanted me to stay the night with her, and when I said no, she just . . . I don't know, she started this vendetta. She made the whole thing up.' His face was pleading. 'For God's sake, Clara, I'm telling the truth!'

Clara looked at him sadly. 'But that's the thing, I have no idea whether to believe you, and I don't want to live like that, wondering whether I can trust you or not. I just can't.'

A miserable silence fell between them. At last Luke spoke. 'Do you think I'm like him?' he asked quietly. 'Because of what happened with Sadie. Do you think I'm as bad as my father?'

'I don't think your father has anything to do with the mistakes you made, Luke,' she replied. 'But I do think you can change, I think you can learn from this. I hope you can.'

After a while they got up and continued walking, and by the time they started to make their way back towards The Willows, they had both known it was over.

When they got to her car, they stopped and faced each other.

'I have something to tell you,' he said. 'I've had a letter from my sister, from Emily.'

Clara gasped, shock rendering her speechless. 'Seriously?' she said at last. 'I mean, my God! Are you sure it's her?'

He nodded and smiled properly for the first time. 'She sent a photo. She's got a kid, a girl aged twelve. She'd seen the trial on TV and now everything's out in the open, she wants me and Tom to meet her.'

'And your parents?'

He looked down and shook his head.

So Hannah had been lying about Emily after all.

The sun slid lower, a throbbing red orb on the horizon now, and around them the late summer evening was heavy with the sound of crickets, the scent of scorched grass. She drank in the beautiful view she knew she would never see again. 'I'm happy for you, Luke,' Clara said quietly. 'I really am. I'm glad that something good has come from all of this.'

At last they'd hugged goodbye, and she'd seen that he was trying to be brave, that he was doing his best to let her go. She'd taken one last long look at The Willows before she got back in her car and drove away.

Now, five months later as she stood outside the courts, she put her phone back in her bag. The future stretched out before her and for the first time in a long while she felt an undeniable feeling of hope. Everything had changed. She'd found a new, better-paid job and moved into a shared house with some friends in Greenwich not too far from where Zoe lived. She'd even, in the odd snatched moments after work and at weekends, begun jotting down the beginning of the novel she'd always wanted to write. She would be thirty later this month, and it felt as though her life was starting anew. It was a good feeling.

Suddenly the traffic cleared and she saw, on the other side of the road, a familiar figure standing by his car, talking on his phone. Mac. He looked up and smiled, and she raised her hand and waved, stepping towards him, to where he was waiting for her, her heart lifting at the sight of her friend.

34

London, 2017

As Clara began to cross the road towards him, Mac hastily hung up his phone, put it in his pocket and, despite the dead weight of panic bearing down upon him, forced himself to smile. It was the fifth time Hannah had contacted him from her remand centre and every time she did so his fear of her, of how she might punish him, deepened.

When they'd met six months before it had been the start of a brief but intense affair, appearing as she had out of the blue, a welcome distraction from the futile misery of his growing infatuation with Clara. It had been at the opening night of a friend's photography exhibition, and the attraction he'd felt for the pretty brunette serving behind the bar had been instant and intoxicating.

Soon they were meeting once a week. The sex had been, frankly, the best of his life, but he'd sensed with some relief that she didn't want the relationship to develop into anything more. At first he'd been hesitant to confide in her about his misery over Clara, but she had been so sweetly sympathetic, so gently encouraging that bit by bit he'd told her of the hopelessness of it all, including his anger at Luke's one-night stand with Sadie. He'd quickly grown to rely on her steady support, her wise advice.

He noticed that she didn't like to talk about herself, the questions he asked of her when they first began to meet always gently batted away. She was older than he was and he sensed she had a private life beyond their weekly meet-ups, so he got used to not prying. And anyway, she was such a good listener, there was so much he wanted to tell her about his own unhappiness. 'Poor Mac,' she'd say, stroking his hair, kissing his face, pulling him into bed. 'Poor lovely Mac.'

And then, a revelation, a shock so great, so unexpected, it had knocked the breath from him. They'd been in bed, their naked limbs entwined, and he had just begun drifting into sleep. 'I have something to tell you,' she had said. She sat up, her long brown hair spilling over her breasts, her lovely eyes fastened on his face, her shadow thrown huge across the wall behind her.

'What?' he'd said sleepily, then smiled. 'Sounds serious.'

'It's about your friend, Luke.'

'Luke?' A jolt of surprise. 'What about him?' And he'd recall later how he'd felt the first stirrings of unease, like a gust of cold air ruffling his hair, making his scalp prickle.

'He's my half-brother,' she said. 'Oliver is my father too.'

He'd given a short startled bark of laughter. Because surely it had to be a joke. And then he'd looked into her eyes and realized that it wasn't. His first thoughts, of course, were that she was quite mad, and he'd felt a pull of disappointment that this lovely woman who'd seemed to understand him so well, who had been such a comfort, was in fact completely insane. And how was he going to disentangle himself from this? What sort of scene would there be? 'Erm, listen, Hannah, I . . .'

'When I was seven years old,' she went on calmly as though he hadn't spoken, 'I found out that Oliver Lawson was my real father, that he'd had an affair with my mother. She died when I was a few weeks old and he gave me away to the people who I would grow up believing were my real parents.'

He'd sat up then. 'What the fuck are you talking about? I've known Luke's family for years. I would know, I would – fuck, you're not joking, are you?'

'No,' she'd said. 'No, I'm not.'

'Christ! I don't . . . wait. You knew I was a friend of Luke's when we met . . . that's why you approached me?'

She leant forward and took his hand and he saw now that tears were spilling from her eyes. 'Oh Mac, I'm so sorry, I'm so sorry for lying to you. I never thought I'd grow to have such deep feelings for you, that I'd start to fall for you the way I have. I just wanted some help, I thought you could help me and I understand that you might hate me now but . . .' Overcome, she'd buried her face in her hands, weeping quietly.

He had stared at her in disbelief. 'No,' he said, tentatively putting his hand on her shoulder. 'No, shush now, I don't hate you . . . no, I, OK calm down, don't cry, just tell me from the beginning.'

And so she had. How Oliver had taken advantage of one of his young students, how he'd got her pregnant then abandoned her, wanting nothing to do with Hannah when she was born. 'Rose found out,' she said. 'She found out and she arranged to meet my mother near where they all lived, at Dunwich, you know the cliffs there?'

'Yes,' Mac said his unease deepening.

'My mother met her up there, she had me in my buggy with her. Rose was the last person to see her alive.'

'She . . . *what*? Hannah, what are you saying . . . ?'

'The papers said it was suicide. But I . . . I don't know, I don't think . . .'

'Oh, come on now! You can't be serious . . .'

But Hannah continued to tell him her story, the long sad tale of her childhood, how she'd tracked down the Lawsons, spied on their wonderful life, watched as her father doted on her siblings without a second thought for her. '*My* father, Mac, the father who'd given me away like I was rubbish.' She'd wiped her tears. 'Mac, even if you don't believe that Rose killed my mother, her death was still Oliver's fault, because of the way he treated her, the way he threw her away, threw both of us away.'

He'd stared at her. 'So what do you want with me?' he asked at last. 'Why am I here?' He was still trying to get his head around how completely he'd been duped, how entirely he'd believed their meeting had been mere chance.

She'd leant forward. 'I want you to help me teach Oliver a lesson. I want to make him see that he can't treat people like that, his own daughter, and get away with it.'

Mac had begun to search around for his clothes then. 'I'm sorry but I think you better go now.'

'I'm telling the truth!' she cried. 'My mother was Nadia Freeman. Her body was found washed up in the sea at Dunwich in 1981. It would have been in all the local papers. Look it up if you don't believe me. Nadia Freeman was my mother. And Oliver Lawson is my father.'

He couldn't look at her. 'I don't want any part of this. I don't think we should see each other again.'

He didn't hear from her in the weeks that followed, but he thought about her often. Could her strange tale be

365

true? He could go to the library in Suffolk, look Nadia Freeman up in the local papers archive, but even if someone had died with her name, it didn't mean Oliver or Rose had anything to do with it. All the same, something kept nagging at him. He had always thought Hannah seemed vaguely familiar, and as soon as she began telling him who she really was, he had realized why: she was the absolute spitting image of Luke and Oliver. He couldn't believe he hadn't seen it before, but now that he had, it was undeniable. Every day his unease grew. She'd been so convincing. She hadn't seemed insane at all.

At the end of the second week he got a call from Luke. 'All right, stranger? Where've you been hiding? What you up to this weekend?'

'Oh you know . . . work. Not really got any plans, why?'

'It's my dad's birthday this weekend. Me and Clara are going up there for the party. You fancy it? I know you said you were planning on going up to see your mum soon anyway. Clara was only saying this morning that she misses you. Come, it'll be fun.'

He realized as soon as he got to The Willows and saw Clara that it had been a mistake to go there. She looked incredible. He wasn't even sure what it was about her that pulled her to him so. She was nowhere near as beautiful as Hannah, yet she was everything. When she saw him she gave a cry of delight and went to hug him, her familiar scent filling his nostrils, the feel of her small, compact body in his arms. It was agony. He'd hoped that the short time away from her would have helped, but he realized he loved her more than ever.

Towards the end of the evening he'd stood at the edge of the party, drinking solidly, morosely, by himself. When Luke bowled over to him, bright-eyed and flushed with drink, enthusiastically slapping him on the back, he had looked at him and said quietly, 'What's happening with that girl from work? Sadie? Did you really finish it with her?'

Luke's eyes had widened. 'Yes! Of course I bloody did! Jesus, Mac, I told you that. It was one night, months ago, the worst mistake I've ever made. I just want to forget it ever happened.' He'd glanced around uneasily.

Mac had nodded. 'Yeah. OK, I just wanted to make sure.'

But still, anger had burned inside him as he'd watched Luke wander off to where Clara was talking to his mother, draping his arm around his girlfriend's shoulder with casual propriety. When an extremely drunk Oliver had approached Mac a few minutes later, wine bottle proffered to top up his glass, Mac had said, raising his voice over the music and voices, 'Oliver, do you know anyone named Nadia Freeman?'

And the expression in Oliver's eyes had told him all he needed to know. 'What?' he said, the colour instantly draining from his face. 'What did you say?'

'Natalia,' he had almost shouted. 'Natalia Fellum.

Just a girl I met in London the other day, said she used to live locally. Oliver? Are you OK?'

'Yes, yes, sorry, I thought . . .' he took a large gulp of wine. 'Um, Natalia? No, doesn't ring a bell I'm afraid.' And with that he'd patted Mac on the shoulder and staggered drunkenly off. But Mac had seen it: that initial reaction of pure, unbridled fear. He had seen it, and he had known.

In the days that followed, his thoughts kept returning to Hannah. He was surprised how much he missed her; there had been a connection between them, a sympathy, a sense that she was as alone as he was in her own way, that they shared a singular misery, a longing to make peace with something impossible. Since the party he'd found himself brooding on Luke's selfishness, his undeserved good fortune, more and more. Finally, late one night when he'd been drunk and wretched, he'd texted Hannah. *What did you want me to help you with?* he wrote.

Her reply had been instant: *Can we meet?*

At first the plan had sounded so outlandish that he'd refused. 'Are you joking? No fucking way.'

'Three days,' Hannah had said. 'It's only three days. Long enough to teach Oliver a lesson, that's all, make him see that I haven't gone away, that I'll never go away.'

'Hannah . . .'

'He threw me away, Mac. Like rubbish. He threw me away, and my mother too. She died because of him.'

'Yes, but . . .'

'Listen. You love Clara. Don't you?'

And he'd looked at her, the only person in the world he'd ever admitted that to. 'Yes. Yes, I do.'

'And Luke cheated on her, treated her like shit. The woman you love. Do you really want Clara to stay with him? With Luke out of the way, you could be alone with Clara, let her find out about Sadie, show her how much she means to you.' Tears had filled her eyes. 'Please, Mac, please. You're my only hope, I feel as though I'll never get closure on this if I don't do something.'

Mac had thought about the guilt that had been plain to see on Oliver's face and put his arms around her. 'It's OK,' he said, 'it's OK, take it easy.'

'Look, I'm not going to hurt him. I just want Oliver to admit the truth, jolt him out of his smug little life, make him face up to what he did.'

'How are you going to get Luke to your flat?'

'You don't need to worry about that,' she'd said. 'I just need your help with a few things first.'

And he hadn't asked too much, because he hadn't really wanted to know. The next night he'd gone round to Clara and Luke's flat, and while Luke had cooked them dinner, he'd sat with Clara, listening as she talked about the holiday they were saving up for, how wonderful it was now that they were living together. The next morning he had phoned Hannah. 'OK,' he'd said. 'I'm in.'

It had begun to go horribly, terrifyingly wrong, very

369

quickly. After Luke went missing, Hannah seemed to change overnight. Gone was the hurt and vulnerable woman he thought he knew and in her place was someone very different. After the second day he had phoned her. 'Is he OK? Are you going to let him go tomorrow like you said? Rose and Oliver are beside themselves, job done, so you can let him go now, right?'

In a new, harsh voice, completely unlike her usual one she'd said, 'No, don't be stupid. I need you to do something for me. I need you to tell me everything you know about Rose and Oliver's movements from now on.'

'What? How am I supposed to do that?'

'Find out. Ask Clara. Every time Clara speaks to Rose, every time Rose phones Clara, or the police speak to Rose, or Oliver and Rose come to London, or whatever, you tell me. Got that? Everything, every detail, you tell me.'

'What if I don't?'

She'd sighed irritably. 'Look I'm pretty close to stabbing this whining prick in the face anyway. Jesus Christ but he never lets up. You give me the slightest reason to lose my temper, and I'll do it. If you want to see him again, I suggest you do as you're told.'

He'd had no choice. 'OK, OK, relax, I'll do it.'

'Good. Does Luke have any photos of his sister Emily in his flat?'

'Emily? What's she got to do with this?'

370

'Just answer the question.'

'Erm, yeah, he mentioned them to me once when he was drunk, said he keeps them in his office at home, but I've never seen them. He told me he never looks at them, still too cut up about it, I guess.'

'OK. You need to go round there and take them.'

'What? Why?'

'Just do it. I'll give you Luke's keys.'

When he'd tried and failed to find them her fury had been terrifying. 'Christ you're useless,' she'd spat. 'I'll find them myself. By the way, are you any good at doctoring photos? Photoshop, that sort of thing, I have some old pictures Emily gave me years ago of her with her family. I want you to replace her face with mine.'

'Emily?' he'd said, his unease deepening. 'You didn't say you'd met Emily . . . When? I don't understand.'

'Can you do it?'

'Well yes, but . . .'

'Good. Then I've got another job for you.'

And things had gone from bad to worse, as he'd realized that what Hannah had passed off as a little trick to scare Oliver, to make her presence known, was far more twisted and sadistic. When she started to meet Clara, he'd almost lost his mind. 'You need to stop, now,' he said. 'You need to stop or I'll go to the police.'

'Why? I need to keep up with what the police are doing, and anyway it's fun hearing about what a mess my father's in.'

371

His threats were useless. Every one he made countered by her promise that Luke would die if he didn't keep quiet. He believed her. Even worse, she might hurt Clara. He was trapped.

In desperation, he'd followed Hannah from her meeting with Clara and taken the photograph of her. It was the only thing he could think of to hold as currency over her, a way of warning her, if he needed to, that he could go to the Lawsons and the police whenever he wanted. She'd looked up at the last moment and seen him. He'd run, then, jumping on to a train just before it left the station. Back at his flat he'd downloaded the photograph to his laptop for safekeeping, then dropped it in to Mehmet in the kebab shop below. 'Can you hold on to this for me?' he'd asked.

'Not a problem, my friend.'

He had been right to fear that Hannah would come looking for it, and though she'd taken his camera with the photo on it, she hadn't, of course, been able to find its copy on the laptop. He knew he had to tell Clara the truth, yet every time he opened his mouth, he couldn't find the words, terrified that she would hate him for what he'd done. It had been a desperate, spur-of-the-moment decision to show her and Tom the picture, leading them to finally work out the truth without him having to implicate himself.

But it would never be over, he knew that now. He had expected Hannah to expose him during her trial, had been terrified that she would reveal the part he'd played in it all. But to his surprise she'd kept quiet. For weeks hope had flickered in his heart. It looked, for a time, as though he might get away with it. But then the phone calls had started. She seemed to have become even crazier while on remand, more vengeful and hate-fuelled than ever, and he realized now why she hadn't implicated him in court: it was to have something to hold over him. She told him she'd thought of new ways to punish the Lawsons, and that it was down to him to help her. 'You know what'll happen if you don't,' she'd said, moments before he'd cut her off. 'I'll make sure Clara knows you were in on it from the start.'

He looked up now as Clara walked towards him, and as he watched her a warmth of emotion came to him. The love he felt for her was the one certainty in all of this; despite all that had happened, all the wrong he had done, it was still the one, undeniable truth: Clara belonged to him. Over the past five months as they'd waited for the case to go to trial, he'd fallen more deeply in love with her than he'd ever thought possible.

'Are you OK?' Clara asked, putting her hand on his arm. Such a friendly, affectionate gesture. It didn't mean anything, he knew; she didn't feel about him as he did about her. But maybe one day she would. Her love for Luke was finished, that was clear. Maybe the friendship she felt for him would develop into something more.

He swallowed back his fear and regret and forced himself to smile. Perhaps she'd never find out, perhaps it would all be OK. 'Come on,' he said, putting his arm around her. 'Let's get out of here, shall we?'

35

London, 2017

Hannah slammed the payphone receiver down and allowed the waiting officer to lead her back to her unit. How fucking dare Mac hang up on her like that? Spineless. He was utterly spineless.

She had been on remand for months now, though the trial was finally nearing its end. She would be found guilty of course, and her sentence would be a long one, but she didn't particularly care. She was neither more nor less happy in prison – it made little difference to her. And in the meantime she had plenty to occupy her mind. Plans to make. It wasn't over between the Lawsons and her, not by a long shot, she had big things in store for them. And not just the Lawsons, but Clara, too.

The way she'd ingratiated herself with Oliver and

Rose – 'like a daughter to them,' Mac had told her once. The Lawsons were *her* family, and always would be; Oliver didn't need another daughter, he had one right here. Then there was the way she'd stuck her nose in where it wasn't wanted, tricking her way into her flat, laying it on thick in court while the jury lapped it all up. There's no way she was getting away with that.

The door banged shut behind her and as the lock turned she took a seat on the narrow bed and smiled. It wasn't so very bad here. After all, it gave her plenty of time to think. They didn't have much on her: assault, kidnapping, stalking, blackmail. It could have been worse. It was supposed to have been worse. But even if she got ten years or more, it really didn't matter; the Lawsons, Mac, Clara, they'd all get what they deserved in the end.

Acknowledgements

Huge thanks to Hellie Ogden, Will Francis and the rest of the team at Janklow & Nesbit UK. Thanks so much to my editor Julia Wisdom, her assistant Kathryn Cheshire, Felicity Denham (publicity), Laura di Giuseppe (marketing), Stefanie Kruszyk (production), Ellie Game (cover design), Anne O'Brien (copy editing) and everyone else at HarperCollins who has played a part in the making of this book, I'm grateful to you all. In America I am indebted to my editor Danielle Perez, her assistant Jennifer Snyder, Fareeda Bullert, Dan Walsh, Emily Osborne and Sarah Blumenstock at Berkley/Penguin Random House. My thanks also go to Emma Parry at Janklow & Nesbit US. Thank you to Marcus Jones, Laura Espinel Gonzalez, Alex Pierce and especially to David Holloway.